SHADOWFELL

JULIET MARILLIER

EMBER

Also by Juliet Marillier

Wildwood Dancing

Cybele's Secret

Text copyright © 2012 by Juliet Marillier
Cover art copyright © 2012 by Jonathan Barkat
Map copyright © 2012 by Gaye Godfrey-Nicholls of Inklings Calligraphy Studio

All rights reserved. Published in the United States by Ember, an imprint of Random House Children's Books, a division of Random House, Inc., New York. Originally published in hardcover in the United States by Alfred A. Knopf, an imprint of Random House Children's Books, New York, in 2012.

Ember and the E colophon are registered trademarks of Random House, Inc.

Visit us on the Web! randomhouse.com/teens

Educators and librarians, for a variety of teaching tools, visit us at RHTeachersLibrarians.com

The Library of Congress has cataloged the hardcover edition of this work as follows:
Marillier, Juliet.
Shadowfell / Juliet Marillier — 1st ed.
p. cm. — (Shadowfell ; 1)
"A Borzoi Book."
ISBN 978-0-375-86954-9 (trade) — ISBN 978-0-375-96954-6 (lib. bdg.) —
ISBN 978-0-375-98366-5 (ebook)
[1. Fantasy. 2. Magic—Fiction. 3. Voyages and travels—Fiction. 4. Insurgency—Fiction.
5. Orphans—Fiction.] I. Title.
PZ7.M33856Sh 2012 [Fic]—dc23 2011041050

ISBN 978-0-375-87196-2 (pbk.)

Printed in the United States of America
10 9 8 7 6 5 4 3 2 1

First Ember Edition 2013

Random House Children's Books supports the First Amendment
and celebrates the right to read.

To my grandson, Angus

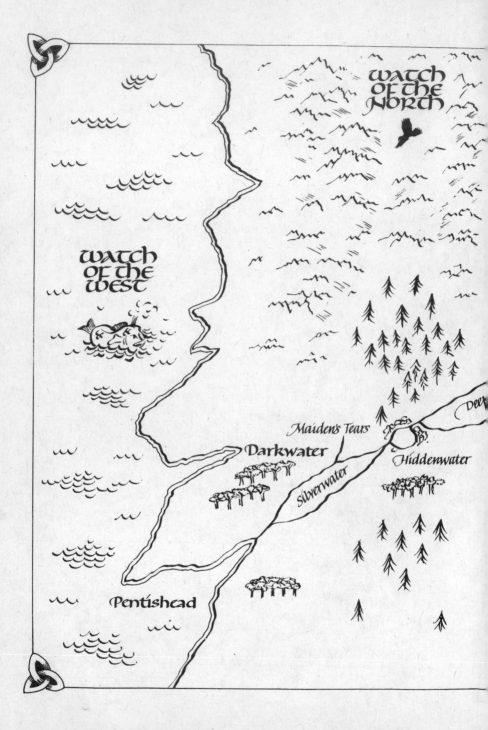

WATCH
OF THE
NORTH

WATCH
OF THE
WEST

Maiden's Tears

Darkwater

Silverwater

Hiddenwater

Deer

Pentishead

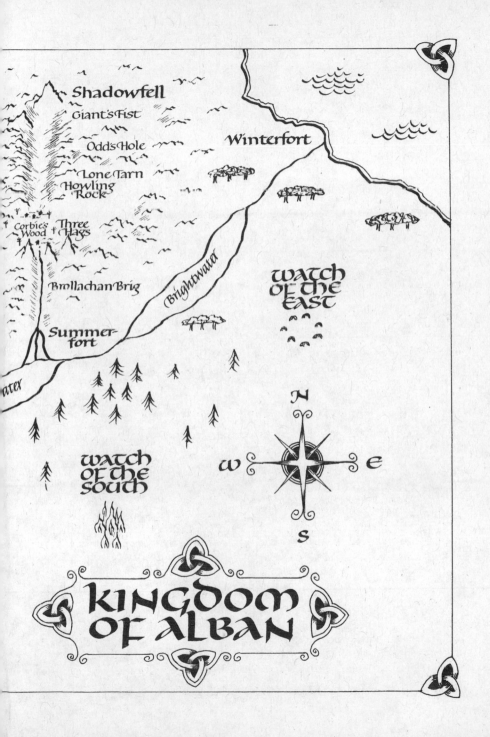

Shadowfell

Giant's Fist

Odds Hole

Lone Tarn
Howling
Rock

Winterfort

Corbie's
Wood

Three
Flags

Brollachan Brig

Brightwater

WATCH
OF THE
EAST

Summer-
fort

water

WATCH
OF THE
SOUTH

N

W   E

S

KINGDOM
OF ALBAN

CHAPTER ONE

AS WE CAME DOWN TO THE SHORE OF DARKWATER, the wind sliced cold right to my bones. My heels stung with blisters. Dusk was falling, and my head was muzzy from the weariness of another long day's walk. Birds cried out overhead, winging to nighttime roosts. They were as eager as I was to get out of the chill.

We'd heard there was a settlement not far along the loch shore, a place where we might perhaps buy shelter with our fast-shrinking store of coppers. I allowed myself to imagine a bed, a proper one with a straw mattress and a woolen coverlet. Oh, how my limbs ached for warmth and comfort! Foolish hope. The way things were in Alban, people didn't open their doors to strangers. Especially not to disheveled vagrants, and that was what we had become. I was a fool to believe, even for a moment, that our money would buy us time by someone's hearth fire and a real bed. Never mind that. A heap of old sacks in a net-mending shed or a pile of straw in a barn would do fine. Anyplace out of this wind. Anyplace out of sight.

I became aware of silence. Father's endless mumbled recounting of past sorrows, a constant accompaniment to our day's journey, had come to a halt, and now he stopped walking to gaze ahead. Between the water's edge and the looming darkness of a steep wooded hillside, I could make out a cluster of dim lights.

"Darkwater settlement," he said. "There are lights down by the jetty. The boat's there!"

"What boat?" I was slow to understand, my mind dreaming of a fire, a bowl of porridge, a blanket. I did not hear the note in his voice, the one that meant trouble.

"Fowler's boat. The chancy-boat, Neryn. What have we got left—how much?"

My heart plummeted. When this mood took him, setting the glitter of impossible hope in his eyes, there was no stopping him. I could not restrain him by force; he was too strong for me. And whatever I said, he would ignore it. But I had to try.

"Enough for two nights' shelter and maybe a crust if we're lucky, Father. There's nothing to spare. Nothing until one of us gets some paid work, and you know how likely that is."

"Give me the bag."

"Father, no! These coppers are our safe place to sleep. They're our shelter from the wind. Don't you remember what happened last—"

"Don't tell me what to do, daughter." His eyes narrowed in a way that was all too familiar. "What's better than a drink of ale to warm us up? Besides, I'll double our coppers on the boat. Triple them. Nobody beats me in a game of chance. Would you doubt your father, girl?"

Doubt was hardly the word for what I felt. Yes, he had once been skilled in such games. He'd had a reputation as a tricky player, full of surprises. Sorrow and reversal, hardship and humiliation, had eaten up that clever fellow, leaving a pathetic shell, a man who liked his ale too much and could no longer distinguish between reality and wild dream. Father was a danger to himself. And he was a danger to me, for strong drink loosened his tongue, and a word out of place could reveal the gift I fought to hide from the world every moment of every day. He'd talk, and someone would tell the Enforcers, and it would all be over for the two of us. But I was heartsick and weary—too weary to fight him any longer.

"Here," I said, handing over the bag. "I hate the chancy-boat. The only chance it will give you tonight is the chance to squander what little we have. If you lose this money, we'll be sleeping out in the open, at the mercy of whoever happens to pass by. If you lose it, you'll lose what little self-respect you have left. But you're my father, and I can't make your choices for you."

He looked at me directly, just for a moment, and I thought I saw a glimmer of understanding in his eyes, but it was gone as quickly as it had appeared. "You hate me," he muttered. "You despise your own father."

I could have told him the truth: that I hated his weakness, that I hated his anger, that the days and months and years of looking after him and keeping him out of trouble and protecting him from himself had worn me down. But I loved him too. He was my father. I loved the man he used to be, and I still hadn't given up hope that, someday, he could be that man again. "No, Father," I said, plodding after him as he strode ahead, for the prospect of a game and a win had put new life in his step. "I'm cold and tired, that's all. Too tired to mind my words."

As we made our way closer to the lights of the chancy-boat, which rocked gently in the dark water beside a small jetty, I was aware of pale eyes watching me from the branches of the pines. I did not allow myself a glance toward them. Small feet shuffled in the fallen leaves and pattered along behind us a way, then skipped off into the woods. I did not allow myself to turn back. A whisper teased at me: *Neryn! Neryn, we are here!* I closed my ears to it. I had been hiding my secret for years, since Grandmother had explained the peril of canny gifts. I had become adept at concealment.

I stiffened my spine and gritted my teeth. Maybe there would be nobody on the chancy-boat but its captain, Fowler, who had some understanding of my father's situation. Who would want to spend such a chilly night playing games anyway? Who would be visiting such an out-of-the-way place as Darkwater? We had come here because the settlement lay so far from well-traveled roads.

We had come because nobody knew us in these parts. Except Fowler, and we had not expected him. But Fowler wouldn't talk. He was a bird of passage, a loner.

Before we set foot on the jetty, I knew the chancy-boat held a crowd. Their voices came to us through the stillness of the night, discordant and out of place under the dark, silent sky. Nobody was about in the settlement, though here and there shutters stood half-open, revealing the glow of lamps within the modest houses. The rising moon threw dancing light on the waters of the loch, as if to show us the way on board the fishing vessel that housed Fowler's place of entertainment. The chancy-boat went from loch to loch, from bay to bay, never two nights at one mooring. They said Fowler had been a peerless warrior in the old time, the time before King Keldec. I'd heard tell that he had fought in far eastern realms, where the sun shone so hot the land was all dust, and the wind made eldritch creatures out of heat and sand. To be a warrior in Alban now was to be an agent of Keldec's will. It was no calling for a man of conscience.

I felt a strong desire to stay in the settlement, to crouch beside a wall or in the lee of a cottage and wait for it all to be over. The prospect of an evening on a boat full of drunken, combative men made me shrink into myself. But I couldn't leave Father on his own. There was nobody else to stop him from drinking too much, from speaking when he should be silent, from wasting our last coppers in a futile attempt to win back the pride he had lost years ago. So I followed him along the jetty, over the creaking plank, and into the crowded cabin of the boat.

The place stank of sweat and ale. The moment I stepped through the door, I could feel men's eyes on me, assessing me, wondering why my father had brought me here and what advantage could be taken from the situation. I stayed just inside the entry, trying to make myself invisible, while Father greeted Fowler with a too-hearty clap on the shoulder. Within moments he was seated at the gaming table with a brimming cup of ale before him. The drink was cheap—ale made men take risks they might avoid when their heads were clear. A copper changed hands. *Let him not squander all of it,* I prayed. *Let him not lose too soon. Let him not get angry. Let him not weep.*

Once play started in earnest, they all forgot me. I stood in the shadows at the back, watching as the games progressed. Father was watching too, working out other men's strategies, their strengths and weaknesses. He would not join in until he had their measure.

Most of the players had the look of seasoned travelers: reserved, cautious. The ones standing behind them were making all the noise—local fishermen, perhaps, or smallholders. There was a silent fellow at the back, on the opposite side of the cabin from me, his hood shadowing his face. Beside him stood a burly red-faced man. Seeing me looking, he grinned, and I lowered my gaze.

They were playing stanies, which Father had the knack

for. The rattling fall of the playing pieces on the wooden table, the calls of *Spear! Crown! Oak! Hound!*, the occasional dispute over the timing of a call or the angle of a throw, all were familiar to me. Father had played game after game of this in the past and had won most of them. But that was then, in another age, before his sorrows tore out his heart and with it his good judgment. All the same, he wasn't playing yet, but sat there drinking his ale and watching the others, biding his time. Perhaps he would confound me by staying sober, by playing as he used to, so quickly and deftly that nobody could match him. Perhaps he would win, and our money would double and treble, and we would be able to pay for both food and a bed for the night.

The games went on, and still Father sat watching. I saw Fowler refill his cup. The cabin was warm from the press of bodies. I was finding it hard to keep my eyes open. Every part of me ached with tiredness. I must not fall asleep. Father needed a guardian, and the only one was me. Besides, I did not like the way that big fellow was looking at me, his eyes greedy.

"Here, lass." Fowler, a sharp-eyed ferret of a man, slipped between two bulky farmers and put a cup of ale in my hands. "Drink this—you look dead on your feet. No payment needed. You can sit over there if you want, out of harm's way."

It was so long since anyone had been kind to me. I let him usher me into a tiny alcove furnished with a wooden bench. I sank down on the seat gratefully and took a sip of the drink. My stomach was empty; the rough ale went down like honeyed wine. Gods, it was good! I made it last; likely this was all the supper I would get.

From the alcove I could not see Father quite so well, but if there was trouble, I should be able to reach him quickly. And I was at least half-shielded from the intrusive gazes of those men. All the same, I must be vigilant. I must not allow my mind to wander, despite the utter relief of sitting down, despite the sweetness of the ale, despite the way my body was urging me to rest. . . .

I started, realizing I had been drifting on the verge of sleep. Oh gods, how long had I sat here in a daze? Father's voice came to me, slurred with ale now and raised in anger. "'Nother round! Who's man enough to take me on?"

I rose to my feet and saw him waving his arms wildly. The man beside him shrank back to avoid a blow to the face. "Come on, what are you, a pack of cowards?"

There was a silence. The quality of it set every part of me on edge. I would have to stop him. He was drunk, and in this mood he might do anything at all. I would have to elbow my way through the crowd of men and get him out of here.

Before I could move, one of the men said, "You've got nothing left to wager, fool. Your purse is empty."

Gods, had he already gambled away every coin we had while I sat here oblivious?

"Father," I began, my voice cracked and tentative.

"I need no stake," Father rumbled, half rising. His fists were clenched; his face was flushed. How much ale had they given him? "I'll win. I can beat anyone. I'll take whatever you put up."

"No stake, no play! That's the rule!"

"If you can't put up a price, you're out of the game, fellow!"

"And not before time," someone muttered.

I made myself push forward through the crowd. "Father, it's time to go," I said, tugging at his arm. My voice was lost in the general hubbub.

"Li'l surprise for you," Father said, getting unsteadily to his feet and draping a heavy arm around my shoulders. "See? I have got a stake—my girl here. What'll you wager against her? No paltry coppers, mind. It's silver pieces or nothing."

My heart faltered. I stood rigid, unable to move, unable to speak. I was dreaming. This couldn't be happening. But it was real, for I saw the eyes of the men opposite Father widen with shock.

"Steady on, fellow," someone muttered. "You don't mean that."

"Speak up!" Father shouted, gripping me harder. "Who'll take me on? I'll beat every last one of you!"

My body was cold stone. "Father," I whispered. "No." But he did not hear me. His mind was on the silver he would win, silver that would buy him ale for a whole turning of the moon, a purse that would restore his pride.

Muttering had broken out all around the circle. I was the object of every eye once more. I could see men undressing me in their minds, but nobody spoke. I snatched a panicky breath, praying that even the basest of them would be above accepting such an appalling proposition.

Fowler stepped forward, clearing his throat. "I can't allow—" he began just as the big red-faced man at the back reached into his pouch and brought out something that glinted in the lantern light. Silver coins. I swallowed bile; my gut twisted in terror. He was going to play.

A black-clad arm reached past him. With a dull knocking sound, three silver pieces fell from a long-fingered hand onto the table. "I will play you," said the man in the hooded cloak, turning my heart to ice.

"No," I managed. "No, Father, please don't do this—"

"Hold your tongue, Neryn!" said Father, and sat down again, releasing me.

I gazed across the table at the challenger, but the hood concealed his face so well I could not even see his eyes. He could have been anyone.

"Toss for the call," said Fowler. It was too late for him to stop this now. Once a wager was accepted, the rules required the game to proceed. "Single round, or best of three?"

"Your choice," Father said, glancing up at the hooded stranger.

The man held up three fingers. Someone got up hurriedly, and the man took the vacant seat, opposite Father at the table. A hush descended. I could not seem to breathe properly; my chest felt as if there were a tight band around it.

"Challenger throws first," Fowler said. "When you're ready."

I could not look. I clutched my shawl around me, as if the threadbare length of woolen cloth might shield me from a world gone all awry. My heart sent out an incoherent prayer. The stones clicked together in Father's hand, and I heard his opponent make the call: "Owl!" A clatter as the pieces fell across the circle chalked on the tabletop, and a babble of excited talk. The owl symbol had come up closest to the center, so it was a clear win.

"First round to— What's your name, friend?"

"Never mind that." The hooded man was gathering up the stones, ready for his own throw. If he won the second round, I was forfeit. He had not spared me a glance.

"Opponent throws second," said Fowler. "When you're ready."

Father sat silent. This time I watched, my heart in my mouth. The hooded man weighed the pieces in his hand, and as he cast them, Father made his call: "Shield!"

A murmuring from the crowd as the stones fell.

"Shield's closest to the center," one man said.

"Not from this side, it isn't," another countered, bending to squint at the lie of the playing pieces. "Spear's the same measure out—look, one finger's length. Makes the round void. Throw again."

"Rubbish," growled Father, and my stomach clenched tight.

"Don't you fellows know the rules?" Fowler's voice was all calm authority. "In a dispute about placement, Shield outweighs Spear, provided neither piece is touching the margin of the circle. Second round goes to the challenger."

A small cheer went up. Someone lifted a tankard in celebration; someone clapped Father on the back. Drunk and incapable as he was, he had won the second round, and there was still a chance to stop this before my freedom was lost.

"Father," I said, leaning close to whisper in his ear, "please don't go on with this. Ask that man to let you out of the game. Tell him it was a mistake. Nobody in his right mind would agree to such a thing. Father, don't do this to me—"

He swatted me away as if I were a troublesome insect. "Leave me be, girl!" His eyes were on the three silver pieces. My price. Fifteen years as his daughter. Nearly three years as his guardian and attendant, his minder and companion on the hard road to self-destruction. Oh gods, this couldn't be real. I would never complain about cold and hunger again, if only this could be a dream.

"Challenger throws the third." Fowler's voice had an edge in it. "You sure you want to go through with this?"

Father did not speak, simply gathered up the pieces.

"So be it, then. When you're ready."

In the silence before the throw, it seemed nobody breathed but me, and mine was the shallow, uneven breath of utter panic. *Make this not be happening, oh, please, please. . . .*

"Flame!" came the hooded man's call, and an instant later the stones hit the tabletop. I heard the universal gasp of horror and knew without the need to look that Father had lost.

No time. No time for anything. Father shouting, a bench toppling, a fist connecting with someone's jaw, a string of oaths. Now several men were throwing punches, knocking over seats, grappling with one another, as if they had only been waiting for an excuse to fight. Someone crashed into me, sending me reeling into the red-faced man, who grabbed me and seized the opportunity to clamp one hand around my breast and slip the other between my legs. In the press of bodies, nobody noticed. In the general din, my protest went unheard. The man's hand was creeping up my inner thigh. I put my hands against his chest and pushed, and he laughed at me. Struggling in his grasp, I heard Father's voice raised above the others: "Filthy cheat! Liars and swindlers, the lot of you!" A pair of combatants lurched across the cabin, scattering others in their wake, and the fellow who was holding me let go abruptly. I staggered, caught off balance, and fell to my knees. The fighters reeled into me, crushing my hip and shoulder against the wall; in a moment I would be trampled. The cabin was full of surging bodies and flailing arms. I struggled to catch my breath. *Out. Oh, please, let me out.*

A hand reached down, fastened around my arm, and hauled me upright. Someone interposed his body between me and the crowd, then shouldered a way out of the cabin, drawing me along with him. As we stepped out into the cold quiet of the night, I saw that it was the hooded man, the man who had just won me in a game of stanies. I shrank away, but he kept hold of my wrist. "Come," he said. "Make haste."

"No! You can't make me go! He didn't know what he was doing. He's not in his right mind! You can't—"

The man headed across the plank, his hand a manacle around my wrist. Rather than topple over and fall into the water, I followed. Above the noise from the chancy-boat, I heard my father's voice, shouting.

"Please," I gasped as we reached the shore and my captor marched on toward the settlement without so much as a glance at me. "You must know how wrong this is. He didn't mean it. He needs me. Please don't do this."

The man stopped so abruptly that I crashed into him. He spoke in a sharp undertone.

"That's what you want, is it? A life on the road, a father who's prepared to sell you to a stranger for the price of a few jugs of ale?"

I stood shivering and silent in his hold, for the moment unable to answer. My life had shrunk to a wretched thing indeed. I had let this happen. I had passed the bag of coins over to Father. I had become as weak and hopeless as he was. "He needs me," I whispered. "Don't make me go, please."

"Move," the man said, and strode on, pulling me along with him. "And keep quiet."

Gods, he was going through with this, the wager, the win; he was taking me with him and I'd have to share his bed and do his bidding and . . . It was unthinkable. "But—" I began.

"Shh!" He made a sharp gesture, drawing his fingers across his throat.

After that I did not try to talk. Besides, I needed all my breath to match his pace. We strode through the settlement in silence, passing between the houses and up a steep path toward the deeper darkness of the forest above. The noise from the chancy-boat faded away behind us. I managed a glance back over my shoulder, but the jetty looked deserted. Nobody was coming after me. I thought of Father waking in the morning and realizing he had gambled away his only daughter, the last of his family. I could not find tears. I could not find words. I was hollow as a gourd, a rattling, empty thing that had lost all its meaning. With my captor's hand a tight bracelet around my wrist, I set one foot in front of the other and moved on.

We were almost in the shelter of the trees when a new sound came up the hill, a sound that froze the blood in my veins. My companion halted and turned, still holding on to me. Thundering hoofbeats, jingling metal. A troop of riders came into view, moving fast along the road into the settlement. The moonlight made them spectral and strange in their dark cloaks and concealing masks. I had not thought I could be any more afraid, but I was. I must have made some small sound, for my captor hissed sharply in my ear, *"Shh!"*

It was early for the Cull: not yet quite autumn. But there they were, hammering on shutters, kicking in doors, riding to every hut in the settlement to rouse the occupants with barked commands and—now—flaming torches that revealed here a cottager being dragged out by his hair, there a child snatched from its screaming mother; here a pair of household goats being unceremoniously put to the knife, there a furiously protesting dog silenced with the kick of a booted foot. The king's Enforcers. Three years ago they had destroyed my grandmother for her canny wisdom; three years ago my brother had died in a valiant attempt to defend our village from the cruel and arbitrary violence of the Cull. Three years ago my father's heart, already weakened by the loss of my mother, had finally shattered under the grief of those deaths. Dear gods, how many such tales unfolded down there tonight? How many years of sorrow were being wrought before our very eyes?

My companion tugged at my arm, jerking his head toward the darkness of the pines a little way up the hill. He was right: if we had any sense, we would vanish now, in silence, before the king's warriors had the chance to notice us. But—

I motioned, pointing to the jetty, the boat, the men probably still brawling on board, unaware of the dark thing unfolding not far away. Perhaps the fellows I had thought to be fishermen had wives and children in those cottages, little families even now being torn asunder. And my father . . .

Someone had seen the boat with its lanterns alight. Someone was striding down the jetty toward it. Another man came up with a lighted torch, and a moment later a flaming arrow arched through the air, flying over the inky waters of the loch to land on board the chancy-boat. A scream welled up in me. Before it could burst out, a hand clamped itself over my mouth.

The boat went up like a midsummer balefire, hot and bright and all-consuming. Perhaps men dived overboard, their bodies aflame; perhaps I just imagined that. My gorge rose; my eyes felt as if they were bulging from their sockets. My knees sagged.

"No sound," the man whispered in my ear. "If you scream, they find us." He took his hand from my mouth.

"Father!" I whispered. "He can't swim! I must save him! You must let me go—"

His voice was a murmur. "Go back down there and you add the two of us to tonight's toll. Come. We must move on."

I couldn't drag my eyes away; my feet seemed rooted to the path. The fire was raging, burning the chancy-boat to the waterline. If Father survived that, he would drown in the depths of Darkwater. If by some miracle the water did not take him, the Enforcers would. I stared at the bright flames, aching to do the impossible, to fly down there and snatch him from certain death, to spirit him away to a safe place, the kind of place that didn't exist anymore.

"Come," whispered my companion, and instead of seizing my wrist again, he offered his arm as support. "Quick."

A little whimper came from my throat. Gone. All gone. I was the last of my family. I remembered my grandmother telling me, *You must be the woman I cannot be, Neryn.*

"Come," said the man again. I took his arm, and together we fled into the darkness of the forest.

CHAPTER TWO

THE NIGHT WAS HALF OVER BEFORE WE STOPPED walking. What kept me going, I did not know, for I had been dropping with weariness when Father and I came into Darkwater. It was not Neryn, fifteen years old, an orphan and possessed of a perilous gift, who climbed the hill above the settlement and descended a path skirting fields where cattle stood dreaming in the moonlight, then headed up again, up and up by a precipitous track that took us right over into the next valley. Neryn was too drained, too forlorn, too shocked to put one foot in front of the other. The girl who walked on, following the man who had won her in a wager, was a shadow, an empty carapace. She went by instinct, the shouts of the Enforcers still ringing in her ears, the flash of the fire still dazzling her eyes, anticipation of what was to come a cold weight in her belly. She went on because there was no going back.

We stopped at last in a sheltered clearing with three big stones in the center. Pines stood tall and shadowy around the perimeter, keeping watch in the night. Everything was moving around me, as if I were drifting in the middle of the sea or caught up in a mass of swirling black clouds.

"Sit," said my companion, at which point my legs gave up the effort to hold me and I collapsed beside the rocks where he had put down his pack. My body began to shake, its trembling quite beyond my control.

The man busied himself while I huddled into the meager warmth of my shawl and watched him. Now that my mind was not entirely bent on keeping my body moving, I remembered that I was this person's property, to do with as he pleased. It seemed he was making camp—he was gathering fallen wood, building a fire, getting out various foodstuffs as if he planned to prepare a meal. Perhaps there would be no more walking before dawn.

I could think of only one reason why he would have accepted the wager, and that reason clawed at me, a terrifying prospect. I had never lain with a man before. Although Father and I had been living rough, his presence had protected me from unwanted attentions. Long ago, I had dreamed of meeting a man I could love and being properly hand-fasted with prayers and blessings. The world in which such dreams were possible was long gone. And here I was with this taciturn stranger, who would expect me to lie down with him by this campfire and let him do what he wanted to me. He did not seem a gentle sort of man.

Evidently he was in no hurry for it. The fire was burning steadily now, and despite myself I edged closer to its warmth. He had water in a skin, oats stored deep in his pack. I watched as he mixed these in a little iron pot, which he then balanced on a strategically placed stone in the fire. Every move was practiced and purposeful.

"You'll be hungry," he observed.

"I'm not— I can't—" My teeth were chattering, and not only with cold.

"Sit closer."

"I—I don't—" I stared down at my hands, unable to put into words what held me trembling and incoherent. The porridge was starting to cook; the smell made my mouth water.

I heard his footsteps as he approached me; I shrank into myself. A moment later his cloak dropped down around my shoulders, heavy and warm, and the footsteps retreated. When I looked up, he was seated on the other side of the fire, facing me. I blinked. It was the first time I had seen him without the deep, concealing hood. What I had expected, I was not sure. Certainly not that he would be so young. He looked no more than five or six years my senior. It was not a handsome face. His nose had been broken at least once, and there was a puckered scar on his chin and another from a wound that must have come close to taking out his right eye. His scalp and chin wore matching dark stubble. A pair of deep-set gray eyes looked across at me, offering very little.

I pulled the cloak around me, but its comforting weight and the warmth from the fire failed to keep the chill from my bones. I cleared my throat, making myself speak. "Wh–what do you want from me?" I managed, and saw something change in his face, as if, remarkably, it had not until now occurred to him why I was so scared.

"You have nothing to fear from me," he said. "Neryn, is it?"

"Mm." I drew a gasping breath. "So you—you—"

"I have no designs on your person, believe me."

"There were other men there who wouldn't have hesitated." A profound relief swept through me as I remembered the touch of that red-faced man's hands. "I'm in your debt." If he had not accepted Father's challenge, if he had not escorted me off the boat and out of the settlement, I would have been burned, drowned, or taken by the Enforcers.

"My existence holds sufficient complications without adding that particular one," my companion said evenly. I did not know if the complication he referred to was being owed a debt, or taking an untouched girl of fifteen summers to his bed. "Warm yourself, eat, sleep. With me, you're safe."

"Then . . ." I watched as he retrieved the pot and poured half the porridge into a metal pannikin. "Then why did you accept the wager? Why didn't you leave us alone?"

He brought the pannikin around the fire to me, offering a bone spoon. "Eat," he said. "It's not much, but it's hot."

Lumpy and undercooked as it was, the porridge tasted like food for the gods.

"Take it slowly or you'll burn your mouth," the man

said. He was eating from the pot, using a piece of bark as a spoon. "How long since you last had a hot meal?"

"I can't remember."

"Been on the road awhile, then?"

I did not answer. Questions were dangerous even when a person didn't have secrets to hide. A person could be killed on the strength of giving the wrong answer or revealing a little too much information.

"Do you have kin? A home, somewhere to go?"

It was hard to believe I was safe here, though the food, the fire, and the warm cloak were conspiring to lull me. The knowledge of loss, the sick, bleak thought that I was all alone in the world, lay inside me somewhere, along with an image of my father burning, his mouth open in a silent scream of pain. The sight of the Enforcers in that settlement, doing their cruel work, had awoken dark memories of another time, another raid. But my body was a traitor; it soaked up the warmth and tugged me toward sleep. "No," I said. "If I had, I wouldn't have been on the chancy-boat."

"Worldly goods? Did you leave them on the boat?"

I motioned to the small bag I had carried over my shoulder. "That's all I have."

He used his fingers to wipe the last of the porridge from the pot. My share was already finished. "You asked me before why I took the wager. Let's say I did it to give you a choice. Where were you and your father headed?"

"Nowhere. You saw what he did, how he was. We're

wanderers. We go where we might find food and shelter for the next night." *And keep one step ahead of the Enforcers.* I would not say that aloud. If those years on the road had taught me anything, it was that nobody could be trusted. Nobody.

"Mm-hm," muttered my companion. "You plan to keep doing that now he's gone?"

That was blunt to the point of cruelty. What could I say? I hardly knew what tomorrow might hold, for tonight my world had turned upside down.

"Why wouldn't I?"

He gave me a penetrating look. "If you've been on the road awhile, you already know the answer to that."

Even as he spoke, an idea formed in my mind, born of something my brother and his friends had spoken of in hushed voices. A secret. A secret too perilous to share with this stranger, even if he had saved me from dying in flames along with my father. There was a place I could go. A good place. A place that might or might not be real.

"North," I said, giving him a small part of the truth. "There's a place a kinsman of mine once spoke of, in the mountains. I will head that way." Something made me add, "I've had enough of this realm of distrust and fear. I'm coming to think rocks and trees make better companions than men and women."

"Mm-hm." I could not tell what he thought of my statement. He passed me his waterskin. I drank and passed it back. "North," he said eventually. "On your own. How far?"

"Far," I said. "I'll cope. I know how to look after myself."

24

"Mm-hm." He regarded me levelly. In his eyes I saw my ragged, weary, half-starved self, a pitiful stick of a girl with defeat written all over her. He said nothing.

"Without Father it will be easier," I said, and to my surprise hot tears began to run down my cheeks. I had thought myself beyond weeping. "He was once a fine man," I murmured, wiping my face with a corner of the cloak. *Stop talking, Neryn*, I ordered myself. *Don't speak about the past. Don't tell him anything at all.* "I should thank you," I said. "What is your name?"

He threw a handful of twigs onto the fire, watching them flare up. "That's of no importance."

"You know my name." But then, he only knew it because he'd heard Father use it, back on the chancy-boat. And there were many reasons why a person would want to withhold his real name. "Never mind," I said quickly. "I shouldn't have asked."

"Flint," my companion said, not meeting my eye. "That's what they call me."

If I had been asked to pick a name that suited him, I could hardly have chosen better. "Then thank you, Flint," I managed before a yawn overtook me. Gods, I longed to lie down and rest. I needed to let the tears fall freely, without anyone watching. I wanted to think of the good times, before the shadows engulfed my family. I needed to remember Father as he had been, a bright-eyed, clever man who used to whirl me around in his arms, laughing.

"Don't be tempted to go back down there." Flint's tone

was somber. "There'll be Enforcers on the lookout for a few days at least, in case someone they missed tries to slip back in to check on family or lay the dead to rest." He glanced at me, and I thought he guessed how much I longed to do just that. It was wrong to leave Father's body, drowned or burned, perhaps both, to drift alone in the depths of Darkwater. Perhaps he would be washed ashore, carrion for wild creatures to feed upon.

"I won't go back," I said, and it was the truth. I knew how hopeless a quest that would be.

"Listen," Flint said, not meeting my eye now but stirring the fire with a stick, making sparks rise into the night. "You know, and I know, how hard it is to make a journey like that alone. Summer's over and the Cull's under way. You should be safe enough here for a day or so; this spot's well off the known tracks. Tomorrow I have to attend to some other business, but I can be back before dark. It happens that I'm going north too. Travel with me until our paths part ways and you'll have protection on the road." He sounded diffident.

He had been kind tonight, in his brusque fashion. But everything in me rejected this suggestion. "I don't know you," I said. "I'd be a fool to trust you."

"You'd be still more of a fool," Flint said, "to go on alone. I said before, I want nothing from you. This is a simple offer of help. You need help."

"Thank you, but I'll do well enough on my own."

My lids were drooping. The fire flickered strangely, and beyond the circle of light I saw figures darting in and out of the shadows, slender winged beings with hair like streams of light. I heard their voices: *Neryn! Oh, Neryn!*

"What?" Flint turned his head, following my gaze.

"Nothing." My heart was suddenly hammering. Let him not be able to see them, let him not realize what I had been looking at. I must divert his attention. "You said you were giving me a choice. Is that the choice, stay here or go on?"

"The way things turned out down there, the choice was between life and death," Flint said calmly. "But, yes, you have another choice now. I hope you'll leave your decision until morning, and make it after some consideration. All I'm asking is that you wait for me here one more day. Stay safe, lie low until I can come on with you. After what's just happened, it makes perfect sense for you to take a day to rest. You're exhausted. Not thinking straight. Lie down, sleep. I'll keep watch. Tomorrow you'll see this differently."

"But—"

"Rest," Flint said. "You're safe here."

Keep away from me, I willed the uncanny presences. *Don't let him see you.* I dared not glance back to the place where I had spotted them. I wished, not for the first time, that I were an ordinary girl with no canny gifts at all.

I lay down with Flint's big cloak wrapped around me and my shawl rolled up as a pillow. In my mind, I saw myself at four or five, in the garden of Grandmother's cottage, sitting quietly by the berry bushes as two of the Good Folk filled a tiny basket woven from blades of grass. The basket took four berries, no more, but they were small folk, and this would be a feast.

"A blessing on your hearthstone, wise woman," said the little man, doffing his cap.

"And a long life to your wee bairnie there," said the little woman, looking at me and bobbing a curtsy.

Grandmother only nodded, and I was too enthralled to utter a word.

The two of them walked away under the bushes and vanished between a pair of white stones, as if they had stepped into another realm. Which was precisely what they had done, Grandmother explained. That was the day she told me about sharing, about kindness, about secrecy. It was the day I began setting out bowls of milk and crusts of bread, and hoping I would encounter the Good Folk again soon. I had not yet learned that other people could not see them as easily as I did. Nor did I know, innocent as I was, that under the king's law, speaking to uncanny folk was punishable by death.

I would remember all my loved ones tonight. It seemed especially important to do this, to keep them in my heart, now that Father too was gone. Mother had left us long ago. My memory of her was always the same: the two of us on a pebbly beach. I made a creature from weed, sand, and shells; she sat by me, gazing out to sea, dreaming her dreams. Her hair was lifted around her head by the breeze, a soft nimbus of honey brown. I remembered how happy I had been that day. I had thought the sun would shine on us forever.

My brother, Farral. One year my senior, and cut down fighting to protect his own. I remembered a time when, at the age of three or four, I had come upon a little bird that had perished in the sharp cold of winter. As I'd held the tiny frozen corpse in my hands, my brother had gently explained that the spirit of the little creature was winging overhead, safe in a realm beyond cold and hunger, and that I should lay its remnant in the earth to feed and nourish the new life of spring. My brother had dried my tears and helped me dig the hole. And he was right: in spring, a little plant with feathery blue-gray flowers had grown there. Grandmother taught me its proper name, but I always called it birdie-wings.

"Father," I murmured, struggling to conjure up a happy memory in place of the hideous, screaming image I could not erase from my thoughts. "Oh, Father, I'll miss you. . . ." And I saw a man walking away down a long, long road, so long that the end of it was lost in the gray distance. As slow tears bathed my cheeks and soaked my makeshift pillow, I sank into sleep.

When I woke, Flint was gone. The fire had been banked up. Warmth touched my face from coals glowing under their blanket of ash. The cloak was still wrapped around my body, keeping out the crisp chill of early morning. The sun had not yet risen, but the sky was lightening toward dawn.

Flint had taken his pack with him, including the roll of bedding he'd had strapped on top. But it seemed he'd been speaking the truth about coming back by dusk, for next to my bag was a neat pile of items that did not belong to me.

I got up, hugging the cloak around me, and went to investigate. A woolen tunic, well worn but serviceable, big enough to cover me to the knees. A cloth bundle that, unwrapped, proved to hold a supply of traveler's way-bread, a feast that set my belly rumbling. I allowed myself a small piece—the sweetness brought back long-lost memories of home—then rewrapped the rest and stowed it in my bag. And he had left me a knife; its edge, tested on my hand, raised a line of bright blood. My own knife had been traded last winter for a meal and a night's shelter. Father's knife had drowned with him. Flint had given me more than a weapon. He had given me the ability to make fire.

I delved into my bag and found the sheath I had crafted for my old knife. To an ordinary traveler it would have looked like nothing much: sewn hide with a sun pattern pricked onto the surface, and at the opening a decoration made from crow feathers and smooth river pebbles, tied into a cord with very particular knots. Thus I set a layer of protection between the cold iron of my weapon and any being who might be harmed by it.

It did not take long to pack up and be on my way. I filled my waterskin from the nearby stream. I extinguished the fire, spreading out the ashes and scattering soil on top. I checked that we had left no other signs of our presence. I squeezed the tunic into my bag and slipped the knife into my belt. Flint's cloak, I would wear. It seemed unlikely I would ever get the opportunity to return it to him. When all was to my satisfaction, I stood still a moment to get my bearings.

North. The place Farral had mentioned lay deep in the mountains, due north of our home village, the village that no longer existed. To reach it, I must first travel eastward up the great chain of lochs that girdled Alban's highlands. I must walk all the way to Deepwater, then skirt the shore of that freshwater loch until I reached the river Rush and a track that led up to the peaks called the Three Hags. There, I must cross a high pass and go along a valley. At the foot of some formidable mountains was a rock formation known as Giant's Fist. Find that and I could find Shadowfell. If it existed. If it was more than a wishful dream.

Save for the very last part, the way would be familiar enough. Father and I had traveled it in reverse when we fled Corbie's Wood and the ruins of our old lives three years ago. And I had become skilled at pathfinding.

But it would be a long journey, and the season was turning. Flint had been right: food and shelter would be difficult to find, especially on my own. If I did not reach the Three Hags Pass before the first snow, I would be in trouble. And, yes, the company of a fit and capable man would have made things easier. But it would take more than vague talk of choices to make me throw my lot in with a stranger, however helpful he might seem. Why had he been on the chancy-boat in the first place? And why decide to take Father's wager when the idea of it was abhorrent to him? He couldn't have known the Enforcers were coming. Could he? If he had, he'd surely have warned Father and the other men.

I set my thoughts on the journey ahead. In summer I might have offered folk a day's labor in return for a bowl of soup and a night in the shelter of a barn. Father and I had been living that way for some time. But not in autumn, for autumn was the time of the Cull, and dangerous for a lone traveler. Turn up on someone's doorstep asking for help and I'd be peppered with questions about why a girl of my age was on the road by herself. If I could not find good answers, folk would leap to the conclusion that I was on the run from the Enforcers. Distrust always clouded the minds of Alban's people these days. In the seasons of the Cull, that distrust reached its height, fueled by terror. It spread through every settlement, every small hamlet, every lone farmhouse. They did not call people like me *canny* now. The word they used was *smirched,* as if our gifts would sully and spoil if they were not ripped out by the roots. Only the king's inner circle could use magic.

There had been a time before. My grandmother had told me about it: a time when a woman who could weave cloth as soft as thistledown, or a man who could play the whistle fit to rival the soaring lark, was looked on by the community with love and pride, not turned in to the Enforcers as if they carried some kind of plague. Grandmother had spoken of a woman who could set her hands to a broken bone and mend it in a moment, humming under her breath as she sat with eyes closed and head bowed. She had told of a man who could gentle a wild boar so it lay down meekly with its head in his lap. I'd especially loved the tale of a girl who had gone out to the field every morning to talk to the sprouting oats, telling them of sun and wind and rain, and of how well they would nourish hungry children when their time of sacrifice was come. At harvest festival those were the loveliest, sweetest oats ever reaped in Alban.

Sometimes I found it hard to tell which of Grandmother's stories were true accounts of how it was before Keldec came to the throne and which were ancient wonder tales. Keldec was crowned king in the year of my birth. Fifteen years was not so long for people to have forgotten the old ways of thinking. But they had. By the time I was old enough to begin understanding what being canny meant, it had become necessary for me to hide my gift. I learned that fear turned friend into foe in an instant, and I learned to keep secrets.

So there would be no working for food and shelter. I was used to foraging in the woods, and I had a fishing line. But in the end I might have to become a thief. An egg here, a bannock there. It wouldn't be the first time.

Before I reached the track to the north, my journey would bring me close to Summerfort, a lesser stronghold of King Keldec and site of the midsummer Gathering. The thought of it set terror in my heart. It brought back the memory I most longed to forget, the dark thing I had seen through a chink in the wall of my grandmother's house the day the king's men came for her. I thrust the images down, for I must start today's walk strong of heart or I would not get far. *Think of good things, Neryn. Think of small acts of kindness, such as a man's gift of a warm cloak. Think of Grandmother's love and wisdom, not her terrible ending. Feel her strength in you; follow the journey as she would have done, with courage and open eyes. Fix your mind on Shadowfell.*

Last night I had thought Father quite gone, drifting away from me down that last shadowy path. Now I felt him walking along beside me, stooping to lift drooping foliage out of my path, holding my hand as I traversed stepping-stones across a surging stream, telling bad jokes to lighten my spirits. Foolish; those memories were from long ago. Of recent times he had seldom had the heart for such gestures. For many moons now we had walked to the accompaniment of a muttered diatribe, a catalog of the sorrows and injustices that had left us poor, homeless, and outcast.

I had wearied of his endless dispiriting talk. I had become expert at not hearing him. My blisters and empty belly had made compassion run thin. Now, as I picked my way along a barely discernible track under the pines, I felt his shade close by and regretted that I had not been more understanding. Perhaps, as I had long suspected, he would have preferred that I had died and my brother lived. But he had protected me in his own fashion. For my sake he had kept going.

I hoped he was at peace now. "I love you, Father," I whispered. "I honor you." I tried to say *I forgive you*. But the words would not come.

* * *

34

DISPATCH: FOR THE EYES OF KING KELDEC ONLY
Darkwater district, early autumn

*My respectful greetings to you, my lord king.
The Cull is under way in the west. Cleansing of all
settlements in the area of Darkwater was completed
with no resistance. I am confident that this district will
cause us little difficulty in future seasons.*

*Boar Troop has moved on to Clearwater and points
south, with Stag Troop heading northward up the coast.
As we discussed at the council, the Cull in the western
isles will be delayed for another year. My investigations
confirm that the likelihood of finding large numbers
of smirched in that remote location is low, while the
practical challenges of conducting the exercise in such
difficult terrain are significant.*

*You will recall, my lord king, a conversation we
had on a matter of particular personal interest to
yourself. I can tell you that certain intelligence has
reached my ears concerning that matter. When last we
spoke together, you generously indicated that, should
this occur, you would give me leave from my regular
duties to pursue that line of inquiry, provided the Cull
proceeded to plan.*

*Acting on this, I have placed responsibility for Stag
Troop in the capable hands of my second-in-command,
Rohan Death-Blade. I will operate alone for the
foreseeable future. I will report direct to you whenever
circumstances make it possible to send a secure dispatch.
The task I undertake may require me to travel widely*

*through the autumn, and at times I will be beyond
reach. Rest assured, my lord king, that I will return
to court by the end of the season, or as soon as possible
thereafter. I hope to bring with me an unusual weapon
for your armory, my lord, a weapon that should please
you very well indeed.*

   Owen Swift-Sword, Stag Troop Leader

CHAPTER THREE

SEVEN DAYS WALKING, SEVEN NIGHTS SLEEPING in the forest, and I crested a hill in late afternoon to catch my first glimpse of Silverwater, its broad expanse glittering in the sunlight some miles ahead. I moved from the still darkness of the pines into beech forest and found a camping spot by a rocky outcrop among the trees. A small stream gurgled its way down the hill. There was one great oak standing among the beeches, a dark-leaved, broad-armed goddess of a tree. I found a flat rock, set down my bag, and spread the cloak beside it. I lowered myself to a sitting position and, wincing with pain, eased off my shoes.

My feet were afire with blisters. These had been good shoes once, given to me by a girl whose family had sheltered us in a remote village up north. These shoes had carried me many miles, uphill and down, across streams, through bogs, over fields, and along steep fells. They had been with me through spring rain and summer heat, autumn chill and winter snow. They had been patched and mended, relined and strengthened. This season's hard journeying had tested them to their breaking point.

I foraged, barefoot, beside the stream and came back with a handful of fern roots and a scattering of acorns. I could not make a proper poultice, for my small bag carried only essentials. My supply of powders and salves had run out many moons ago, and I had lacked the time and resources to replace it. Perhaps that was just as well. Few healers practiced their craft openly in Keldec's Alban. The line between herbalism and magic was too thin for comfort.

I made a fire, my new knife striking a ready spark from my old flint. Wary of attracting unwanted notice, I kept the blaze small. When the fire was burning well, I went foraging again, returning with wild onions, which I made into a soup. Some of Flint's waybread was still in my bag, saved for the times when I could not fish or forage.

As I stirred my brew, I felt eyes on me, watching from the high branches of the oak, from the shadows between the beech trunks, from the bouncing waters of the little stream. I sensed the presence of observers hidden in every chink and crevice of the great rocks that sheltered me. Close. Closer than I had ever felt them before.

It was said the Good Folk had gone into hiding, fearful of Keldec's long reach. Rumor had it that they had fled Alban altogether, choosing to dwell on the misty islands of the far west or in the cold, empty north. Neither theory was true, or I would not be aware of them now, all around me in this clearing. The little hairs on my neck stood up; my spine tingled with the strangeness of it.

"Best if you don't come near me," I murmured, trying not to look directly at any of them as I sat drinking my onion brew. "You and I, we're trouble for each other. I want nothing to do with you." It sounded harsh and discourteous. And I did not even know if they would understand me; I had never spoken to them directly before. Now it seemed necessary to warn them.

A pointed silence followed, in which I could almost feel their disapproval. In my mind, my grandmother spoke: *Always share what you have, Neryn. Look after the Good Folk and they will do you no harm. If you hear people complaining that someone stole the eggs from right under the hens, or drank the cow dry before milking time, it will be because someone forgot that rule.*

Well, there were a few mouthfuls of the brew left. With some regret, I moved to set down the little pot at one side of the clearing, wedging it with stones so it would not spill. It looked a meager offering, the amber liquid barely covering the bottom of the pot. And there were many of them; I need not look straight at them to know that. Sighing, I took the cloth-wrapped waybread from my bag, broke off a piece, and laid it beside the brew. "I'm a friend," I said, my voice just above a whisper. "I offer you a share of my meal, such as it is. But I don't want companions on the journey. Stay in your safe place. There were Enforcers at Darkwater. The Cull's begun." I wondered if anyplace was safe.

My little fire warmed me as I chopped fern roots and soaked them in water, then mixed them with the acorn flesh

I had crushed between stones. I would fill a cloth with the resultant pulp and put my feet in it for a while before I ·tried to sleep. It couldn't hurt, and perhaps it would help. Maybe, farther on, I would find birch trees, from whose bark I could make a lining for my shoes. I eyed them, seeing the holes, the places where sole had parted from upper, the frayed cords that no longer tied up.

As I worked, I saw from the corner of my eye that the pot of onion brew was already being investigated. Small hands were turning Flint's waybread over and over; a furred being in a red cap took a sharp-toothed bite from a corner—snap! A skinny creature with fingers like long twigs snatched the treasure away with a hiss.

"Share," Long Fingers said. "*Ssshaaaare.*"

"Break it up, then, break it up!" urged Red Cap, and a chorus of voices chimed in. They would get a crumb each, at most. A creature with a tube-shaped snout leaned over to suck the brew direct from the pot, and another gave it a smack on the head.

My makeshift poultice was ready. I sat down with Flint's cloak over my shoulders and the fire warming my face, and wrapped the cloth around my feet. It was awkward, the lack of a binding component making the thing too ready to slip at the slightest movement. I kept perfectly still, wondering what would happen when my meager offering was gone. Would they be angry and turn on me? Would they vanish without another word? Every part of me was on edge with anticipation, but for what I did not know. Their presence, so close, felt both wondrous and perilous. I had seen their kind as shadows passing in the woods or as eyes in the night. Seeing them was my gift and my curse. I had heard their eldritch voices. But they had never come so close before. The squabbling division of the unexpected bounty went on awhile, and then silence fell, a silence so sudden and profound that, against my better judgment, I turned my head to look directly at them.

They sat in a neat circle, as if holding a council, but every one of them was facing me. I felt the weight of all those eyes: little beady eyes; large lustrous eyes; narrow eyes; long-lashed, lovely eyes; eyes of every shape and color I could imagine. The smallest was no larger than a hedgehog, and indeed somewhat resembled one. The tallest, standing, might come up to my waist. One or two were still nibbling on fragments of waybread. Their gaze was neither friendly nor inimical, but deeply Other.

The silence was full of expectation. Plainly, I was expected to make a speech of some kind. With my feet wrapped up, I felt at something of a disadvantage.

"Greetings." My voice had a nervous wobble in it. It was one thing to see Good Folk more or less wherever you went, but quite another to be surrounded by them and attempting a conversation. "I'm afraid I can't get up. I have blisters. Thank you for letting me shelter here with you. I regret that I didn't have something better to share."

"The brew was sufficient," said a little woman in a

leaf-colored cloak, dabbing her lips with a spotted ker-chief. "Besides, such gifts are not offered for the purpose of nourishment, or our kind would all have perished from hunger long ago. They're given as a sign of trust, and accepted in the same spirit." She gave her companions a withering look. "Though there's one or two let their appetites take the place of their common sense."

"Your friends were welcome to my food. But I will need to forage soon enough. What I have won't last long."

"Aye, you'll be hungry tomorrow," said the little woman. "Closer to the loch there's nettles to be found. And you'll see some wee toadstools at the foot of the great oak. Take care which you pick, or you'll set your guts in a twisty tangle."

"There's fine fish to be had," put in Red Cap, revealing that although he looked somewhat like a pine marten, he spoke much as I did. The voice was undoubtedly male, but I noticed the creature bore a sling on his back, and from it peered tiny bright eyes. "Along Silverwater, past the big man's house, a fall known as Maiden's Tears tumbles down toward the loch. Above it lies a pool where they rise by moonlight to be taken. Their flesh will keep you strong. We will show you."

A chorus of protest rang out in many voices, high and low, rough and sweet, sending my flesh into goose bumps with their strangeness. "No!" "No show, no show!" "Fool, Red Cap, fool! What are you thinking, to trust such as her?"

"Never mind," I said, a shiver of foreboding running through me. "I'll be going on alone."

"We would expect no less." The being who spoke looked something like a human girl of about my own age, but she stood no taller than a young child and was as delicately formed as a wildflower. Her gown flowed around her, drifting gossamer. Her hair was a shimmering fall of silver light. Her eyes were large, lustrous, and wholly inimical. "I know what is in your mind, Red Cap, and I know who put it there." She shot a glare at the little woman in the green cape, who gazed steadily back at her, unperturbed. The silver girl turned to me. "Traveler, do not expect our aid. No matter what gifts you may set out for us, the time is long gone when the Good Folk involved themselves in the petty struggles of humankind. Your troubles are of your own making."

Fragile as she looked, her voice was strong as oak wood and chill as a stream under winter ice. It was pointless to protest that I had not expected any help, indeed had not dreamed they would come so close. It was useless to explain that I'd never have accepted an offer to have them accompany me, since that would have put them at the same risk I faced every day. She believed me some kind of enemy. Well, I was human and Keldec was human, so perhaps her animosity made sense. It hurt all the same. In my mind was that sweet, magical day in Grandmother's garden, and the two little folk with their basket of berries.

"You'll be moving on in the morning, then." It was one of the others that spoke, a creature in a dark, glossy cape made all of feathers. Its tone was flat, but its sharp eyes examined me keenly. Its features held something of a man's and something of a crow's; they were disconcerting, and I tried not to stare.

"I will, yes."

"A warning. Red Cap spoke of a fall, Maiden's Tears. The fish are good, aye. But if you go that way, 'ware the urisk. He will call for help, you ken. Bitterly. Endlessly. Take no heed of that, for if you speak to him, he will follow you on your journey. He will dog your footsteps. He will never let go. A creature such as that is eaten up by loneliness."

"Thank you for the warning." Perhaps I would forgo the fish.

Long Fingers had moved out of the circle to investigate my decrepit footgear. "Shoes," he observed. "Broken."

"Leave them!" The silver girl spoke sharply, and the creature shrank back. "Enough of this. Leave the shoes and leave the girl. She's nobody. A wanderer, a vagrant. This was a misguided venture from the first."

"You make your judgment quickly, Silver." Though she spoke quietly, something in the voice of the green-cloaked woman stilled them all. It was as if she had made them draw a long breath together.

"One look is enough." Silver—aptly named—had frost in her voice. "One word. If matters were as you believe, we would know. We would see it. It would be apparent in an instant. This girl can't even mend her own shoes. How could she—"

Suddenly I felt my weariness like a weight on my shoulders, and with it a flicker of anger. "I can mend them. All I need is some birch bark."

Someone hooted with laughter, as if such a notion were utterly ridiculous.

"I said I'll mend them!" My voice was as brittle as a dry twig. "Thank you for your company and your good advice about fish and the urisk and so on. It's obvious my presence is causing some dispute among you, so you'd best leave me to get on with things by myself. I'll bid you good night." Let them take their debate about what I was or wasn't somewhere else. It was plain enough that my company was unwelcome to them.

There was a general twittering and whispering, but I caught no words in it. In the growing dark, the circle of eyes took on an eerie glint, as if they carried their own light within.

At length the little woman in the green cloak spoke. "You're not afraid on your own?" she asked.

"Of course I'm afraid." Sitting, I could look her straight in the eye. She seemed formidable, her small size doing nothing to diminish the strength and shrewdness of her gaze. Her nose was a sharp beak, her hair a cloud of gray-green fuzz through which her pointed ears protruded. I felt as if she were looking right inside me, into my secret thoughts, and that turned my heart cold. "It's culling time," I added, "and the Enforcers are around every bend in the road, behind every wall, listening for every careless word. I shouldn't be talking to you. I should be pretending not to see you."

There was a brief silence, then Red Cap observed, "You set out supper for us."

"My grandmother taught me to share," I said, tears pricking my eyes. "It was a good lesson. She said that even if you think you have nothing at all, there is always something you can give to another. She taught me early to respect your kind."

If the Good Folk felt any warmth toward me after this, it did not show on their faces. Indeed, most of them were looking at Silver, as if waiting for her lead. Only the green-cloaked woman had her gaze on me.

"Good night to you, Neryn," she said. "Safe journey."

"And to you," I replied, wondering how she knew my name.

"Nowhere is safe," said Silver. "Not for your kind, not for our kind, not for anyone. In this benighted realm, all is turned to darkness."

"The wolves howl," put in Long Fingers.

"The winter bites," said Red Cap, and as he spoke, there was a wriggling from the sling on his back, as if whatever was there had burrowed down deeper.

"King's men come with cold iron," said the crowlike being. "They seek out our hidden places."

"I know that, and I am sorry for it. If it were in my power to help, I would. But all I can do right now is follow my own path."

"You will be cold."

"Lonely."

"Hunger and thirst will walk the road with you, every step."

"The wind will chill you. The rain will soak you. Your shoes will break apart."

"Many trials lie before you." Even the woman in the green cloak had joined in now. "You will be tested to your limit."

"Enough!" I snapped. "My father died not long ago, I've lost the last of my family, and I'm tired. I'm terribly tired. Stop making me sad and let me sleep."

They vanished as if they had never been, fading into the stones and the water and the darkness of the forest. I felt instantly ashamed of myself, but when I whispered, "I'm sorry," there was only the night, and the call of a bird, and silence.

I dreamed the Good Folk were in their circle again, with a furious debate raging among them.

"Her? A wee lassie with holes in her shoes? You're off your head!"

"What about the way she shared her food with us? If that's not the Giving Hand, then I'd like to know what it is!" The creature who spoke resembled a small bush, for it was all over twigs and leaves, with eyes like ripe berries set deep in the foliage.

"Sorrel speaks wisely, as always," said the woman in the green cloak. "You felt the girl's presence, as we all did—don't deny it. It was powerful. Compelling. A pull the strongest of us would find hard to resist. It makes no difference if she's a wee lassie or an old woman of seven-and-seventy."

"The Giving Hand?" A wispy, big-eyed being spoke, its voice all scorn. "Easy enough to give when you've plenty to spare. Didn't you see that supply of waybread? Let's see how giving the lass is when she's half-starved and too weak to forage."

"And even if you're right, Sage," said a little man in a rattling cape of nutshells, "what's one out of seven?"

Red Cap cleared his throat. Now he was seated by the banked-up fire, and he had a miniature version of himself in his arms, up against his shoulder. The infant from the sling; perhaps he was soothing it after a nightmare. "It's a start, that's what it is," he ventured, eyes going from the little woman, Sage, to Silver and back again, as if he were not sure which of them might bite first. "Give this lass time and we'll know one way or the other."

Sage folded her arms, her head to one side, as if she were thinking hard. "It wouldn't want to be too much time," she said. "Whether she's what I think she is or not, her gift puts her in danger. Let her fall into the hands of king's men and we might lose our only chance."

"This is utter nonsense! I can't believe so many of you have let yourselves be caught up in such foolishness." Silver spoke with sharp authority. "You're meddling in matters that lie far beyond your understanding. Ancient things. Weighty things." A pause. "Perilous things."

"Aye," put in the big-eyed being, "you'd stir up what's best left sleeping and bring down disaster on all of us."

"When has our kind ever joined with their kind in a venture that did not end in catastrophe?" asked Silver. Clearly no answer was expected, but the bushy creature, Sorrel, spoke up.

"In the war between the Sea Folk and the brollachans," he said smoothly, as if he had only been waiting for the opportunity to provide this information. "A human fellow. A Caller. But for his leadership, the brollachans would have been wiped out in the north, and the human folk of the isles along with them. It's in the long songs. Even you cannot argue with those, Silver."

"A story. That's all it is, an old tale. Those times are gone. To do this would go against everything we are; it feels wrong, it smells wrong, it's as wrong as an eaglet in a dove's nest. Human folk got Alban into this sorry state. Let human folk get it out again. It's not our fight, it's not our quest, it's not our business."

"Alban is our home," Sorrel said. "Since time before time, since long before humankind set foot on this shore."

"What will you do when the storm comes?" put in Sage, her eyes fixed on Silver. "Defend your home or lie down and let it fall to pieces around you?"

The answer to this, I did not hear, or if I did, it was gone when I awoke. But everything about the dream seemed real: the harsh urgency of the Good Folk's whispered interchanges, the cryptic references to me and my journey, the dark blanket of the night, and the cries of owls in the trees above. I wondered if it had been no dream at all. Perhaps, thinking me asleep, they had decided to debate my worth or my future or whatever it was, and I had been just sufficiently awake to hear them. *One out of seven.* Seven of what?

Next morning, when I rolled out of the warmth of the cloak, I found that my footwear had been repaired, the torn uppers cobbled together with tiny, fine stitches and the linings replaced with a flexible substance like tightly packed cobweb. When I slipped the shoes on, they were no longer too small but fitted me perfectly.

I knew it was perilous to accept fey gifts. The king's wrath fell swiftly on anyone found to be in possession of such an item. A wooden spoon that happened to have a magic symbol carved on the handle, or a piece of weaving that was a little too expert, could see a house burned to the ground with the occupants still inside. No matter if the spoon had been carved by someone's old grandfather, or the weaver simply happened to be clever with her hands. Under this king, suspicion was as good as proven fact. And Keldec's will was absolute.

I wondered, often, what kind of man it would take to carry out an Enforcer's duties. Did the king use fear to keep them obedient? Did he offer rewards they could not refuse? It seemed to me it would be better to die standing up to a tyrant than to survive as a tool of his will. If I ever had to face the Enforcers, I hoped I would be as brave as Grandmother had been.

"Many trials lie before you," I muttered to myself. "You will be tested to your limit." True, maybe, but as a piece of advice, not especially helpful. As for the shoes, clearly mended by no human hand, I had to wear them. With autumn closing in, and many days' walking over rocky hillside and untracked forest ahead of me, I simply could not do without them.

I remembered the settlement of Silverwater clearly. It lay on the shore of the freshwater loch: a collection of mud-and-wattle buildings with roofs of thatch, all surrounded by a drystone wall. The most substantial building was fashioned of shaped stones and had a small tower. It was the home of the district chieftain, Dunchan. A long time ago the folk of his household had given Father and me two nights' shelter. We'd earned our keep by shoveling cow dung the first day and cleaning out a privy the second. Father had done most of the work; back then, he'd been a strong, fit man, though given to bouts of melancholy. In that household the meals had been good and few questions had been asked. We'd done the work we were given, kept ourselves to ourselves, and, on the third day, moved on.

I could reach that place by tonight. The loch was in sight, and if my memory served me well, the settlement was about a half day's walk along it. Maybe I should change my plan. If I told a convincing story, perhaps Dunchan's folk would give me work over the cold season, and I could move on north in springtime, when there would be good foraging in the woods. That made sense, provided they believed I was no threat.

I glanced down at my shoes with their fey mending. Walk into Silverwater wearing those and I'd be handed straight to the authorities. Even a tolerant household like Dunchan's could not afford to ignore such plain evidence. And what about the Cull? I had no idea which way those Enforcers were headed after they'd worked their evil in Darkwater. The path of the Cull was different every year; the order in which settlements and farms were visited was never the same. Some escaped altogether, though nobody could ever be sure that would happen. The element of surprise let Keldec cast his net more effectively. Folk never knew when the Enforcers were coming. To seek shelter at Silverwater might be to bring down disaster on that household.

Before the sun was at its peak, I reached the loch shore. I did not walk on the path by the water, for it was busy. Cull or no Cull, life had to go on. I saw men fishing, boys with geese, a girl with a small herd of goats. And from time to time I saw folk scrambling to the side of the track when drumming hoofbeats announced the arrival of a group of black-cloaked Enforcers riding their big, dark horses. They went in pairs, harnesses jingling with silver, leather-helmed heads high, round shields blazoned with the Stag of Alban: the king's emblem. Mostly they were traveling eastward, as if returning to Summerfort, where Keldec's household spent the warmer part of the year. A shiver went through me. The king might still be in residence there now. My journey would take me right by that place, close enough to be almost sure of meeting Enforcers on the way. I would not hasten the day when that might happen. I kept to the precipitous slopes of the forest, letting the trees shield me.

I made good progress along the shore, and before dusk I saw, framed by beeches, the settlement of Silverwater down the hill below me. There was the cluster of cottages, there the long wall, there the chieftain's house with its modest tower. And in the yard, between barns and outbuildings and stock pens, something out of place. I halted in the shadow of the trees.

A small crowd was gathered in that open space: men, women, and children, the chieftain's whole household, and perhaps the villagers as well. They stood in complete silence, faces ashen. Stationed around them were Enforcers with weapons drawn. No running. No screaming. No burning. But where a lovely oak grew in the very center of the open ground, an oak I remembered well from my brief stay here, for its shade had been enjoyed by chickens and dogs and children alike, a dark matter was unfolding. A glance showed me the rope hanging from a strong bough, and Dunchan of Silverwater standing very still below it, balanced on a stool. A masked Enforcer stood behind him. As I watched, cold to the bone, the Enforcer slipped the noose over Dunchan's head and drew the knot tight.

"No," I muttered. "Oh no." Dunchan's wife was in that silent crowd, his children, his loyal servants and men-at-arms, a whole household of good people. I imagined folk hushing their little ones, fearful that a cry at the wrong time would bring down the same fate on them.

I wanted to shut my eyes. I wanted to turn away. Part of me protested: *This is not my story, these are not my folk. I'll just turn my back and walk on. I'll pretend I didn't see this.* But I kept my eyes open, and I stood witness to the hanging of a good chieftain. When it was done, the Enforcers backed off and Dunchan's friends cut him down. His wife knelt over him and closed his eyes. The Enforcers were keeping their distance; it seemed this one execution was all the punishment they had come to deliver. Already some of them were riding out through the gates, though five or six remained.

Silence would have saved Dunchan's wife. She chose another path. She did not collapse on her husband's body, weeping. She stood up, head high, and hurled defiant words at his killers. With my heart in my mouth I watched her do it, and I saw an old man fighting to keep a child—the chieftain's little son, I guessed—from running forward as she spoke.

She was killed with a single expert stroke of the sword. Her head rolled away, coming close to the feet of the frozen onlookers. The killer gave his weapon a desultory wipe on a tuft of grass, sheathed it, and spoke a few words to the crowd. The old man had his hand clapped over the child's mouth; I saw a woman edge in front of them to shield them. *No more,* I willed the Enforcer. *Let there be no more evil done here.*

The executioner turned away, mounted his horse, and

headed for the gate of the settlement. He was the last of them. As he rode off down the track and out of sight, the preternatural stillness of the crowd broke. The old man released the boy. The lad did not go to his mother, where she lay in her blood. He did not go to his father's lifeless corpse. Instead, screaming out a great cry of rage and defiance, he pelted after the Enforcers, as if one boy alone could prevail against them all. Three or four men ran after him, arresting his wild progress. He fought them at first. At length he wept, and the old man, perhaps his grandfather, held him as the storm raged. Others moved to gather up the sad remains of the chieftain's wife, to blanket Dunchan with a cloak, to tend to little ones who had seen what no child should ever see.

Time for me to move on. There was nothing I could do here, except grieve for the woeful place Alban had become. What would happen to all those folk now their lord and lady were gone? I had heard that Keldec liked to put his own favored men in as local leaders, never mind the tradition of families and clans. Someone had to keep the smallholdings going; someone had to provide leadership in times of trouble. I wondered what Dunchan had done to earn Keldec's disapproval: harbored a fugitive, expressed doubt about the king's rule, used magic? This had been a good chieftain, well loved by his people. Two days' stay had been sufficient for me to see that. As I walked on, I imagined the open space within the encircling wall, empty save for the lovely bare-limbed tree. In my picture, a great patch of red stained the hard earth. A dog slunk past, giving the stain a wide berth. From within the dwellings there came a sound of weeping. And from the top of the little tower a new banner flew: the proud stag of Keldec, King of Alban.

I walked as far as I could along the loch shore before darkness forced a halt. I did not make fire. With Enforcers so close, I could not take that risk. I spent a chilly night in the meager shelter of a rock shelf and moved on before dawn. I had learned a lesson. There would be no seeking a bed in any habitation of men.

By the next night I had reached the waterfall the Good Folk had called the Maiden's Tears. It was as they had described it: a splashing, exuberant beck cascading over mossy rocks. White-bellied fish swam in the darkness of the still pool above, and when I lowered my line into the water, the faint moonlight seemed to draw them to the hook. I muttered thanks to the gods for this bounty, killed the fish quickly, and enjoyed my best supper since Flint's lumpy porridge. There was neither sight nor sound of the urisk, of whom the Good Folk had spoken such a dire warning. I had heard of such beings before; Grandmother had said they were the loneliest creatures in all Alban, and always lived beneath waterfalls.

I wrapped myself in Flint's cloak, pulling the folds up over my ears, and fell asleep with the coals of my cooking fire glowing warm red-gold in the soft shadows and with the wash of the water soothing me.

In the darkness of midnight, a piercing cry sliced through my head, jolting me wide awake. Against every instinct, I made myself hold still. The wailing went on and on, setting my teeth on edge and chilling my blood. There were no words in it, but I felt the creature's grief, its profound loneliness, its longing for a hand of friendship.

If you speak to him, he will follow you on your journey. He will never let go. There had been no need for the Good Folk to warn me. I had known this wisdom since I was a child of three. Farral and I used to play a game of urisk, taking turns to emerge from hiding, wailing and reaching out clinging hands, while whoever was the victim tried to stay still and silent. Now, with the real creature crying within a few paces of my campsite, I trembled as I lay huddled in the cloak. I must not move; I could not speak the words of comfort I longed to offer. *It's all right. When I pass this way, I will visit you. I will stay a little while and talk to you.* It would have been so easy to help, so simple a thing, but I could not. Give an urisk any encouragement at all and it would be with you every moment until the day you died, clinging, twining, hanging about your shoulders, slipping into bed next to you, a chilly, vaporous, constant companion. If I tried to help the being, it would follow me. And any creature that followed me not only would put me at greater risk from the Enforcers but would be at risk itself.

Humankind and Good Folk were forbidden, under king's law, to speak together, to be in the same place together, even to set eyes on each other. This law had long puzzled me. My brother had told me Keldec feared magic, but that couldn't be true, for the only place where magic was allowed was at his court, among his inner circle.

I slept no more but lay silent, with the urisk's voice, now shrunk to a pitiful weeping, filling my mind with sad memories, a parade of loss and grief, from the small sorrows of a child—a favorite toy lost, a hurtful remark by a friend—to the deaths of all my dear ones, each in turn. I thought of that good chieftain Dunchan of Silverwater and his brave wife. I thought of the folk who had died under the harsh blows of the Cull, in Darkwater and in hundreds of other settlements like it. For a little, as the crying went on, I felt something close to despair. It was a long journey. I did not really know if the place Farral had spoken of existed. I would have to cross the mountains, and the leaves were already turning to red and gold. I was, in truth, only a wee lassie, as the Good Folk had said. This was foolish. It was impossible. . . .

A tear welled from my eye, falling to lose itself in the wool of Flint's cloak, and I caught myself up sharply. *Just hold on until dawn,* I told myself. For in the tales, when the sun rose, the urisk faded. *Hold still,* I ordered myself. *Keep silent.* And, remembering the terrible night when the Enforcers came to Grandmother's cottage, I thought, *You know how good you are at that.* Breathing into a fold of the cloak, I made myself think of Flint, my unlikely savior. What his true motives had been, I had no idea. But he was proof that here and there in Alban, kindness still existed.

The lamp of that good memory lit my way through the lonely hours of night. With the rising sun, the urisk fell silent. When I rose, I found a circle of wet footprints all around me. Each was as long as a man's but narrow, with the marks of webs between its three toes.

From the Maiden's Tears, it was two days' walking to the eastern end of Silverwater. Here the terrain opened up to grazing land. Beyond those fields lay a line of barren hills, with a track running up to the lonely tarn named Hidden-water, a place of dark memories. There had been a battle there once, chieftain against chieftain, clan against clan, son of Alban against son of Alban. Many had fallen. When Father and I had passed through that place, coming the other way, the air had been full of voices, as if a whole troop of dead warriors lingered in the loch's stony basin, the echoes of their dying cries sounding from the rocks all around. I did not want to go there again, but there was no other way.

I waited under the last fringe of trees until dusk fell, studying the terrain ahead and fixing in my mind the places of hiding. When I judged it to be dark enough, I moved. I went like a shadow, darting from one place of concealment to the next, every part of me alert to danger. A group of rocks, a drystone wall. A midden heap, a stack of turf drying under a makeshift shelter. There were strips of walled pasture, outbuildings in which sleepy hens clucked or restless cows shuffled in their straw, and a farmhouse with light glowing from behind closed shutters. A foot set wrong might bring dogs out to the attack, or worse. I thought of eggs, of barley bread, of fresh milk and butter. I went on. When I was clear of the last farm, the last warm lamplight, the last sleepily bleating ewe, and the rocky hillside loomed before me, I scrambled into the shelter of a shallow cave and curled up to rest. Somewhere nearby I could hear water flowing. If I remembered rightly, that was the stream known as the Churn, and the path to Hiddenwater lay beside it. I would move on before dawn.

The ground was hard. I couldn't sleep. Cold pierced through to my marrow; even Flint's thick cloak could not keep it out. I couldn't make fire. That would be like lighting a beacon to show that I was here. My body was all aches and pains. Worse, my mind was playing tricks on me. I had seen nothing of the Good Folk since the night they had argued about the seven of whatever it was, though sometimes, coming along Silverwater, I had sensed a soft footfall behind me and, turning, had peered into the forest to see nothing more than shifting shadows. Here on this inhospitable hillside, I could not escape the sensation that I was being watched. Once or twice, as the long night wore on, I thought the gurgle of the stream held voices, a flow of words in which the only one I recognized was *Neryn*. An owl flew overhead, hooting strangely. Such sorrow was in its cry that tears sprang to my eyes.

Stop it, I told myself sternly as my teeth chattered with cold. *There's nobody out there, and if there is, you're not going to let them know you know. Now sleep, or you'll be too tired to go on in the morning.* But sleep would not come.

After what seemed an endless night, I rose to the first

lightening of the sullen, cloud-veiled sky and set off along the track to Hiddenwater. As if it had only been waiting for me to emerge from my bolt-hole, the wind got up, and by the time I came over the crest of the hill and headed down the steep path to the loch shore, the water before me was whipped to a turmoil of angry gray. Hiddenwater was a small loch. It lay in a steep stone bowl, with a narrow track hugging the water's edge. I must walk halfway around it to reach my path onward.

The spray hit me as I came down the track, drenching my clothing. The water was on my right, a sheer rock face on my left. Where ravines split the stone, their surfaces were a nightmare of treacherous gravel. Not a scrap of vegetation could be seen; it was as if no plant dared set root in this benighted place. The water lay in deep shadow. The stark slopes were brooding presences, hanging over the loch. The only path was the one that ran along the shore. I must hope that on such an inclement day, and so early, nobody else would be abroad.

Rain had begun to fall, shrouding the grim gray landscape in shifting sheets of moisture. Whatever spirits were condemned to haunt this desolate place, they surely led a wretched, forlorn existence. It seemed a corner of Alban deserted by all good powers.

"If you're there," I murmured, "ancient ghosts or whatever you are, please know that I mean no disrespect when I walk through this scene of your loss. I honor your memory. I ask you to let me pass unmolested."

I could barely keep my feet against the gale. It tore at

me, making my nose and eyes stream. I hugged the cloak around me, pulling the hood down over my face. I had not thought I could be any colder, but this wind cut deep. There were voices in it, not lifted in sorrowful wailing like the urisk's, but screaming of loss and futility, of old wrongs that could never be put right. *Hear us!* they howled. *Hear our call! Our lifeblood stains the water! Our bones lie shattered on the rocks! Our spirits cry out for justice!* They were all around me.

I breathed deep. My feet in their mended shoes went forward. But I heard my grandmother's voice, soft but strong, whispering in my ear. *No matter how bad things are, you always have something to give. Never forget that, Neryn.*

Gods aid me. What could I give in a place tenanted by sad ghosts? I could hardly offer them food. Besides, my supplies were dwindling. I shrank from the screaming presences. All I wanted to do was run forward, get away, find a hiding place, somewhere I could not hear them.

Likely every traveler who passed this way did that: rushed on by with fingers in ears. But I need not do it. I need not be every traveler. Now that Father was gone, my path was my own to make. Where it led me depended on how much courage I could find within myself. *You will be tested to your limit,* the little woman of the Good Folk had said. If I was afraid now, with eldritch voices howling in my ears, perhaps I should see it as a test: the first of many.

I stopped walking, bracing myself against the force of the wind. "I hear you," I said. "What do you want from me?"

Through the veils of wind-whipped rain, they appeared all around me, warrior-shades clad in the garb of long ago, their hair shaggy and wild, their faces bone white, their bodies sliced and hacked with the wounds of the battle in which they had fallen. The shouting had died down, to be replaced by a steady muttering. It came from every side, the same words over and over. "The song . . . Sing the song of truth. . . ."

I stood frozen, unable to speak, let alone sing. I knew it. Of course I knew the song, but . . .

Somewhere between the howling of the gale and the ragged voices, a fragment of melody came to my ears, a thready whistle squeezed out between lips that had long forgotten how to savor a goblet of mead, how to kiss a sweetheart, how to say *Well done* or *Farewell, friend.*

I knew the tune as I knew my own heartbeat. Everyone did. But nobody sang the song of truth aloud, not anymore. The king had forbidden it. I'd heard of a woman who was put to death after someone overheard her humming the melody as she worked in her kitchen. It hadn't always been so. In older times folk had sung the song proudly at village festivals, at gatherings of clans, at burial rites of elder or warrior or infant taken in harsh season. The men and women of Alban had worn this tune as close as their own skins. Its beloved measures had been lodged deep in every heart.

The fragile sound faltered, as if the whistler could not quite remember how the tune went. It seemed to me that if this was forgotten, this precious last fragment of what had once made us strong, we were all doomed. Softly, I began to sing: *"I am a child of Alban's earth. . . ."*

In an instant they were still, their shadowy eyes fixed on me, and the song swelled and rose and grew to thunder as twenty, fifty, a hundred ghostly voices took up the strain. My voice became a clarion call, borne on that warrior chorus. The words our king had forbidden, the words I loved with all my heart, burst from me with the force of a flame catching dry timber:

> *I am a child of Alban's earth,*
> *Her ancient bones brought me to birth,*
> *Her crags and islands built me strong,*
> *My heart beats to her deep, wild song.*
>
> *I am the wife with bairn on knee,*
> *I am the fisherman at sea,*
> *I am the piper on the strand,*
> *I am the warrior, sword in hand.*
>
> *White Lady, shield me with your fire;*
> *Lord of the North, my heart inspire;*
> *Hag of the Isles, my secrets keep;*
> *Master of Shadows, guard my sleep.*
>
> *I am the mountain, I am the sky,*
> *I am the song that will not die,*
> *I am the heather, I am the sea,*
> *My spirit is forever free.*

The song came to an end, and silence fell. The air was full of anticipation.

"What would you have me do?" I asked the ghostly army, for it was clear the song alone was not enough, or they surely would have faded away with its echoes.

"Fight. . . ." The word came out of them like a great sigh. "Fiiiight. . . ."

In their ghostly eyes I saw a flame burning, as if the passion they had shown in their last bloody encounter had not been extinguished by their years of lonely exile here in the place of their fall. But fight? Me?

"I am no warrior," I said. "Look at me. I'm a . . . a vagrant, a nobody." I dropped my gaze, suddenly unable to meet their eyes. Their need was powerful in them; perhaps only that held them in the realm of the living. Was it possible that I was the only person ever to stop and listen? Could I be the only one who had heard their cry for justice?

"I can't. . . . I don't know what I can do," I whispered. How could I fight? The greatest warrior in all Alban could not stand against the might of Keldec. And that, without a doubt, was the fight they meant. "I want to help," I said, risking a glance up at them. "But I am powerless."

Oh gods, their faces, on which the blaze of hope kindled by the song was already starting to fade; their eyes, already losing the brightness of their awakening . . . How could I bear this? I sank to a crouch, lifting my hands to cover my face, for their sadness was like a knife straight to the heart and I could not look at them.

I did not complete the gesture. For there, in a crevice between the rocks at my feet, I saw a tiny plant growing. Three fronded shoots of soft green cradled a single flower no bigger than my thumbnail, a five-petaled bloom, white as first snow, fragile and perfect. So unlikely a survivor. So delicate, to stand against the scourging wind, the biting cold, the drenching rain. It was surely the only living thing in this place of death and sorrow. Apart from me.

I rose to my feet and drew a ragged breath. "I'll try," I said.

A ripple passed through the spectral crew. As I spoke, they stood taller, their pallid faces lighting with a fragile hope.

"I can't fight with sword and spear as my brother did, but I'll stand up for justice. I don't know how, but I promise I'll find a way."

As if a silent message had passed between them, each member of the ghostly army made the same gesture: a clenched fist placed over the heart. Through the falling rain their voices came to me as one: "Weapons sharp. Backs straight. Hearts high."

Then in an instant they were gone, dissipated to nothing as, somewhere behind the clouds, the sun edged over the horizon. I was alone on the bank of Hiddenwater, shivering in my wet clothing.

I drew a deep, unsteady breath and made myself walk on. The gray water beside me rippled and stirred uneasily. My heart was thumping and my palms were clammy. In my mind the warrior voices sang on, lifted in a chorus of hope and faith, grand, powerful, indomitable. Yet here was I, an ordinary girl whose life was all fear, flight, and concealment. What had possessed me to stand up and accept a challenge I surely could not meet? The battle I had agreed to fight was for Alban's freedom. That meant a new king and a new rule. The thought made me tremble. It was huge, monstrous, terrifying. The strongest fighter, the most powerful mage, could not stand up against Keldec. His might was absolute. The Cull accounted not only for the canny but also for anyone heard to question the king's rule. Those chieftains not cowed into obedience could expect the sort of treatment Dunchan of Silverwater had suffered. The populace was beaten down into submission. The iron fist of the Enforcers was everywhere. And if their unthinking brutality proved insufficient punishment, Keldec had one more weapon in his armory: magic. For though it was forbidden for ordinary folk to use canny skills, those skills were a tool in the king's hand, and he used them cruelly indeed.

This was the man I had just sworn to fight, a man whose power was a hundred times greater than mine. I was fifteen and all alone in the world. I was tired, hungry, and cold, and there was a long way to go. If Shadowfell was where Farral had thought it was. If it was what he had believed it was: a place where folk dared to speak the truth, a place where they could plan a future free from tyranny. I prayed that Shadowfell was more than a wild dream born of a desperate hope that someone, someday, would be strong enough to stand up for what was right.

I had to keep my promise. I had to fight, and the first step in the battle was finding Shadowfell. Those ghostly warriors had believed in me. They had shown their faith in me. I must have faith in myself and keep going. Sing the song. Keep weapons sharp, back straight, heart high. One person might not stand against Keldec and his Enforcers. But if enough of us did so, there would be an army.

CHAPTER FOUR

NIGHTFALL FOUND ME CLOSE TO DEEPWATER, longest in the chain of lochs. The oak forest that cloaked the banks would offer shelter and concealment for the next few days' walking at least. At the far end of Deepwater lay the king's summer fortress. I must pass close by that place to reach the track to the north. Dwell too much on that and I might lose my hard-won courage.

I risked a fire, for my clothing was wet and I could not stop the trembling that ran through my body. There were places in these woods where rock or tree canopy had kept fallen timber reasonably dry, though striking a spark was a challenge. My hands were shaking from cold. I took off Flint's cloak—gods, how would I have managed without it?—and hung it over a rock near the fire, where it steamed alongside my tunic and shirt. I put on the garment Flint had left. It had been rolled up in my bag and was a little less damp than my own things.

I had tried to forage along the way, but my efforts

had supplied no more than a handful of wizened berries and a scant bunch of herbs. I boiled up the leaves to make a rudimentary soup, which I drank slowly, savoring the warmth of each mouthful. When I was done, I set the little pot down with some of the mixture still in it, and beside it I arranged the last three berries on a fallen leaf. I did not think I had imagined the stealthy tread of small feet behind me today, especially once I had entered the forest.

I wrapped the damp cloak around me and settled to rest. Already the oaks were shedding their summer mantles, and I slept half-buried in a rustling blanket of leaves. Soon the forest would no longer provide safe concealment. I was wood wise; I had learned the skills I needed while Father and I were on the run. What I had not been taught by Grandmother about foraging and making shelter, I had worked out for myself as Father and I crisscrossed the highlands, always keeping one step ahead of trouble. We stayed no longer than a night or two in any single place, fearing our presence might bring unwelcome attention on those who sheltered us. We never talked about why the Enforcers might be interested in us. Often enough they came close to us, covertly, thinking we would not know them in their plain dark clothing, without their silver brooches and their jingling harness. But we knew: their ill deeds hung over them like a bad smell. We used what skills we had to vanish into the forest; we let Alban conceal us.

Once or twice folk had whispered that the king's men were asking after a traveler in the north, a fellow with a good hand for stanies, wandering with a daughter who was somewhere between girl and woman. Had anyone seen this pair? If they did, they were to report it straightaway to the nearest Enforcer. Lie about it and the punishment would be grievous indeed. Nonetheless, some folk had been brave enough to warn us. Not of recent times.

I walked for one day, two days, three. I developed a cough that would not clear. Each night in the forest the spasms kept me awake longer and hurt more. Each morning, as I awoke to another day of chill and damp, I found it harder to catch my breath. There were herbs that might have eased the symptoms, but they did not seem to grow here, and even if I had been able to find them, I could only have made the simplest of infusions.

Hope is easy enough to find on a sunny day, when a person's clothing is dry and her belly is full and the prospect of a good night's rest lies ahead. It is much harder to keep that flame alight when autumn closes in and the rain falls in sheets, drenching every tree and bush and turning the ground to a treacherous quagmire. It is still more difficult when the wind gets up, chilling the air and sending every creature scurrying for what meager shelter it can find.

Staring into my little fire one night, I acknowledged

that I would soon be in serious trouble. I was dizzy with hunger. My chest ached. I always felt cold, even though I spent all day on the move, climbing rock walls, making precarious crossings over gushing streams, darting into cover if I saw any sign of human activity. For even here, up in the woods, there were tracks used by local cottagers, places where pigs were driven out to forage for nuts and roots, signs that folk had been burning charcoal or gathering firewood. The closer I came to Summerfort, the harder it would be to stay unseen.

I reached a place where the track dipped down to run along a lower part of the hill, a stone's throw from the broader way that followed the loch shore. This was a well-made earthen road suited to carts and riders, and it was busy. Among those who passed along it were groups of Enforcers, most of them heading eastward. They were riding to Summerfort, I guessed. Perhaps they would report the progress of the Cull to King Keldec, if he was still in residence there. He would be proud of them.

It made me sick to see them ride by. I kept well clear of the road and moved as quietly as I could. One wrong step, one cracking twig or sliding foot, and I would be in custody in the blink of an eye, forced to answer hard questions about what I was doing out here on my own.

Four days, five days, and still no sight of Summerfort. The leaves fell all around me; the branches above me grew bare and stark. This was taking too long. What if I could not reach the pass before the winter snow came? But I couldn't press on today. Riders had been going by since early morning. If I came too close, my coughing would give me away. I found a hollow barely big enough to accommodate a fox and crouched there in the hope that the way would clear so I could move on. As I waited, the sky opened, releasing a downpour that dwarfed the previous rain. I huddled under Flint's cloak, watching the road, where the deluge had slowed but not halted the stream of riders traveling eastward. Water dripped from the foliage to pool around me. My bones ached with cold.

There was no making fire. I had neither heart nor strength to look for food. I could not remember how it felt to have a full belly. It seemed to me I would never be dry and warm again. I cursed Father for dying; I cursed him for believing he could change our world with a wager.

"If only you were here," I whispered into the chill as the light faded to dusk and the endless curtain of rain turned all to shadowy haze around me. He couldn't have made the rain stop; he had no canny powers. He couldn't have conjured supper from nowhere or stopped the Enforcers from riding by. But if he had been here, I would not have been alone.

I stayed where I was for a night and a day. On the second night the rain stopped and I risked moving on in the dark. My limbs were like an old woman's, stiff and cramped. I crept through the woods, struggling not to cough. Each furtive footstep sounded to me like an intrusive crash, alerting the whole world to my presence. Perhaps Keldec had sentries right here on the hill. Maybe the

Enforcers who had ridden past yesterday were waiting just around the next corner. When an owl flew out from the trees ahead, my heart jolted in fright.

The walk felt endless. It felt pointless. Why in the name of the gods had I promised to fight? I could hardly manage to put one foot in front of the other. *Remember the song,* I told myself. But that seemed a long time ago, and I was too tired to remember.

At last came a watery dawn, and there, a hundred paces or so before me, was the broad valley of the Rush, the river that cut through the mountains on its headlong progress to Deepwater. Once I reached the crest of the hill, just over there, I would be looking down on the stone keep, the wall, the hard-packed practice areas of Summerfort. There would be guards everywhere.

A voice spoke right behind me, making me jump in fright. "You'll be wanting a wee sit-down and maybe a brew."

I whirled around. Standing quiet as shadows amid the damp ferns of the forest floor were two small figures. The little woman in the hooded green cloak: Sage. The odd creature with the leafy pelt: Sorrel. He extended a fronded hand, beckoning. I did not move.

"A brew?" I croaked, thinking how good it would be to wrap my hands around a warm cup, to soothe my aching throat with a hot drink. "You can't make fire here. We're too close to Summerfort. They'd see the smoke. And we should keep our voices down."

"Still heading north, are you?" Sage's eyes were fixed on me in piercing question.

Had I told them this? "Up the valley of the Rush."

The little woman looked at her companion, then the two of them gazed at me. "You'll not get far in that state," she said. "A few steps out from the forest, just far enough for king's men to catch sight of you, and then you'll collapse in a dead faint. If you won't accept help when it's offered, you're more fool than I took you for."

"I must go on," I whispered.

"Not without a brew and a warm-up," said Sorrel. "Come this way."

"I told you—"

"Aye, we heard you. *They'd see the smoke.* From your fire, maybe. Not from mine."

"Come on, lassie," Sage said, reaching up to take a fold of my cloak between her bony fingers. "You're all shivery-shaky. It's not far."

Their fire was a little higher up the hill, in a depression between great rocks. It was so tiny I doubted it would warm so much as a beetle. There was no smoke at all. On the flames was a small pannikin, and there was Red Cap, stirring the contents with a long stick. He still wore the sling. I could see the small ears of the infant sticking up from it. None of the others seemed to be around. I crept into the shelter and realized I was wrong on one count, for the flames' warmth was a blessing on my chill body. I sank down, easing my bag from my shoulder.

"Aye, that's it," Sage said, eyeing me as I stretched out my hands to the fire. "You can't go on anyway, with king's men on the road. You may as well be warm and fed."

Before I could say much at all, Red Cap was ladling a mushroom broth out of his tiny pannikin into even smaller bowls fashioned of interwoven leaves. He put one of these in my hands. "Eat up," he advised, and applied himself to his own meal. Sorrel drank his share straight from the bowl. Sage ate tidily, using an implement fashioned from an acorn cup.

I hesitated, my mouth watering, my mind on old tales about people who wandered into the realm of the Good Folk, accepted tempting treats, and found they could never return home again.

"Get on with it, then," Sorrel urged. "You're skin and bone, girl."

"You'll take no harm from the brew," put in Sage, quicker to understand why I held back. "Eat your fill."

So I ate, though my sore throat made it hard to swallow. The food was good. It was astonishing that such a small pot could provide sufficient for all four of us, but it did. When Red Cap had drunk half his bowlful, he loosened the sling, lifted out the baby, and sat it on his knee, then proceeded to feed it the remainder of his meal by dipping his finger in and letting the infant suck off the broth.

As soon as I was done eating, I got to my feet again.

"I should go on," I made myself say, though I longed to stay by the fire. "Thank you for helping me—"

"Sun's up," Sorrel observed. "King's men will be watching. Besides, you're dripping wet. Bide awhile, dry yourself, and watch who comes and goes down there. If you have to run in the open, don't do it without thinking."

"That could be the best way to do it," I said. "Before I lose my courage."

"A plan, that's what you need, and common sense," said Sage. "Do what the wee mannie tells you, Neryn. Rest, dry those wet things, get some heart back."

I sat down again, or, rather, my legs gave up the effort to support me. "How do you know my name?"

Sage gave me a beady-eyed look. "We know what we know," she said, which was no answer at all.

"Where are the folk who were with you earlier? Silver, and the man in the nutshell cape, and all those others?"

"Ah." Sage had her hands held out to the fire's warmth. She gazed into the flames. "We had what you might call a disagreement. The three of us came this way. The others . . . well, they followed Silver, as they generally do."

Had I been the cause of this? Had I parted friend from friend? I hoped not.

"Our kind, we're solitary folk mostly, you understand. Get more than two of us together and we're uncomfortable. Get more than three of us together and you'll likely have a dispute."

"There are three of you."

"Aye, well, three's not such a bad number. In the old tales it's all threes. And we're not your run-of-the-mill folk." She glanced at her companions. "Silver and her band were eager to leave you to your own devices. Keen to send you on your journey alone."

"They were right," I said, "though today I am very glad of your fire, your food, and your companionship. The king's laws forbid all of this. You should go home and leave me."

"Home? What home does she mean, Sage?" If Sorrel had been possessed of visible eyebrows, he would have lifted them at this point.

"I don't rightly know, Sorrel. The old home under the earth? Or a new wee home, with a bittie wall in front and flowers growing over it, maybe?" Sage's unswerving stare had never left my face. "Would that be your picture of it, Red Cap?"

"With this king ruling Alban," Red Cap said, "we've got no more home than you have, lassie. We're all of us set adrift, letting the storm carry us where it will." As he spoke, he was tucking the young one back into the sling, his hands deft and gentle.

"I'm sorry," I said after a moment. "What is the old home you mentioned, under the earth? Is that a . . . retreat? A portal to your own world?" Rumor had it that many of the Good Folk had slipped through into that other place, never to be seen again by humankind.

Their eyes were full of sadness.

"We're all bairns of Alban," said Sorrel eventually. "We live in the same world as you, lassie. The world of the king's brutes, the world of the poxy mind-scrapers with their fell tricks. As for that other place, aye, it's real. It's a hidey-hole. There's more than a few of our kind went away there when they saw your king's mischief at work. Sorrel and Red Cap and I, we could do the same. But we're small folk. Most times, we pass without notice."

A shiver went through me, not so much cold as foreboding. "I'd best move on as soon as I can, then. Being with me puts you in danger."

"Because of your gift, aye."

"That's what keeps me running. We were warned long ago, my father and I, that the Enforcers might be looking for me. So we learned to lose ourselves in the woods or in the mountains. We learned to hide, to be invisible, as far as an ordinary man or woman can be. A few times they nearly caught up with me."

"So we've heard," Sage said. "Makes a body wonder what gift it might be that they're so interested in. Not that the Cull doesn't stamp hard enough on anyone with a spark of canny knowledge, but this . . . it's different."

If she'd been a human woman, I'd never have spoken of this. But I was beginning to think Sage could be a friend. And it seemed she knew a lot about me already, without ever being told. "My gift is to be able to see your kind, even when you are merged into rocks or bushes or water. I know most people can't see you unless you choose to come out and show yourselves. It's a simple enough gift."

"Simple, that's what you think?" Sage lifted her brows at me.

"I don't see how it could be dangerous. I don't understand why the Enforcers would especially want to find me." I remembered the day we had heard they might be looking for me. Shocking news, that had been, sickening, fearful news. But Father and I had been numb from our losses, and we had simply thanked our informant for the whispered warning and slipped away. "They may still be looking for me, so I must keep moving on. But you're right, it would be foolish to rush out there without a plan. If you think my things will dry . . ." I eyed the tiny fire.

"They can't get any wetter," observed Sage. "Spread yon big cloakie over the rock, hook the shawl on a branch, and sit you down a while longer. Then we'll go higher and take a look."

"How did you come by that?" Sorrel asked, looking at the cloak.

"Why do you ask?"

"Doesn't seem quite right. Something about it."

"It's a man's cloak. A stranger gave it to me, back in Darkwater."

"Oh, aye." That was all the creature said, but I saw his eyes move to the dark swath of wool from time to time, as if trying to work out what it meant.

They had questions, then, and I offered answers where I could. I told them about the urisk, and how I had made myself lie still as a log on the ground until the sun had lightened the darkness of the forest. I told them how all my sorrows had come back to me, hearing that mournful voice, and how I had made myself remember something good, so

I would not give in to its pleading. I did not speak of Flint. I did not mention Shadowfell.

When my account was finished, my three listeners exchanged looks that were heavy with meaning. Sage held up seven fingers; Sorrel held up two; Red Cap nodded. But when I asked them what this signified, they busied themselves with tending to their fire and had nothing to say.

In time the rain ceased, patches of clear sky appeared, and watery sunlight filtered down between the branches of the oaks, where leaves clung in last defiance of the turning season. My clothing dried—perhaps I should not have been surprised that my companions' little fire did the job so well. At one point Sage went off into the woods, returning some time later with a bunch of the herbs that had eluded me. Red Cap brewed a tea to soothe my aching throat.

"You'll not get far with that cough," Sage observed, watching me drink the draft. "If you can't keep quiet, how can you hide from folk who mean you harm?"

"I'll keep away from the farms until my cough is gone."

"There's not a lot of eatables to be gleaned up the Rush valley," Sorrel said.

"I'll be all right for a while. You've fed me well today."

Plain on their faces was the conviction that I would be far from all right, but nobody said a word.

"I can fend for myself," I said firmly. "You said we could go up and take a look out over the valley. Can we do that now?"

"Aye, we will."

They led me to a vantage point shielded by great stones. From here I could look down over the broad valley of the Rush. The river slowed its breakneck pace on this last part of its course, dividing into three separate streams that flowed into Deepwater. And there, on the far side of those streams, close by the loch shore, was Summerfort: a formidable fortress of stone. A wall enclosed both the keep and various other buildings, sufficient to house a large contingent of warriors as well as all the folk required to maintain a royal household over the summer. There was no banner flying atop the keep. I breathed more easily for that, for it meant the king was not in residence.

When we had first left our home village, or what was left of it, Father and I had fled down the valley of the Rush, up into these woods, and away. I had not expected to pass this way again. Stunned by shock and grief, I had thought only of running, hiding, putting as many miles between myself and Corbie's Wood as I could. When Father and I had looked down on Summerfort, warriors had been performing complicated maneuvers on horseback, moving across the expanse of hard-packed earth that formed the keep's practice ground.

"Getting ready for the Gathering," Father had muttered. "Even that, Keldec's made his own. Set his stamp on the very heart of us. Celebrations? Games? It's all blood and fear now, and the sort of games no man would play if he had any choice. Come, Neryn, let's walk on." We had passed by like a pair of ghosts, silent and wary. I had not asked for further details, and Father had not offered them.

Well, Father was gone now, and here I was, on a journey I had never thought to make. There would be no slipping by Summerfort under cover. Sometime in the last three years, the area all around the fortress walls had been completely cleared of trees. Where beech and birch had stood, softening the grim stone, there remained nothing but a scattering of stumps. One or two had sprouted hopeful clusters of new leaves, which now shriveled under autumn's cold fingers.

"Not a lot of cover in those bittie trees," put in Sorrel helpfully. "Besides, the water's up. No getting over the ford, not on foot. You'll have to cross the king's bridge up there."

It was true. The rain had swollen the Rush. Here and there the flow had broken the banks, and the three streams looked both broad and deep. To attempt a wade across would, at the very least, make me a target for the sentries atop the Summerfort tower. More likely I would be swept downstream and drowned. From where we stood, we could not see the king's bridge, but I knew it was always guarded. When Father and I had come down the valley, the sentries had waved us across. That seemed altogether remarkable to me now, though at the time I had been too wretched to think much of it. Perhaps Father and I had looked the way we'd felt: powerless, incapable, numb with grief. No threat.

"Best have a story ready," suggested Sage, "and brazen it out. Walk on the track, hold your head up, and when you get to the bridge, don't let on what you're thinking. It'll be risky, mind."

"Risky, aye," put in Red Cap. "But not as risky as trying to slip by unseen and being spotted. If king's men catch you, it's all up."

"Is there no other way across the river?"

My companions exchanged a look, but did not speak.

"Another bridge, higher up? A different path that will lead me to the Three Hags?"

Sorrel cleared his throat. "There might be."

"How do I reach it?" What was it they were not saying?

"You'd go up this side of the Rush, half a day's walking," Sorrel said. "There's a track. Folk live up that way, here and there."

"Where does the track lead?" I asked, hearing the reservation in Sorrel's tone. Sage's eyes were troubled. Red Cap was scratching his furry head, as if wondering whether I was crazy. Clearly there was a reason why this way had not been mentioned earlier.

"Nowhere," Sage said flatly. "You wouldn't be wanting to go that way. Folk don't cross the Rush up there. Your kind of folk, I mean."

"But there is a bridge?"

"Oh, aye. If you can call it that." There was a weighty pause, then Sage added, "Do what you think best, lassie. You can go by the big track and hope nobody stops you.

Or you can take the wee bittie path and hope it's not a foolish risk."

"Which way would you go?"

"Ah," said Sage. "It's not for me to choose."

Time was passing. If I did not move on soon, I could be stuck out in the open at nightfall. I must get past the farms by dusk. "I'm not asking you to choose, I'm asking for your advice!" I heard how sharp that sounded. "Please," I added more softly.

"It's your own path that lies before you," Sage said. There was a weariness in her tone. "You'll make your own choices, for good or ill."

"If you wanted *my* advice," put in Sorrel, "I'd bid you take the three of us along with you. Any path's easier when you're not on your own."

Tears welled in my eyes, and I blinked them away. "You mustn't leave the safety of these woods. Where I'm going, there's scant cover—it's all rocks and open hillsides. It's cold and bare. And while I might pass for an ordinary traveler, the first sight of you would tell any sentry that you're . . . Other."

The three of them hooted with laughter.

"Shh!" I hissed. Gods, they'd alert every sentry in the valley at this rate.

"You forget," Sage said, "we have the knack of blending. An ordinary man might look at us and see only stones or water or leaves in the sunlight. If we couldn't blend, we wouldn't have been in Alban since long before

85

your grandmother's great-grandmother was a bairnie in the cradle."

There was no disputing this. Most men and women in Alban had never seen one of the Good Folk. Most people were not like me. "Sometimes I think my gift is a curse," I murmured. "All it seems to do is bring down trouble. Please don't come any farther up the valley—being with me must put you in danger."

"True, no doubt," said Sage. "We know you're set on going forward alone, and perhaps that's the way it has to be. Go safely, and find what you're searching for."

They were fading before my eyes, blending into the shadowy hues of the forest.

"Goodbye," I said, shouldering my bag. "Thank you for your kindness." But they were already gone.

I chose the path on the near side of the Rush. The smaller bridge, the one the Good Folk had not seemed to want to talk about, was a lesser terror than the king's bridge, with its guards, and this track a more likely prospect than the broader way, on which I would be visible to all who rode by. The dark gray of Flint's cloak would blend well with the stony terrain beyond the forest fringe. Unlike the other path, this one lay somewhat above the valley floor, following the natural curves of the hillside. That would allow partial concealment from watching eyes down below. Of course, if sentries were posted to observe comings and goings in the Rush valley, this would be a good position for one. I must be prepared for anything.

Smoke was rising from hearth fires somewhere up ahead. Perched in unlikely spots on the rocky hillside were meager dwellings, low to the ground as if hunkered down against wind and rain. They looked smaller and poorer than the farmsteads dotted across the valley floor. Down there I could see cattle grazing in walled fields, and well-tended vegetable patches. People too: a girl herding sheep with two dogs working to her whistled commands; a man with a cart piled high with bulging sacks, heading back toward Summerfort. I tried to be a shadow, a nothing, a mere alteration in the color of the rocks. *Don't see me,* I willed them.

I walked for some time, passing one modest habitation after another, dodging behind a shed when a woman came out to throw scraps for a flock of scrawny chickens, hiding between rocks when a man rode by on a stocky farm horse with a child perched in front of him. I waited until he was out of sight, then crept out and went forward again. I saw the king's bridge in the valley below me: guards at either end and a trickle of folk crossing over.

Later, a band of Enforcers appeared below me, moving down the valley toward Summerfort. They rode in a precise formation of pairs, and I crouched behind a tumbledown outhouse until they had passed, fearful that one of them might glance up and spot me. Thank the gods I had not chosen to go that way. They carried the shadow with them, those men. Just so had they departed my home village three years ago, a tidy, orderly group, turning their backs on the chaos they had wrought. Turning their backs on the bones and ash, the blood, the twisted bodies and tangled minds that were all that was left of a place where folk had lived and worked and raised their families for countless years. It was because of her that they did it, because of Grandmother and her canny gift. So I had hidden, and watched, and witnessed the unspeakable. If I was caught today or tomorrow or another day, if I came face to face with an Enforcer, I must lock that memory away so tightly that no trace of it could show in my eyes. I must shut it in so deep that no vestige of it could tremble in my voice. I must lie as I had never lied before.

I had a story ready. I was an orphan, my fisherman father having drowned at sea not long ago. I was making my way to the home of my only remaining kinsfolk, who lived in a remote settlement in the north. My name was Calla, and the name of the place was Stonewater.

It was not so far from the truth, I thought as I walked on. Our village had been in the north, though not so far north as Shadowfell. But when we lost everything, Father and I had turned our backs on our shattered home. As for the time before the Enforcers came to our village, it seemed far away now, like a lovely dream or a wonderful bedtime story. I imagined Mother sitting beside my bed, humming an old tune as I fell asleep. Her hair bright in the lamplight, her eyes a tranquil blue, her face . . . I could not remember her face. Father had told me I looked like her, but the wan, gaunt features I sometimes glimpsed in the water as I bent to drink surely bore little resemblance to hers. If I had no clear vision of her, I did remember that she was a happy person, given to smiles and song. I could almost feel glad that she was gone, for the Alban of now was not the peaceable land of my early childhood, and if she had survived, she might have found little cause for joy.

My thoughts on Mother and what might have been, I rounded a corner and walked straight into a man coming the other way.

CHAPTER FIVE

HE GRABBED ME, SHOUTING—NOT WORDS, ONLY an agitated babble. His grip was strong as iron.

"Let me go!" I gasped. "Please."

My captor turned me and pinned me against his chest, facing forward. His strange, flat voice kept up its flow of sounds, as if he was trying to speak but could not make himself understood. Through my shock and fear, memory rose in me.

"It's all right," I said shakily, even as the man's hands bit into my arms and his voice rose in a harsh wail of agitation. I struggled for a reassuring tone, the kind I might use to pacify an overwrought child. "I won't harm you. I won't harm anyone here. Please let go of me."

A new stream of sounds issued from him, louder, wilder. Holding me as a toddler might a rag doll, he started walking along the track. My heart pounded. I fought for breath. His arm had slipped up around my neck, and with each step he took, my feet left the ground. We were heading toward a cottage tucked into a pocket of flat land beside the path. Several other dwellings were strung out along the way ahead, and as the man continued to shout his nonsense, I saw a shutter open here, a door there, only a crack, as if folk wanted to know what was happening but were not prepared to come out and look. I did not call for help—could not, for I was half-strangled. My captor manhandled me up to the door of the cottage.

"Mawa?" he called. "Mawa, wha'oo? Gar! Fa gar! " He crashed his shoulder against the door, making it shiver in its frame. The force of the blow jarred my whole body, making my head spin. Spots appeared before my eyes.

"Mawa!" he shouted. I heard anger and fear in his rough voice as he drew a great breath, readying himself for another assault on the door. Before he could throw himself at it, there was a sound of running footsteps from the path alongside the cottage, and a woman came into view, white-faced, holding up her skirt for speed.

"Garret, no!" she cried out. "Let her go! Friend, Garret, the lady is a friend."

"Gar!" he said again, but his arms had slackened their death grip on me, and his voice was quieter. *Girl. Found girl.* Perhaps all his words made sense, if only one took the time to interpret them. Oh gods, I hoped I was wrong about him.

"You can let go of her, Garret. She won't hurt me."

"Huur . . ." He had picked up only one word of the woman's speech.

"I won't hurt her," I said, my voice coming out as a rasping croak. "And I won't hurt you. Let me go. Please."

The woman was beside us now, easing his hands off me, gazing up into his face, making sure he was listening. "Friend. No hurt. Garret, inside now." She opened the door, which was not bolted, and shepherded him in, then stood on the threshold glancing up the track to the doors and shutters from behind which her neighbors were no doubt watching everything.

"I'd best go on," I muttered. "I'll get you in trouble." A bout of coughing shook me.

"Inside." She reached out and took my wrist, drawing me within the house and shutting the door firmly behind us. "I'm sorry. Did my husband hurt you?"

I must have gaped at that, for she drew her shawl around her and lifted her chin as if challenging me to make comment. She was young, perhaps not much older than I was, but her face was that of a person carrying a heavy burden.

"I'm fine now," I said, though Garret's vicelike grip had bruised my arms and hurt my throat. "He did no harm. I should go on. You don't want me in your house." My gaze went to the shutters. Garret had seated himself on the floor by the well-screened hearth and was attempting to build a tower from firewood.

"Hahss," he echoed.

"He doesn't mean any harm," the girl said, moving to set a kettle on the fire. "I hope you understand that. I hope you won't . . ."

Her husband. This man-child playing on the floor, this big, strong infant with his handsome, unthinking face. For he was a good-looking man, or had once been, his features well balanced and regular. I guessed that his eyes had not always darted about as they did now. I imagined that his mouth had not always been slack and open, with a thread of spittle at the corner.

"Wipe your mouth, Garret," the girl said, and when he simply looked at her, she crouched down beside him and lifted a corner of her apron to dab gently at his lips. The look on her face made me want to weep, for it was tenderness, pride, and anguish all in one. "There, sweetheart," she murmured. "You sit quiet now and I'll make you some honey brew." She rose to her feet, straight-backed and dignified in her old clothes. "He likes his honey brew."

She moved to the well-scrubbed table and began to assemble ingredients, a tiny pot of honey, a pinch of dried herbs, a green apple. "You won't tell, will you?" she said. It sounded as if she were forcing the words out. "That he grabbed hold of you? Most of the time he's good. Most of the time I can keep him out of trouble. But I was up tending to a goat that's ailing, and he wandered off. You see how he is."

"I won't tell," I said. "I'm not stopping here; I must get on. He did me no harm. Mara, is that your name?"

A wintry ghost of a smile crossed her lips. "How did you know that?"

"He said it, didn't he? *Mara, where are you? I found a girl.*"

Mara surprised me by sinking down on a chair and putting her face in her hands. I thought perhaps she was crying.

After a little she spoke. "You understood him. How? When I tell people he still makes sense, they don't believe me. Everyone says he's . . . all gone, shrunk away to nothing." She lowered her hands, gazing at the ruin of her man.

There is always something you can give. What could I give here, when there was no mending the wrongs of the past? A smile? A song? No, I could give something far more precious to me: time. Never mind that it was a half day's walk to this bridge. Never mind that I must reach it before nightfall. This was more important.

I seated myself on the floor opposite Garret. He had found a little wooden cart by the hearth, with cunning wheels that turned on pegs, and was pushing it across the floor. I caught it, turned it, and pushed it back to him.

"Is this your cart, Garret?" I asked.

"Beha," the man said. "Beha cah."

A silence. "Brendan's cart," the girl translated.

"Beha!" Garret was excited now, anticipating a treat. He scrambled up onto his feet. "See Beha!"

"Sit down, Garret." The girl's voice bore a well-practiced evenness of tone. "Brendan's not coming today. Another day. Later."

"Beha come!"

I saw how tired she was. I saw the pallor of her delicate face, the lines of exhaustion that aged her, the fragile strength that would not let her give up.

"Is there nobody to help you?" I murmured, thinking of all the work of house and fields, and the terrible, never-ending task of watching over her damaged man.

"We do well enough, Garret and me. He's strong. He can lift things I can't manage, or hold a creature still while I tend to it. He just needs telling what to do." Her glance went up, almost despite her, to a hook in the rafters, and I saw there something quite unexpected: a graceful little knee harp, suspended from a cord.

"Yours?" I asked her, wondering how long it was since she had had time and inclination for making music.

"Garret's. He was a fine player, before. Folk came from all around to hear him." Her flat tone held a world of pain. "That was what drew their attention. His playing was so beautiful, some began to think it must be . . . canny." Her voice cracked. "So the Enforcers came for him, but seeing what a big, strong man he was, they didn't kill him. They thought to turn him to the king's will and make him into a fine, obedient warrior. You've heard what they do, I suppose. The mind-scrapers." Her voice had fallen to a murmur.

I had not only heard it, I had seen it with my own eyes, trapped as I had been in the wall of Grandmother's cottage and forbidden so much as to squeak. I nodded, wondering that Mara was prepared to speak so openly to me.

"They brought him back next day, and he was like this. No warrior, nor even the man he had been, but . . ." Mara faltered to a halt, watching Garret as he pushed the little cart along the hearth. "It's hard for people to understand," she went on. "He barely sleeps at night. I sing to him, tell him tales, hold him, and soothe him. If I'm lucky, he'll drop off for a bit before sunup. As for the harp, I can't get it down; he'd only break it."

"Who is Brendan?" I asked, knowing it was none of my business, but wanting, suddenly, the reassurance that she was not quite alone.

"Our son. I sent him away, to my mother's village. Garret misses him. But it's too dangerous. He doesn't know his own strength, you see. What they did to him, it was meant to make him obedient. But sometimes their magic goes awry, steals some part of a man that there's no getting back." She tipped her chopped ingredients into a small pot and added water from the kettle, using her free hand to bat her husband's curious fingers out of harm's way. "No, Garret, hot!" She stirred the mixture with a wooden spoon. "Brendan's only three years old. He's best off out of this. We don't see him much."

"See Beha!" Garret's voice was insistent, woeful. "Beha!" He drummed his feet on the floor.

There was a basket of straw at one side of the hearth, perhaps bedding for an animal. I plucked out a handful and began to weave the strands together, pretending I did not see the pair of bright eyes within the basket, eyes that most certainly did not belong to a cat or rabbit or motherless lamb. "Look, Garret," I said.

He was instantly fascinated, edging over to sit right beside me, his gaze intent on my busy fingers. I twisted and knotted and bent the straw to make a little figure with legs, arms, and a head, then put it in his hand. "Garret," I said. "Man." As I made a second, slightly smaller manikin, with a head of long, wispy hair, Mara sat down at the table, watching in silence. I wondered how long it was since anyone had given their time to Garret, how long since she had been able to rest for a few moments knowing he was safe and happy. I thought of that last season with Grandmother, when Father was out laboring on farms to earn our keep, leaving me to tend to her. The exhaustion of the road was nothing beside the bone-shattering weariness of those endless days and nights of constant watchfulness. She had seldom slept more than an hour at a time. She had lost control of her bodily functions. She would rock to and fro, weeping, making me wonder if, deep down, there still burned a tiny spark of the brave, wise woman she had once been.

"Mara," I said, handing Garret the second little figure. "Woman."

Garret smiled. He made the two tiny people do a little dance along his leg, and a whistle emerged from him, an attempt at a tune. "Beha," he urged. "May Beha!"

As I fashioned Brendan, a very small straw person, I imagined Mara and Garret's son in fifteen years' time, a young man finding his path in the world. I thought of him in twenty-five years' time, with a wife and children, and parents he hardly knew. "Brendan," I said, putting the finished manikin in Garret's hand. "Your son. Your boy."

From the basket of straw the strange eyes watched, unblinking. Perhaps this sad pair was not entirely alone. There was an infinitesimal rustling sound.

"Mice," said Mara a little too quickly. "They're everywhere this autumn. Will you take some honey brew? It'll warm you for the road."

I rose to my feet. For now, Garret was happy with his little straw family. "Thank you. I shouldn't linger here." Mara's eyes met mine across the table, where three cups of brew stood gently steaming. "You've been kind," I added. I would not tell her about Grandmother. She need not know that I understood all too well what it meant to see a loved one come to this. "I honor you for your courage and goodness."

Mara wrapped her hands around her cup. "Not so good," she murmured. "I look at him sometimes, and I wish . . . Never mind."

"It can be hard to go on." I had tended my grandmother for a scant two seasons before an ague killed her. Garret looked strong and healthy; he could live for forty years.

"He's my husband." She spoke with devastating simplicity. "I'm all he has."

Not long after, with my supplies replenished by a gift of bread and cheese that Mara had insisted I put in my bag, I was at the door of her cottage, my cloak around my shoulders, my belongings on my back.

"If I could shelter you here, I would," Mara said. "But folk distrust us. If they weren't afraid of Garret's temper, they'd have cast us out long ago."

"You've already given me more than most folk would," I said. "Best if I move on now. How far away is the bridge?"

Mara turned pale. "You mean the old bridge? The one up that way?" She jerked her head toward the north, up the track.

"That's right."

"Nobody goes there, not anymore." Her tone was hushed. "Try it and the river will send you back down again, stone-dead. You can't get across up there."

My heart sinking, I looked down the valley toward the king's bridge, which was the only other way. The guards were checking all travelers before they passed over. Their weapons glinted in the weak autumn sunlight. "I'll have to chance it," I said. "Goodbye, Mara. Thank you."

"The gods guard your steps," she said, her voice a mere whisper.

Behind her in the doorway, Garret suddenly loomed. He had tucked his straw family into the neck of his shirt; their faceless heads peeped out over the coarse homespun, blind witnesses to my departure. He uttered a series of sounds that I took to be a farewell.

"Goodbye, Garret," I said, managing a smile. "You're a good man, and I wish you happiness."

From one of the houses farther along the track there came the sound of voices, and Mara pulled me back inside the door. "Wait," she muttered.

Two men emerged from the house. There was a further exchange of words. One went back in and the other headed along the track toward us. We waited, the door closed to a crack, the three of us silent. The man kept walking, passing Mara's cottage without a sideways glance and disappearing in the direction I had come from. I breathed again.

"Go now," Mara said. "I doubt if anyone here will

challenge you, but that fellow who passed, Donal, will likely report that he's seen a stranger in these parts. You'd best make haste."

"Report," I echoed. "To whom?"

"Sentries. Guards. Word always gets back to the Enforcers, one way or another." Her tone was flat.

There was a tight feeling in my stomach. "I've brought down trouble on you," I said.

"I'll have a story ready. Besides, even the Enforcers are wary of Garret. He protects me well, in his way." She hesitated. "It's quite a walk to the old bridge. Looks as if you don't have much choice of ways, with Donal heading down toward Summerfort. Don't try to cross at night. That place, it's . . . there's a thing there, an uncanny thing. Underneath. That's what they say, that it won't let anyone go over."

Given a choice between a troop of Enforcers and an uncanny thing under a bridge, I knew which I would pick. "Thank you, Mara," I said. "I wish you well."

"Travel safely." The door creaked shut.

Beyond the straggling row of houses, the path became steeper. My fey-mended shoes were still sound, but my legs soon grew weary. My pack felt as if it were full of stones. A veil of clouds shrouded the sun; it would rain again before nightfall. I could not stop coughing. I might just as well have rung a bell to let folk know I was coming. I did not stop to rest, for it seemed to me that if I sat down, I would find it hard to get up again. I hoped my choice to stay awhile in Mara's cottage had not cost me the chance to get across the bridge before dark.

I had been lucky, and I knew it. Garret could have killed me before I said a word. Mara could have made him hold me captive while she called in the Enforcers. The fee she would have earned for that would have kept her and Garret in food all winter. Most folk would not have hesitated.

I kept on walking. There was nothing I could do to help her, nothing anyone could do to turn Garret back into the healthy, whole man he had been before he was given over to a mind-scraper. Officially, mind-scrapers were known as Enthrallers, and in a way that was apt, because what they did turned folk into thralls, wholly obedient to the king's will. Except when it went wrong and the person ended up like Garret, a fine man reduced to an infant.

Mind-scraping was a scourge. Of all the terrors confronting the folk of Alban, it was the worst. And yet, Grandmother had told me, it was an ancient art, which had once been a power for good. I'd struggled to believe this. Long ago, she'd said, such work had been known as mind-mending. It had been a canny gift of unusual power, shared by only a handful of folk in Alban. As the years passed, fewer and fewer were born with the gift, and fewer and fewer learned the right use of it, until it was all but forgotten.

A mind-mender could lay hands on a sleeping person's head and make a way into their thoughts; in this, the craft was no different from an Enthraller's. But a mind-mender's purpose was not to exercise control. It was to heal. A mind-mender could comfort the troubled and bring solace to the grieving. He could provide balm to the dying, hope to the despairing. A mind-mender's gift would come in the form of healing dreams, for as short or long a time as they were needed. The sleeper did not remember these dreams, Grandmother said, but their power to set matters right was profound.

It became even harder for me to believe this when I saw Grandmother herself fall victim to the Enthrallers. That night showed me mind-scraping at its cruelest. I had known and loved my grandmother as a strong, wise old woman, the heart of our community. I had seen what was left of her afterward. If there was ever such a thing as mind-mending, it must have existed in a forgotten time, in a realm of light and goodness and courage. I wondered, later, if the story had been a fine imagining designed to comfort me. How mind-mending had become warped and debased into the evil art of mind-scraping even Grandmother had been unable to explain. All she'd said was that Keldec used magic for his own ends, in his own way. I supposed that if even one mind-mender had still existed when he came to the throne, the king could have bribed or coerced that person into serving his ends. If so, that mind-mender's spirit must surely be dark as the grave.

I walked on, and the path became even steeper. The river valley was narrower here. The main track was still visible as a pale ribbon, and the Rush was a swirling pathway, now close to the foot of this hill where I walked. The light was starting to fade. I hoped the bridge was not too much farther. A spasm overtook me and I stopped to cough, bent double on the perilous track. Gods, it hurt! When the fit was over, I took a moment to adjust my pack, and in the quiet I heard footsteps behind me. My heart performed a panicky dance; cold sweat bathed my face. I made myself breathe.

The footsteps ceased. Not those of a man, I thought. Little, pattering steps. *Let it not be Sage and her friends*, I prayed.

I pressed on. My legs hurt, my back ached, my head was dizzy. My feet were losing the knack of finding safe spots to tread. Curse this weakness! I must get there in time. If I could cross the river, if I could reach the main track farther up the valley, where there would be some cover, I had a chance of reaching Three Hags pass without being stopped. A burst of shivering ran through me; the wind was rising. *Don't think about the bridge, Neryn. Don't think about the dark, and the wind, and falling down.*

The path rose higher; the slope to my right became a cliff. Down below, the Rush roared between its banks as if desperate to break free. I crested a rise and teetered, for the path no longer skimmed the edge of the drop but sloped sharply down. And there, some distance ahead, was the bridge.

The Rush raced along the foot of the cliff. On the far side of the river stood an odd looming mass of rocks that put me in mind of Grandmother's old tales about stone monsters that rose up in anger and crushed unwary passersby. And spanning the gap between cliff and stony mound, a distance of some fifty paces, was a single log of wood. A veritable giant of a tree must have furnished this trunk, and I could not imagine who had moved it into place, or how it had been done. It was the work of ancient gods, maybe. The thing stood high above the raging river.

One step at a time, Neryn, I told myself. *Get there first, then walk across and don't look down.* Once over, I could camp for the night. Those old rocks looked full of chinks and crannies, and there were plants growing there, deep among the stones. I would join them.

The footsteps again, furtive, careful. "Don't follow me," I said quietly. "It's not safe."

Someone shouted. A man's voice, and now a man's steps, booted feet closing in fast behind me. My heart leapt into my throat. I skidded and slithered and stumbled down the path, fixing my eyes on the dark line that was the bridge. One false step would send me tumbling into the icy waters of the Rush.

"Down there!" someone shouted. A second voice called, "Don't lose sight of her!" *Run, Neryn!* I came up suddenly against a rock that projected out from the cliff face, almost blocking the path. "Stop!" someone yelled, much closer now. I edged past the obstacle, my feet shuffling sideways on the path. I did not look back. I did not look down.

Twenty paces to the bridge. Mist was forming above

the river; before me the pathway darkened. My feet slipped on the pebbles. I fought for balance, my heart thumping. Not far ahead, the pathway broadened. One end of the great log rested on this natural shelf; the other lay on the rocky hillock across the river. Below the bridge, far, far below, coursed the Rush.

"You!" The voice was right behind me, no more than ten paces away. "Hold still or I'll put an arrow in your heart!"

Chapter Six

"Run, Neryn!"

Suddenly Sorrel was beside me, though where he had come from I did not know. Every twig on his body stuck out, as if he were a hedgehog raising its prickles in defense.

"Quick!" Sage's voice; I would recognize it anywhere. Half turning, I saw her little form, green-cloaked, and her fist brandishing a miniature staff as she took up a stance beside Sorrel. "Move, girl! Get over that bridge and don't look back."

I ran. Five paces, ten paces, and I was at the bridge. Three stone steps led to the great log. As I climbed them, an eldritch light flashed behind me, and a man let fly a string of startled oaths. A moment later a bowstring twanged. There was a grunt of pain. I turned my head.

"Neryn, don't look back!"

Sage's command was not to be ignored. I moved onto the log while behind me light flickered, weapons clashed, men shouted and cursed. I was about six paces out along the bridge when there was a metallic clanking noise, followed by an uncanny drawn-out screech of pain. Sorrel. Oh gods, Sorrel. I looked back.

They were on the ledge. One man had Sorrel in his grip, held by something around the little creature's neck. A chain. An iron chain. Sorrel was writhing in pain, his leafy hands clawing at the metal. His screams pierced through me. I took a step toward him, then halted.

Sage had stationed herself at the end of the bridge, staff in hands, a stalwart small figure keeping the warriors at bay. A stream of fire issued from the tip of her weapon, and while she stood there, the two warriors could neither step onto the bridge nor stop me with an arrow. She was protecting me, winning me safe passage across. While she guarded my way, she could not help her friend. Cold iron is the true enemy of the Good Folk. It burns them as no fire can.

With tears blinding my eyes, I turned my back and fled over the bridge. I did not look down. My feet moved by instinct alone. I ran as I had never run before, the terrible screaming filling my mind. I ran until I was almost at the end of the bridge. Then I could run no more, for a huge dark figure was on the log before me, blocking my path, an apparition of shadows and mist, elusive, shifting. From deep within that smoky mass, a pair of inimical eyes glared out, sizing me up.

The being spoke. "Wha dares set foot on Brollachan Brig?"

My voice was the squeak of a field mouse in the wildcat's path. "Neryn. I am a friend, and I wish you no harm. Please let me pass."

"Whaur's ma fee?" The body swirled and swayed, and I felt myself swaying with it, this way, that way, over the chasm.

There is always something you can give. Bread. Cheese. Clothing. A flint. None seemed likely. A kiss? A promise? Both seemed perilous. Should I offer to solve a riddle? No, that way lay disaster. My heart hammered. My throat went dry.

"WHAUR'S MA FEE?" Within those shadows I could make out a massive form, lantern-jawed, with fists the size of platters. It was clad in a tattered black garment, and in place of sword or dagger, its broad studded belt held an assortment of sharpened bones. Its mouth gaped open, revealing rows of pointed teeth.

How about the truth? *I'm tired, I'm cold, I think two friends just died so that I could cross your bridge.* Did the brollachan, if that was what it was, have any compassion? I looked into its eyes, and in my mind I heard Sage's voice, clear and strong. *Don't bear Sorrel's hurt on your own shoulders, lassie. We're all children of Alban.*

"Tell me the fee and I'll pay it if I can." I straightened my shoulders, trying not to wobble too far to one side or the other. The wood was slippery under my feet.

"Aye, weel, that depends. Ye could dance a jig, mebbe." The brollachan began a dance of its own, swinging its massive fists, kicking out with its heavy feet. In a moment it would sweep me bodily off the bridge. Behind us, at the far end, the light from Sage's staff had gone out and all was silence.

"Please," I gasped, ducking a sweep of the creature's arm, "I'm not very good at dancing, as you can see. Is there some other way I can pay—cooking supper, or . . . or answering a question, or . . . singing a song?"

"A sang, ye say?" The brollachan was suddenly still. I snatched a breath, my chest aching. Foolish suggestion. My whole body was trembling. I had hardly enough breath left to squeeze out a couple of pathetic notes. "And what sang might that be?"

I grasped for anything I could remember about brollachans. They lived alone. They were morose in temperament and quick to anger. Mostly, they lived in the far north. This one had strayed a long way from home.

"A song that will give you heart," I said. "A song to lift your spirits."

"There's nobbut ane sang pleases me."

"And what song is that?" Perhaps I could do this after all. If I could keep my balance long enough. I made the mistake of glancing down and caught a glimpse of the river, a narrow ribbon far below. I teetered, stretching out my arms.

"Ah—" The brollachan raised its hands, palms up, in a gesture curiously human. Its knobby fingers were anything but human, tipped as they were with long yellow nails.

"'Tis an auld, auld thing. A wee scribbet like you wouldna ken the tune."

"Try me," I said.

"No' sae fast. A lassie doesna cross Brollachan Brig sae easy."

"What would you have me do?" My head felt strange, as if I were about to faint.

"A game o' catch. Here!"

Before I could draw breath, something left the creature's hand to come hurtling toward me. I caught it. A ball. A furry ball that squirmed in my hands, uncurling partway to show four neat paws, a triangular nose, a pair of gleaming eyes.

"Dinna drop him," said the brollachan. "Your turn to throw, dinna dawdle!"

I threw. The little creature sailed through the air, and I prayed I had not tossed it to its death. A pair of huge hands emerged from the misty strangeness of the brollachan's body and caught it. In an instant it was in flight again, higher this time, so I had to go on tiptoe and stretch up my arms to grab it. It squealed and bit me, and I nearly dropped it. My body was drenched in the cold sweat of sheer terror. I would not plead for mercy. If the brollachan wanted a game, I would give it one. "Sorry," I murmured, then hurled the creature back at it as hard as I could.

"Guid toss!" The brollachan sent it back to me at ankle level and moving fast. I bent, grabbed it, and lost my balance. Time seemed to slow, letting me feel the moment I knew I had tipped over too far to recover: my churning stomach; the black spots dancing before my eyes; the knowledge that my life had been pointless, every wretched, sorrowful moment of it. . . .

A hand fastened around my ankle, and I was dangling headfirst above the void, swinging from side to side, with my cloak and bag hanging below me and the little creature still clutched in my hands. My heart was in my throat. The river shone up at me, as if to say, *Next time, Neryn.*

"Oops," said the brollachan, hauling me back onto the bridge and flipping me upright. "We canna hae that. Not before ye sing the sang. Come ower, then. Ye've a guid hand wi' the pookie, though ye could do wi' a better grip on your wee slippers."

It backed along the bridge, and I moved forward. The light was fading fast. As we neared the rocky hillock at the far end, the brollachan began to shed its garment of mist and strangeness, becoming more solid in form. By the time I stepped off the bridge, every part of me shaking, the being before me was discernible as a man-shaped entity, though this would be a man rough-hewn, and bigger than the tallest, broadest warrior I had ever seen. It towered over me.

I set down the creature we had used as a ball. It was something akin to a cat, but its tail was as thin as a rat's and hairless, its ears were huge, and its eyes were round and strange. It sat up and began to wash its face with a paw, apparently none the worse for wear.

"Ye're ower," the brollachan said. "I'll hae the sang now."

Accompanied by the rushing of the river and the cries of birds overhead as they winged for shelter, my voice rose, fragile and shaky.

"I am a child of Alban's earth. . . ."

"Ahhh," sighed the brollachan. I'd guessed right. The old forbidden song was indeed the one it had wanted. It stood still as stone while I pressed on through one verse, two verses, three, praying that I could stay on my feet until the end. My head was feeling quite odd.

I reached *"I am the mountain, I am the sky"* before I faltered. I was bone weary. I simply could not remember the words. My mind was full of Sage and Sorrel, almost certainly lying dead on the other side of the bridge. Perhaps Red Cap had been killed before they even reached me. What about the baby? Perhaps Mara, who had made a choice to take me in, and poor innocent Garret were even now being interrogated by the Enforcers. I deserved to be thrown down into the river for the hurt I seemed to cause folk whenever they tried to help me.

"I'm sorry," I whispered. "I'm too tired and sad to sing the last verse."

There was a long, long silence, and then the creature raised its lumpy hand and beckoned. "Come ye doon under the hill, then. Sit awhile by ma wee fire, and ye can sing it when you're ready."

I hesitated. "Are you telling me I'm safe? You won't throw me in the river?"

"Likely I willna. Meantimes, best we get oot o' this chill."

I allowed myself one glance back across the bridge, but on the other side all was shadow. I sent up a silent prayer for friends taken before their time. Then I turned away, following the brollachan between the dim rocks and into a twisting tunnel that wound its way toward the heart of the hill. The light was low. My companion was a darker patch among the shadows, its shuffling footsteps moving on ahead. I was beyond finding this strange. For some time now, I had felt as if I were in a waking dream. Only my aching chest and the tears in my eyes told me it was all too real.

I had expected a dank cavern, a bolt-hole full of spiders and gloom. But the brollachan's lair proved to be spacious and comfortable, as caves went, and the wee fire it had mentioned was a cheerful blaze, the smoke venting up through a chink in the cavern's roof.

"Sit ye doon, then." The brollachan set the pookie on a collection of old blankets, and I sank down gratefully beside the little creature. I watched as the brollachan fetched a blackened kettle, which it set on a stone at one side of the fire. The pookie had its eyes fixed on the big creature as it fossicked in a corner, then returned with a meaty mutton bone. This it laid in the coals. There were bones all over the cave, piled in heaps, hanging on the walls, forming a decorative pattern around the central hearth. "I'm fond o' banes," the brollachan commented, noticing me looking.

"I see that." My voice was unsteady.

"Ye thinkin' I might eat ye up for supper?"

"It did cross my mind, yes. I seem to remember that, in the tales, brollachans sometimes do eat people."

"Ye canna see yersel', wee one. There's hardly a scrap o' meat on ye. Nae worth the trouble."

I opened my mouth to say something, but the cough overtook me and I struggled for breath.

"Ye're no' weel," observed my companion when the spasm was over. "Best ye dinna sing mair, for fear it'll be the death o' ye. But the sang needs finishin', a' the same." It sang the last verse with surprising sweetness, the deep notes of its voice ringing around the cavern. The pookie did not care for it; it curled into a ball again, tail tucked over folded ears.

"That was beautiful," I said when the song was finished.

"Aye, 'tis a grand auld sang. I like best the third versie, that about the Big Ones, the Lord o' the North and them."

"The Big Ones? You mean the Guardians?" They were in the ancient tales, figures from a distant past, like powerful, benevolent spirits.

"Aye, the Four Guardians." The brollachan regarded its fingers, as if to be sure of the number. "Alban's heart. Alban's hope. Dinna forget the sang, and dinna forget the Big Ones. Wi'oot them, this land would be nobbut a heap o' rocks." Its tone suggested the White Lady and the others were alive and well and living just over the hill.

"I'm not sure what you mean," I said with some caution. "Those are very old stories, the ones about the Guardians. Are they a symbol of Alban as it was? Or Alban as it should be?"

The brollachan made a noncommittal noise, which I took to mean *Maybe yes, maybe no.* The pookie had uncurled and now came to settle by me, not quite touching. Its eyes were on the mutton, which was sizzling on the fire. The kettle was steaming.

"Ye'll tak' a bittie supper?" the brollachan inquired.

"Gladly. I have some food to share." My pack had survived my near plunge from Brollachan Brig. I fished out Mara's bread and cheese and set them on their cloth wrapping.

"The pookie's partial tae cheese." Indeed, the catlike creature had transferred its interest to my provisions the moment they were uncovered. It was already hunkered down by the cloth, nibbling steadily. The brollachan took the mutton bone out of the fire, heedless of the heat, and split it neatly with its bare hands, offering me half. Fat dripped onto the cavern floor, making my mouth water. It was a long time since I had eaten meat.

We ate in silence awhile. Despite my hunger, I could manage only a few mouthfuls of the rich food. I knew that if I had any more, I would be sick. I sat quietly while the brollachan demolished its own meat, my leftovers, the small amount of cheese the pookie had left, and half the bread.

"Neryn," the brollachan said eventually. "That's your name, ye said?"

"It is. I will not ask for yours."

"Ye could guess, if ye like."

"Is there a penalty if I can't guess right?" Let this not be another trial, not when I had begun to feel safe at last.

"Ach, no, lassie, 'tis for amusement only. The nights get ower lang doon here, wi' only the pookie tae keep me company. I'll gie ye a clue. 'Tis a name for a lonely fellow. A deep-down solitary sort o' name."

"How many guesses do I get?"

"Three. In the auld tales, it's all threes."

Sage. My heart clenched tight, remembering. "If I guess it in three," I said, "will you do something for me?"

The brollachan stared at me, taken aback.

"A favor. It shouldn't be too hard."

"Guess first, and then I'll answer ye."

"Deep," I suggested.

"A fine guess," the brollachan said, "but, no, that's no' the name."

I thought of caves, of strength, of the old song ringing from the stones. "Echo," I said.

"Ach, that's grand!" said my companion, a broad grin revealing his many sharp teeth. "I like it weel. But, no, that's no' the name."

"Hollow," I said.

There was a little silence. "Ye got it," the brollachan said. "'Tis a good name for a body on his ainsome."

"Thank you for letting me know it, Hollow." Had it been a lucky guess, or had the natural magic of this place put the right name into my mind? "Have you been living here long?"

"Lang enow. Came here wi' ma wifie, but she's gone. Gone tae dust."

There was nothing to say. His loneliness filled the cavern; the warm firelight did nothing to dispel the shadow of it.

"There's the pookie, o' course. Keeps my feet warm o' a winter night. But that's no' the same. No' the same at a'."

For a little, the only sounds in the cavern were the crackling of the fire and the faint thrum of the pookie purring. Then Hollow stirred himself from his reverie.

"What was it ye were wantin' done, lassie?"

"Will you go back over the bridge and see if my friends are still there? Two of the Good Folk were with me, and I'm very much afraid they are both dead. They held back the men who were chasing me. They bid me go on. I don't like to think of them lying out there all alone and—"

Hollow had lifted his hand. "What's that ye say? Men chasin' ye? A wee lassie? Why would they do that? Ye should hae callit oot tae me. I would hae made short work o' them."

"I wish I'd known that. All I'd been told was that there

was an uncanny presence at the bridge. Hollow, will you do it?"

"Ye didna gie me an answer, Neryn. Why would men be after ye? Did ye dae some ill?"

I shivered. "I couldn't stop my friends from following me and getting killed. That's ill enough. As for why the king's men are pursuing me, I have half an answer, but if I tell you, it could put you in danger."

Hollow's wide mouth opened in a toothy grin. "Even a king's man canna best a brollachan. Come on, gie me this half answer and I'll cross ower the brig and see what's what for ye."

I had to trust him with part of the truth, at least. He had sung the song; he had saved me from falling; despite his perilous games, he seemed a friend. Briefly, I explained my canny gift, and how for years I had seen the Good Folk as I traveled but had done no more than leave offerings for them. "But this journey has been different," I said. "Since my father died, I've spoken to several of your folk—not brollachans and the like, but smaller beings. Some were hostile, but three of them became my friends and they protected me at the bridge. They held off the attackers until I could get across. I had warned them not to follow me."

"Why would ye dae that, if ye needed them?"

"If I'm caught, anyone who is with me is likely to be caught too. They'd be punished for helping me evade capture, or for any reason the Enforcers took it into their heads to invent."

"But ye're nobbut a wee lassie."

"I come from a place called Corbie's Wood." I saw in Hollow's eyes that, even isolated as he was, this name meant something to him. "You'll know, maybe, that it was one of the villages destroyed by the Cull. We stayed on awhile. My grandmother could not be moved. When she died, we got a whispered warning. Someone had told the king's men about me, hinted that I was . . . unusual. What folk call smirched. We've been on the run ever since, slipping from place to place, trying not to attract notice." That had not been easy toward the end, with Father unable to tell reality from fantasy. He had truly believed he could win that final wager. "Father's gone now too," I added.

"So ye're a' on yer ainsome, just like me."

I nodded, unable to speak.

"I did wonder," Hollow said, "how it was ye stood up tae me, when I could hae knocked ye off the brig wi' ane push o' ma wee finger. As for your gift, there might be mair tae it than ye think, lassie. We'll talk o' that, but first I'll keep my side o' the agreement." He rose to his feet. His head almost touched the cave roof. "Bide ye here awhile. Dinna be afeart o' the shadows; they canna harm ye. Sit quiet; ye look weary tae the bane. I willna be lang."

The shadows cast by the fire did indeed move oddly, making shapes on the stone walls that suggested all manner of creatures: a bat, a heron, a newt, a running fox. I sat quietly as I had been bidden, stroking the sleeping pookie as it purred deep in its throat. I considered all the folk who had been kind to me, both human and uncanny, and knew how lucky I was. Kindness was in short supply in Keldec's Alban. Reaching out the hand of friendship was perilous when any passing stranger might be a spy. But Mara had not alerted anyone to my presence, I was sure of that. It was her neighbor who had done it. I had seen something of myself in Mara, and I knew I would never betray someone to the king's men, not unless they ripped the truth out of me with their instruments of torture. I hoped that even then I would have the strength to keep silent.

Through the aperture above the hearth, faint moonlight showed. I prayed that if my friends had perished out there, their deaths had been quick and clean. I cursed myself for not running back, for not trying to protect them, for not standing up to my pursuers, for making the impossible choice: to save myself at the expense of the Good Folk. I prayed that none of them had been taken prisoner. They could escape human snares and traps easily, using earth magic. But if a man had cold iron, he could bend them to his will. Did every Enforcer carry a chain on his person? Or had they expected that I might have fey help and come specially prepared?

After some time I heard Hollow's deep voice from the tunnel. "Mind yon corner. Go slow, slow. . . . Aye, that's the way." My heart leapt. Someone was with him. Someone had survived.

They emerged into the firelight and I jumped to my

feet, hope and horror warring in me. Hollow bore a limp form in his arms. Sorrel's leafy pelt was all broken stems and patches of red, raw skin. And now, behind Hollow, came the figure of Sage, her face ashen, her eyes swollen, her mouth a grim line. Against the gray pallor of her skin, her nose looked more beaklike than ever. She still carried her oak staff, but it was in two pieces. Her cloak was scorched and ripped.

"He's awa' hame," Hollow said, coming to lay Sorrel down on the blankets. "Couldna dae mair than bear him ower. I'll mak' ye a brew." He glanced at Sage, who was standing by the fire now, staring into the flames as if she hardly knew where she was. "Neryn, talk to yon wee wumman. Show her a's well wi' ye. I'll say this, ye hae braw friends."

I said nothing at all, simply went over to Sage, knelt down beside her, and took her in my arms. She stood rigid a moment, then collapsed, her knees buckling, her small body racked with sobs. I held her, blinking back my own tears. This was my fault. Her friend was dead; but for me he would have lived. Her staff was broken. She had seemed so strong, and now she looked defeated.

Hollow busied himself with various dried leaves, making a brew. After some time, Sage stirred in my arms and stepped back, disengaging herself. "You're safe, then," she said. "He'd be glad of that. We won you another day, at least."

"I'm sorry—" I began.

Her hands went up in a gesture curiously like one

Hollow had used earlier. "No, no, none of that. We did what we did so you could run ahead and be safe. Sorrel would have been mightily annoyed if you'd turned back and fallen victim to king's men. That wouldn't have saved his life. It would likely have been the end for all three of us."

"What about Red Cap?" I made myself ask. "And the little one?"

"Red Cap's no fighter. We bade him stay hidden, well clear of it. He'll take the word to Silver and the others, let them know you got across, tell them we've lost one of our own." A pause.

I opened my mouth to say sorry again, and shut it without a word.

"This journey you're on," Sage said. "You'll be tested hard, to prove your mettle. That part you must do on your own. The journeying, the getting there, we can help you with." She looked over at the still form of Sorrel. "And we will, lassie. Even if it kills us."

"Drink up," Hollow said. "Dinna speak a word mair until it's a' gone."

Some time later, when the brew was finished, and Hollow had asked a lot of questions about Sorrel, and Sage had answered them by telling us stories of the times her friend had been brave, and the times he'd been foolish, and the times when he had annoyed her to the point of screaming, I realized how wise the brollachan was. Perhaps his long, lonely days and nights had given him time to ponder death and loss and acceptance. For when the tale, with its tears and smiles, was all done, and Hollow had drawn a blanket gently over Sorrel, I saw that some of the animation had come back to Sage's face, and some of the life to her beady eyes.

"Ye could sing him that sang," Hollow said now, looking at me. "That fine auld sang. Tae send him on his way."

So I did, all four verses, and when I was done, Sage wiped her eyes and said, "It's a long while since I heard that. Hag of the Isles, eh? If that old one still walked the earth of Alban, I'd ask her to mend my staff for me. A powerful mender, she was, in her time. But they're all gone now, the Big Ones, gone deep down where they can't see a human king making a mockery of their fair land. More's the pity."

"Ye'll be wantin' tae sleep," Hollow said, eyeing her. "I'll help ye lay the wee fellow tae rest in the mornin'."

"Ach, no. I'll sit by Sorrel. I won't leave him alone in the night." Sage looked over at me.

"I'll keep vigil with you," I said.

"Aye, weel, it's rare enow for me tae have the company o' ane fine lassie, let alane a pair o' them," said Hollow. "I willna waste the time in sleepin'."

"You said something before about my canny gift, Hollow," I ventured. "That it might mean more than I thought. Could you tell me what you meant?"

"Before he starts on that," said Sage, "there's something else you need to know. One of those two men, I burned with my staff. He's dead, and Hollow here sent him down the river. The other fellow, I couldn't finish. I hurt him, but not so badly that he couldn't run. So he ran. You'll need to move on quick, Neryn."

I had known this might happen. All the same, I felt chilled to the marrow. "He ran back toward Summerfort?"

A mirthless smile appeared on Sage's lips. "I gave him no choice of ways," she said.

"Naebody crosses Brollachan Brig," Hollow added in his deep rumbling voice. "Naebody dares."

"I did."

"Aye, weel, ye didna flinch at the challenge. Ye proved yourself. 'Twere plain to me at first eyeblink that ye were somethin' apart."

"How, apart?" My mind was racing. What was best? Head off at dawn and hope I could walk fast enough to get into the woods higher up the valley before that man sent a troop of Enforcers to look for me? Hide in Hollow's cave and hope nobody would dare fetch me out? Maybe my pursuers had known whom they were following, and maybe they'd only been investigating a report of a suspicious stranger in the area. But they'd seen me in company with uncanny folk, and those folk had taken up arms to defend me. I could expect to be hunted down. Maybe I should leave right now. The moon was up; perhaps I could find my way. A spasm of coughing overtook me. When I had caught my breath again, Hollow said, "I'll tell ye a tale. A lang, lang time since, in the far north, there was ane summer when the Sea Folk rose up, urged on by a wicked queen, and took it upon themselves tae wage war on the brollachans who lived in the shore caves nearby. So evil was this queen, she had her folk breakin' and crushin' and killin' in every corner o' that place, and human folk were drawn into it too, what wi' their boats being sunk and their nets slashed and their bairnies stolen from the shore before their very eyes. Now ye may know, Neryn, that human-kind doesnae trust a brollachan. Folk like me, we're in the tales your kind tell their bairnies tae frighten them awa' frae spots such as high cliffs, slippery ledges, and holes in the ground. And my kind, we're nae sae fond o' your kind, what with the way ye stamp all ower the land, regardless of wha' cam there afore ye. So the war raged on, and every-body suffered for it.

"It wasnae until a fellow steppit forth frae the human folk o' that place that the tide turned. Corcan, the lad's name was. He'd always said, from the time he was nobbut a bairn, that he could see and hear uncanny folk a' across the isle. When Corcan was sixteen or so, he went awa' journeyin', naebody knew whaur, and when he returned, he wasnae the same. He'd grown quieter, wiser, older than his years. Turned oot he'd been off learnin' his craft as a Caller, and when he got back hame and saw the trouble his folk were in, he put what he'd learnit tae verra guid use. He callit the brollachans, and the brollachans came tae him, because o' what he was. Then, against their na-tures, human and brollachan fought side by side tae defeat the Sea Folk and send them back oot tae their lonely isles, never mair tae set foot on that shore. Some say the Lord o' the North himself was callit forth that day, but I dinna know if any call would be powerful enow tae summon a Guardian.

"Ye know about canny gifts, lassie. They come about frae a coupling o' oor kind"—he glanced at Sage—"and your kind. Good Folk and humankind dinna oft lie doon in the same bed, but frae time tae time it happens. Ofttimes the gift will come oot in the family lang years after. Sudden like, there's a bairnie wi' a rare talent for singin' or dancin' or fightin' or understandin' creatures and their ways. Once in a lang, lang while, there's a Caller: a body who can summon the Good Folk in a' their forms and bring them tae work on a task together. Ye need tae understand, we're a' shapes and sizes, a' sorts and kinds, and we dinna mix much. We keep oorselves tae oorselves. It's no' in oor nature tae band together and fight, or build, or plot and plan. But if a Caller summons us tae a task, we must obey. We canna refuse the call." He looked at me, his small eyes assessing. "Wi' a gift like that, ye could be marchin' oot tae war wi' a great army at your biddin'."

There was a telling silence, in which it became apparent to me that this astonishing statement had not surprised Sage in the least.

"*Me?*" My voice came out as a shocked squeak. "You think *I* am one of these Callers? But that's ridiculous. I didn't call Sage and Sorrel to me. I didn't call any of the Good Folk I've met on the way. They just appeared. My gift is to see and hear uncanny folk, not to . . . command them." Such a notion shocked me to the core. No man or woman should wield such power. In the wrong hands, it could wreak unimaginable evil.

"What's your opinion on the matter, wee wumman?" Hollow looked at Sage.

"I believe you could be right, brollachan." Sage sat with one small hand resting on the blanket that shrouded Sorrel's still form. She was solemn as an owl. "I've had my eye on Neryn since she was a smaller creature than I am, digging in her grandmother's vegetable patch and learning which were the good herbs. Even then I sensed she was something rare. Though I have to tell you, my opinion is not widely shared among my own kind. We've long disagreed about just what you are, Neryn, and how important you might come to be. If wretched Silver and her band hadn't been so stubborn about it, we could have stood in numbers against your enemies just now, and this braw wee fellow wouldn't be growing cold here beside me. I *told* her. . . ." Sage fell silent for a little, her face shadowed.

"Callers don't come along often," she said eventually. "Two hundred years could pass with none such walking the hills of Alban. It's uncommon enough for a girl or a boy to have the knack of spotting us and hearing our voices, but not so uncommon that there would not be a few such scattered somewhere in the settlements and farms of the highlands if a body went looking. That's a good gift to have, right enough, though in these times, dangerous. Calling starts off the same way, with a rare ability to see our kind even when we are in hiding. To draw us out. Without the right training, it may never become more than that. But if a body does what Corcan did—finds a teacher, learns, and practices the skills—this can become a powerful gift indeed. A gift that can win or lose wars. A gift that can bring about great changes. You'd think human folk would remember that. But your kind have short lives and short memories. Like as not such a phenomenon's forgotten entirely between one Caller and the next."

I could hardly think what question to ask first. It seemed desperately unlikely that I was what they thought I was. On the other hand, if it were in any respect true, it could transform my future entirely. It could make Shadowfell not simply a refuge, but . . . No, it could not be true. I would have had some inkling of it before now. "Why would you believe this of me?" I asked them.

"We feel it in the truest way," Hollow said. "In our banes. The moment I clappit eyes on ye, wobbling ower the brig, I knowit what ye were."

"Then why did you make me dance and sing and play games?"

"Just testin' ye, tae see if I was right. I wouldna hae let ye fa'."

"I don't think you can be right," I said. "I've never heard of Calling. I have no understanding at all of how it's done. I am in my sixteenth year: a woman, not a child. If I had such a powerful gift, surely there would be more sign of it."

"The signs are there," Sage said quietly. "Sorrel saw them too. Others disagree, as you know. There's many don't have faith in you; there's many think me addle-headed to pursue this. Ask me for proof that I'm right and I could not give it to you. It's for you to prove yourself, and that will take time. But ask yourself why king's men want you so badly. And ask yourself why you're still alive, after three years of running. Your gift makes you valuable beyond measure. And it helps keep you safe."

I felt a prickling all over my skin. I shrank from the immensity of this. I did not want it to be true, yet the more I thought about it, the more possible it seemed. When the ghost-warriors of Hiddenwater had sung the song and bidden me fight, it was not an ordinary girl they had seen, but someone who could rally folk, someone who could make a real difference. A gnawing horror gripped me. "If the king heard someone might be a Caller," I said, and now my voice was small and shaky, "he wouldn't want that person killed. He'd want her working on his side. Doing his bidding. He'd want her rendered obedient." I made myself draw a steadying breath. "I'm a danger to you both," I said. "I must move on at first light. I can't use this gift, I don't know how, I'll bring trouble on anyone who tries to help me."

"A bairn doesna learn to run before he can walk," Hollow said.

"Or sing verses before he can speak his mother's name," said Sage, nodding agreement.

"Or wield a broadsword before he can feed himself wi' a spoon."

"Or weave a blanket before he can tie up his shoes."

"What are you telling me? That I should learn how to be a Caller, as the young man in the story did? Who could teach me?"

A long silence, broken only by the crackling of the fire.

"I dinna ken," Hollow said eventually. "That tale, it's auld. Auld as these stanes."

"I've heard of none skilled in a Caller's art since the time of my grandmother's grandmother," said Sage. "If there's any left in Alban, they're hiding away. And who'd blame them for that?"

"More likely there's nane," said Hollow. "Nae wonder king's men are after ye, Neryn."

"But how could they know what I was? I didn't even know myself." The people of Corbie's Wood had known only that my grandmother had been teaching me her healing craft. While that was enough to make me suspicious to the Enforcers, it was hardly sufficient to explain their continued pursuit of me. Could it be that my father, incautious after too much ale, had at some point hinted at my ability to see the Good Folk? Had this reached the ears of someone who knew about Callers? The thought set a sick feeling in my belly.

Hollow had settled to rest, his imposing form stretched out all along one side of the hearth, his head pillowed on a massive arm. "Ye could talk about that a' nicht lang and still be nane the wiser," he said. "Ane thing's sure: ye must move on at cockcrow. Whaur ye headin'?"

"North. Up the valley."

"Now that ye know what ye are," Hollow said, "are ye fleein' awa', or gaein' forward?"

"I'm going forward, Hollow. On my own." I hesitated. "Sage, you said something about proving my mettle. I'm not sure how to do that. Are there certain tests I must pass? And what comes next? You must know I'm not simply wandering about, I am going somewhere, but . . . if it's true, if I am a Caller, then . . ."

"If you are," she said, "my guess is that soon enough it'll be plain to you what's next. As for tests, a Caller needs to show some particular qualities. They're known as the virtues. A body cannot be told what they are until she's proved herself; it's set out in the Old Laws."

"But if I don't know what they are, how can I— Never mind." I thought for a little. "These virtues. Might there perhaps be seven of them?"

"There might," Sage said with a crooked smile. "I cannot tell you more. Just do what you need to do, when you need to do it. Take good care on the path up the valley. There's open country between here and the place where the river threads the needle. Country where a lone traveler would be easily spotted. And once you reach the narrow place, you'll have no choice but to walk on the road. Quite sure you don't want me to come with you? I've hidden you more than once before when you were in trouble, though at the time I expect you were just glad to find a clump of bushes in a convenient spot, or a handy patch of shadow."

With Sorrel's body lying beside us under its blanket, I knew I must refuse, though I'd have welcomed her companionship on the journey. "Thank you twice over, then. But I must go on alone."

Hollow had sat silent a long time, listening. "I'd come

wi' ye masel', lassie," he said now, "if I could. But I canna leave ma post. There's naebody else tae guard the brig. Ye understand?"

"Of course." I imagined going up the valley with a brollachan as my companion. He'd make a fine bodyguard, no doubt of that, and good company of an evening. On the other hand, the first glimpse anyone got of him—and he was hard to miss—would bring down the king's men like a swarm of ants to a honeycomb. It would bring Enforcers with cold iron. "I'll leave at first light."

CHAPTER SEVEN

THE MOON WAS A PALE HALF CIRCLE WHEN I bade my companions farewell next morning. The sun had not yet risen. I felt the air's chill deep in my chest and struggled not to cough. I tied a cloth around my neck and pulled it up to cover my mouth and nose. I would keep my hood up and walk as fast as I could.

I knew the way. Eventually I would come to the spot Sage had referred to as a threading of the needle. There the valley narrowed to a steep defile, river and road passing between sheer rock walls. The road was barely broad enough to accommodate the wheels of a cart. The defile was close to two miles long. In that place there would be no hiding. Coming the other way, a person might, in a pinch, essay the Rush by boat. But not going upstream.

I thought I might reach the defile by midmorning and wondered whether someone could ride there from Summerfort before then. Was it really possible that Keldec's people knew I might be a Caller? If so, I was in worse danger than I could possibly have believed. A Caller could change the great tide of events; she could draw together humankind and the Good Folk and get them to work side by side. A Caller could be a great asset to the cause of Alban's freedom. She might also be a truly terrible weapon, if turned to the king's will.

Imagining what Keldec might do if he acquired the capacity to command the Good Folk, I felt my belly churn with nausea. Maybe I had it in me to be this Caller and maybe I didn't, but if there was the least chance Sage and Hollow were right about me, I must not allow the king's men to catch me. I owed it to everyone who had shown faith in me to get to Shadowfell safely. Once there, perhaps I would have time to find out exactly what I was and what I could do.

As for virtues, how could I show them when I had no idea what they were? As I walked, I tried to remember the clues sprinkled through that conversation I had overheard when half-asleep. Something about a hand. The Giving Hand, that was it. Had my sharing of my meager food supplies been sufficient for me to pass a test of generosity? Unlikely, since one of the Good Folk had scorned my gift, saying I would find it harder to share when I was starving. So I might not have demonstrated even one virtue yet. *The Giving Hand*. There was something familiar about that expression, but if I had heard it before, it was so long ago I could not recall where.

The sun rose higher. Clouds were massing in the west, heavy and gray, threatening a downpour. My feet were leaden and my head ached. My chest was so tight I was struggling to breathe. I followed the course of the river, delaying the moment when I must step onto the road. In these parts the valley was a barren wilderness, the slopes almost devoid of foliage as their pitch steepened, the level ground beside the Rush home only to low, scrubby bushes and tough grasses. There were signs that rabbits had been about. I saw a small flock of goats grazing not far from the riverbank and ducked behind a crumbling drystone wall, my heart thumping. Goats could not tell tales, but goatherds could. When I was fairly sure the animals were on their own, I took time to scan the way ahead once more. On the far side of the road, a farmhouse stood low and gray against the hillside, smoke threading up from its chimney. And farther up the valley, there at last was the entrance to the defile. Dear gods, let there be no guard post.

I leaned back against the low wall, closing my eyes. Now that I had sat down, I could feel the ache in my limbs—not the satisfying pain of a physical task achieved, but a deep-down pain, the kind that is a warning of illness. My head felt hot; my vision was odd too, spots moving before my eyes, obscuring the way ahead. I must not be weak. I could not stop out here in the open, a sitting target. I forced myself to get up. It wasn't far to the place where the defile began: a mile or two at most. Then two miles through. I could do it. I must. As soon as I reached the other side, I would be able to take shelter in the tracts of forest that grew in the lee of the hills.

I stood there a moment with everything swaying and shifting around me. I fished out my waterskin and took a mouthful, forcing it down. Then I gritted my teeth and walked out into the open.

Something was wrong with me. The simple act of walking felt almost beyond me, as if I were dragging my legs through heavy mud. I fixed my gaze on the point where the valley walls closed in on each other, casting a heavy shadow on the ground beneath and throwing the river into darkness. I would keep going. I would reach that place and walk through to safety.

By the time I reached the entry to the defile, the sun was almost at its midpoint. If that man had alerted the Enforcers at Summerfort and people had ridden up the road in search of me, surely they would be here by now. There was no sign of anyone. Anyone human, that was. There were Good Folk everywhere: up on those steep slopes, under the rocks, in the chinks and cracks. Without even looking, I felt their presence. There would be no speaking to them here. The last thing I wanted was to put anyone else in danger.

I drew in a deep, shuddering breath and let it out again. *Here I am,* I thought. Sick and weary as I was, it felt like a battle cry. I stepped onto the king's road.

I had walked perhaps a hundred paces into the shadows of the defile when I heard the clop of horses' hooves and the squeak of cart wheels on the road ahead of me, approaching steadily. I pulled the cloak around me and kept going. What was that story again? I struggled to remember it. Calla. A drowning. Relatives in the north. The place . . . was it Stillwater?

The cart came into view, a looming shape in the shadows of the deep vale. A solid farm horse, a man sitting hunched on the bench with a sack around his shoulders for warmth. As the cart neared me, I shrank back against the rock wall, for there was barely room for the vehicle to pass me safely. The man narrowed his eyes at me but did not stop.

Sucking in a breath, I hitched up my bag and walked on. Two miles to a precarious kind of safety. Two miles to a place where I could find cover. There were farms higher up the valley, of course, but at least I would not be walking over open ground, exposed to every eye. Tomorrow, or the day after, I would reach the Three Hags. Once over the pass, I would be close to Corbie's Wood. The chill fingers of memory clutched at my heart. Going home would be the hardest thing of all.

At last I saw a brightness up ahead, as if the high walls of the defile were leaning back, opening up. Nearly there. My head was spinning. My feet refused to walk in a straight line.

A sound from behind me. Hoofbeats on the road. Horses—two, three, more—moving at a canter. No time to think. No time to make a plan. Nowhere to hide. My heart banged like a drum; my skin was all cold sweat. I could not run fast enough to outpace them. I pressed myself against the rock wall, knowing I was in plain view. One look and I would be taken.

Hard stone was against my cheek, against my body. Within it I sensed a long, slow beat, a grave answer to the panicky thudding of my heart. There was a presence here, huge, old, wise beyond count of years. Crazily, a snatch of rhyme ran through my head, part of a childhood game almost forgotten: *Stanie Mon, Stanie Mon, nod yer heid; Stanie Mon, Stanie Mon, fa' doon deid!* A stanie mon was a being of stone, a creature Farral and I had used to frighten each other with at bedtime. A story. A fantasy.

The deep heartbeat filled my body with its rhythm. It was strong beyond any human strength. It felt entirely real.

A rider came in view on the road: a tall, cloaked figure on a formidable horse. Behind him were others, riding two abreast. The first man gave a sharp call, pointing toward me.

I shut my eyes and pressed my face against the rock wall. If I truly was a Caller, if such a gift existed, let it work for me now. "Stanie Mon, Stanie Mon, wake frae sleep," I whispered through chattering teeth. If this did not work, I would be facing a mind-scraper before sunset. I would be lost. "Stanie Mon, Stanie Mon, hide me deep."

In an instant everything went dark. Stone was all around me, trapping me within its bulk. I could not move so much as my little finger. I was blind, deaf, paralyzed. I could not breathe. I managed a squeak of terror, and sensed a response, as if the heaviness that surrounded me relaxed a little. I sucked in an unsteady breath. Had I just worked a charm that would kill me? Oh gods, oh gods, it was so dark:

not the darkness of a moonless night or a house with the lamps quenched, but a profound and chilling absence of light. It was as if the world had been sucked away, leaving me in a place where I was the only living, breathing creature. "Stanie Mon," I whispered into the faceless black. "When it's safe, please let me go."

Nothing changed. Nothing moved. I strained my eyes for the least dim flicker of light. My body was a mass of tightly knotted pieces; my heart juddered in my chest. There was nothing I could do, nothing. Nobody knew where I was. I might remain here until I was no more than a walled-up set of bones. How long had I been here already? How long would those riders linger once it became plain that the figure they had seen standing against the rock wall was no longer there? With the heavy darkness pressing on me, with the stones a finger's breadth from my body, time no longer made any sense.

Not much of a choice, said a little voice inside me. *One: you get buried alive. Two: an Enthraller turns you into a weapon for evil. Seems to me you'll be doing Alban a favor if you give up the struggle right now. Why fight when you can't win? There's no rhyme or reason to that.*

Rhyme. That last time, I had not spoken in verse. Could it be as simple as that? I took a few long breaths, forcing my trapped body to a semblance of calm. My mind cast wildly for rhyming words. "Stanie Mon, Stanie Mon, when the way's clear"—my voice came in a shaking whisper—"Stanie Mon, Stanie Mon, free me frae here."

Darkness was absolute; the rocks hugged me close as a

shroud. The silence drew on. Then, in its own time, came a vibration from the rocks, like deep, slow laughter. And then light. I squeezed my eyes shut, momentarily dazzled. The stones released me, and I sprawled helplessly onto the hard-packed earth of the road, bruising hip, knee, and hand. There was a shifting sound. By the time I gathered myself and looked up, there was nothing to be seen but a blank stone wall. I scrambled to my feet, looking one way, then the other, along the road. The riders were gone. I was safe. Safe for now.

Every instinct screamed, *Run!* But I could not run. My legs were like jelly, and my chest had a band around it, squeezing ever tighter. Which way had my pursuers gone, on up the valley or back toward Summerfort? There was a confusion of marks on the road, the prints of hooves and of boots. But I was used to reading such signs. Someone had paused to dismount here; someone had taken a good look at the place where I had stood within the rock only an arm's length from capture. And then, when they couldn't see me, they'd split up. Four sets of hoofprints headed back toward Summerfort. One went on.

By the time I emerged from the defile, my legs would barely carry me. I must find shelter; I must find a place to hide. Here the valley broadened again, though it was not the open flatland of the river mouth but a ribbon of farm-land beside the Rush, lying between wooded hillsides. Elder and willow clothed the lower slopes, and above them stretched a band of oaks. Higher still, the rise became bare rocky fell. An eagle passed overhead, its wings catching sun between clouds, flashing golden brown. Leaves lay in heavy drifts beneath the bare-limbed trees; the forest would not hide me as well as I had hoped.

I was cold. I was cold deep in the bone, my whole body shivering, my joints aching. As I scanned the terrain, trying to spot a place that might conceal a cave, a hollow, an overhang, anywhere I might creep in and shelter, it began to rain, at first a scattering of droplets, then a steady, soaking fall.

No outcrops close at hand, no thicker growth of trees, no place to hold a desperate wayfarer. I swayed, knowing I was close to fainting. I had no chance of reaching the deeper parts of the forest today.

If my head had not been so muddled with fever, I might not have taken such a risk. As it was, I saw a farm not far away, its back against the forest, its face toward the road. I would not approach the homestead. Smoke was rising: it was tenanted. I would not go near those walled inner fields, where pigs rooted about and a house cow stood in patient silence. I would not seek shelter in the small outhouses that stood near the dwelling, sheds in which I might stumble on chickens or geese or pigs. But there was a barn standing at some distance from the other buildings, its big doors closed, its yard empty. Halfway along the side there was a low opening, perhaps designed for stock to go in and out. I crept closer, sidling from wall to shed, from hawthorn bush to outhouse to woodpile. I bit my lip, expecting the sudden barking of a watchdog or a shout of challenge. Nothing. Nobody came out. The cow turned her head to look at me but kept her silence. A ragtag flock of chickens was crouched in the lee of the barn, huddled against the rain. A scrawny cockerel perched on a wall nearby, keeping watch. He eyed me; I willed him not to sound an alarm.

The ground on this side of the barn was a quagmire, the smell of pigs overwhelming. My feet slipped and slid; I was in danger of falling headlong. I crept forward. Here was the opening, with animal tracks going through. I slipped under, came up inside. It was quiet in the barn, dim, dry. Sacks of something, a cart, harnesses on the wall, scythes and pitchforks neatly stowed at one end. Pigeons maintaining a quiet conversation somewhere up above. And at the other end, a deep, luxurious heap of straw. I stumbled over, dug out a shallow nest, and collapsed into it. Wrapped in my damp cloak, I sank into exhausted sleep.

"Up! Move!" Cruel hands seizing my arms; someone hauling me up to stand. Groggy and confused, still half-asleep, I would have fallen but for my captor's hard grip. Where was I? What had happened?

"Give us your name! What are you doing here?" the man snapped. A second man stood nearby with a pitchfork in his hands, the prongs aimed at my chest.

"N-nothing, I—I—" The well-prepared story—*My name is Calla; I am an orphan*—would not come out. The barn . . . I had fled in here for shelter. Now it seemed to be night outside. My neck was on fire with pain, my limbs were numb, my head throbbed. I could hardly draw breath, let alone say anything coherent.

"What do you mean, nothing? How did you get up here? Who sent you? Where are you going?" My captor shook me; my head wobbled like a rag doll's.

"Calla," I managed. "Stonewater. Just going . . . move on."

"Stonewater? No Stonewater in these parts. You're lying." Another shaking, harder than the last. There were others here: a third man, with a length of sharpened wood in his hands; a grim-faced woman; a boy of six or so, holding a lantern.

"Account for yourself, girl, and tell the truth this time," my captor ordered. "If you needed shelter, why not come to the door and ask?"

No good answer for this. Say what I knew was true—that there was nobody in all Alban who could be trusted to offer a wayfarer a safe bed for the night—and they could call it speaking out against Keldec's rule. I stared down at the floor, thinking vaguely that I must be quite ill or I would be able to tell better lies. I had often done so in the past to secure a night under cover.

"Her shoes." The woman spoke in a stunned whisper. "Finnach, look at those shoes. If that's not uncanny stitching, I'll eat my grandmother's bonnet."

All of them looked at my shoes. In the uneven light from the lantern, their faces were uniformly pale, their eyes dark with horror.

"Smirched." The man with the pitchfork spoke the word as if it tasted foul. "She's smirched. Gods have mercy on us. You know what happened to the folk up at High Reach Farm when they were caught with one like her in their house—"

"How dare you come in here?" The woman stepped toward me, her voice quivering with fury and fear. "How dare you? Every moment you spend under this roof puts us at risk! Get out! Take your filthy self off and your tricky shoes with you!" She spat at me. I felt the spittle dribble down my cheek. With my arms pinioned, I could not wipe it away. *Do what she wants,* I willed my captor. *Let me go.*

"No, no," said the man named Finnach. "Think, woman. We should turn her in. She's the one they want. She's the lass that's running from the Enforcers. There'll be silver in this."

"Turn her in?" The woman's voice was sharp. "Let the Enforcers know we've been harboring a smirched girl in our barn? What do you want, to see the whole place go up in flames and all of us with it?" Beside her, the child stood immobile, his eyes fixed on nothing in particular.

"Didn't you hear what that fellow said earlier?" Finnach looked at the others, as serious as a lord pronouncing judgment. "*Come and fetch me the moment you see her.* Those were his words. It's all very well to talk about flames, but what if we don't tell him and he finds out about it? We'll be strung up in a neat little row and saying our last goodbyes, that's what. Tie the girl up, then go and fetch the man in the cloak."

"Me?" asked the fellow with the pitchfork.

"Yes, you, Ollan."

"What, now? In the dark?"

"Aye, now, in the dark, you lumpie." Finnach shifted his grip on me. "And be quick about it, before she can get up to any tricks. Light another lamp, and away up to Seven Pines Farm with you. That's where he's staying, isn't it?" A pause. "No, wait. I'll go up. You tie the girl and guard her until I get back. There's a good payment in this if we do it right."

His hold slackened. I made a wild dive for freedom, my mind filling with those last images of my grandmother. *No, please, no . . .* Terror gave my limbs a momentary strength, and surprise made the men slow. I was almost at the entry when my legs gave way and I fell heavily to the earthen floor.

"Iron," said Finnach as the other men dragged me up again. I hung between them, limp as a sack of grain. "Rope'll be no use. Whatever stitched those shoes could unravel a rope and set the girl free in the twinkle of an eye. A body such as her will have uncanny friends in every corner. Fetch that chain from the hook over there, and some iron tools. Bind her and fence her in. That should hold her until I bring the Enforcer."

Chapter Eight

THEY SAT ME ON A STOOL AND BOUND ME TO the post behind it with ropes. They took the chain down from the wall. Perhaps it had been used to hang up dead things. Now they wound it about the post and around me. It lay heavy on my shoulders and pressed tight on my chest. They fenced me in with a makeshift barrier constructed from iron implements: scythes, axes, and the like. They went through my bag and took away the knife Flint had given me. "Stolen," I heard one of them mutter. "Has to be. What would a girl like her be doing with a weapon like this?"

The woman had gone, and the boy with her. I could not blame her for her hostility. I could not blame any of them. For their own survival, these folk had no choice but to hand me in.

I could not stop shivering. I saw Grandmother, sitting straight and proud, and two Enforcers coming to tip her head back, force her mouth open, and pour a potion down her throat, a mixture that would send her into a deep sleep. From my hiding place in the wall, through the chink, I saw the Enthraller come in, a man with deep-seeing eyes and a soft, terrible voice. He had tiny glass vials strung around his neck, one for each victim, to hold what he had stolen from them. I did not hear the charm he sang over her that night, for while he worked his magic, I stopped my ears with my fingers, as she had bidden me do in those desperate moments between the Enforcers' arrival at Corbie's Wood and the hammering on the door. I did see her wake. I saw the change in her face. I heard her stumbling, slurred words. I saw her wise, bright eyes turned dull and lifeless. Gone. Gone forever. Dear gods, let me face this with the same dignity and courage as she did. I fought down a longing to die now, quickly, before they came to take me away. That was a coward's wish.

"Weapons sharp. Backs straight. Hearts high," I whispered to myself, trying vainly to control the tremors that coursed through me. What if there was an Enthraller up here in the valley and he did it to me this very night? By daybreak I might be another like poor Garret, only I would have no loving family to tend to me. Or the mind-scraping might work as it should and I might wake up as an obedient servant of Keldec's will. It was unthinkable. "Weapons sharp. Backs straight. Heart high."

"Cease your muttering, girl," snapped one of the men. "We'll have none of that canny stuff. This is plain folk's land."

There was no point in trying to reason with them, no point in defending myself. I could not give my true name. I could not tell them where I'd been going or why I'd had to shelter in their barn. They feared for their safety, for their farms and livestock, for those they loved. All Alban lived in fear. "I mean you no harm," I murmured.

"Hold your tongue!" the fellow responded, making a sign of ward with his fingers. "I won't listen to your wicked lies." The two of them were half turned away from me, as if they thought I could work a charm on them merely by looking in their eyes.

We waited. The barn was full of cold drafts. The men blew on their fingers, and one went to fetch a couple of sacks, which they wrapped around their shoulders. I sat trembling on my stool, weighed down by iron, watching the shadows move in the lantern light. Deep inside me, silently, I sang the ancient song. *I am a child of Alban's earth. . . .*

After a long, long time, men's voices came from outside. I tried to breathe slowly. I tried to sit up straight. I hoped I could look into the Enforcer's eyes and answer his questions with some semblance of calm. Tomorrow I might be a witless castoff, a ruin of a girl who needed help to use the privy, to put on her clothes, to use a spoon. Today I would be someone my grandmother could be proud of. I sucked in a gasping breath and willed myself to stop shaking.

Finnach entered first, bending to get under the opening in the barn wall, coming through with a lantern in his hand.

After him came a man in the dark cloak of an Enforcer, a man wearing boots and gauntlets. He straightened, and the stag brooch that fastened his cloak glinted silver in the lantern light. The king's token.

"The girl's here, as you see," said Finnach. "Is she the one?"

The Enforcer stepped closer, scrutinizing me. The light touched his features: deep gray eyes, a nose that had been broken in the past and had mended crooked, a scar here, a scar there, dark hair severely cropped. He folded his arms, and his steady gaze met mine, shocking in its familiarity.

"That's her," said Flint. "Get those bonds off and find me a blanket. The king won't be well pleased if the girl perishes from cold before she can give any answers."

I sat frozen, my mind reeling. Flint. Flint who had helped me, Flint who had left me his cloak and his knife and his food. Flint who had told me he wanted me to have a choice. Flint, an Enforcer? How could that be? It made no sense. Why had he let me go that first time only to close the trap now?

He was taking coins out of a pouch at his belt and counting them into Finnach's hand. "That's for now," he said. "There'll be more later, provided I hear you've held your tongue." A grim glance at the other two men. "That goes for every person on this farm. You don't talk. You don't speak a word to anyone about me, or her, or what's been said tonight. You never saw us. You never spoke to us.

If I hear you've talked, it won't be silver on the palm, it'll be iron in the belly. Understood?"

A muttered chorus of "Yes, my lord" as the three men hastened to clear away the barrier, remove the chain, and unfasten the rope that bound me. I had sat still so long in the cold, I could not get to my feet. Tears of pain and frustration ran down my cheeks. I hardly had the strength to feel anger, but it was there somewhere, deep down, along with the memory of the chancy-boat burning.

One of the men brought a blanket. Judging by the smell, it had last been worn by a horse. Flint shook it out, draped it around me, then scooped me up, one arm around my shoulders, the other hand under my knees, as if I weighed no more than a child. He took a step toward the opening in the wall, then turned back. The three of them flinched.

"Don't forget," Flint said. Then, without waiting for a response, he ducked under the opening and we were outside, where a tall horse stood waiting. An Enforcer's mount, dark as night, saddled in good leather, with silver rings on its bridle.

"I . . ." I struggled to draw breath. "Where . . . ?"

I might as well have stayed silent for all the notice Flint took. He hoisted me up, a long way up, until I sat sideways in front of the saddle. I swayed, close to falling. "Hold on," he ordered. I clutched the horse's mane, wondering if the plan was to ride all the way to Summerfort tonight. Flint swung up behind me, pulled me back against him, and took up the reins. "Sit still," he said. At some signal too subtle for me to detect, the horse moved off, leaving the barnyard behind. No galloping, no wild flight. We went at a sedate walk, and when we got to the road, a pale thread in a night now full of stars, the horse did not turn south toward the king's fortress, but north up the valley.

"Wha—"

"Quiet." It seemed Flint was not going to offer explanations. Perhaps I did not want them. My imagination could supply enough unpleasant possibilities. When we had gone on some considerable way, and I could see the lights of a dwelling drawing closer, he said, "Tonight, as far as the farm up there. Tomorrow, farther. That's all you need to know."

I imagined a troop of Enforcers waiting at the farm, ready to prize answers out of me. I imagined a night spent in drugged sleep while a mind-scraper turned my thoughts inside out. With Flint's body warming mine and the horse moving steadily on in the darkness, I thought of betrayal and how it came so easily—in a word, a glance, a gesture.

Weapons sharp. Backs straight. Hearts high. I heard Sorrel's hideous scream as the iron touched him. I saw his limp body, and Sage's wise little face suddenly aged by grief. I considered how acts of kindness could spring from the unlikeliest sources. A woman whose husband's misfortune had cut them both adrift from the fabric of community; a lonely creature under a bridge. *Courage,* I told myself. *Be that woman Grandmother said you must be.* In the back of my mind was the defile, and the rhyme, and the stanie mon.

Perhaps it was true. Perhaps I really was a Caller. I wished I could slow my thumping heart.

We reached the farm and halted before the door. Flint dismounted and lifted me from the saddle. Something was wrong with my eyes; I could see two or three of him, and when the door opened and a shaft of light spilled out, I shrank back from it, my head shrieking protest. There was a terse conversation, Flint giving orders, someone murmuring agreement. Then I was in a big kitchen, and a grim-faced woman was stripping off my clothes, helping me into a tub of hot water, scrubbing me, washing my hair, speaking hardly a word save for "Lean forward" and "Lift your arm." I sat in the bath and let her do it. My body was a traitor, soaking up the heat, filling with a sleepy sense of well-being, despite everything. It was so good to be warm at last. My mind was a blank, drifting.

The water began to cool and she got me out. I could not stand up on my own. The woman dressed me in someone else's garments: a shift, a gown, a shawl. She put a comb in my hand, sat me down on a stool, and went out, taking my filthy clothing with her. My big cloak, the one Flint had given me the day we first met, she had draped before the fire to dry. My shoes too she had left behind, placed neatly together by the hearth. My fey-mended shoes. I wondered how much Flint had paid this household for its silence.

He came in after a while. Even without his Enforcer's cloak and gauntlets, he looked formidable. I was struggling to get the knots out of my hair. This was the first time it had been properly washed for many moons—the kind of shelter folk had given Father and me had not included warm water and cleansing herbs.

Flint stood by the table and watched me in silence, his arms folded. I could see only one of him now, but he wavered in and out of focus. I tried to guess what he would say when he finally decided to speak. He would ask me about the shoes, perhaps. Try to make me tell him I had friends among the Good Folk. Beat out of me the names of everyone who had helped me. Or maybe hand me over to a mind-scraper right away. A shiver ran through me, despite the warmth of the chamber. Tears built behind my eyes, and I willed them back. Stupidly, what seemed to hurt most was that I had almost trusted him.

"You're cold," Flint said.

I shook my head. The comb snagged in a tangle, and I pulled at it with more violence than I intended.

"You lied to me," he said. His tone was flat.

I looked at him, but his expression was expertly guarded. He had, no doubt, conducted hundreds of interrogations before and had it down to a fine art. I did not answer. What did he expect, that I would come straight out with a confession?

"You said you could look after yourself." His eyes were no longer on me but turned toward the hearth, where my shoes sat side by side. "You've done a pretty poor job of it so far."

Had I told him that? It seemed so long ago, the night Father died. Now I was sick, weak, dispirited, afraid. I had allowed myself to be caught. I could not argue with him.

I wanted to tell him that he had lied too. He had said that with him I would be safe. How dare he say that when all the time he was an Enforcer?

"Here." Suddenly he was standing right beside me, a knife in his hand.

I shrank away, lifting my arms to shield myself.

"Your hair," Flint said. "You won't get that out by combing." With a swift motion of the knife, he severed the knotted lock, catching it in his free hand. He stepped back and sheathed the weapon. I breathed again.

"We won't be staying here," Flint said, resuming his stance by the table. "We'll be moving on."

"Now?" I croaked, imagining stepping out of the door into the cold night, getting on the horse again, and riding all the way to Summerfort.

A glimmer of expression crossed his impassive features. "In the morning. I told you."

I couldn't bear this. My stomach was in knots of anxiety. If he was going to hurt me, if he was taking me in for questioning, let him get started on it now so I need not endure this fearful time of waiting. "Move on where?" I managed.

"One step at a time." His voice had fallen to a murmur. "Tonight, eat, sleep. That's all."

"But—"

"Don't waste your strength arguing. Do as I tell you and keep your mouth shut."

"But I—"

The door opened and the woman came in, followed by a tall, thin man. The man dragged the tub of water out; the woman took foodstuffs from a shelf and assembled a meal of bread, cheese, and onions, with a jug of ale. All the while Flint stood there in silence, watching her, watching me. His presence made the whole room feel dangerous.

I had no appetite. I swallowed a morsel of bread and a sip of ale, then began to cough uncontrollably. Nausea churned my belly. I struggled up from the table and staggered over to the hearth, where I stood with my back to the rest of them, struggling to keep down what little I had eaten. After that, it was all a blur. Someone carried me to a corner, someone put me into a bed, and darkness rolled over me.

Flint's mount was as tireless as its master. The miles of the Rush valley passed beneath its hooves as the last leaves fell from the oaks and the winds of autumn whistled down from the mountain passes, singing songs of snow. The days were a tangle of waking dreams. The nights saw me fall into exhausted sleep in one makeshift camp after another. Later, I could not have said how long we traveled, five days or five-and-twenty.

My cough grew worse. I was hot and cold, sleepy and restless. My body ached; I could not remember a time when I had been so weary. Somehow, at the end of each day's ride, there was a fire, food, somewhere to lie out of the wind and rain: under an overhang, or beneath a shelter of fallen branches, or in a cave. I was beyond wondering where, why, how. When I became so weak that I could not go into the woods to relieve myself without collapsing, Flint took to coming with me and holding me up, his gaze averted, until I had finished. I was past caring.

If Flint was worried that his prize might die before he could do whatever it was he planned to do, he hid it expertly. Only, sometimes, I saw a flicker in his eyes as he knelt to lay a hand on my brow, to feel if it burned hotter than before. He went about the routines of making and striking camp with orderly calm, as he'd done on that very first night, the night we walked out of Darkwater, setting our backs to the scene of flame and death. But it seemed to me each day saw his mouth set a little grimmer and his eyes a little narrower.

At a certain point I ceased even to notice this. I simply lay shivering and shaking, and the only thought in my mind was, *I want to die.* And not long after that, the traveling stopped, and I was in a house or hut, and in a bed, and there was a little fire on a hearth, burning steadily. I thought maybe it was a dream, a wishful sort of dream, and that I would wake soon on the horse's back with long miles to go before nightfall.

I woke, then I slept. It was light, then dark. Perhaps I dreamed, but those dreams were like none I had experienced before; they were twisted and strange, and I could not tell what was real and what was not. I did not know where I was, and I did not care. I would open my eyes a crack to see Flint there with a cup of water or a bowl of gruel, and I would swallow obediently, my throat tight and sore, then close my eyes and sink back onto the pillow. I would feel myself being lifted and taken out to the privy, brought back in again, tucked under the covers. Sometimes he wiped my face with a cloth dipped in warm water; sometimes he bathed other parts of me. He made a somber nursemaid.

There were sounds: a bird screeching outside, small creatures rustling in the thatch, shutters rattling in the wind. There was light: the flames of the fire, always burning, as if Flint feared a chill would carry me off; the warm glow of the lamp in the evenings. There was the profound darkness of night, and the knowledge that he was there, sleeping on a bench by the door, guarding the house. Guarding me. Wasn't he supposed to be the enemy? That couldn't be right. He was keeping me safe.

DISPATCH: FOR THE EYES OF KING KELDEC ONLY
Three Hags district, late autumn

My respectful greetings to you, my lord king, along with my profound regret that there was no way of sending word to you earlier. It has become necessary for me to go to ground, beyond reach of Summerfort and my comrades. The matter of which I wrote earlier is still unfolding, but unforeseen complications have delayed its resolution. It is a delicate mission. Undue haste could precipitate disaster. Rest assured that, should the venture bear fruit, a season or two's delay will weigh nothing against the strategic advantage to be gained.

The autumn being now well advanced, I anticipate that this dispatch will not find you at Summerfort, my lord king, but that it must be carried to you in the east. That will take time. Since Stag Troop must depart for Winterfort soon, I am entrusting the message to the capable hands of Rohan Death-Blade, who leads the troop in my absence.

     Owen Swift-Sword, Stag Troop Leader

*   *   *

At last the fever abated, leaving me limp and weak, but lucid. I lay in bed, watching Flint as he brought in firewood, chopped vegetables at the table, concocted herbal brews. Sometimes he went away for a while, returning with a hare or bird to skin or pluck and prepare for supper. He didn't talk much; he hadn't for a long time. His blunt features seemed thinner. The glow of lamplight on his face served only to accentuate his pallor.

The past began to return to me, but I could make little sense of it. Flint was here, and I was here. But where, exactly? And why? On the few days when it was warm enough, he opened the shutters to let a patch of sunlight fall across my coverlet. But the window showed me only the limbs of a leafless birch, and beyond them pale sky.

I thought perhaps I had nearly died. Under the blankets, my stomach was hollow between jutting hip bones. My knees and elbows were sharp as an old woman's. If I looked in a mirror, I imagined, I would see a ghost's face staring back. How long had I lain here helpless? There were a hundred questions I wanted to ask, but I could not find words beyond *yes, no, thank you.* The moment I began to question, Flint and I would be enemies again. But I grew a little stronger with each day, and there came a morning when I sat up on my own, looked across at Flint, and said, "I'm hungry."

He smiled; his eyes lit up; briefly, he was a different man. As quickly, he clamped control over his features and the smile was gone. "There's porridge," he said. "It seems a fitting breakfast."

It took me a moment to recall that our first meal together had been a lumpy porridge cooked in the camp near Darkwater, when the worst fear I had of him was that he would take me to his bed. "Where did you get the oats from?" I asked.

"Don't waste your strength asking about oats," Flint said, turning his back on me and busying himself at the table.

What should I use my strength for, then? Asking questions whose answers I was not sure I was ready to hear? I gazed around the hut—anything other than stare at Flint—while I considered this. I knew the place well by now. It was so small I could see almost all of it from my bed. Everything here was rough-hewn, from the blocky table to the hard bench on which Flint slept, a bed devoid of blankets and pillows—his cloak lay folded at the foot, and a rolled-up sack was at the other end. My bed, by contrast, had several blankets and two feather pillows. A shelf by the table held a cook pot, a few platters and cups, various implements. Beside them was a row of bags containing foodstuffs. The limp form of a rabbit hung from a string, waiting to be skinned for the pot. Close to the door, weaponry stood against the wall: a bow and quiver, a sword in a black scabbard, an ax that did not seem the kind with which one would chop firewood.

What should I say to him? Each possible question gave rise to a myriad of others. Anything I said, beyond a simple query about oats, might give away what I must keep secret: where I was headed, to whom I had spoken, who had helped me. I wondered if I had rambled in my fever dreams. I wondered whether, in the throes of a nightmare, I had spoken the word *Shadowfell*.

Flint removed a pot from the fire, spooned the contents into a pair of bowls, brought one over to the bedside. He set down the bowl, then reached to wedge the pillows behind my back with a deft touch born of long practice. He found the shawl that had lain across my bed and wrapped it around my shoulders. He did not once meet my eye.

"Eat," he said, sitting down on the stool beside the bed and dipping a spoon into the porridge.

"I'll feed myself. I must start sometime."

Without comment, Flint put the spoon in my hand. Willing myself to be strong, I took a careful mouthful. He had fed me too many meals to count. Time after time he had seen me turn my head away, unable to eat the smallest morsel. He had cooked broth after broth, gruel after gruel, only to see me retch them up onto the bedding. I would eat this without his help if it killed me. I took another spoonful. Flint held the bowl, his gray eyes as steady as his hands.

"Good," he said when I was finished and had lain back on the pillows, worn out by my effort. "I'll cook the rabbit tomorrow and make you a broth. We have a supply of foodstuffs, running somewhat low at present. I supplement it with my traps. The oats were here the night we arrived."

So he'd answered my question after all. That surprised me.

"You should eat your porridge," I said. "It'll be cold."

"That's the least of my worries," said Flint. He took my bowl over to the table and brought his own, then stood looking down at me, making no attempt at all to eat.

"Where are we, exactly?"

"How much do you remember?" Flint asked.

I made myself meet his gaze. "It's coming back to me slowly. I was sleeping in a barn, and some people found me. They fetched you, and you paid them and took me away. We slept at another farm. Then there was a long, long ride. I think I've been quite sick. My dreams were odd. Confusing. There is a lot I don't remember at all."

"It was a long ride, yes. We came up the Rush and over the pass, then down into an area close to a burnt-out settlement."

My heart was suddenly all bruises. I could no more have shielded my expression than taken the moon down from the sky. All I could do was close my eyes.

"You should rest," Flint said. "This is too much for you."

I drew in a long breath and let it out again. "I'm all right. Please go on." Corbie's Wood; it had to be. Somewhere just out there lay the bones of my brother, his ribs smashed by an enemy spear. There lay my grandmother in the grave we had hastily scrabbled out for her. Father and I had fled our home with earth under our fingernails.

"This hut is attached to a farm," Flint said. "It's high on

the hillside and invisible from the main track. The place is tenanted in summer, when the sheep are herded up here for grazing. At other times of year it is used for different purposes. To house folk who need a bolt-hole, for example. You were too sick to go on. I had thought . . ."

He seemed to have lost the thread of what he was saying. I opened my eyes and he turned his gaze immediately away. I waited.

"I had thought it possible you might not survive." Flint's tone was constrained.

This made no sense. He had captured me. He had paid good silver for me. Then, when it would have been less than a day's ride to take his prize back to Summerfort, he had brought me the other way. He could have delivered me safe and sound to the king's fortress before I got so sick I almost died. But here we were a stone's throw from Corbie's Wood.

"Over the pass," I murmured. "So far." There was a powerful longing in me to walk among the scattered remnants of my birthplace. To stand by the graves. To speak words of farewell and comfort, the words there had been no time for back then. To sing my dear lost ones the old song. My chest ached with the feeling. I thought of the care with which Flint had tended to me. I considered the undeniable fact that, without him, I would have died. The truth trembled on my tongue. I bit it back. He had been kind, yes. But there was no getting around the fact that he was an Enforcer. Was it possible he had saved me not out of some feeling of compassion or responsibility but for another purpose entirely?

Flint was gazing into his porridge bowl with some intensity. "Winter is close," he said. "It was a calculated risk. If I had waited for you to recover before leaving that first place of shelter, it might have been too late to cross the pass before the first snow. And there were additional reasons for moving on." He dipped in his spoon and began to eat, as if this were a perfectly ordinary conversation.

I drew a deep breath, summoning my courage. "What are your intentions for me?" I asked.

"It's my turn to ask a question," said Flint coolly. "When you headed up the Rush valley, were you still going to the same place you spoke of that night in Darkwater? A place of shelter, where you would have rocks and trees as companions?"

Gods, he had remembered everything. But perhaps that was part of his job. I had told outright lies often enough in the past to escape tricky situations. Lies would not work with Flint. He would see right through me. I scrambled to find a half-truth. "The burnt-out village, Corbie's Wood," I said. "I lived there once. Everyone is gone, the houses are destroyed, but . . . there must be some places of shelter, caves, old huts. . . . That was where I planned to settle, to fend for myself." I heard how unlikely it sounded. Flint would think me devoid of any wits at all. And yet, if sickness and foul weather had not both descended on me at once, I could have survived on my own. Those years on the road with Father had taught me many skills. Now, in my weakened state and with winter fast approaching, my intention seemed ridiculous. Unless I allowed my otherworldly friends to help me. Unless I used the gift I barely understood. A vivid memory flashed through my mind: myself pressed in panic against a rock wall, muttering rhymes to Stanie Mon, and the rock embracing me, protecting me. The Enforcers had ridden back to Summerfort. All but one of them, and here he was.

"You couldn't have done it," Flint said bluntly. "Even without this illness, you'd never have survived winter up here in the mountains. Where are your traps and snares? Where are your bow and arrows, your skinning knife, your fishing spear? What cave or tumbledown ruin can provide sufficient shelter when ice lies black on every pond and hard frost crackles the earth under your feet?"

I cleared my throat but said nothing. This was not the manner of speaking I expected from an Enforcer.

"You asked me about my intentions for you," he said. "Once before you asked a similar question and I gave you an answer. That answer is unchanged."

I was growing tired; the good meal, the warm bedding, the luxury of being able to breathe properly, all were combining to make me crave sleep. Had I asked this before? What had he said? I delved for the memory of that night above Darkwater and a strange conversation conducted when I was shattered with weariness, numbed by the loss of my father, terrified of the future. Something about choice. That he was giving me a choice.

"I don't understand," I whispered, resisting the urge to close my eyes and surrender to sleep. "What choice can you possibly offer me?"

Flint was silent. He went over to take a kettle off the fire and carry it to the table. Eventually he said, "You should sleep now. Do you need the privy?"

"No." I looked down at my hands on the coverlet. They were pallid, white gray, the bones stark under the skin. Corpse hands. I thrust them under the blankets. "Thank you for looking after me," I made myself say. "I know that but for you I would have died."

A long silence; my eyelids drifted shut.

"I understand it's hard for you to trust," he said quietly. "You're not alone in that."

I opened my eyes, turning my head to see him standing by the fire again, his gaze on me, his expression somber.

"There is a choice. You are weary; now is not the time to speak of it." After a moment he added, "You have a long road to tread before you are well enough to travel again, even accompanied. You don't like it that I am the one you need to keep the wolf from the door; that comes as no surprise. But I am the one you have. At some point we'll both have to risk telling the truth."

Chapter Nine

The days passed, and with each day I was a little stronger. As if by mutual consent, Flint and I did not talk again about the future, or about our reasons for being where we were. Instead, we worked on my recovery together. Stormy weather meant he would not let me go out of doors except to the privy, but he devised a set of tasks for me, which I performed several times a day under his eagle-eyed scrutiny. Walk to the door and back ten times. Bend and stretch ten times. Circle the arms, circle the shoulders. Time for rest, then repeat the entire exercise. As I grew stronger, he added more difficult elements.

I wondered whether, in his other life as an Enforcer, his duties included training new recruits.

By now I was going out to the privy on my own, and even occasionally bringing in a small armful of firewood from an enormous stack beyond the hut's back door. On a day when the rain had cleared at last and the sun was making a brave attempt to break through the clouds, I walked a short distance along the hillside, thinking I might fix the direction of Corbie's Wood, or even perhaps see what was left of it. But the rocky outcrop that sheltered our modest dwelling also blocked out a view down into the valley. I'd need to climb higher up the hill, as far as the band of trees I could see up there. My memories of home did not include this hut; it must be farther from the settlement than I had thought. There was no sign of the horse that had carried Flint and me on our long and taxing journey. And there was no sign at all of the Good Folk, either familiar or unfamiliar, though I stooped to examine chinks between the rocks and crouched to peer under low bushes, half hoping, half dreading that they might be here.

I came back in to find Flint polishing his sword, which lay along the table. The lamplight caught its dark shine.

"Don't stray away from the hut on your own," he said as if he had eyes in the back of his head. "This may be an out-of-the-way corner, but that's an unnecessary risk."

"Where is your horse?"

He glanced up. "Gone. It's too hard to provide fodder up here." Seeing my eyes widen, he added, "She's being looked after. Not in these parts. Such a creature, stabled at one of the local farms, would be bound to attract questions."

I considered this odd statement for a while. I thought of various things to ask and discarded them one by one. Finally I said, "Then . . . when you move on . . . you plan to go on foot?"

He eyed me. "That depends on a few factors. Where

I go. When I go. Whether the snows are here. Whether you're strong enough to walk the distance."

I moved over to sit on the edge of the bed, for my legs were tired. It sounded as if he expected me to go with him. "So there's some doubt about where you go next," I said.

Flint moved his polishing cloth along the gleaming metal in strong, even strokes. "There's always a choice," he said. "North or south. Uphill or downhill. Advance or retreat."

I must have allowed some of my irritation to show on my face, for he set down the cloth and came over, leaning against the wall close by me.

. "This particular choice can't be made until you're fully recovered," Flint said. "I'm hoping you will be fit before the tracks become impassable. We can't afford to be trapped here over the winter."

I said nothing.

"You could tell me where you were going," Flint said. "If I knew that, I could help you get there. I can see you don't trust me, and that keeps you from being open about it. If it helps, imagine me as one of those dogs that follow you about even when you curse and shout at them."

I looked at him and he looked at me. I realized I was finding it increasingly difficult to see him as the enemy.

"Have I cursed and shouted?" I asked.

"Not exactly. You talk in your sleep."

A shiver ran through me. I must not forget what he

was. If I trusted the wrong man, I could jeopardize every-thing Shadowfell stood for. Perhaps I already had.

"Now you have that look on your face again," Flint said. "As if you have closed up the shutters."

I told myself not to hear the kindness in his voice. I bade myself not look into the gray eyes, whose expression was somewhat less guarded than was customary.

"You're the king's man," I said flatly. "Tell me why I should trust you."

He folded his arms. "I wear the stag, yes. On the other hand, I'm here and I've stayed here all this time. You are here with me, and I haven't set a hand on you except to tend to you in your illness."

"Because you want something from me."

"Neryn." Flint's voice had gone quiet. Despite myself, I lifted my head. His eyes were turned on me, steady and sure. If he was dissembling still, he was indeed expert at it. "It's easy enough for me to guess where you are headed. That place is some days' travel from here, and the journey will take you across terrain unsuited to riding. It's late in the season; there may be storms and the nights will be chill. You'll need to be well enough to go on foot and make camp by the wayside." And when I simply stared at him, unable to tell whether he really had guessed where I was going, Flint added, "If I go with you, I can ensure you get there safely. If you'd waited for me, that morning above Darkwater, you'd have been there long before now."

That silenced me. He had known where I was going even then? How could that be?

"You wonder, I think, why I brought you over the pass instead of taking you straight back to Summerfort." His voice had dropped to a murmur, as if even in this isolated place, with the two of us behind closed shutters, there might be someone listening for secrets. "If I told you I never intended to hand you over to the authorities, would that help you trust me?"

"If I could believe it, yes."

"I don't expect the whole truth from you, though it would help me considerably if you'd give just a little. Of my own circumstances, I'll tell you only what you need. We both understand, I think, how perilous knowledge can be when there are those who would wrench it out of us forcibly. Know simply that I am here to guard you. To watch over you. And to ensure you reach your destination."

So you are not a king's man? I could not ask him that. With his silver stag brooch and his air of authority, with his kindness and his promises to keep me safe, it seemed he both was and was not. Could he be some kind of spy? That would make sense of more than a few things. But where did his loyalty lie?

It felt as if we were playing a game, a dangerous and difficult one. Every day I performed my exercises under his supervision. I ate what was put in front of me and rested when I was told to. I began to help with domestic tasks—preparing food, tending to the fire, washing clothes and hanging them on a line by the hearth. Once or twice he took me outside, well wrapped, for a brief, closely supervised walk.

The air was bracingly cold; I could not stay out for long before my chest began to hurt and he bundled me back inside to recover by the fire. But slowly and surely I was getting better. Soon we would have to talk again about what came next.

Flint did not ply me with hard questions. From time to time he would remind me that if I were more open with him, we'd both be better placed to discuss the next step. He was patient, working away at my reserve as water works at stone, drop by slow drop.

A wary trust developed between us. His kindness seemed real. With every day that passed, he seemed less Enforcer and more friend, a man not given to smiles, laughter, or confidences but who was steady, capable, and considerate. He never once raised his voice or lifted a hand against me. And he was patient. He worked me hard and praised my small successes; when I grew too tired to go on, or failed to complete my required exercise for the day, he gave me breathing space, then encouraged me to try again. If he was worried about how quickly the autumn was passing, he said not a word about it.

Of course, it might all be a ploy, designed to win my trust. If that were so, Flint was expert at dissembling. But then, a spy would be. There might be no telling what he truly was: Enforcer or lone warrior, king's man or rebel. Or none of those. The puzzle was often in my thoughts, but I found no answers to it. Despite the questions that lay between us, we became easier with each other. It was a long time since I had smiled, a long time since I had felt contentment. I had almost forgotten how to be happy, in those years on the road. But here in the hut, where all was order, warmth, and quiet, I began to feel a kind of peace.

"Flint?"

"Mm?" He had gone out earlier to fetch a basket of carrots and turnips from a store beneath the hut. Now he was chopping them into a pot while I cut up onions to flavor the brew.

"When you were a little boy, did you play a game called stanie mon?" I could not ask him about recent times, his family, where he had lived before he became an Enforcer. Nobody asked those kinds of questions anymore, and I thought Flint would be the last man to provide answers even if they did. But the distant past seemed safe. "I'm not sure if my brother and I invented it or learned it from someone else."

I had said a little too much. Flint was quick to notice. "Your brother?"

"He died a few years back. At Corbie's Wood." *Died in his blood. Died in his innocence. My lovely, pigheaded, valiant Farral.*

Flint's knife moved steadily. After a while he said, "He must have been quite young."

"He almost reached his fourteenth birthday," I said. The tears that welled in my eyes had little to do with the onions. Curse it. It was Flint's childhood I had planned to talk about, not my own. My brother's story was dangerous to tell. Farral had been too young and too angry to recognize the strength of silence. But I had learned that lesson long ago, and I should have known better than to speak of him.

"Neryn," Flint said quietly.

I stopped cutting the onions and looked straight across the table at him. His gaze was perfectly steady, his eyes clear as a forest pool under a winter sky. They were beautiful eyes. I had not noticed what a fine-shaped mouth he had, thin-lipped, tucked at the corners, a mouth on which I had only once seen a smile. The rest of his face was plain enough, with its crooked nose and its scars. His hair had grown over the course of our stay in the hut. His face wore an untidy beard and his head a short, dark crop, ill tended.

"What?" he asked, the knife stilling in his hand.

"Nothing." I felt as if I had been caught peering into something secret, private. As if I had set my foot over the threshold of a forbidden place. My thoughts confused me.

"A look like that isn't nothing. You were scrutinizing me."

"I was attempting to guess how many days we've been here by the length of your hair."

Flint ran a hand over his head. Briefly his features registered surprise. "More than a turning of the moon," he said. Then, "You have tears in your eyes."

"It's the onions."

He put down his knife and looked at me with the same assessing gaze I had turned on him. "Tell me about your brother. Did he die of an illness? An accident? Or was he killed when the folk of Corbie's Wood stood up against the king's men?"

He knew about that, then. "He died on an Enforcer's spear." I heard the bitter edge in my voice. "It broke my father's heart. And they burned everything anyway. Farral sacrificed himself for nothing." My hands were tight fists on the table before me. I bowed my head, knowing I should not have spoken thus in anger, but knowing too that I had wanted Flint to hear it.

In the silence that followed I could almost feel him thinking.

"Then you must make sure you do what he could not," Flint said, so quietly I wondered if I had imagined the words.

My grandmother's voice sounded in my memory: *You must be the woman I cannot be, Neryn*. She had meant: be a wise woman; be a person who understands the uncanny; be a carrier of ancient lore, strong in spirit. Be someone who does not crumple under tyranny. Stand up against the king's men and make that stand count for something.

The hut felt alive with peril. There was absolutely nothing I could say.

"*Stanie Mon, Stanie Mon, fa' doon deid*," Flint said conversationally. "I seem to recall a rhyme like that. Part of a jumping game, I believe."

I lifted my head, looking over at him. "You're full of surprises."

"It was one of the things you muttered in your sleep."

What else had I said? He might have learned my whole story during those days and nights of tangled dreams. Even now that I was almost my old self again, my sleep was still visited by a wild unrolling of confused images, sometimes frightening, often troubling, always vivid. I had wondered if this was what a person felt after being mind-scraped. I had even thought . . .

"Flint," I said.

"Yes?"

"While I was so sick . . . did anyone else come here? Someone must have fetched the horse. Brought supplies, maybe."

"Why do you ask?"

I hesitated, searching for the right words. "When I had the fever, I lost the sense of how much time was passing. But I know you were gone sometimes. You went out to check and reset your traps, to gather and chop wood, to fetch water. Perhaps for other reasons too. Even if this hut is well concealed, it is hard to believe you saw nobody during all that time. The folk on the farm must know we're here."

Flint poured water from a jug into the pot of vegetables. His eyes were narrowed, his brows crooked in a frown. "There's a lad I can trust," he said, not looking at me. "He came up once or twice with supplies, yes. Not inside. And he took Shadow. The horse."

A lad. That did not sound like an Enthraller.

"You look confused," he said, eyeing me.

I shook my head. "Just one lad? Who else knows where we are?"

"Nobody knows," Flint said quietly. "Just the boy. And even that is a risk, for us and for him. The sooner we can move on, the better." After a little, he added, "If anyone finds you, be sure it won't be through any careless act of mine."

"What about when you were gone? Someone could have come in while I was here on my own."

I could hear Flint's sigh. "You don't have much faith in my capacity to keep you alive, do you? Believe me, if I had not been obliged to leave the hut in order to provide food, I would not have done so. The door was fastened securely; folk would not have known how to open it. I kept my outings brief. I have been trained in certain skills; I can assure you that nobody saw me."

"But—"

"If anyone had been here in my absence, I would have known."

I was silenced. So, no mind-scraper. Not unless the whole thing was a pack of lies.

"Does this training of yours also include the capacity to tell convincing untruths?" I asked. We were deep in it now; I might as well keep going.

A smile; not the unguarded one that changed him so, but a bitter, crooked travesty. "Oh yes," Flint said. "I have great expertise in that. But I won't lie to *you*. The worst I will do is withhold what you need not know."

"Your words are a kind of maze," I said. "A puzzle, a trick. This expertise of yours, I imagine it allows you to sound completely convincing while telling me whatever suits your purpose." Part of me already trusted him. Part of me was all too ready to believe he would take me safely to Shadowfell, then leave with no questions asked. But the years of flight and silence lay on me like a heavy cloak. I could not easily set them aside. "I could go on alone," I said. "You could give me directions if you wanted to be helpful. Then you could reclaim your horse and go back to Summerfort, or wherever else your work takes you." It was hard to picture: Flint bidding me a courteous goodbye, then returning to the violent, bloody duties of an Enforcer. I did not want to think about it.

"You're fitter than you were, but you're far from ready to do this on your own. Besides . . ."

"Besides what?"

"Let's just say I have a vested interest in making sure you reach your destination in one piece," Flint said. "Don't press me for more."

"We can't go on playing this game forever," I said. "Can't you explain why you're helping me? I know knowledge is dangerous, but there's nobody else to hear you, and I don't need the whole story, just enough to make sense of this."

"Every step I take falls under a shadow of danger." Flint's voice had sunk to a murmur. He glanced around the chamber as if there might be spies in the corners, watching us. "Every time I open my mouth, I raise the stakes higher. You said once that you wanted to live alone, without any companionship save rocks and trees. That makes sense to me. Retreating, falling silent—it's the only way to be safe. But we cannot live like that. Your brother died fighting injustice and cruelty. You said his sacrifice was in vain. It's not so. Every man or woman who makes a stand helps keep the flame of freedom burning."

After that, I had nothing to say. Nothing at all. I sat staring at him, my eyes no doubt as big as saucers, and he gazed back steadily.

"If the weather is clear tomorrow, we'll try a longer expedition outside," Flint said, and now his voice was level and calm. "I judge that we have perhaps ten days, maybe a little more, before it becomes too dangerous to stay here. We have a lot of work to do."

That night I dreamed of Flint. He was riding back down the valley, his dark cloak billowing out behind him, storm clouds gathering over him, his face sheet white, his mouth set in a tight line. All alone. The vision swirled and changed, and I saw him in a great hall full of men and women in fine clothing. He knelt, bowing his head, then looked up, his gray eyes clear and calm. The eyes of a truthful man. "My lord king."

Keldec, I did not see. But I heard his voice. "Ah, my long-absent friend. You are returned at last."

"As you see, my lord king."

"And with a tale to tell, I trust?"

"Yes, my lord king. A tale that is for your ears only."

When I woke, that was all I could remember. Coming so soon after the strange conversation in which Flint had spoken eloquently in support of those who rebelled against Keldec's rule, the dream confused and unsettled me. I ate my breakfast in silence, and Flint made no attempt to start a conversation. When we were finished eating, he said, "The day's clear. Put on your cloak and shoes and we'll try a longer walk."

"Now?"

"The sooner, the better, Neryn. The boy's coming up later today; let's get this done while there's nobody about."

I tied my shawl around my shoulders, then fetched my cloak—Flint's old cloak—from the peg where it hung beside his black Enforcer garment. "How do you know he's coming today?" I asked.

"A signal. I need to speak to him briefly. I'll do so outdoors. He won't see you."

"But he does know I'm here."

"As I told you, the place is used to shelter folk who need it. The lad knows I'm not alone. No more than that. The less I tell him, the safer for all of us. Ready?"

"Just my shoes . . ." I reached for them, but Flint was ahead of me.

"Sit down."

I sat on the edge of the bed. He knelt beside me, holding each shoe in turn as I slipped my foot in. As he tied up the cords, I waited for him to make some comment on the tiny, neat stitches, the unusual lining, the fact that the shoes were remarkably unscathed from the trip along the lochs and up the valley. But he finished fastening them in silence, then, when I would have got up, he put his hands around my feet for a moment. The warm strength of them jolted something deep inside me. Part of me woke up, a part I had not known existed.

"Neryn."

"Yes?"

"I'm sorry. Sorry I can't tell you more. Sorry we have to move on when you're still not yourself. Sorry I can't give you time. But there is no time."

My heart was thudding; my cheeks were warm. I could think of nothing to say, but I managed a nod.

Flint rose to his feet. "Come, then," he said, holding out a hand. I took it, and we went outside together.

We walked up the hill. Flint set a good pace, and quite soon my legs were aching, but I gritted my teeth and went on. Our breath made little clouds in the cold air.

"Fix on a goal you can manage," Flint said, pausing while I caught up. "That rock up there—another ten steps. When you reach it, choose the next goal."

I climbed to the rock. I chose the next goal, the trunk of a long-fallen pine, from which limbs had been hewed, perhaps to fuel our hearth fire. By the time I reached it, I was breathing hard.

"Rest now," Flint said. "You've done well. If you feel faint, bend over and put your hands on your knees. It might help to wrap your shawl over your mouth and nose. The air's chill; you've been used to the fire."

The kindly tone was misleading. He waited exactly as long as it took for me to get my breath back, then said, "Now we'll walk up as far as the trees. You go first." As I began to climb, he spoke from behind me. "You can do it, Neryn."

The band of trees was about thirty paces away, straight up the steep path. A goal. I would do it. I would be strong enough.

At ten steps I felt Flint's arm come through mine. "That's enough on your own," he said.

His body was warm against me. His touch gave me strength. We walked up to the trees. Their leafless limbs were alive with little birds searching for dried-up berries or nuts the martens had missed. We turned to look down the hill. Now that we were clear of the rocky outcrop shielding the hut, the valley was revealed below us under a sky streaked with high cloud. Down there, about a mile to the north, lay a blackened, empty place. A broken wall. The crumbling ruins of houses. A row of sad hawthorns. I remembered helping decorate them with ribbons, in spring, to honor a deity whose name was no longer spoken. There had once been a fair wood around that place. Many of the trees had been burned along with the settlement, but an outer ring still stood, sad witnesses, mute guardians.

"Corbie's Wood," I breathed, slipping my arm out of Flint's.

Gods, there were the remnants of Grandmother's house,

and there the lone blackthorn beneath which Farral had died. There was the spot where the Enforcers had camped after the rout was over, waiting to see who would come back, waiting to see whether they had missed anyone. Far up the hill on the other side of the valley was the cottage where we'd found refuge, Father and I. The place where I'd tended to Grandmother over those last sad seasons; the place from which Father had gone out, day by day, to find what work he could to keep us from starving; the make-shift home to which he'd returned, each time sunk deeper into despair. My heart ached with grief.

Flint laid his hand on the small of my back. His touch made me start with some violence; I had been far away. The hand was instantly removed, and that, somehow, was the worst thing of all. I stood cold and alone, looking down over the ruin of my old home, not knowing how to tell Flint I needed the warmth of human touch, an arm around my shoulders, a hand in mine. I longed to believe, just for a little, that I had a friend.

"We'd best walk back now. You'll get cold," Flint said.

"I want to go down there." My voice was thick with un-shed tears. "When it happened, there wasn't time . . . we couldn't . . ." I had not dreamed this could hurt so much.

"It's not safe."

I looked again at the place where Corbie's Wood had been. Nothing lived in that deserted spot now save sad ghosts.

"Flint."

"Yes? Come, we must keep moving; tell me as we go."

I slipped my arm through his again, unasked. In a landscape of death and loss, he was alive, warm, strong. "When you said we would move on . . . you meant going north, didn't you? How could we do that without passing by Corbie's Wood?"

"There's a track up beyond those trees that follows the ridge and comes down farther north. You may even remember it. You and your brother must have roamed about these hills in summer, as children do. It leads past a place called Lone Tarn. That way's safer. More remote." He glanced at me. "It's a hard walk."

"I'll manage," I said.

We were passing an outcrop of rocks cloaked in thorny bushes when Flint made a little sound under his breath. A moment later I found myself thrust down into hiding.

I crouched between the rocks where Flint had put me; there was no need for him to say, *Be quiet*. I didn't see him unsheathe his knife, but it was in his hand as he moved on down the hill.

I waited, imagining the possibilities. Local people hunting for me in the hope of winning a payment in king's silver. Wild dogs, hungry wolves. Enforcers. No, Flint would not have left me on my own. I made myself breathe slowly.

"Neryn."

I nearly jumped out of my skin. Not Flint's voice, but that of someone smaller and stranger. "No!" I whispered. "Not now!"

"Now, yes, now!"

"Quick, before he comes back!"

Faces peered from the cover of the thorny plants. Eyes peeped out from the chinks and cracks of the hillside. Voices spoke from pools of rainwater. From the time Flint brought me here, I had seen not a trace of the Good Folk. Now they were everywhere. "Now, now, talk now!" they pleaded. "Now, while *he* is not near."

"Shh!" I hissed. "Keep quiet and stay hidden. This is not the time."

"Danger! Peril!"

"Hide yourselves *now!*" I ordered.

And now the wind brought voices from down the hill, Flint's and that of a younger man.

". . . early," was all I caught of Flint's speech. *You're here early.* The boy. It was only the lad come before Flint expected him. I breathed again.

". . . message . . . coming up toward the pass. Many . . ."

"How long . . ."

The men's voices faded; they had moved away. The Good Folk had obeyed my command and merged back into the land, invisible to human eyes. I knew they were still there watching me. My skin prickled with their closeness.

I waited, crouched in my bolt-hole and growing colder by the moment. I imagined myself walking in Corbie's Wood. I pictured myself kneeling by Farral's grave—a grave marked by a pile of stones placed there long after the Enforcers had moved on, satisfied that the place had been

185

cleansed of both the smirched and the rebellious. We had come out from hiding then, we sad survivors, and laid our dead to rest. We had hidden the pieces of our broken lives in our hearts and crept away. In my mind I sang the old song for my brother. *Hag of the Isles, my secrets keep; Master of Shadows, guard my sleep.*

"Neryn."

Flint was here. I struggled to my feet. My cramped legs did not want to hold me. He caught my arms to stop me from falling.

"I'm sorry," he said. "I did not mean to be so long. It's safe now. Come, let's get you home."

"Home," I croaked. "I'd laugh at that, if I were capable of it." Gods, my legs felt like jelly. I clenched my teeth and took a step.

"I'll carry you," Flint said.

"No! It's only a cramp." I made myself move forward. "Is he gone?" I murmured as we headed back down to the hut.

"Mm." Flint's answer was not much more than a grunt. After a moment he added, "We'll talk inside."

Once in the hut, with the door closed behind us, I resisted the urge to sink down on the bed. I hung up my cloak, then went to sit on the bench by the table. I wanted my strength back. I wanted the old Neryn back, the one who could walk many miles between sunup and sundown, and make her own fire, and catch her own supper.

Flint was a somber-looking man at the best of times.

Right now he was grimmer than usual, his mouth a thin line, his jaw tight, his eyes forbidding questions. He put a log on the fire, filled the kettle, set it to boil. He took off his cloak—the silver stag gleamed in the firelight—and hung it beside mine. He came to stand by me, arms folded. Neither of us had said a word since we came in.

"I thought I heard you talking to someone up there."

I had not expected this. He must have exceptionally sharp hearing. The voices of the Good Folk were small, and I was sure I had not spoken above a whisper. "I was saying a prayer for my brother," I told him. A half-truth.

"Mm-hm." Flint just leaned there, looking at me.

"Was that the boy who usually comes here?" I asked.

He nodded.

"What did he want?"

"Nothing important," Flint said.

Now that was more than half a lie, I thought. "I heard him say something about someone coming up toward the pass."

"I could deny that, as you denied that you were talking to someone. We could keep playing this game until time caught up with us."

I said nothing. His approach to information was to share only what he thought I needed to know. He did not need to know about the Good Folk.

"You look tired," Flint said. "You'd better rest."

"I will be strong enough," I muttered, not sure if I was angry with Flint, or with myself, or with King Keldec and the whole benighted realm of Alban. *A day,* I thought. *Just one day when I don't have to think about any of it. One day when I can go outside and walk around and feel the sunlight without looking over my shoulder. One day when I can talk to Flint, and talk to the Good Folk, and talk to anyone who comes by without guarding every word.* It didn't seem much to ask. But it was. It was impossible.

"Rest first," Flint said. "We'll have another walk later. But . . ."

"But what?"

Now there was a look on his face that really troubled me. It was an Enforcer look, and his tone matched it. It was all hard edges. "Tomorrow I must be away all day. I need a promise from you, Neryn. You mustn't leave the hut while I'm gone. Not even out to the privy—you can use a bucket. If anyone comes, if you hear anything at all, you must stay inside and keep silent. Not a sound. Do you understand?"

"I understand why people are afraid of Enforcers," I said, making myself look him in the eye. "Where are you going? It's because of that boy, isn't it? The message he brought?"

Flint sighed. "You need not know the details. Just as I need not know exactly what you were doing before, when I left you on the hill up there. I find myself hoping . . ." He lost the thread of what he was saying, or perhaps thought better of it. "I'll brew you an herbal infusion. Warm you up."

"Whatever the message was, it's upset you. Is someone

coming here? Someone who is a threat to me?" I thought again. "Or to you?"

He was setting cups on the table, his movements precise. For a man with such big hands, he was remarkably deft. I liked watching him work. "You understand why I cannot tell you that," he said.

I did, of course. What I didn't know, I couldn't pass on. "If you can't tell me that," I said, "tell me what you were going to say before. *I find myself hoping* . . . Hoping what?"

He kept his attention on the brew he was preparing. "Hoping for one day, a single day, with the world to rights. A day when I need not worry about whether you are safe; a day when I can open doors and shutters and let the sun in. A day when there are no battles to be fought, when right and wrong are as clear-cut as light and dark." Flint grimaced. "It will be a long time before we see such a day. Never, perhaps." He went to fetch the kettle from the fire.

I considered this remarkable speech while Flint finished making his brew and set a cup before me on the table. It startled me that his thoughts had run so close to mine. He seated himself opposite me, his own cup between his palms. He was avoiding my gaze.

"Right and wrong are clear-cut," I said eventually. "Aren't they?" But in my mind were the times I had stolen food to keep myself and my father from starving, and the night Father had wagered me away. I saw an image of myself running over Brollachan Bridge and leaving my friends behind, at the mercy of my pursuers. I heard Sorrel screaming.

"I have not always found them so."

"What about when you were a child, Flint? Children see things clearly and simply. Until . . ." *Until they witness the unspeakable, and the conviction that right will always triumph fades away forever.*

"That's irrelevant."

The most formidable of shutters had closed over his features, forbidding further comment. I had never seen a look like that on anyone's face, and it chilled me. He was too young to wear such a look, surely. He had been a child once, with a child's innocent delight in the world. This was the face of a man who had forgotten the meaning of joy.

I sipped my drink, which was a healthful concoction of various green herbs, and said nothing. The fire's warmth was spreading through the hut now, chasing away the chill. Flint sat staring into space. The silence drew out.

"I want to make you a promise," I said.

"Promise not to go out the door tomorrow. That's all I need."

"What you said . . . I had been thinking something very like it. About a day when all is to rights, a day that is a perfect gift. You'll have that day eventually, Flint. And I'll have the day I wish for, a day without fear, a day of sunshine, a day of open speech." Suddenly it felt desperately important that he should believe this. "That was what my brother died for. I'm afraid of death. I'm afraid of a lot of things. I don't know if I can be as brave as Farral was. But I do have hope. Without hope, I don't see how anyone can keep on going. You will have your day of freedom, and so will I. Maybe we'll wait a long time, but that day will come." After a silence, I added, "Perhaps I've said too much. Perhaps not as much as you wanted." I had no idea what he thought of my speech.

"Promise me you'll stay in the hut while I'm gone," Flint said. "Say it, Neryn."

"I can't promise. Anything could happen. What if the place caught fire?" And, when he glared at me, "I promise to apply common sense. I know I shouldn't go out on my own. I'll use your wretched bucket."

The hard frost in Flint's eyes thawed slightly. "I can see that's the best I'm going to get from you. Now rest. Don't argue about it; lie down on the bed and shut your eyes. When you've slept and eaten, we'll go out again."

I slept, and dreamed of Flint. Flint seated at the table, writing. Even in the dream, I thought that was odd—where would he procure parchment, ink, and quill? How was it that a man like him knew how to read and write? He labored over the task as if he found it not only difficult but distasteful. When it was done, he packed his materials away, rolled up the parchment, and sealed it with wax melted over a candle flame. He put the scroll into his pack, blew out the candle, sat awhile with his eyes on nothing in particular. There was a new look on his face, the look of a man edging ever closer to an abyss.

The dream changed. I was on a rocky island, a wild, lovely place where sea and sky formed a perfect unison, a landscape of myriad shades of gray and blue and green. Seals basked on a promontory; gulls wheeled overhead. A little boy of five or six was playing alone on a beach of pale pebbles. His dark hair was ruffled by the wind. His gray eyes were all concentration as he balanced stones in a circle atop a flat rock. "Stanie Mon, Stanie Mon, stand up ta'; Stanie Mon, Stanie Mon, doon ye fa'!" His arm swept across, sudden, brutal; the stones clattered and fell. The boy crouched there a moment, as still as if he too were of stone. Then he began to set his men upright again, each in its turn. A cloud covered the sun, cloaking the child in shadow.

When I woke, the fire had been built up and Flint had a meal ready. My dreams clung close. There were questions I wanted to ask. Had he been raised in the western isles? Who had taught him to read? A man who had become an Enforcer must have many ghosts in his past. His memories would be hard to carry. A man could not do the king's work and stay whole in mind and spirit.

I ate; I could not do otherwise when Flint was watching me with a hawk's keen eye. Later we went out walking again and he showed me where the track to the north began, at the upper edge of the band of woodland. I sensed that the Good Folk were close by, but Flint's presence kept them in hiding.

When night fell, I slept the sleep of complete exhaustion,

and if I dreamed, those dreams were fleeting fragments. I woke soon after dawn to find Flint fastening the straps on his pack. He was already in his cloak and boots. The bucket stood in the corner and a pot of porridge steamed by the fire. I sat on the edge of the bed, rubbing the sleep from my eyes.

"I have to go." He came over and crouched down in front of me, taking my hands in his. "I will do my best to be back before nightfall, but if I'm not, don't be concerned. There's sufficient food here for a while, and I've brought in a supply of firewood." He hesitated. "If . . ."

"What? If you don't come back?" It was too early for this. I was half-asleep, unable to mind my words or school my features as I should.

"I will come back," Flint said. "I give you my word."

I looked into his eyes and could see no trace of uncertainty there. "Be careful," I said, realizing that only a matter of days ago I would not have dreamed of speaking to him thus.

Flint's mouth twitched. It could have been an attempt at a smile. "Careful," he echoed. "I am always careful, Neryn. You, I think, are more impulsive. Please keep your promise." He rose to his feet. "I must go. Be safe."

After Flint left, I did as he had told me and barred the door. The shutters were closed fast. By the light of the oil lamp, I ate my breakfast, washed the dishes, tidied the bed, put more wood on the fire. The stack Flint had left me looked sufficient for days. I shivered. How could he be so certain he would come back? Out there, anything might happen.

Then there was nothing to do but sit and think. Where had he gone? What was he doing? My mind went to the night he had purchased me from my captors and chosen to take me north, not south. To freedom, not captivity. It seemed he had been among those Enforcers who had pursued me through the defile and seen me vanish before their eyes. He had sent the others back and come on alone. Had he known then what I was? Perhaps he had known from the very first. Perhaps he had been sent to apprehend me that night at Darkwater, but had disobeyed his orders and saved me for some reason of his own. An act of direct defiance, an act that could see a man summarily executed. I wished I knew where he was. He might be in terrible danger.

This was driving me crazy. I was thinking in circles and going nowhere. I would work on getting stronger. Gods forbid that I should be a burden to Flint when we moved on. Nine days now. I must be ready in time. I would be ready.

I went through the sequence of exercises he had given me. I rested. I performed the exercises again, thinking that although my arms and legs ached, I could in fact complete the sequence more easily than I had a few days ago. Flint was a good trainer.

I boiled up the kettle and made a brew. Without thinking, I set two cups on the table. I sat and stared at them, imagining Flint as I had once dreamed him, riding down to Summerfort with a face like death. Let that not have been a prophetic vision.

I prepared a meal for later, using what I could find within the hut: barley, dried meat, herbs. I set the pot at the side of the fire to cook slowly. "Come home safe," I muttered to myself, "and you get a hot supper."

I opened the shutters a sliver, trying to judge how much time had passed. Perhaps not so very much. I considered the fact that there was nothing to stop me from packing a bag and heading off for Shadowfell on my own. I realized that even if I had been completely recovered, I would not have done it. This was a development I did not want to think about.

While the food was cooking, I lay down on the bed awhile, hoping I might sleep some of the long day away. I had just closed my eyes when a sharp rattling against the shutters brought me bolt upright, my heart pounding. A moment later something bounced off the roof with a thud. Then someone knocked on the door: a little knock, low down near the ground.

"Neryn! Neryn, open the door!"

Not a sound, Flint had said. If a man or woman had come to hammer on the door, I would have kept silent. But that was no human voice. The tiny knocking was not made by human hands.

"You can't come in," I said. "Go away."

"Oh, no, no, no, no! Talk to us! Hear us! Danger! Peril!"

A chorus of voices now: high, squeaky ones; lower, softer ones; sharp ones; hollow ones; all kinds. I did not hear Sage's wise, droll tone among them.

"I can't open the door," I said. "I can't come out. I promised."

A silence followed this, then there was a dispute on the other side of the door, conducted in fierce whispers.

"We can come in," someone said. "Open the door."

I stood silent, weighing this up against my promise to apply common sense. "I can't see you," I said. "If I can't see you, how do I know I can trust you?"

"We'd as soon not come in." That voice I recognized. It was Silver's, Silver who had resolutely refused to believe I might be a Caller. "The warrior's smell lies over everything. Leave your door bolted if you will. We will send one *through*."

I had not considered the ability of the Good Folk to merge. The bottom of the door bulged slightly in one spot, and then, in an eyeblink, a small figure was standing there, inside the hut. I had seen this being before among Silver's followers: part man, part bird, and standing about as high as my knee. He sketched a bow. "We bring a warning," he said, and glanced around the hut as if fearful that enemies might be concealed in a corner somewhere. "You must come with us. You must come now."

"Come now, come now!" echoed a chorus of voices from beyond the door.

"What warning?" I felt cold. The Good Folk had a deep

196

knowledge of the affairs of Alban. If they sensed something wrong, if it troubled them enough to bring them through my door despite their doubts, then I would be a fool not to listen. "I am safe here. And I promised Flint I wouldn't go out. I've been ill."

"We saw, we saw. Do not trust him! Even now he betrays you."

"Betrays you!" came the chorus.

I reached out, slid the bolt across, and opened the door. "You'd best all come in," I said.

They entered in a silent line. Most of them were familiar from that remarkable night in the woods by Silverwater. The being with long sticklike fingers was here, and the wispy big-eyed creature. A number of others followed. Silver came in last, casting her gaze around the hut as if it harbored a bad smell. No Sage. No Red Cap.

When they were all in, I locked the door behind them. That set them shuffling with unease.

"Please sit down," I said, and settled myself on the floor. After a moment they sat, forming a somewhat restless circle. "Now tell me."

"No time to waste!"

"Pack up and flee! Come with us!"

I lifted a hand and they fell silent. "You said, *Even now he betrays you.* Tell me what you meant." I did not want to hear it but I must. I prayed that they were wrong.

"We have seen him, Neryn." Silver's calmly authoritative voice. She sat straight-backed and still, with her filmy cobweb gown lying around her in delicate folds. "Up the valley toward the pass, with a troop of his own kind. King's men. Enforcers. They came through last night and made camp, waiting for him. He walked up this morning to meet them."

Chapter Ten

"You're wrong," I said. How could I explain without revealing what must remain secret: that Flint was almost certainly some kind of spy, a rebel in the guise of a king's man? I hesitated, and the silence drew out. I felt the weight of the Good Folk's gaze. They were judging Flint, judging me, finding both of us wanting. "I know he is a good man," I added. It was not a strong argument. "He has his own reasons for talking to the Enforcers. He wouldn't lead them to me. He has helped me, looked after me in my illness. If he were going to hand me over, he would have done it long ago and saved himself that trouble."

"You sound sure," said the bird-man. "But how can you be sure? What do you know of this fellow save what he himself has told you?"

"Enforcers are expert liars," put in the man in the nutshell cape. "They imbibe deception with their mother's milk."

If this was not literally true, I recognized the general

idea as something I had often considered when weighing up Flint. I tried not to think of that. But doubt had begun to creep into my mind.

"If you had seen what we saw," said the bird-man, "you would know we speak the truth. You would not hesitate to pack your bag and flee."

Now I was cold. My chest felt tight, as if a stone had lodged itself somewhere near my heart. "What did you see?" I made myself ask.

"They joked and laughed. They shared a meal by the campfire."

"That is no more than I would expect. Flint is—" No, I could not tell them outright what I believed about him. This secret was not mine to share. "He is their comrade-in-arms. He is an Enforcer, yes, but . . . he means me no harm. I'm almost sure of it." I had thought it probable Flint had gone to meet a fellow Enforcer today to make a report or exchange news. A whole band, I had not expected. "He might be putting them off my trail," I suggested. Then, as Silver looked at the bird-man, and the twiggy creature looked at the wispy one, and all around me faces showed disbelief, I added, "A meeting doesn't mean a betrayal. He's my friend."

A telling silence.

"He is an Enforcer." Silver's tone was calmly authoritative. "He cannot be your friend. After they had shared their food and spoken together, the group struck camp, mounted their horses, and headed off. Not back toward Three Hags pass and the road to Summerfort, but on toward Corbie's Wood. Your *friend* rode with them. Far from putting them off your trail, Neryn, he is leading them to you. If you do not leave here now, you are a prize fool. It makes me doubt, yet again, that Sage's claims about you can be true."

Through the dawning realization of a betrayal, I felt a rising anger. "If you doubt me, why are you here?" I challenged. "Why bother coming to warn me? If I'm not a Caller, then it should make no difference to you whom I trust or where I go."

"Red Cap brought us the news that Sorrel was lost," the bird-man said. "Later, Sage came to fetch him. She told us something of your journey. Then the two of them were off again. They didn't say where they were going, and we didn't ask. As for why we're here, it was a bird brought me the news that you'd got a new friend, a fellow so hung about with iron that this place reeks of it, even while he's not here. . . ." He hesitated, glancing at Silver.

"What came to our ears was cause for concern," Silver said. "Make no mistake, I still doubt greatly that you are all you claim to be. I still believe Sage is a muddled old woman. But you stopped to hear the warriors of Hiddenwater. You kept silent before the urisk's pleas. You stood up to the brollachan. You came on up the valley, and word soon spread that something of an unusual nature occurred in the defile. When that news came to our ears, we knew we could no longer afford to dismiss Sage's claims entirely. We were taken aback to discover that you were keeping company with an Enforcer; shocked that you were sick, weak, and confined in this hut with him, at the mercy of his hard fist and his persuasive tongue. While he was here, we could not come close to warn you. Now we come almost too late. By allowing this man to befriend you, you have placed yourself in deadly peril."

"What have you told him?" demanded the bird-man. "What does he know of your plans?"

"Not much. I've been careful. Anything Flint knows, he knew before he rescued me in the valley." Oh gods, was this really true? Had he been lying all the time, lying so skillfully that I had come to believe every word? I remembered a dream in which he had knelt before the king and turned on Keldec a gaze so open that the most doubting person in Alban could not believe him a liar. Just so had he often looked at me; I had thought that gaze a measure of his true worth. The memory of it made my throat tight.

"Rescued?" Silver's tone was all scorn. "If you still believe that man is your friend, he has indeed cast a spell over you. He has nursed you back to health for one reason only: because the king wants you whole and well and useful. If a chieftain is offered a prize pig for the midwinter feast, he does not expect it to be all skin and bone, halfway to death already. The warrior has waited until he could be sure you would survive the journey back to Summerfort, and on to the king's court at Winterfort. He has fattened you up for the kill."

"Not for the *kill*," put in the little man in the nutshell cape.

"It is a manner of speaking," Silver said lightly. "Neryn, this man has prepared you for the king. That is the plain truth of the matter. The king wants you. In his hands you will be a tool of destruction."

A silence. I thought I could hear the beating of my own heart, where panic and grief struggled for ascendancy. I must be calm. I must think this through. "You said before that you still doubted my gift. But you just contradicted yourself. If I'm not a Caller, I can't become a tool of destruction. If the king wants me, either he's making a big mistake or I really am what Sage believes me to be."

"I'd have thought a Caller might have the wit not to be captured by a king's man and held by him in a place so full of iron that we could not come close," said Silver sharply. "If this *rescuer* of yours had not gone off this morning and taken his weaponry with him, you'd still have been here when dusk fell and he returned with his band to take you away."

"She's right," said the bird-man. "Lucky for you that he left you alone, and that we were near at hand. Pack up now and come with us. We will lead you forward."

"But what if you're wrong? They might be heading this way for some other reason. It might have nothing to do with me." Oh gods, perhaps they were riding for Shadowfell. Maybe this was a mission to attack and destroy. "It might be safer for me to keep my promise and stay here in hiding until Flint comes back." I heard myself babbling, saw the expressions on their faces. I had been fooled. Tricked. By an expert. And yet I could not quite make myself believe it.

"Stay here and wait for this man at your peril," said Silver. "Have you forgotten what happened to your grandmother?"

Now I was as cold as ice. "No," I whispered.

"This Flint is the king's minion. The king would harness your gift and turn it against us. He would use his mind-scrapers to make you obedient to his will. You would call us to you. We would come because we cannot do otherwise. A Caller must be obeyed. Keldec's henchmen would destroy us."

I looked around the circle, taking in their diminutive forms, their small, earnest faces, and perhaps there was a question in my eyes.

"Not all of our kind are small and weak," said the nutshell man. "Call now, and you bring to your aid those who are close by, those who have chosen to remain in the forests and lochans and rocky reaches of the highlands. Call when you have learned more, and you bring out larger beings, a trow maybe, or a water horse. Call when your gift is stronger still, and you call a power from the ancient heart of Alban."

"You cannot be speaking of the Guardians."

"Aye, the Big Ones," said a dozen small voices.

"It is said in the lore," added Silver in explanation, "that a Caller proven can summon even them."

"But they were immensely powerful, almost like gods," I protested. "And besides, from what I heard, they are long gone from Alban." *Gone deep down,* that was what Hollow had said.

"Aye, they went deep," said the bird-man. "But not so deep a Caller can't wake them and bring them back. Or so the tales tell us."

That was true. In the story Hollow had told me about Corcan and the war with the Sea Folk, he'd mentioned one of the Guardians, the Lord of the North. I did not remember Hollow saying this grandly named being had been summoned by Corcan, only that perhaps he'd been there and perhaps not. It was an old tale; there was no telling how much of it was true.

"Daw speaks the truth," Silver said, nodding toward the bird-man. "With the Big Ones at his command, this king of yours would have greater power than any man has enjoyed since the time of the oldest tales." Silver folded her graceful hands on her knee, turning her wide, lovely eyes on me. "Or so he imagines. That is why the warrior has not harmed you, Neryn. That is why he took time to win your trust. That is why he nursed you to health, bidding his fellow Enforcers keep their distance until you were ready for handing over. That time has come. In the king's hands, your gift will be turned to great evil. Used for his purposes, you could be the bane of all Alban."

"Spoken with rare tact," put in Daw dryly. "We should be helping the lassie get away, not frightening her with tales of ill-doing. Come on now, you, pack her bag. You, fetch her shoes. And, you, fill up a waterskin from the jug there, and let's be on our way. Lassie, you'll need your warm cloak."

I got to my feet. I would not cry. I would not shed a

single tear. Flint. Flint, an enemy. Every gentle touch, every kind word, had been a lie. I made myself walk to the peg, take the cloak, wrap it around my shoulders. Pride said I should leave it behind; common sense told me I needed its warmth for the journey to come.

I unbolted the door and opened it, feeling the cold air on my skin. Despite everything, the hut felt like home. It felt like a haven. I could not make myself take the first step away from its warmth and light.

A pattering of feet around me; the brushing of several small bodies against me. "Time to go," someone said.

Still, I hesitated. Each time the Good Folk had offered to walk with me in the past, I had said no, for the sake of their safety and mine. This time felt different. Flint's betrayal had laid a weight of sorrow on me, and I knew that even after all his work to get me well, I was not fully recovered from my long illness. Attempting to reach Shadowfell alone might stretch me to my breaking point. If I could not go on, either I would die of cold or the Enforcers would find me.

"You understand the risk you take if you walk with me?" I asked quietly. I wanted them to come; I wanted their arguments and their gruff kindness and their little warm presences. If they were with me, perhaps I would not think of Flint.

"We weren't born yesterday, lassie," said Daw. "Now, which is it to be? Go, or stand on the doorstep until king's men come?"

I closed the door behind me and walked away. The

fire would die down. The supper would congeal in the pot. The lamp would run out of oil. Flint would come home to a cold, dark house. Home. To think of it that way was foolish beyond belief. Had my dreams turned me soft, making me long for a friend and a hearth fire more than I longed for justice and a way forward? I would not think of Flint. I would not think of him going down the valley to meet his cronies, and sharing a meal by the fire, and telling them how clever he'd been to lull me into trusting him. I would not think of him leading them back to fetch me while I made a fool of myself tidying up and preparing a meal for him. I would think only of setting one foot in front of the other and moving on.

We reached the band of woodland above the hut, passed quietly under the trees, and moved onto the track Flint had spoken of. My companions maintained a steady pace. As for me, fear was a sharp whip to keep me moving. If the Enforcers were on horseback, they could be here long before nightfall. *Flint* . . . I set my jaw tight, narrowed my eyes, and walked on. Gods, it was cold out here. The ridge above us seemed impossibly high, the pathway that snaked up onto the fells dauntingly steep. How far was it to Lone Tarn? I thought I remembered the place, though Farral and I had given it our own name. We had skipped stones over the water. We had challenged each other to climb the rocks and jump down from ever-higher ledges. It seemed a very long time ago.

We climbed up over the fells. Here we were exposed

to view. The valley lay below us, the Rush a strip of sullen gray under a sky of gathering cloud. There was Corbie's Wood by the river, a black stain in its circle of leafless trees. *Goodbye,* I thought. *Goodbye again.* It was oddly hard to breathe.

I wondered which way Flint would think I had gone. He had told me he would take me this way, the more covert way, where we would be concealed from watchers in the valley once we crested this hill. But perhaps he'd expect me to go the other way, now that I had left him behind. Down into the valley, along past Corbie's Wood, and then from farm to farm until I caught sight of Giant's Fist. My steps faltered. I looked back down the hill, and my companions halted in their line. The two who walked last held small boughs of pine, thick with needles. With these they swept the path behind them, erasing our footprints.

We had not come far. The roof of the hut could be seen below the little wood, nestled under its protecting rocks, with the bare birches standing guard. A thin thread of smoke arose from my fire. A group of rooks flew overhead and settled in the trees, cawing.

"Move on," said Daw. "No time to stop and look. They will come."

The cold air was hurting my chest. "Wait a moment," I said. I took off bag and cloak, then wrapped my shawl around my head and over my mouth and nose before putting the cloak back on. When I reached for the bag, I found that two small beings were carrying it between them.

"Still not yourself," observed Silver, scrutinizing me. "You cannot walk far."

"I'll walk as far as I have to."

"Hmmm." The tone was of extreme doubt. "Come on, then."

The procession wound on across the fells. The track soon dwindled to a pebbly goat path. Above us the clouds darkened, their bellies heavy with rain. I tried not to think of my lonely, cold trip up the lochs. I was with friends. It was only a few days' walk to Shadowfell. I could do this.

On the crest of the hill, we crouched down behind a row of jagged rocks—or I crouched down, as the tallest of my companions was concealed even when standing. I looked back down the valley and saw, in the direction of Three Hags pass, a distant smudge on the road. Perhaps riders. Perhaps merely a herd of goats. It was too soon, surely, for Flint and his cronies to be in sight.

"Come close," whispered Silver. The Good Folk bunched up tighter, so we were in a huddle behind the rocks.

"If that's the king's men," said Daw, "they'll be straight up to your wee house, and on after us."

"It's a shame you cannot call something larger and stronger," observed a doglike creature. "If you could bring out a giant, maybe, or a big monster of some sort, you could bid it carry you all the way to where you're headed. With only us to aid you, you'll be taken in a trice."

"Aye," said a little man in a yellow scarf. "It's a sad thing if you're lost simply for want of time."

I cleared my throat. "I did call a stanie mon," I said. "At least, I think I did. In the narrow part of the valley, coming up. The Enforcers would have taken me, but I . . . well, I spoke a verse, and the rocks moved over to hide me. And later, when it was safe, they let me go."

Round eyes gazed at me.

"She callit a stanie mon!" someone muttered. A murmured argument broke out all around me. "That's six of seven!" "No, it isna!" "Which one's it supposed to be, then?" "The one about bein' brave, ye gomerel!" "Stirrin' up a big lump o' rock, that's no' brave, it's foolish!" "No, it isna!"

"We heard that something out of the ordinary had taken place," said Silver, ignoring them completely. Her tone was as assured as ever, but the look in her eyes had changed. Was there now a reluctant respect there? "We had not realized it was . . . quite so unusual. This means you can call help. The kind of help that'll make your journey a great deal easier. A strong creature to bear you along and frighten off your enemies. Did that not occur to you?"

There was a little war going on inside me. "I don't think that's a good idea," I made myself say, though the prospect tempted me. "I don't know how to use my gift wisely yet. I was almost entombed in the rocks when I called the stanie mon. Besides, if something as big as that came out to carry me, we'd be seen for miles around."

This was greeted with murmurs and nods, to my surprise.

"She's right," someone said. "A stanie mon might get a prize for strength or endurance. Not for a running race. And he couldn't blend, not if he was carrying a lassie. Once, maybe. Not over and over."

"What about a loch beastie, then?"

"A loch beastie? What are you thinking, laddie? We're not at Deepwater now. There's one wee tarn up yonder. Then nothing until she gets to the Folds. Any beasties up here will be like tadpoles with wee fangs on them."

"The Folds?" I had not heard this name before, and perhaps I had not been meant to hear it, for the one who had spoken was quickly hushed by five or six others.

"A place near where you're going," Silver said, making a trifle of it.

"You don't know where I'm going," I felt obliged to point out. It was freezing up here. The wind was rising, the clouds were darkening. And back down the valley, the disturbance that might be riders on the road was getting bigger.

My companions had fallen silent. The weight of the situation hung over us all.

"A new plan," said Daw, taking charge. "We get to a haven and go to ground. We bide there until they've passed. Over the hill, halfway along toward the tarn, there's a place. Neryn, take my hand and hers. You two, keep that bag up off the ground. Now go!"

Walking with the Good Folk was not like walking with Flint. The memory of how that had felt—his arm in mine, the warmth of his body, the strength of his presence—lingered close, despite my efforts to banish it. His treachery made my heart sore. It made my gut hollow and empty. I fought to maintain the anger that would keep me walking, but it was hard with the day growing colder and the path ahead stretching on and on, uphill and down, over sliding pebbles and sucking mud patches and rocks all jutting edges and deceptive holes. All the time the Good Folk kept pace with me, taking turns to hold my hands, whispering among themselves. Their bright eyes, their warm paws, their murmurs of encouragement, gave me heart and kept me moving.

We followed a narrow track that lay just below the ridge. From time to time one of my companions would climb back to the crest to look down into the valley. We would wait, then move on.

It was on the third such patrol that Daw, perched between the stones on the ridge and looking over, motioned urgently to the rest of us, summoning us to climb up. We scrambled up beside him. We had come farther than I thought. Corbie's Wood lay well behind us, dark and still amid the skeletal trees. Smoke was rising somewhere back there. Not from the ruined settlement; there was nothing of it left to burn. From up the hill beyond that place. And down by Corbie's Wood there were riders moving about as if searching.

"King's men are near at hand," said Silver. "But he has led them the low way."

"That smoke." I made myself say it. "It could be the hut. Where we—where I was staying. They may have split into two parties. One could be close behind us."

"And even if you are wrong," said Daw, "when they find no trace of you on the low road, they will think of this path. Come, we must make haste."

"How far to this haven?" I asked Silver. I did not know how long I could keep going.

"It is not so near," Silver said, "and not so far. Gentle!" The little woman she called to was sweet-featured, fair-haired, and dressed in a gray hooded robe. She carried a curiously woven bag over her shoulder. "You'd best give Neryn one of your cordials."

"I shouldn't— I've heard—" I stammered as the little woman opened the bag and took out a minuscule stone bottle sealed with a bark stopper.

"Alban's full o' tales, lassie," Gentle said, fishing out a nutshell cup. "This willna send ye to the Otherworld, nor bind ye to us in any way whatever. It will do nae more than give ye strength to walk."

It was one risk against another. Drink the draft and accept the consequences, or perhaps fail to reach the place of safety before the Enforcers came. I took the little cup and tilted it to my lips. There was one sip of the draft, and it was like a fire in my mouth. I struggled not to spit it out.

"Swallow it down now," murmured Gentle, her eyes shrewd. I heard in her voice that she had done this more times than anyone could count. "Ye'll feel stronger soon."

"What's in that?" I spluttered.

"Ach, nobbut an herb or two," said Gentle, wiping out the cup with a twist of grass. "It willna kill ye." She glanced at Silver. "Give the lassie a bittie time, then we'll go on, aye?"

We waited. Down at Corbie's Wood, I thought I could see the Enforcers gathered in a group now. I wished for better sight, the kind some folk had as a canny gift. I imagined them: dark cloaks, dark horses, men conferring. *Ride on up the valley, or leave the horses and try the path over the hill?* I thought of Flint telling them I was more likely to take the less obvious path: this one, the one he had told me about that allowed a person to skirt the settlements on the way north. How could he have done this? If anyone but the Good Folk had brought me the news of his betrayal, I would have refused to believe it.

Life was creeping back into my cramped limbs. My mind felt clearer, though beneath the effect of Gentle's cordial, I knew I was exhausted.

"I'm ready to go on."

Gentle looked me up and down. "Aye, ye'll do."

"On, then," said Silver. "Rain's coming. The path moves away from the hilltop now. There'll be no watching out for king's men. Go as quick as you can."

*   *   *

214

The path descended into a shallow valley between barren rises studded with oddly shaped rocks. This must be the way Farral and I had used as children when we made our expeditions to Lone Tarn, but I did not remember its being so eerily empty, the slopes so steep, the open spaces so bare and lonely. In a place of such profound silence, I felt like an intruder.

"Quicker, Neryn," muttered Silver. "Move those legs."

"A pity you cannot summon a flame beastie," observed the doglike creature, whose name seemed to be Blink. "A fair set of wings, those creatures have. Such as that could pick you up in his claws and carry you to the hiding place in a flash."

"Aye, a flash that would toast her like a bannock left too long in the fire," said Gentle. "Keep your good ideas to yourself and let the lassie do her best. It's not far now."

Not far meant different things to different folk. Twice more, as we made our way across the difficult terrain and the clouds massed overhead, plunging us into near darkness, Silver called a halt so we could rest for a little, and Gentle gave me another dose of the cordial. Each time the draft brought new strength to my limbs and hope to my heart, but I could not fail to notice that each time the effects wore off more quickly. Weary and sore, I felt a flood of relief when a huge rocky outcrop loomed into view, its shape that of a wolf crouched to spring. I stood swaying, with Daw on my left and Gentle on my right.

"Howler," Daw said.

"What?"

"Howler. Howling Rock, some folk call it. This is our place. Follow Silver around and down."

I hesitated, watching as Silver skirted the flank of the great wolf, then disappeared as if by magic. "Are we going to . . . to another realm? I must be able to get back, I must be able to reach . . . the place where I'm headed."

"It's no' the Otherworld, lassie." Gentle grinned at me, flashing pearly teeth. "It's a bolt-hole, that's all. Anyone can step in here if he can find the place. Come, take my hand, I'll lead ye in."

"Are you sure—"

"Aye, we're sure. This place, it's a very useful cave, no more and no less. Come on now, you're dead on your feet."

It was true. I had hardly another step left in me. I followed Gentle around the rock and into a narrow fissure concealed by creeping plants. Then there was a tunnel, dark as night, curving deep into the heart of the stone until it opened in a chamber illuminated from above by a small triangular aperture I guessed might be at the crown of the wolf's head. The cave floor was soft earth. Gentle released my hand.

"Sit down, Neryn," said Silver. It was an order, and I obeyed, swallowing tears of relief. Silver began rapping out a series of instructions. "Blink, fetch wood. Sheen," she addressed a flickering being of indeterminate form, "make fire. You boys"—she pointed to a pair of sturdy-looking fellows who might almost have passed for unusually short human lads—"food. And make sure you don't give Neryn anything she can't safely eat. Daw?"

The two of them moved away to consult together. Then Daw left the cave, heading out into a deepening dusk, and the rest of the band went about transforming the place into a suitable shelter for the night. Silver came over to where I sat on the floor.

"I'm sorry," I said. "I never wanted to be a burden to you. Where did Daw go?"

Silver sat down beside me, her gossamer garment falling into soft folds around her. One pale bare foot peeked out from the embroidered hem. She had walked the mountain track without any shoes. Gentle came to settle on my other side.

"He went to spy on your pursuers," Silver said. When I stared at her in surprise, she added, "Daw is a bird-friend. He may fly over, or he may summon a crow to be his eyes. We do not use such skills unless we must. It taxes us."

Blink and some others were building the fire, using wood they dragged across from a corner. The flickering being stood ready to wake it to life.

"They'll see the smoke," I said. "The Enforcers." A moment later I recalled the fire Sage and Sorrel had made, which had burned hot and smokeless.

"Our fire will not betray you," Silver said. "And our footsteps have been concealed. Only the most skilled of human trackers could find us here. We will stay in this place overnight, and we will not leave carelessly. You must eat, drink, and rest. And we must talk."

That was certainly true: I had a hundred questions for

them. Yet I could hardly set my mind to asking, with my heart still aching from Flint's betrayal.

"There are many farewells behind you," put in Gentle quietly. "And many ahead of you, Neryn. You will need to be strong."

I thought of tending to Grandmother; of the years on the road with Father; of the long, cold trip up the lochs to Summerfort. I remembered calling the stanie mon. I saw myself stepping out of the hut this morning and shutting the door behind me for the last time. "I am strong," I said.

CHAPTER ELEVEN

WE WERE ASSEMBLED INSIDE HOWLER, ALL OF us in a circle around a little glowing campfire. I was exhausted and sick at heart. I wanted to give in to my sadness, to curl up and grieve for the good friend I had thought I had, a rare, strong friend, who all the time had been my enemy. I stiffened my spine and ordered myself to set all that aside. Time was short, and there were too many questions still unanswered.

"Your help has been most welcome today," I said, framing my speech with some care. "I notice how you are all working together, even though you have some disagreements within your band. From what I've been told, that's unusual for your kind. I'm hoping that means some of you do believe I am a Caller, or at least that I can be one, given the right teaching. I would like to know more about the use of such a gift. I know the old story of Corcan and the war between the Sea Folk and the brollachans. Corcan went off and undertook some training before he came back as a leader. Who would have taught him? I understand there may be some . . . special qualities . . . a person must demon-strate before starting that training."

This provoked a furious muttering around the circle, of which I could make out little except the familiar dis-putes about how many of the seven I might have shown already.

"You mean the virtues," Silver said in her cool voice. "They'll come out in you or they won't. There's no way to prepare save following your own path. What troubles me is that you were so ready to trust the warrior when the fel-low reeks of the king's evil. Would a Caller be so gullible? I ask myself."

I felt my face flush. "She might," I said, "if she didn't know much about where she was going or how to get there, or about how to use her canny gift. From the start, Flint seemed to be helping me. The night we first met, he saved me from the Cull. When I thought he would hand me over to the king, he brought me up the valley to a place of hiding instead. When I was sick, he looked after me. I don't understand why he would do all that unless he was a friend. He could have sent me to the king that first night at Darkwater."

"No doubt he has his own ways, Enforcer ways, dark and devious. And yet you defend him. The man wears the king's badge. He does the king's will. Are you so much under his spell that I must repeat for you what we saw this morning?"

"No," I said. The truth about Flint could not be as sim-ple as the Good Folk seemed to think, but there was no doubt today's betrayal made him my enemy again. "I believe you."

"As for *why*," said Daw, who had come in from his spying mission to report that the Enforcers had camped for the night down in the valley, "on that matter, we cannot agree among ourselves. Silver believes the fellow took you somewhere safe to fatten you up, to prepare his special gift for the king. I'm of the opinion that perhaps he wanted you to lead him somewhere. Someplace where there are folk the king has a particular dislike for."

"Flint knew about that place already," I told them. "He said he knew where I was going and could help me get there."

"He's a king's man," Silver said. "He lied. What if I told you your black-cloaked friend has been sending messages up and down the valley, using a lad to carry them? Scrolls all tied up neat with cord and sealed with hot wax, the kind a man might dispatch to his leader? According to our spies, one of those went off not long after the two of you reached what you call your place of hiding. I could guess what might have been in that message, and for whose eyes it might have been destined."

One blow after another. In my dream, Flint had been seated at our table, laboring with pen and parchment. Perhaps I had not dreamed it but seen it, half waking. I imagined what might have been in that missive. *There's a change of plan; the girl is sick. When she is sufficiently recovered to travel, I will convey her to you.* It still didn't explain why he had brought me so far north.

"Can you tell me, at least, whether Corcan had to show these virtues you mentioned? I realize you can't tell me what they are. Sage gave me the same reply when I asked her."

"Oh, Sage," said Silver with a gesture of contempt. "She'd tell you whatever suited her purpose. But she was right on that score. A Caller must have all the virtues before he can begin to learn his craft. As to what those virtues are, if I told you, it would make little sense to you. They're in an old rhyme."

"Aye," said Gentle, "a wee versie a mother might sing to her bairn at bedtime."

"It's not so much the words themselves that make sense," said Daw. "It's the sense a body chooses to make of them."

"Seven virtues, yes?"

More muttering and whispering; more sidelong glances, mostly in Silver's direction. Nobody was prepared to speak out. Perhaps she had already reprimanded them for letting me hear what should have been kept secret.

"Silver," I ventured, "what would happen if I tried Calling before I had all the virtues? Before I'd been properly taught?"

A silence. Then Silver said, "It would be like giving an infant a sharp knife to play with."

"Worse," said Gentle. "You might harm not only yourself but scores of others along wi' you."

"When I called the stanie mon, it did not do any harm that I know of."

"You were lucky," said Silver, her tone severe. "Don't think to try it again. You've no inkling of its perils. Better that you had perished along with your family than that you use this gift unwisely."

That silenced me. The weight of my losses, the old ones, the newer ones, settled over me, a cloak of sadness.

After some time, Gentle spoke quietly. "You havena done so badly, lassie. You're on your way, and you have a good heart. And from what we heard, if you hadna used your gift that day wi' the stanie mon, you wouldna be sitting here wi' us now." Silver made to interrupt, but the little woman lifted her chin, defiance in her eyes. "You'll find your true path forward, dinna doubt that." She stared at Silver, and Silver stared back, displeasure written all over her graceful form.

I did not want to be the cause of dissent within their band. Bonds of friendship were rare enough. "I am hoping it won't take too long," I said quietly. "Where we are headed, I'll be much more useful if I've made a start on a Caller's training, at least."

There was an odd silence, as if I had said something troubling.

"What is it? What's wrong?"

Silver cleared her throat. "You say, *where* we *are headed*." Her voice had lost its combative note. She sounded almost apologetic. "We can go no farther with you."

"But . . ." I faltered, remembering the long, cold nights, the lonely plodding days of my journey up the lochs. "I had thought . . ." Once, twice, three times I had bid the Good

Folk leave me to go on by myself so I would not lead them into danger. Now I wanted their company so badly it hurt.

"We canna go on wi' ye, lassie," said Gentle. "None of us here"—she waved a hand around the motley circle of beings—"can pass the place ye call Lone Tarn. That's the far edge of our Watch."

"Your Watch?"

"Aye," said Gentle. "Past Lone Tarn, it's the Watch o' the North. We canna go up there, nor talk to those that bide there. It's forbidden under the Old Laws."

I must have looked blank, for several voices chimed in with explanations, all speaking at once.

Silver raised a hand for quiet. "The Laws of the Guardians, Neryn," she said, her tone telling me this was a matter of profound solemnity. "They divided up the land of Alban into four Watches. When the Guardians walked among us, in the old days, each dwelt in one Watch, and those who lived there looked to their Guardian for wisdom and guidance and the settlement of disputes. Now the Big Ones are gone away, but still we keep their laws. We cannot travel outside the borders of our own Watch."

"Tell me more about where they've gone," I said as I struggled to accept that tomorrow I would be on the road alone once again. "The Big Ones."

"'Twas your king, Keldec, that drove them away," said Gentle. "The Guardians came to this land long, long ago. They ruled over all of our kind, from sprites to brollachans to sea beasts, and for the most part their rule was wise.

Then humankind came to Alban. Man wasna always cruel. But he could be thoughtless, heedless. There have been bright times and darker ones. This king, Keldec, is darkest of them all. He came wi' cold iron and fell magic, and closed his fist around the heart of the old land." A shuddering sigh arose from the listening circle. "The Guardians went deep," Gentle said, "and the smaller folk, our folk, were set adrift. But still some of the old order held strong. The last of the Old Laws remained, and that was the rules of the Watch. We bide within our own Watch. We guard its borders; we tend to its heart and spirit; we keep the lore."

"I see. Are there Good Folk across the border? Folk that are known to you?"

"Maybe there's folk there will help you," Daw said. "But we cannot be sure of it. And there's no sending a message to seek their aid."

"But you can fly, can't you? Or send a bird to be your eyes? Couldn't you—"

"There's no flying over or burrowing under or using magic to pass across," Gentle said. "The law's the law. It's akin to the old customs and the old songs. When you're in the dark, you need a lamp. The law is our lamp."

"I understand," I said, my heart heavy. I had traveled alone before. Why did this feel so hard? "I can do it. But I'm weaker than I should be after my illness. I wonder if . . . Gentle, could you give me some of the cordial to take with me? I would use it sparingly. With that, I'd have some hope of reaching the place." Even now I could not bring myself to speak the name Shadowfell.

Gentle shook her head. "No, lassie, I canna. 'Tis a powerful brew, and effective, aye. But the more ye have, the more ye crave. Already I give ye three cups, and ye can feel that need in ye, the wanting, for the brew gives a rare feeling of well-being, a sense that all's well and ye can climb mountains. A lassie could die for the wanting of more. It's best ye move on without such help, for if ye have more, it'll be no boon, but bane."

There was no answer for that. I felt the craving in my stomach, not so desperate that it would drive me to beg or steal, but a warning of what might have happened if these folk had not been so wise. I could not blame Gentle for having offered it, for without the brew I might not have reached this place of safety. Tonight I would sleep in shelter. I would lie down among friends. Tomorrow lay before me, full of shadows.

I don't think I can do it was in my mind, but I did not say it aloud. It came to me that courage might be my only weapon once the Good Folk left me, and I could not afford to throw it away.

"There is another answer to this." The voice was that of a creature who had thus far been silent, a little wizened thing with a face like a dried-up turnip, and dark liquid eyes. It hobbled forward, gnarled hands on a diminutive ash stick. Its body might have been of any shape; it was shrouded in a faded patchwork garment that swept down to the floor. Its hair was white as swansdown and stood up in tufts. "There is another path."

Silver subjected the being to a withering stare, which it met without flinching. After some time, the sylph sighed and nodded. "Tell her, then," she said. "Neryn, this is Blackthorn. He is the elder of our clan. We have debated long over you. *If* you are a Caller, and *if* you can be trained adequately, then you could wield considerable power. You understand, I think, that while that power could be used to do great good, it could equally be the source of great evil." She did not need to add that this was why she doubted me so; my wary trust in Flint must seem to her an indication that I would easily slip down the latter path. "Blackthorn will present you with another choice. A safer choice."

What could be safe in Keldec's Alban? "Very well," I said. "Please tell me." And I inclined my head courteously to the tiny being, showing the respect due to an elder.

"When it became plain this king meant to crush every drop of goodness out of Alban and its people," Blackthorn said, his voice remarkably deep and resonant for such a small being, "the Big Ones went away. Away down, away in. And so did many of our people, the great and the small, the powerful and the weak. Many are in retreat. Only a few of us choose to stay here in the sad and sorry place that Alban has become under this king of yours."

"Not mine," I protested.

"Keldec is of humankind, as are you. But he is no Caller,

and though he is a man of power, a power he wields with cruel force, there are some weapons he does not yet have at his disposal. You are one of those weapons, Neryn, or you will be if you follow the path of a Caller. That makes you valuable. And it makes you dangerous. As Silver said, we have spoken of this, seeing your bond with this Enforcer. Some of us think you should not go on."

I sat bolt upright, shocked. "I must go on!" I exclaimed. "I can't give this up! That would be letting Keldec have his way—it would be giving up the fight for Alban!"

"Bide awhile, lassie," Gentle said. "Hear Blackthorn out."

I nodded, though my heart was cold. The Good Folk did not believe in my mission. Even they did not think I could do it.

"We can offer you a place to go, a safe place deep down among our kind," Blackthorn said. "There you can live with no fear of this king, for it is beyond his reach, hidden by ancient magic. It is a good place, Neryn. There are no other human folk there, but you would have our kind as companions, and I do not think that would be unwelcome to you. You could live out your life safe in the knowledge that Keldec could never use you as a tool for ill. I see doubt in your face, and I understand that. Know that what we offer is a great privilege. Perhaps once in five hundred of your years is a man or woman given a place among us. Choose this and you may not keep Alban safe, but *you* would be safe, Neryn, and you could not be the instrument of Alban's final downfall."

"If I agreed to this," I said, feeling suddenly old and

tired, "would the rest of you, those who did not go into hiding, keep fighting for freedom? Would you band together and perhaps join the struggle alongside any of my own kind who might try to rebel against Keldec?"

In the silence that followed, the Good Folk exchanged glances that told me the answer more eloquently than any words could.

"It depends on a Caller, doesn't it? Just as it did with the Sea Folk and the brollachans. Without a Caller, Good Folk and humankind won't work together and the Guardians will stay in retreat. And that would mean Keldec would rule unchallenged."

"And his son after him," Daw said with some bitterness. "A wee lad made in his father's mold, no doubt."

This was a dark choice indeed.

"I would say take your time to decide." There was compassion in Blackthorn's voice. "But there is only until dawn. If you choose to go on, you must go swiftly."

It was little enough time to choose the path of the rest of my life. But in the stillness of the firelit cavern, I knew I needed no time at all. "I respect your offer," I said shakily. "I am honored by it. But I can't accept. The place where I'm going—I think you know what it is, though I won't speak its name aloud—it may be the only place in all Alban where folk are attempting to stand up for what is right. I wanted to go there even before I knew I was a Caller. It seems to me now that I might have something to offer them, something more than just thinking the same way they do. You're wrong to doubt me. I would die before I let the king use me for ill purposes." I looked around the circle of small folk and thought perhaps they were not surprised. "I'm going on. My brother died in the fight to bring justice to Alban. I know the risk is high, but I must do this."

"Aye," said Blackthorn. "That's what we expec—"

Light flickered across his face as something flashed at the tunnel entry. His eyes widened, and in an eyeblink every one of my companions vanished. I scrambled to my feet, my heart pounding. There by the entry was Flint, a patch of dark on dark. He had entered this secret place without a sound. The firelight glinted on the silver stag brooch that fastened his cloak.

I stared, frozen with shock. Flint stared back, his face white as linen. His mouth was bracketed by grooves that suggested a long, hard journey. Shadows danced, sending a wavering pattern across his features.

"You're alive," he said. He did not look at the clutter of minuscule cooking pots on the coals, or at the tiny woven baskets that had held nuts or berries or grain, or at the marks on the earth where many small beings had been seated only moments before. He only looked at me. "You're safe," he said, and I heard in his voice the smile his exhausted features could not summon.

An incoherent sound came from my lips. I took a step backward. *Safe.* The man must think I was stupid.

"Neryn, you can't imagine I would . . ." He lifted both hands, palms toward me, a gesture of surrender. "You promised you'd stay," he said. "You broke your word."

I found my voice. "Where are they? Your troop of Enforcers, the men you went down the valley to fetch this morning? Outside in the cold, waiting for you to hand me over? Or are they in the tunnel listening, just as you were? How dare you try to lull me into thinking you're a friend? How dare you talk about promises?" I would not let these tears fall. I would be strong. I would be brave. No matter what came next.

"Neryn." Flint ran a hand over his head, making his short hair stand up on end. "I'm by myself. There's nobody waiting out there. Neryn, I thought you were . . . I thought you might be . . . hurt. Injured. Alone in the dark, up on the fells with no shelter. What possessed you to go off on your own? I told you to stay in hiding!" He glanced around the cave now, as if he had only just noticed its oddities.

"Is that true?" I challenged. "Are you really alone?" The expression on his face, the tone of his voice, warred with the stark fact of his betrayal. He sounded like a man telling the truth. He looked just as he had not long ago, when he had been my friend.

Flint sighed. "It's true. I've been tracking you for some time, thinking any moment I'd find you lying under a rock somewhere, breathing your last. I have nobody with me, I swear it." He looked at the pots and pans now, each no bigger than a child's cupped hand. "Unlike you. You have your own cook, it seems, and someone to cover your tracks. I nearly lost you."

There was a silence, during which I wondered how much he had heard, how much he had seen, before the tell-tale glint of flame on silver had given him away. I wondered if there was any point at all in pretending.

"I have a supply of food," Flint said. His voice was under better control now. He sounded like a traveler making a polite offer of help to a new acquaintance. "My pack is outside. I see you have a fire of sorts. Are you hungry?"

It came to me that in the long time of my illness, I had become used to his voice, the changes in it, the light and shade of it. I could tell when he was holding something back. I could tell when he was hiding something. He was not doing that now.

"What I want," I said, "is a proper explanation from you, an honest one. Cook supper if you want, but talk to me while you're doing it."

"What about—" Flint cast his gaze around the cavern, where not so long ago the Good Folk had sat in solemn council.

"We'll be on our own," I said. "You're carrying cold iron. In this sort of place, that's not likely to make you friends."

"Didn't you have a knife? I seem to recall giving you one, long ago."

"I seem to recall being apprehended and handed over to you as a captive," I said. "They took the knife, along with most of my other possessions. And before that, I—" No, I would not tell him how I had sheathed the knife in such a way that uncanny folk were shielded from its destructive influence. "I kept it hidden," I said.

"Mm-hm. You promise not to disappear while I fetch my pack?"

I sat down by the fire, wondering at myself. He had gone along the valley to meet his comrades; the Good Folk would not lie to me. He had ridden back with them. How was it that even now I wanted to trust him? I longed for an explanation that would set all to rights. "I will be here," I said. "Fool that I am."

He cooked. I watched. If the Good Folk were watching too, from within the walls of Howling Rock, they were doubtless thinking, *I told you so.* As for Flint and me, for a long time our conversation was limited to the occasional wary glance.

"You thought I would bring men here to take you prisoner," Flint said when his pan had been bubbling on the fire for some time. He was hunkered down watching it, the firelight lending his wan face a deceptively cheerful glow. "You believed that of me."

"How long were you here before I saw you?" I asked.

"You mean, what did I hear? A little. Not a lot."

"What, exactly?"

"You were offered a refuge and you turned the offer down. A response that was exactly what I would have expected from you."

I stared at him, and he looked back across the fire, his eyes giving nothing away.

"Your friends doubt me," he said. "So you doubt me."

"You're saying I'm mistaken, then." I felt anger rising in me, overwhelming my long-practiced caution. His being here was a disaster. Why, then, did it feel so good to see him? "You're not working for the king. You didn't look after me so I could be handed over to him in good health. You didn't charm me into thinking you were my friend. You didn't go down the valley to talk to your fellow Enforcers. You didn't lead them on to Corbie's Wood."

Flint's gaze was on the task at hand: transferring half the contents of his cook pot into a bowl for me. The meal looked identical to the one he had prepared the night we first camped under the open sky together. My gut was churning with anxiety; food was the last thing on my mind.

"The truth can be so easily twisted," he said.

Now I was angry, too angry to watch my words. "Gods help us, Flint! Enforcers destroyed my family! They laid waste my home and everything I held dear! I've been running from them since I was twelve years old. I've seen what people do in the king's name. It's taken the whole time since we first met for me to be able to trust you even a little bit. And now this. What do you expect from me, that I should accept what happened today and act as if it were nothing? You've offered no explanation at all. Of course I doubt you. I know where you went this morning and whom you met with. I know that meeting was on good terms. I know you rode back up here with them. And I've been told you were sending out messages all the time we were in the hut together. Trust goes two ways. If you expect me to have any faith in you, it's time to give me the truth."

My whole body was shaking. My heart was pounding. How could I have let myself speak like that? I had always been so careful, holding my secrets close, saying only what was strictly necessary for safe passage from one place to the next. The risk I had just taken could cost me my future, my freedom, my chance to do some good with my gift. I looked at Flint, and he gazed steadily back at me, his eyes the color of a storm at sea. In his plain features I saw nothing but honesty. *They imbibe deception with their mother's milk.*

"I went down the valley to meet with them," he said quietly. "The boy brought a message that they were coming. I spoke with them. The purpose of that meeting I cannot tell you, but it was not to make arrangements for you. I had no choice but to ride back in their company; to do otherwise would have aroused suspicion. That is the truth. As for my tending to you in your illness, is it so hard to believe a man might want to help a friend in trouble?"

Struggling for a response, I blurted out the first thing that came to me. "Did the hut burn down?"

Flint passed me the bowl of porridge. "Why do you ask that?"

"I saw smoke. I thought they had come up and burned it." After a moment, I added, "That made me sad."

He raised his brows in surprise. "Sad? You developed an attachment to that place?"

I did not reply, for I could not think how to explain the

way I felt. That modest hut had been a haven of safety in Alban's madness.

"It was still standing when I left to search for you. Some burning was carried out, yes. Not there." He grimaced. "No thanks to you, I should add. The pot you left on the fire was scorched black."

"I left in a hurry." I remembered the care with which I had prepared that meal, almost as if it were a magical charm to bring him safely back. Gods, what a fool. And now here I was, eating his porridge again and still not getting proper answers. Absently, I dipped my spoon into the bowl and took a mouthful.

"So did I," said Flint. "Finding you gone . . . Well, never mind that. You are alive."

"I need more from you," I said.

Flint waited.

"That night at Darkwater, the night my father died, had you been sent to look for me? What did you know about me then? Did you know the Enforcers were coming to raid the settlement?"

He drew in a long breath, as if to steady himself, then let it out in a sigh. "You don't pose easy questions," he said. After a glance around the cave he added, "Are you quite sure we will not be overheard?"

"No," I said. "But I am sure those who might hear us are friends and will not use what they learn to ill purpose."

"Very well. You may not like my answer to the first question, because it is both yes and no. Yes, along with my regular duties as an Enforcer, I had for some time been looking for a vagrant, a man in impoverished circumstances who was skilled at games of chance and a little too fond of strong drink. With him, the rumor went, traveled his daughter, fifteen years old. It was not the gambler the king was interested in, but the young woman, as certain rumors about her had reached his ears. Folk were whispering that she might have an unusual gift." Perhaps seeing me stiffen, he added quickly, "Do not judge until you hear me finish, Neryn. You sought the truth, and that is what I am giving you, as far as I can. I had been tracking you for some time, following one lead after another, but you proved unusually hard to find. When I did catch up with you, the circumstances were unfortunate. A raid was imminent. The way it fell out, I had time only to get you off the boat and into safety. I regret that I could not save your father."

"You bought me for three pieces of silver, for the king. And then you let me go."

In the silence that followed, I could feel how reluctant he was to speak.

"You let all those men on the boat perish," I said. "You could have warned them, and you said nothing."

"My life is full of such decisions."

"What are you?" I found myself leaning forward, staring at him, desperate to make sense of all this. "What is it you do?"

Flint looked down at his hands. They were clenched so tightly together the knuckles were white. "What is it *you* do?" he said. "What is it that so interests Keldec that he allows his most trusted man to scour the highlands searching for you, neglecting his duties as a troop leader?"

I put my hand over my heart, which threatened to leap out of my chest. "His most trusted man," I said shakily. "If that is what you are, wouldn't the king be rather displeased with what you're doing now? Or is this an even bigger web of lies than I've been led to believe?" I had gone so far now, there seemed no point in holding back.

"That part is true. My orders were to find you by whatever means I could, to keep you safe once I had you, and to bring you back to court. The first and the second I have done, or had done until you took it into your head to bolt. The third I will not do. I am an Enforcer, yes. I am a king's man. But my true loyalty lies elsewhere."

I found I was holding my breath.

"Your unusual friends offered you a haven just now, a place where you would be protected for the rest of your life. I wish I could offer the same. I wish I could promise the kind of existence folk lived in these parts in earlier years, where the worst of their concerns was getting the harvest in or dealing with a malady among the sheep. These are testing times. They are times when each of us is called upon to show his true mettle, to find a . . . a spark within."

I sat quiet, hearing the strength in his voice, and the pain.

"I ask you to trust me, even though I cannot tell you everything you want to know," Flint said. "I swear to you that at some time in the future, a time when all is changed, you and I will speak openly together. But for now, I will not endanger you by saying too much. Neryn, there is a place in the mountains not so very far from here. It houses a . . . a force, a movement for change. Because of the exceptionally high risk of conducting such an enterprise, the location and other details are known to very few. The movement is in its infancy. It is small, but its goals are grand. You know its name, I think."

I held my breath, waiting for more.

Flint glanced around the cavern, into the dark corners. His voice dropped to a murmur. "I believe you intend to travel to a place called Shadowfell. Should you reach that place, you might find yourself among friends, folk of like mind to your own. They call themselves Regan's Rebels. The name started as a jest. Back then, they could count their number on the fingers of two hands."

He paused, his gaze meeting mine over the fire. "There are more now, and among them are folk with special abilities, folk somewhat similar to you, Neryn. You are reluctant to tell me what your talent is. But I saw you use it, and I believe there is none at Shadowfell with an ability to match it. You disappeared before our eyes, halfway up the valley. Vanished as if by magic. And thank the gods you did so, for I would have been hard-pressed to explain to my companions on that day why you should not be immediately apprehended and conveyed to Summerfort. When you and I were traveling together, there often seemed to be other footsteps walking along beside us, other voices whispering around our campfire at night. And there was tonight. The only time I have heard of a man or woman being so close to . . . whatever they are . . . is in ancient tales, and those tales tell of wonders."

I stared into the fire. He knew everything. Had known all the time. Almost everything.

"If you were a leader," Flint said, his whisper blending with the crackle and hiss of the little fire, "and your adversary was at a distance, and his army was immeasurably greater than yours in both numbers and influence, what might be your most useful weapon?"

It took me a moment to realize he was talking not about me but about himself.

"A spy," I said. It was what I had been thinking for some time, of course. But, looking at Flint's white face and shadowed eyes, I was struck anew how perilous such a life must be. He had said he was the king's most trusted man. Keldec wielded immense power; he was feared throughout Alban. Should the king discover there was an enemy at his right hand, his vengeance would be terrible indeed. One wrong word, one wrong look, and Flint would be facing all I had most feared in my years of flight and concealment. That set a chill deep in my bones. "A spy at the heart of his stronghold," I added, "someone who could win his trust, who could act and speak like a friend and supporter, someone who could convince everyone that he was loyal. And go on convincing them, no matter what happened."

He gave a curt nod. Such was the sadness in his eyes

that I turned my gaze back to the fire, for I could not bear to look at him.

"You're not lying, are you? You weren't before and you aren't now."

Something in my voice must have told him how I felt, for he got up, moved around the fire, and sat down next to me. He put his two hands around one of mine. His touch was warm and strong. "I'm not lying. If I have not told you the whole truth, it is for your own safety and mine. I know you understand that."

We sat there awhile in silence. My thoughts were too big to put into words; a confusion of feelings welled up in me. In the end I said, "I'm sorry."

"I too," said Flint. "Sorry that I cannot offer you a safer world. Sorry we must keep a rein on our words, even here in this strange hiding place. Sorry your destination is still some distance away, for if I could spirit you there right now, I surely would."

"It's close enough. And I'm stronger than I was. I can get there."

"Not on your own. It's a testing walk." He hesitated. "Were you planning to go on in the company of these friends of yours?"

"They can't," I said. "You didn't hear that part of the discussion. There's a sort of territorial dispute, a boundary they aren't allowed to cross."

"I will take you," Flint said. "There should be time, provided we leave at first light." A pause. He still had his hands wrapped around mine. "There are dangers on the way, Neryn. Perils I cannot explain to you, save to assure you they are real and that I can protect you. Please let me do this for you."

"Not for me, surely. For Alban."

"For both," Flint said.

CHAPTER TWELVE

WE MOVED ON AT DAWN, FLINT AND I TOGETHER. The Good Folk did not come out to bid me farewell, and not only, I suspected, because they feared my companion's iron weaponry. Now that I had committed the utter folly of deciding to trust him after all, they would doubtless wash their hands of me.

I'd have liked more answers from him. In particular, I wanted to know about Regan's Rebels—who they were, how they operated, whether he maintained contact with them somehow, what their plans were for the near-impossible task of challenging Keldec. And I wanted to know where that party of Enforcers was now, and why they had come along this valley as if tracking me. Flint had implied that his purpose in meeting with them had nothing to do with me. What was his purpose, then? Why had he led them this way? Concern for my safety did not seem quite enough to explain his grim mood, his haunted look.

I did not ask about that, or about any of it. Flint was right: the more a person knew, the more someone could find out from them, by threats, intimidation, or torture. I was not safely at Shadowfell yet. And he, with his double existence, was surely never safe.

When we had traveled together before, up over the pass, I had been feverish and confused; I remembered little of it save the endless, jolting motion of the horse. Now, walking along by Flint's side, following him through narrow mountain ways, holding his hand as we traversed fields of sliding stones, relying on his support as we balanced over a makeshift bridge high above a mountain stream, I was reminded of how patient he was and how tireless. He chose our way with skill, shaping it to my current ability. He found safe places to rest. He found spots to make a fire and be unseen. When rain fell, he found cover. At nightfall, he made camp with the efficiency of a skilled woodsman. I was weary beyond belief, my body longing for sleep. Flint bade me wrap myself in his blanket and sit down while he gathered wood, kindled a fire, fetched water, and prepared a meal. He would not let me help. "I'll do it, Neryn," was all he said. "You need your strength for tomorrow."

So we went on, through a sequence of tomorrows. Each day saw us farther from Corbie's Wood and nearer, I hoped, to the sanctuary of Shadowfell. We left Lone Tarn behind us. Walking past the expanse of gray water, the great rocks like crouching beasts, I could not find a single happy memory, though I had often come here with Farral in the old days. The place was empty, bleak, beyond even sorrow. I headed on, walking in Flint's footsteps.

We must now be in the Watch of the North, according to what the Good Folk had told me. I would not see Daw and Gentle, Silver and Blackthorn again on this journey, but I kept my eyes and ears open in case others of their kind might shadow our steps in this new Watch. The iron Flint carried had not been sufficient to keep the Good Folk away completely; they had come close to the hut despite his presence. But now there were no pattering footsteps, no half-glimpsed stirrings in the undergrowth. There was no whisper of wingbeats or hooting of something that was not quite an owl. There was nothing at all. Nothing save, one night, a sound from the valley below us like a group of horses moving fast. My heart turned over in dread. Hearing the drumming hooves, I was back in the defile, pressed against the stones with the Enforcers closing in. Flint's hand fastened around mine, and at the same time he laid a finger across his lips, warning me to be silent. We sat immobile by our little fire, which he had made in a hollow between rocks, and after a while the sound passed on, and all was quiet.

"They are closer than I expected," Flint murmured, his warm hand still clasped around my cold one. "I must—" He broke off to sit in brooding silence.

No need to ask who *they* were. A shiver ran through me. Flint got up, releasing my hand, took off his cloak, and put it around my shoulders over the one I already wore. But the chill I felt had nothing to do with the season; it was bone-deep. It was a mistake to imagine, even for a moment, that we were safe.

"Neryn, I may need to leave you at some point. Tomorrow, perhaps, or the next day. I'll make sure I'm not gone overnight."

I did not trust myself to speak, though my heart sank at the prospect of being on my own again.

"Don't look like that. You will be safe, I promise. I'll find you a place where they cannot reach you. Believe me, I wouldn't do this if there were any choice. You heard them; you heard how close they passed. I did not anticipate— The timing is—" He fell silent once more.

I tried to interpret this and could not. Was he saying he'd expected the troop to come along the valley, but earlier? Later? "Why are they—" My voice came out as a nervous squeak. I swallowed, took a breath, and tried again. "Are you sure they're not looking for me? Why are they so close? It's nearly winter; the Cull should be long over."

Flint was gazing into the flames of our little campfire, his features a carving in stone. The silence drew out.

"Flint?"

He shook his head. "With me you are as safe as you can be. At least until we reach our destination. Once there, you will no longer need me." There was a bitter twist to his mouth, and I wondered what was going through his mind.

I thought of various things to say and discarded each in its turn. If he planned to leave me on my own again, there was nothing I could do about it. Here in the Watch of the North, I could not count on Good Folk to emerge and keep me company, to walk on with me and shield me from harm. I'd have to do as Flint bade me and wait for him in some bolt-hole among the rocks. If he did not return this time, I really would have to go on alone. When would we catch a glimpse of Giant's Fist? How many days to Shadowfell?

"I'm sorry," Flint murmured, poking the fire with a stick. The embers glowed, casting a rose-gold light on his blunt features, but his eyes were full of shadows. "What I do . . . the path I tread . . . it brings some choices that test me hard." His lips tightened as if to hold back more words. I guessed he had already said more than he'd intended.

It seemed to me an Enforcer would not have many choices. His job was to carry out the king's will with perfect obedience. I could hardly say this. I could not ask Flint how it felt to do that work—the burnings, the beatings, the summary executions. I knew he was not a bad man. He could be gentle, kind, thoughtful. I had heard him speak with stirring sincerity of the fight for freedom. But if he was accepted as an Enforcer—more than that, as the king's most trusted man—his conscience must be heavy with the deeds he was required to perform. I wondered how long he had been maintaining his double life.

"Can you tell me a little more about the rebels?" I asked. "Who is Regan?" I had given some thought to the way Flint had told me of Shadowfell. Without quite saying it, he had implied that he himself had been to that place. Perhaps he had been involved with Regan's Rebels from the early days. *They could count their number on the fingers of two hands.*

"A leader." He spoke under his breath, as if, even here, to say this aloud might be too risky.

"Young? Old?"

"Young in years. Old in experience. His name is a password to . . . certain opportunities. On the wrong lips, it could be a betrayal. This is perilous ground, Neryn. Best that we speak no more of it."

A silence. Flickering light played around us as Flint stirred the fire. We had eaten well, for Flint had snared a rabbit, which we'd jointed and boiled with wild greens.

"Where did you grow up?" I asked him, remembering suddenly that vivid dream of the solitary child on the seashore. "Here in the mountains, or somewhere else?"

In all things, Flint was measured. He took his time in replying, though I could see the question had surprised him.

"Why would you ask such a thing?"

"I had a dream about you, when you were a child. I recognized you by your eyes, and by your stillness. You were on the seashore. All alone."

Flint grimaced. "And I dreamed of you, Neryn. You and your brother, skipping stones across the water at Lone Tarn. You looked content. There was sunshine on the hills that day."

"That is . . . very strange. That each of us would dream of what we could not possibly know."

He made no comment.

"That has never happened to me before," I said. "Not even with my brother."

"The place you saw," Flint murmured. His arms were draped across his drawn-up knees, his big, capable hands loosely clasped together. He gazed into the flames. "It's in the western isles. That was the place of my . . . learning. I don't speak of my family. There's nobody left."

I nodded. "Then you know how lonely it feels."

He glanced at me, eyes narrowed. "I've been on my own a long time. It suits me. What I do . . . it's no work for a man with . . . ties."

He had begun this speech in the tone of someone talking about putting wood on the fire or folding a blanket. Only the catch in his voice told me perhaps he did understand what it meant to be a son, a brother, a friend.

"You're still young," I said.

Flint looked at me. "You reproach me?"

"Reproach—no, of course not. Who am I to pass judgment? I know nothing about you."

"You know me better than most do, Neryn. I've spoken more than I should have done while we have been together. There's a certain quality you have, a warmth about you, despite all you have experienced. . . . It undermines my best intentions. Become my friend and you embrace a nightmare. I don't wish that on anyone."

I had no answer to this. My mind could not encompass

the loneliness of it. I had been alone; after Father's death I had thought, for a little, that I had no friend in the whole of Alban. But I had the Good Folk. I was never truly alone. And now I had Flint.

"You have no friends, even among those men you work with every day?"

A look came onto his face that frightened me. Flint was good at masks; he was expert at making himself impassive. But he had dispensed with the mask now, and the pain on his features brought tears to my eyes, though I did not fully understand the cause.

"I'm sorry," I said, laying a hand on his. "I shouldn't have asked that."

Flint's fingers curled around mine, and I thought how that did not sit quite right with what he had just said.

"You said that something about me made you speak unwisely, tell too much," I said. "But you've told me almost nothing. I still don't fully understand what you're doing, only that you must walk a line between life and death, trust and betrayal, every moment of every day. I still don't know how you put these two parts of your life together and make them work. I know you can't tell me that. But . . . despite everything, I did think we were already friends, or something close to it. Was I wrong?"

There was a long silence. He kept hold of my hand but would not look me in the eye. Eventually he said, "Neryn, what happened to your grandmother?"

I had never told this story. I had not told it to anyone.

With Father, I had not needed to put it in words. "I— I don't—" I drew in a ragged breath. Flint was my friend. We were alone, safe for now. He had helped me, guided me, been as open with me as he dared. Telling this tale would hurt, but perhaps the time for it was now.

"She was taken by the Enforcers, at Corbie's Wood." My voice came out tight and hard. "They drugged her to sleep, and an Enthraller put his hands on her and worked his foul charm. When she woke—" My voice cracked.

"Go on." Flint's tone was soft as a breath.

"She was . . . not herself anymore. She stumbled out of the bed, and she cried—Grandmother never cried—and she called for me, but I couldn't come out because that man was still there, and there were Enforcers outside the cottage, I had to stay where I was until everyone had gone. . . ." I was back there, huddled in the secret place behind the wall, my eye glued to the tiny crack, hardly daring to breathe lest they find me and do it to me too. *You must stay still as a stone, Neryn,* she had warned me. *No matter how long it takes. No matter what happens to me. No matter what they do.* "After they changed her, she didn't understand what had happened. She no longer had the wit to comprehend even the simplest things. She . . . she couldn't do anything for herself anymore. She'd been so strong before, so wise. . . ."

Flint put his arm around my shoulders. "You *saw* this?" he asked quietly. "When they came, when this man did his work, you were there?"

I nodded. Now that I had finally begun this story, now that I had managed to frame its first words, the truth spilled out of me like water from a broken dam. "I was hiding. They came quickly; there was no time for Grandmother and me to get away. Father was off working in another settlement, and Farral . . . The boys had taken their makeshift weapons and run out to mount a defense. Grandmother knew they wanted her. She made me hide, bade me be silent no matter what happened. She knew they would not fire the cottage; they would have other plans for her. It was . . ." I drew a shuddering breath. "Watching the mind-scraping . . . it made me feel dirty. Sullied. It filled me up with fury. I stood there a long time, all the hours of night, watching her and hearing the noises from outside, in the settlement. The sound of my world breaking in pieces. In the morning, when the men accepted that the charm had failed and went away, I felt as if I were a hundred years old."

"What did you do?"

"I crept out of my hiding place. I cleaned Grandmother up, fed her, sat by her until she fell asleep. I went to the door and looked out, and all around there was burning, and the dead lying in their blood, hacked and broken. I went out to find Farral. He was still alive, pinned by a spear. I hadn't the strength to free him. I stayed by him while he died. There were a few women and girls left in the settlement, and one or two very old men. When Father got back, we buried the dead. Nobody stayed at

Corbie's Wood. Father and I gathered a few possessions and moved up the hill to an old deserted croft. Father took what work he could find; I looked after Grandmother. Two seasons, she lived. Once she was gone, there was no reason for us to stay. Besides, we had a . . . a warning, and Father decided it wasn't safe for us to be in one place for too long. We buried Grandmother up on the hill, and we left."

"I'm sorry," Flint said.

Suddenly I was furious with him. How dare he? I pulled away from him, letting loose a tirade of angry words. "Sorry? What use is being sorry? I know that in your heart you are not the king's man, but when you're at court, or riding out with your troop, you do his bidding. How are you any better than those wretches who put a spear through Farral's chest and destroyed all I held dear?"

After a moment Flint said, "I am no better, Neryn. That is why we cannot be friends. Believe me, if you knew all there is to know of me, you would shun me as you would a plague."

I fought for self-control. Putting that night into words at last had left me wretched and shattered. If I had not been so close to tears, I would not have shouted at him the way I had. Now I was ashamed. "That isn't true," I whispered, wiping my eyes. "I'm sorry I spoke as I did. I hate the things you have to do. But I know that deep down you are a good man. I see it in your eyes. If you were bad, you would not have been so kind to me."

A wintry smile curved Flint's lips. "Kind? That's not a word folk use when speaking of me."

"Have you forgotten how long you looked after me? You did everything for me. If you were frustrated or angry that I was so slow to recover, I never saw the least sign of it. What was that but kindness?" Seeing the look on his face, bitter, self-mocking, I added, "Is it so hard to believe I see some good in you?"

"I could lie to you," Flint said, "but I think you would know if I did. Where you are concerned, I seem to have lost the skill of telling convincing untruths. If Alban were a different place, Neryn, you and I would be friends. Perhaps more than friends. But this is the realm we live in, the time we are born to. There is no place here for softness. Let folk in too close and you offer them up as weapons for your own destruction."

After a little, I said, "We *are* close, Flint. If we weren't, I would never have come with you after you found me that last time. If we weren't, you would never have found the patience to stay with me while I was sick."

"You misinterpret my motives. I wanted to assist you in your journey because I believed you had something of value to offer. You needed to be strong enough to get there. I helped you. That was all." He moved to set another log on the fire, though it was already well supplied. Now I could no longer see his face.

"I don't believe you," I said. "I think we are friends, not in some impossible Alban of the future, but now, in this sad, scarred realm we were both born to. You said I'd loathe you if I knew the truth. Why not tell me this unpalatable truth and let me make my own decision?"

"It makes no difference what you think. When we reach Shadowfell, you will stay and I will leave."

"You're going back to Summerfort?"

"Back to the king. That is what I do, Neryn. I do things that would make you weep. I do things that would make you sick. I do things that would make you as angry as you were that day at Corbie's Wood when you found your brother dying. I am not a fit friend for anyone."

After that there was nothing more to say, and the two of us settled to sleep on opposite sides of the fire. I was a long time awake, listening to the night sounds and trying to untangle our conversation. I was glad I had told Grandmother's story at last, though the memory of that night still made my stomach churn and my heart pound with rage. I murmured a silent prayer for her, and another for Mara and her child-man Garret. I vowed that if I did reach Shadowfell, I would do all in my power to make sure nobody ever performed mind-scraping again. It was an evil practice, corrupt, wrong. Someone, somewhere, must surely have the power to stop it. If not, Alban was doomed.

Restless, I rolled over to catch the firelight glinting in Flint's open eyes as he lay quite still, watching me.

"Cold?" he murmured.

It was always cold these days, with the wind coming straight down from the mountain snow. The nights held a chill to freeze us to the bone.

"I'm warm enough." I already had my cloak and both blankets; I did not want him to give me his cloak as well. To build the fire higher would be too risky. "I can't sleep. My mind is turning in circles."

He rolled onto his back, staring up at the dark sky. The firelight played on the tall stones that surrounded our resting place, making shapes I imagined as creatures of ancient story. "There's no need to be afraid," Flint said. "We should reach our destination in two or three days. And when I need to leave you, I will find somewhere safe for you to shelter. I told you."

"You keep telling me I will be safe." My voice sounded small in the dark. "But what about you?"

A silence. "You fear I will be killed by my own kind and not come back for you?" he asked.

"That wasn't what I meant."

In the quiet that followed, a bird called out somewhere above us, its harsh cry cutting through the cold air of the autumn night. Perhaps there were stealthy footsteps somewhere beyond the rocks that sheltered us; perhaps my imagination conjured them. Flint put a finger to his lips and we waited. After some time, a time when every breath I took seemed one risk too many, he nodded to me, indicating all was safe, and I breathed more easily.

"Only a creature passing," Flint whispered. "Men will not come here by night. Close your eyes, Neryn. You need rest."

I swallowed. "For a long time after that night at Corbie's

Wood, I was afraid to sleep," I told him. "Afraid of what my dreams might bring, and how they might change me. Even now, sometimes I lie awake remembering, and feeling the terror she must have felt to wake up and be a husk of herself."

"Close your eyes," Flint said again. "Think of good things. Playing with your brother. Skipping pebbles. Chanting 'Stanie Mon.' Think of the time when the ones you loved were still alive and well, and how much they taught you. Think about how much of them you carry with you, inside."

Tears welled behind my eyes. Too often when I thought of them, I saw only that they had left me, each in turn: Mother, Farral, Grandmother, Father. Left me to walk on alone.

"You're strong, Neryn. You're as strong as the rocks and the mountains. As strong as the oaks with their roots deep in the ground. You look as fragile as a mountain flower, but looks can be deceptive. If I haven't been prepared to leave you on your own, it's not because I think you weak and incapable. It's . . ."

"What?" His words had caught me off guard; they set a confusion in me.

His voice came to me as the merest whisper. "Because if I see you defeated, then I think I will see Alban defeated, and if that happens, none of us can go on. To guard you is to guard the heart of this land of ours. Sleep now, Neryn. Tonight, at least, your dreams will be good ones."

With that speech he succeeded in silencing me completely. I hardly understood what he meant. And yet his words felt like a warm light on a gray and joyless pathway; they were balm to my heart. "Good night, Flint," I murmured, and settled to sleep.

Chapter Thirteen

THE GOING WAS STEEP NEXT DAY, THE PATHS treacherous as we made our way over bare fells high above the valley. Flint had said he wanted to be off on his solitary mission by midday, but when the sun was at its peak and he started looking for a sheltered place to leave me, there was neither cave nor crevice to be found, only barren open country. We walked on for a while longer, with Flint growing more and more edgy. At last we saw a stand of pines, the only green in the bleak gray of the fells. When we reached the trees, which stood by a gushing beck, Flint was dissatisfied with the cover they offered. We stopped nonetheless to eat and to fill our waterskins. As we sat on the rocks by the stream, a flock of crows flew overhead, cawing. I watched them pass and settle on a lone pine a hundred paces or so to our north along the ridge. Something flickered beneath the tree. A creature? A man? I froze, a warning on my lips.

Now all was still beneath the pine. I narrowed my

eyes, wondering what it was that had caught my gaze. Not a man. Not a wandering sheep or errant goat. No, what I had seen was a discoloration of the land, a slice of darkness that lay behind the solitary tree, barely discernible to the eye. Here, then gone. Here again. A shadow. A mark. An opening.

"Flint," I said, "I think there may be some kind of cave down there, near the pine. It's hard to see. There are rocks partly concealed, and within them a narrow opening."

I had risen to my feet, shading my eyes against the cloud-veiled sun. Flint came to stand beside me.

"I see nothing."

"We should go and look," I said.

"If you say so." Clearly he thought me deluded, but when we had packed up our meager repast, we headed that way, side by side on the pebbly slope. We passed the lone pine, and there before us was an outcrop that had been quite invisible from our vantage point under the trees.

"Odd," Flint observed. "I'd have sworn there was nothing here but bare hillside. I don't see any entry."

"It might be concealed," I said, remembering Howling Rock and wondering if I had stumbled on another of the Good Folk's secret meeting places. I closed my eyes, breathing deeply, and tried to sense the way. To the left, maybe, and lower down.

"What are you doing?"

"Shh." I opened my eyes to meet his bemused gaze. "Let's try around that side."

And there it was, an opening partly screened by the

withered fronds of a creeping plant that had surrendered to the cold, and marked by a pair of white stones. Flint eyed these, perhaps recognizing, as I did, that the stones were an ancient sign. "How could you know this was here?" he asked, then added, "No need to answer that. It's ideal. I'll make a fire for you, then I'd best be on my way."

"Is that wise? A fire, I mean?"

"Weighing the fact that someone might see it against the likelihood of your getting so cold you'll be ill again, I think we'll chance it."

Inside, the cave was dim, dry, and inhabited by nothing bigger than a bat or field mouse. Its shadowy depths seemed to stretch deep into the hillside. I unpacked what we would need while Flint went back up to the band of trees to fetch firewood. When it was stacked to his satisfaction, he headed off on his solitary mission, assuring me he would return by nightfall.

I tended to the fire, draped garments and blankets to dry, assembled the makings of a hot meal. Only then did I go to stand by the lone tree and look out to the north.

The land lay before me in folds of gray, purple, and blue, under a sky heavy with cloud. Not so far ahead arose the foothills of a snowcapped mountain range. I wondered where among those peaks lay Shadowfell. Scanning the terrain, I felt my heart still. There, jutting from a rocky hillside, stood a rough column of stone. Atop its considerable height was a formation resembling the clenched fingers of a huge hand. Giant's Fist. It was just as Grandmother had described it. *Find Giant's Fist,* she had said, *and you will find Shadowfell.*

Flint had been right, then: from here, it was at most two days' walk. All of a sudden, two days seemed endless. How could I wait so long? I wanted to leap, to gallop, to fly, to be there today, right now, between one breath and the next.

But those hills looked so bare and bleak. Could people really live there? Where could they grow food? Where could they shelter? When the snows came in earnest, there would be no way in or out. I shivered, imagining myself reaching Shadowfell only to find that the rebel movement did not exist, that Flint had been mistaken, that it was nothing but a wild story born of desperate, impossible hope.

The ridge we had been following did not lead to those hills; we'd need to descend into the valley and walk some distance along it before we climbed again. The valley floor looked empty of human settlement. This was mountain country, inhabited by wolf and eagle. Folk did not run sheep or cattle in such terrain. A few stands of pine softened the hillsides, but there was little fodder for grazing animals. Surely the Enforcers would not come so far along the valley. Not unless they were heading for Shadowfell.

I must put that possibility from my mind. Let myself dwell on everything that could go wrong and the dream might start to slip away. As I returned to the cave, I wondered where Silver and Daw and their band were now. With Flint gone, I half expected a clan of northern Good

Folk to emerge from the shadows of this uncanny place. But nobody came.

The fire was lit. The waterskins were full. The clothes were drying, and the bedding was unpacked. There was nothing for me to do but sit and wait. I had promised to stay inside the cave, out of sight. I had already broken that promise by going out to look along the valley. I should lie down and rest awhile. But the knowledge that Shadowfell was so close filled me with the need for action, and it was hard to be still.

I stared into the flames of my little fire, remembering all those who had helped me, all who had shared their wisdom. I thought of the ghost warriors by Hiddenwater, lifting their voices in the old song. We all wanted Alban to be free. We all wanted justice and peace. But I had so much to learn. From what the Good Folk had told me, I had barely begun my journey.

I thought of Flint. *Let him be safe. Let him come back before dark.*

The day seemed endless. I sat, I stood, I paced. Once or twice I went out to the tree again to gaze toward Giant's Fist. I was almost there; Shadowfell was almost within my reach. But all I felt was doubt. What if I reached the rebel headquarters, offered to help, and then could not learn how to harness my canny gift? What if there was nobody who could teach me to be a Caller? I had called the stanie mon, no doubt of that. But that had been a fluke. I had guessed at how to summon his help, and it was just lucky for me that my verses had worked.

I might not be so fortunate next time. And what of the mysterious virtues? Perhaps I was doomed never to learn the wise use of my gift. Perhaps I would never be a Caller.

Eventually I lay down and closed my eyes. I did not want to sleep. I feared my dreams. The cave felt empty without Flint; it felt wrong. Stupid to think thus, as if his presence alone could bring sound sleep and peace of mind. An Enforcer. A rebel. How could a man be both and stay in his right mind?

Something moved outside, close to the cave mouth. I sat bolt upright, my skin prickling. A shifting. A subtle change in the light. I rose silently to my feet, heart pounding, gaze fixed on that patch of brightness. Nothing to be seen beyond the ragged strands of foliage that screened the entry. But someone was there; I felt it.

Flint had left me a knife. I had not thought I would need it. It lay next to my bag in the sheath I had made long ago for another weapon. One step toward it, another step, praying that I could reach it without making any sound. A shadow passed the cave entry, then as quickly was gone. Whoever was out there, he was swift and silent.

I backed farther into the cave, the knife held up before me, its point not quite steady. I had never killed anyone. I did not know if I could. I waited.

Time passed and nothing stirred. Perhaps I'd imagined the whole thing; perhaps I had been closer to sleep than I'd realized, half dreaming. Still, I did not move. In my mind

I counted slowly up to fifty. I could hear nothing out there, see nothing. I slipped the knife into my belt, feeling rather foolish, and crept back to the fireside.

A crash outside, and an oath. I froze. The voice came again. "Poxy good-for-nothing cur!" I could hear someone breathing hard. "Now look what you've done! I spent all day gathering that wood." Then a moan of pain. "Ah! My back!"

The voice was an old man's, unsteady, a little querulous. It sounded as if he was just beyond the cave mouth. He must know someone was here: the smoke from my fire would be obvious. I edged to one side, and now I could make out the figure of a man, bent double, with a hand pressed to the small of his back.

A little dog raced into the cave and came to an abrupt halt a few paces from me. The old man straightened, groaning. Through a gap in the screening foliage, I saw his face clearly. His eyes had the milky color of the sightless.

The dog—curiously patterned, as if one side had been painted black and the other white—had begun a shrill, furious barking. As for me, my heart was racing and my palms were sweaty, but I hung on to my common sense. This old man was not the Enforcer I had dreaded. He seemed too infirm to be any threat to me—I could easily outrun him if it came to that. I drew a steadying breath and spoke above the dog's fanfare of challenge.

"Have you hurt yourself?" I moved forward, keeping one hand on the knife in my belt. The dog planted its short legs wide, quivering. Its voice rose to a shriek. "Do you need help?"

The old man was as gnarled as an ancient juniper, with a tangle of dirty white hair to his shoulders. He was dressed in shapeless garments of indeterminate color, clothing that looked as if it were a natural part of him, as bark is of a tree. He stood crooked, weathered to that shape by his years. I was reminded, piercingly, of my grandmother.

"Tripped over the dog, lost my wretched firewood. Hurt my poxy back again. Stick a stopper in your mouth, dog!" The old man's gaze was unnerving. What was a blind man doing coming all the way up here for wood? Was this a trap to lure me out from my safe shelter? "Stop that!" he rapped out.

The little dog fell silent, though when I took another step forward, it growled deep in its throat. "Are you injured?" I asked the old man.

"A girl," he said. "I did not expect to find a lassie hiding in Odd's Hole."

"That's the name of this place? Odd's Hole?"

"You're not from these parts, then?"

I did not think he would expect an answer to this, and I did not offer one. He had indeed been carrying a huge bundle of firewood. The sticks lay scattered all around the cave opening, along with the cord that had tied them.

"Wretched dog keeps getting underfoot," the man muttered. "It's her way of being helpful."

"Perhaps you should leave her at home next time."

He chuckled, then winced with pain. "Can't do that, lassie. She's my eyes."

So he was blind, or so nearly blind that he could not get about on his own. I glanced to left and to right and down the hill. There was nobody else in sight. "Why don't you sit down and I'll gather these up again for you?" I said. "Have you far to walk?"

"Far enough." He lowered himself onto a rock, cursing under his breath, and sat there as I picked up his fallen cargo and tied it back into its bundle. The dog had vanished inside the cave; I hoped she was not eating the last of the provisions. "A brew would go down well," the old man said. "Got a good wee fire there. I can smell it."

There was plenty I could have said to this, but I held my tongue. He was old and tired. Best that I treat him with courtesy and go along with what he wanted, provided it was reasonable. With luck he would leave and not think to tell anyone he had met me. His presence here, so far from any settlement, was surprising. I did not ask him where he lived. Asking questions meant you had to answer questions in return, and I had no answers to give.

When the bundle of wood was secure, I went back into the cave, filled the pot from my waterskin, and set it on the fire. The two-colored dog had curled up on the blankets, but she was not asleep: one eye was open a crack, keeping careful watch on me. The old man came in after me. He settled on the ground with somewhat more ease than he had shown earlier, then extended knotty hands to the fire's warmth and sighed.

I made a brew. The supply of dried herbs was almost exhausted. Just as well Shadowfell was only a couple of days away. Neither of us spoke again until I had put his cup into his hands and settled with my own. I looked at my companion through the rising steam and hoped I had not made a terrible mistake.

"You'll be going four ways, then," the old man said.

My skin prickled. "I don't know what you mean."

"North, south, east, and west." This was delivered with exaggerated patience, as if he thought me rather slow. "You'll be visiting each in its turn."

Perhaps his great age had addled his wits. Or perhaps this was something much more devious. "I would hardly visit them all at the same time," I said mildly. If he thought I would tell him where I was going, he was a fool.

The old man roared with laughter, startling the dog, who leapt to her feet. "Indeed not," the fellow said when he had recovered his breath. "But you'll be making a wee journey."

I said nothing.

"When I say *wee*," he elaborated, "I don't mean short, you ken? In miles, it'll be long. In other ways, even longer. I hope you make a better fist of it than Odd did of his travels."

What was he talking about? Did he know something about me, or was this just an old man's rambling? I grabbed at the only part of it that seemed safe. "Odd—you mean the man this cave was named after? What was his story?"

"Got any food with you?"

I suppressed a sigh. "I may have some cheese," I said, fishing in the bag of supplies Flint had left. "And a little dried fruit."

"That should fill the spot."

As soon as I produced the cheese, the dog fixed her attention on me with unnerving intensity, reminding me of Hollow's pookie. The animal's markings were indeed odd; I had never before seen a creature so neatly divided into sun and shadow, day and night. I gave the man what I thought we could spare, then offered the little hound a scrap of cheese, expecting her to snatch the morsel greedily from my fingers. But she accepted the gift with some delicacy and, when she was done, settled again on the blankets.

"That fellow, Odd," said the old man considerably later, when he had finished dusting crumbs from his ragged garments. "Long story. Not explored the back of the Hole yet, have you?" He appeared to be looking over my shoulder to the inner parts of the cave.

"No." I wanted to hear the story, but I also wanted my unexpected visitor to leave. It seemed important that he be gone before Flint returned.

"Ah. Not much of an adventurer, then."

I said nothing.

"It goes a long way down. A long way in. A long, long way. Folk have told tales about this place for more years than a lass like you could imagine. The cave had a different name once, a name that's forgotten now. Odd had a certain talent, and he heard the stories. His tale's simple enough. He came here to have a look. He went in. He went down. He didn't go properly prepared, and he never came back."

"That's hardly a long story."

"It could be longer." The old man folded his hands in his lap.

"Was there something in the cave? What did the old stories say? Was Odd looking for anything in particular?" *A certain talent,* he'd said. Could that be the same talent as mine?

"He might have been."

"Treasure? A creature of some kind? A portal?"

"I could show you," the old man said, and when I looked at him, suddenly I saw a different person, a taller, more powerfully built figure whose eyes were not the white orbs of the blind but flickering puzzles of light and shade in which fiery red chased night black one way then the other. My heart thudded. What was he? When the Good Folk were nearby, I felt their presence deep within me, as if they were part of me. This man had seemed quite ordinary. As indeed he was now, for from one breath to the next he was as he'd first appeared, blind eyes, wrinkled skin, stooped shoulders, and all.

"I could take you in," he said, smooth as honey.

"Odd's tale suggests that would not be very wise." I worked hard to keep my voice steady. "I'm here for shelter, nothing more." How long would it take me to bolt past him, out into the open, and run up to the concealment of the woods?

"It might be very wise indeed," he said. "Not big on courage, are you? I see you're keeping that little knife within reach of your hand."

I felt a cold, creeping sensation in my spine. "If you can see that," I said, "then you don't need a wee dog to find your way for you."

"Ah," the old man said. "There's seeing and *seeing*."

"As for going farther into the cave, I exercise common sense. I can't think of any good reason to go in there. I can think of quite a few reasons not to."

"Might be a while before I pass this way again. I could lead you in, and I could bring you out. Could be there's something you badly need in Odd's Hole. But if you won't go down, you'll never know."

I bit back the retort that sprang to my lips, words that would have dismissed him and sent him on his way. The virtues. Maybe this was a chance to demonstrate one of the qualities required for a Caller, along the lines of the Giving Hand, but different. A test of courage, perhaps. What exactly did lie in the dark shadows of Odd's Hole? "Would that something be by way of a . . . challenge?" I asked.

The old man grinned, and there in his place was a boy of about twelve, white-faced, dark-clothed, with a flickering light falling across his features that was not made by my little fire. His hair stood up around his head in dark, wild filaments. The eyes were as I had seen them before—

black, red, black, red—drawing my gaze. "It might well be so," the boy said, lifting his brows and giving me an unsettling smile. "Down there"—he motioned toward the back of the cave—"you will find a pool of water. They say Odd drowned in it, drawn deep by what he saw there. Too deep. But you would not drown. Not if I held your hand."

Gods, what was this? A trap? Or a vital part of my journey toward becoming a Caller? What kind of being could hide his uncanny nature thus? He put me in mind of a trickster from ancient story, a being all twists and turns, whose favor could only be gained if one were able to pin down his likeness between one disguise and the next. A will-o'-the-wisp, a player of games, unreliable in every respect.

"Speak plainly," I said, my fingers closing around the hilt of the knife, though I was beginning to think an ordinary weapon would be of no use at all in this situation. "Are you here to help me or to hinder me?" I rose to my feet, taking a step toward the boy, though my instinct was to shrink away.

The dog growled deep. Too deep for such a little creature, surely. I risked taking my eyes off the boy to look at her, and my breath faltered. The dog had grown bigger. Her back was as high as my waist, and her slender body was now sturdy and muscular. Still growling, she drew back her upper lip to show me a set of purposeful teeth. The message was clear: *I can take a full-grown boar on my own. You? One bite.*

"I haven't made up my mind yet," the boy said, and became once more the ancient wood gatherer. "As for what you might find in Odd's Hole, you might find a test and you might find a map. You might see your whole journey set out in that. Of course, sometimes it doesn't help to know what's to come, which friends will die before their time, what grave errors you'll make, who'll betray your trust, whom you'll destroy and whom you'll offend. On the other hand, a map helps us know where we're going. In your case, it'd be four maps."

A test. A test down there in the darkness, in a deep pool. "I can't swim," I said. My voice came out like that of a child, alone and scared. I gathered myself and spoke more strongly. "There's no point in passing a test if I drown."

The grin again, and a flickering series of changes, each so fast I had hardly the time to take it in before it was gone. Either this was a skillful practitioner of magic, or it was indeed one of the beings mentioned in the old tales. Could a canny human perfect shape-changing to such a degree? I doubted it. But if he was one of the Good Folk, why did he show no fear of the naked knife?

"Trying to make sense of me?" the man quipped, as if, despite the blind eyes, he knew how intensely I was scrutinizing him. "You won't. I'm the biggest puzzle in all Alban, and there's no untangling me. One piece of advice, take it or leave it. Before you meet me again, and you surely will, you'd best develop a liking for games. Without that, your journey will surely end in tears. As for drowning, some do and some don't. One thing's sure: if you're too scared to try, there's no passing the test."

"I have a feeling that if I agree to this, I will end up as Odd did, in the Hole forever, stone-dead."

The man laughed, throwing back his head. The sound rang from the cave walls, setting the dog howling. "When Odd went down," he said, "he had no guide. You have the best and only guide, lassie. Show courage and I'll keep you safe. Turn to jelly and I might be tempted to let you fall. But as a token of goodwill, I'll give you a wee rhyme before we go, to put some fire in you. Ready now?"

I stood mute, waiting.

The old man's voice rose in quavering song. As he sang, the words came back to me from long ago, so dear and familiar that I could not believe I had forgotten them. Beneath the man's voice I heard my mother's, singing to a tiny Neryn, barely two, as I sat on her knee, and before us in the water the seals danced their slow, mysterious dance under a sunset sky purple as heather, gray as a dove's wing, red as fire.

Canny Eyes and Strength of Stillness
Guide your path across the land.
Open Heart and Steadfast Purpose,
Flame of Courage, Giving Hand.

He turned his filmy eyes in my direction. Whether he could see me, I did not know. "That's six," he said. "You've got those out of the way already, or so I've been told. There's some wee folk would argue all day long as to whether each requirement had been met, but I'd say that's

274

a waste of time. Now, will we get on with the next part of this or won't we?"

Was it only my imagination or had the cave become unnaturally dark and the air unusually cold? I tried not to shiver. "You're telling me I've demonstrated six out of seven virtues already?" That was not possible, surely.

"Don't be too pleased with yourself, lassie," said the old man. "You're not done yet. That rhyme's got another whole verse to it."

"Tell me!"

"Ah, not so fast." He raised his hands as if to ward me off. "Come down the Hole first, do what you have to do, and I'll give you the rest when it's all over."

There was a story I recalled in which a gullible young man goes down a well to fetch treasure for a mysterious old woman, with promise of a small reward, and then, when the treasure is duly brought to the surface, the crone snatches it and pushes the adventurer back down to his death. But the old man had spoken as if he knew we would meet again. *You'd best develop a liking for games,* he'd said. So perhaps I would not perish in the depths of Odd's Hole. What would Flint expect me to do if he were here? He'd probably be standing guard over me with his weapons drawn and an Enforcer look on his face. But if he were to face this choice himself, I knew he would not refuse it. "Very well," I said. "I'll do it."

My companion rose to his feet. For a moment I saw his profile silhouetted on the cave wall behind him. It was not the shadow of a bent old man, nor yet of a wild-haired boy. The features were proud and strong, those of a warrior, a leader. He turned his head, and the image was gone. "Come, then," he said. "We don't have all day."

I drew a deep, steadying breath. "I'm coming." I slipped the knife into my belt. I picked up a stick from the fire, wondering if there was any chance it would keep burning long enough to light our way there and back.

The dog went first, small again. The old man followed his creature with confident feet; either he had a different kind of sight, or he had done this so many times before that his feet found the way all by themselves. I came last, with my burning brand in one hand and my other hand free to grab the knife. *This place is called Neryn's Folly,* I thought grimly. *She followed an old man and a dog down there one day and was never seen again.*

Soon enough the cavern narrowed to a tunnel, piercing the rock of Alban's spine. A long tunnel. Here and there side passages opened off, or perhaps they were merely shallow caves. The air was cold and fresh, suggesting that somewhere, not so far away, there were openings to the outside. Yet that seemed unlikely, for I sensed we were deep underground.

We walked for a long time, long enough for my legs to start aching with weariness. I recalled that Flint and I had already walked for half a day before I found the cave. He might be back there by now, discovering the place deserted, perhaps thinking I had gone on alone. What if he headed off toward Shadowfell looking for me, and when I emerged from here it was too late to go after him? I banished those thoughts and concentrated on moving forward.

Oddly, the torch I had brought did not burn away to nothing or wink out in the draft, but flamed steadily, lighting our way through the dark passage. The tunnel began to slope downward. First a gentle descent, then a steeper one. The place was damper here. The tunnel walls shone with moisture, and I felt a clammy chill on my skin.

Man and dog came to a sudden halt; with difficulty, I managed not to crash into them. I lifted my torch. Its wavering light revealed that the way had become a set of narrow, precipitous steps going downward. Something gleamed at their foot, pale as moonlight. Pool? Well? Mirror? Perhaps it was all three.

"This is the place." The voice was not the old man's, nor yet the boy's. It was strong and authoritative, and when I glanced sideways, I saw beside me a tall man whose profile was the one I had seen on the wall, cast by shadows. A person of kingly bearing, a being of power. "Go down," he commanded.

"By myself?" My tone matched the trembling of the torch. "Very well."

"Give me the brand." He held out an elegant, long-fingered hand on which dark rings gleamed, and I passed him the flaming stick. For a few moments his eyes met mine, and I saw in them the same dancing colors as before, crimson and sable flickering almost faster than I could follow. Shadows moved across his high-boned features. He lifted his brows. "Don't wait too long," he said, "or you may lose the will to go on. Tread with care. Don't slip."

"Wait a moment." Perhaps I was a fool to challenge him. In this form he not only puzzled me, he scared me. Before such power I was nothing. Why was he playing with me like this? But then, maybe I was nothing, but Shadowfell was something. Alban's freedom was something. And if I could get this right, maybe I could play my part in winning that freedom. In my mind I heard Flint's voice, soft as a breath, strong as stone. *If I see you defeated, then I think I will see Alban defeated, and if that happens, none of us can go on. To guard you is to guard the heart of this land of ours.* "Didn't you say you would hold my hand?" I asked.

"There's holding and *holding*," the flame-eyed man said. "We'll watch from up here."

Nothing for it, then, but to make my way down those steps. They were awkwardly spaced, and their surfaces were not only wet but grown over with some kind of creeping subterranean moss on which my shoes slipped and skidded. There was nothing to hold on to; the tunnel walls looked close enough to touch, but when I stretched out my arms, the rock seemed to shrink away so it was just out of reach.

"Make haste!" the man called, and the dog gave a curt bark, like a warning.

Step by step I went down. *Canny Eyes, Strength of*

Stillness. Open Heart, Steadfast Purpose. Flame of Courage, Giving Hand. And here I was on the lip of a round pool. In its depths was an eerie gleam, as if somewhere beneath the water a flame flickered and moved. An old, old place; a place of the Good Folk. It was alive with magic.

There was barely enough space here for my two feet. No ledge; no handy stone edging such as might be placed around a well to stop an incautious child or animal from falling in. Only this tiny level spot and the water, with sheer rock rising all around. I held myself still as the light moved and changed in the depths. Was it a scrying pool that offered visions of the future? A place of ancient ritual? What was I expected to do?

A sharp bark from the dog, and the rock walls on every side were suddenly alive with light and shadow. Shapes sprang and pranced and dived: here a flying owl; here a mounted warrior, ax raised; here a capering girl with hair like long strands of weed. It was as if a great fire burned behind me, throwing these images onto the stone. I looked over my shoulder, up the steps. The man had one arm outstretched, fingers pointing ahead. In the other hand he held the modest brand I had snatched from my little fire. A mage, then, or something more.

"Keep your gaze straight ahead," he said. It was a command, and I obeyed. On the rocks before me a shadow man fought a desperate, one-sided battle. He was on foot, armed only with something that looked like a stick or crude staff. Against him were three mounted warriors. He turned and ducked and leapt; he swung his weapon high and low; he used trick after trick. I found myself willing him to survive, it looked so real.

The voice came from the top of the steps, calm and cool. "Jump!"

I jumped. The water took me, cold as a winter night, its sudden embrace jolting me to the heart. Down I sank, down and down, until I should have been near drowning, yet oddly I felt no need for air. As I descended, images formed and dissolved around me. Was I in water or fire? Light and shadow flickered, teasing me as I passed. There were faces in the flame, faces dear and familiar, yet never quite captured, for they altered from one moment to the next, until smoke veiled them, or maybe ripples, and they were gone. . . . Gone before I could touch, before I could speak . . . *Stay!* I cried, but my voice was a string of bubbles, vanishing upward. *Oh, stay!*

For I saw my mother, appearing, disappearing, her image fleeting as a dream, beloved, lost. Now I was struggling, thrashing about with my arms and legs, fighting the water that held me close. *Stay! I need to— I want to—*

No. It was a test. Against every instinct, I stopped fighting and surrendered to the water. No stir. No breath. Just like that night, hiding in my grandmother's wall. Still as stone. Still as death. The water drew me down, down into the depths of Odd's Hole.

And there she was, on the shore, singing. I was in her arms, resting against the warm softness of her body. *"Open Heart and Steadfast Purpose,"* she sang, and I felt the gentle movement of her hand against my hair, stroking. *"Flame of Courage, Giving Hand."* She bent her head to kiss my brow. "My girl," she whispered. "My precious girl."

I found words, and spoke them not as the child she held close, the memory-child, but as the woman I was now. "I love you, Mother. You left me early and I've grieved for that. What you gave me was precious beyond all gifts. Maybe you knew, even then, what the future would hold for me." In my mind I made a new picture. The woman in it was very like my mother, but not exactly like, for though she was younger, there was something hard in her, as if she had been weathered by long journeying and touched by experience too terrible to put in words. On her knee, another child nestled. I felt how warm and soft she was in my arms, how fragile and yet how strong. "My girl," I whispered. Then the fire flared up, and the veil of smoke moved across, and they were gone: mother, daughter, and granddaughter alike.

The water again. How deep could I sink before there would be no going back? My body tensed, craving deliverance. *Out!* screamed the voice of my fear. *Let me out!*

Flame of Courage, I murmured, or perhaps I only thought it. *Face this test to the end, or you make a lie of all those who believed in you.*

Eyes closed, limp as a frond of weed, I let myself fall. I fell into the light of a summer's day. It bathed the chalk-white face of my brother, and touched the line of bright blood running from his mouth. He fought for one more breath and spoke the words I had already heard: *Neryn, I'm sorry.*

Neryn-that-was had wept, cursed, pleaded with Farral to stay, begged him not to leave her alone. The last sound he'd heard, as he died, was his sister's anguished wail. Now I knelt, cradling him, and whispered in his ear. "You gave your life for truth and honor. You showed me how to be brave. Pass the flame to me, brother. I will carry it now." I saw the change in his eyes, then the light leaving them as he drifted away, up, up into the blue sky that stretched wide and perfect over Alban's hills. "Goodbye, Farral," I whispered.

I was in the sky too, turned and turned by the four winds, floating. Faces in the clouds. Here a warrior, here a child, here a proud stallion, here a scurrying beetle, here a little dog, a strange old man, a girl watching as her father wagered her for three silver pieces. Fire caught him, making of him a pillar of screaming flame, his mouth stretched wide, his eyes staring, his pain searing through me until I cried out, but the wind snatched my voice and blew it far away.

Oh, this was cruel. Grief weighed me down, stifling the words I should have found. My father's suffering tore at me. I longed to curl up in a ball, hands over my face, and pretend he was not there. But I must face this test with open eyes, with open arms, with an open heart, a heart without bitterness, regret, or blame. I must stand witness, and I must make peace with my lost ones. "Father," I said, choking on the word, "your burden was heavy indeed, and you carried it long. You did your best for me. Walk on in peace now. I love you. I forgive you."

Daughter . . . The word was a whisper, a breath, a sigh, drifting away. He was gone.

Not done yet. Not finished. I sank again through water deeper than memory, down and down. This time, I thought, I would not be able to do it. This time I must close my eyes and ears to it; this time I would surely fail, for some things could never be made right, some things simply could not be borne. *Please,* begged the child inside me, *please don't make me do this.*

But there was no choice. No flight, no refuge, nothing but moving straight ahead to face the darkest thing, the cruelest hurt, the wound there was surely no healing. *Steadfast Purpose.* She'd always had that, right to the end. It had been in her voice when she bade me hide, when she warned me, not a twitch, not a squeak, however long it took, no matter what they did to her, no matter what I saw. It had been in her eyes when they drugged her; it had been there until the moment when she fell unconscious in their grip.

"Grandmother," I said, and the bubble of her name floated up to the light. "Where are you?"

She came twofold. Here was the hobbling, weeping crone of the last days. Bafflement and fear had etched deep marks on her parchment skin; she plucked at her face with restless hands, as if it were a troublesome mask. The stink of incontinence hung about her, along with a musty smell of stale food. However hard I had tried, I had never been able to keep her clean enough. "Neryn," she whispered, eyes darting from side to side. "Neryn, is that you?" I put my arms around her and held on, blinded by tears. "I'm here," I said. "I'm right here."

"Look up, child."

I looked, and though her frail form still trembled in my hold, at the same time she stood before me, straight-backed, clear-eyed, farseeing. Her face held all the warmth of a spirit wise and easy, a heart full of love and life. "So here you are," she said, and smiled.

I could not find a single word. But that was no matter. She took one step toward me, and her arms came around me even as I held the form of her shrunken second self within the circle of my own embrace.

"Dear one," she said. "Dear brave little one."

Now words tumbled out of me. "I should have spoken out, I should have stood up to them, that's what Farral would have done! How could I have stayed there and not helped you, how could I let them—"

"Hush, Neryn, hush. You were a child and you could not have helped. It was as it was, and now it is past, and you cannot change the way of it. If you had rushed to my aid that night, who would have passed these tests and made this journey? Rise up to the light, dear one. Rise up and go on your way."

Then, evanescent as dew on morning grass, she was gone. Gone in a heartbeat. There was too much in me to be put in words. But perhaps that did not matter, since she had always understood.

I rose. Slow as thistledown on the breeze, turning and turning, through shifting shadows I rose toward the surface. As I passed, images came to me, more fleeting than the others but no less vivid for that. Myself at the mouth of a sea cave, looking out to the west. A pair of hands, weathered, wrinkled hands, fastening around mine. An old woman's whisper. *Be fluid as water.*

I rose again and a new image formed. I was in a hall of snow and ice, glittering and pale, mysterious and grand. A fur cloak, perhaps a wolfskin, around my shoulders. Someone standing behind me, though I could not see who it was. A warrior, I thought, with spear in hand; but not Flint, for this figure was slighter. A voice again, a different voice, deep and strong. *Endure as earth endures.*

The water rippled around me, turning to green, gold, silver, white, chasing away the wintry vision. And there I was again, in a gown of blue with my hair flowing loose across my shoulders. A circlet of flowers crowned my head. *See with the clarity of air,* the voice said, and now it was a woman's, powerful but sweet, like the note of a distant horn.

Up, up again. The light danced around me, filling the water with its changeable magic. I waited now for a fourth image, for the old man had spoken of four ways and of four maps. What had those visions been but glimpses of the Guardians? Hag of the Isles. Lord of the North. White Lady. Must I search for each in turn? Were they the key to learning a Caller's art?

My head broke free of the surface and I was in the cavern, with light flickering on the walls, and the steps in front of me going straight up. I flailed with my arms, desperate to stay afloat until I could reach the edge and clamber up, for to drown now, at the end, would be a sorry thing indeed. I kicked out. My foot touched the bottom. I stumbled, then stood straight. The water was only chest-deep. At the top of the steps stood man and dog. The small, bright flame of the makeshift torch turned the man's strong features into a mask with black holes for eyes.

"Climb up," he ordered.

I climbed, leaving a wet trail behind me. My clothing was saturated; my hair lay dripping across my shoulders; my shoes squelched as I worked my way up the steps, one hand holding up my skirt, the other clutching for whatever purchase it could find. When I reached the top, the man slipped off one of his own garments—they were indeterminate in both color and shape—and laid it around my shoulders. Warmth spread through my chilled body; steam rose from my clothing. Sheer relief at finding myself alive almost blotted out my ability to think clearly, but not quite. I was out. I was alive. Had I passed a further test? Demonstrated the seventh and final virtue? The images I had seen as I rose could be interpreted as a map for the journey forward. But this map had shown me three Guardians, not four. Had I missed something? Or was the test not yet over?

"You're close to the end," the man said. "Very close. We'll walk back now."

I walked, following in his steps, and neither of us said a word all the way back to the cavern. By the time we got there, my hair and my clothing were completely dry.

The campfire was down to embers, and there was no sign of Flint. I laid on fresh wood, building it high. Very soon I was going to collapse into a shivering, exhausted heap. Quite likely I would want to weep, not tears of sorrow, but tears that recognized a day of momentous change, a day on which I had forgiven my dear ones for leaving me and released them to their rest.

But I must be strong a little longer. This was not finished. My companion had spoken of games, of tricks. He was holding something back, I was sure of it. A last challenge. A last puzzle. And an answer was coming to me as I watched the flames of the campfire leap and dance before us. Could it be . . . ? Could this really be . . . ?

I drank from my waterskin, then filled the pot and set it to heat. "After all that," I said, forcing my voice calm, "the least I can do is offer you a fresh brew." Let him stay here long enough for me to work this out. Let him sit here with me while I thought it through. The trickster from the old stories, the one with little sense of right and wrong, the one who could change his form at will. He could hide, he could eavesdrop, he could travel fast and covertly, because of his nature. There was only one way to outwit him.

I cast a sideways glance at my companion, who had

settled on a rock, a blind ancient once more. The firelight cast his shadow up on the wall behind him, the bent shoulders, the disordered hair, the old man's profile. At his feet sat the little dog, licking a front paw. "What did you see down there?" he asked.

"My family—" The words dried up in my mouth as the answer to my question revealed itself. I must do it now. Quickly, before he moved. But subtly. Divert his attention, then do it. Trick the trickster. "And I saw myself," I said. "On a journey. Would you like some more food? I'm sure the dog would welcome it." My pack was close to him, its ties open, the herbs at the top. "There might be the remains of a rabbit. Let me see."

I squatted down, making a show of looking in the bag. My right hand was concealed from him by the folds of my skirt; I snatched a stick charred black from the fire. I rose and took a step past my companion. "Where are those cups?" I muttered, and with a speed I did not think I had in me, I brought the charcoal up and drew a line around the silhouette the fire had thrown onto the wall. An old man's head, an old man's shadow. I moved back. He bent forward to scratch the dog behind the ear. And there was his profile, plain on the rock wall: noble brow, strong nose, decisive chin. No old man this, nor even a man at all, but something altogether more powerful.

"I don't know exactly what you are," I said, keeping my voice respectful, for if I was right, this was a being akin to an ancient god. "But I could hazard a guess."

He turned his head to look at the picture I had drawn,

and I wondered if he would be angry. But he seemed more amused. For a moment he was the boy again, with the boy's disturbing smile, a smile that told me nothing at all about his feelings.

"Oh, very sharp," he said, brows lifted. "A handsome profile, isn't it? Someone's raised you on old stories, I see. I suppose you know your quick wits have earned you a favor. Make sure you don't waste it."

"I will save it until it's needed."

"Wise as well as quick." He was mocking me now. "Let's have that brew, and while we drink it, tell me what you learned from Odd's Hole."

"You don't know already?"

"I may be full of tricks and turns, I may be more than usually agile, but I have not yet mastered the ability to be in two places at once. Besides, I asked not what you saw but what you learned. Tell me."

"You spoke of maps," I said, dropping a few pinches of dried herbs into the heating water. "I was given three maps. I'd say one was for the west, one for the north, and one for the east. Water, Earth, Air. I think I need to journey to each and find . . . a certain very powerful entity who may not especially want to be found. Someone who might be reluctant to get involved in a struggle that mostly concerns my kind, not theirs. I need to ask them for wisdom. Teaching."

"How cautiously you speak."

"When one wrong word can bring death, caution becomes a habit."

"And yet you jumped without hesitation. I did not think you would do it."

"I surprised myself." I still did not understand why I had obeyed a command that seemed an invitation to death by drowning. I had not stopped to weigh up the risk. I had simply acted. "Will you tell me the rest of the rhyme now? Down in Odd's Hole I saw my family, each of them in turn. Spoke with them. Made peace with them. Was that my final test?"

"I'll give you the rhyme and you be the judge. The last part goes like this," he said.

> To your lost, your slain, your broken,
> Grant forgiveness, set them free.
> Rise in strength, in truth and honor,
> Live for Alban's liberty.

"Stirring stuff. A call to arms. What do you think?"

My spine tingled with the strangeness of it. I wanted to weep. Farral would have loved those words. "I think it is very curious how an ancient rhyme can fit so well," I said, keeping my voice calm. "Almost as if it were written for me. But others must have been required to prove themselves in the same way."

"Maybe the rhyme is different every time," my companion said, offhand, and accepted a cup of the steaming brew. "Maybe it changes, fits itself to each Caller. Who knows? It does appear you've met the requirements: six virtues in the first verse, only one in the second, but perhaps that one is the most difficult. As for *rise in strength* and so on, it's your choice whether you obey those words; it's what a Caller does, but not everyone with the gift chooses to follow that path. For some it's too much, too hard. As for what you were shown, it's odd that there were only three maps, not four. What about the south?" He grinned, and for a moment his teeth were those of a predator, shining white and sharp as knives.

I swallowed, not wanting to show my ignorance. I might well be wrong about him. "You haven't told me who you are," I said, "and I haven't asked. But it seems to me perhaps I don't need to travel to the south, because the south has traveled to me." *Master of Shadows, guard my sleep,* those were the words of the old song. I could not think of anyone less likely to induce peaceful sleep than this volatile being.

"Good brew," said the old man. "Reminds me of a woman I knew once, can't recall her name, but she'd a rare gift with herbs. Short-lived, like all your kind, more's the pity. I liked her. As for the south, don't think you get off so lightly. We'll meet again sometime, you and me, and it won't be over a friendly cup of tea. There's a long journey ahead of you, much to learn, and some stubborn old creatures to persuade. Me, I don't play by any rules but my own, and I change those when the mood takes me. Before you next encounter me, practice your tricks. I like tricks." He glanced at the charcoal drawing again. "You didn't do so badly."

I nodded, trying to convey gratitude without saying

thank you. To utter such words to a fey being was to place oneself under an obligation that could later prove troublesome. I could hardly believe that I was sitting here talking to one of the Guardians in the flesh.

As if he could read my thoughts, the man said, "The others won't be so easy to find. They're hidden deep, and that's by choice. You've quite a journey ahead of you." He rose to his feet. "Come, dog!"

I unwrapped the garment he had given me from around my shoulders. It was no more than an old black rag. "You'll be wanting this back."

"Keep it," he said, downing the rest of his tea in one gulp and clicking his fingers to the dog. "I'll be off, then. Make sure your fire stays burning, lassie."

Beyond the creepers that screened the cave, the sky had turned to violet gray. Evening shadows lay over the land. I helped the old man get the bundle of wood onto his back and watched him walk away across the fells into the dusk. The little dog scampered ahead, turning every now and then to check that he was following. When they were lost to my eye, I went back into the cave and sat down very carefully by the fire. If not for the obvious signs that it was almost night, I might have been inclined to think the journey into Odd's Hole had been a mad dream. Somewhere inside me there was a burning will to reach Shadowfell, to march into battle, to wave the banner of freedom. At the same time I felt like an old rag that had been soaked, boiled, thumped on the stones, and wrung out hard.

"I can't tell him," I murmured to myself as I sipped at my drink and stared into the little fire. "Not this. Not yet."

When my cup was empty, I got up and wiped the charcoal marks from the cave wall, turning the striking profile into nothing but shadow.

CHAPTER FOURTEEN

DISPATCH: FOR THE EYES OF STAG TROOP
LEADER OWEN SWIFT-SWORD ONLY
Corbie's Wood district, end of autumn

*Owen, sent in haste. Keldec has recalled Stag
Troop to Winterfort under my command. Boar Troop
heads up the Rush valley in response to rumors of rebel
activity. It is late in the season for such a venture, but
the king's councillor overruled my protests. Sending this
with Dugald, who leads them.*

*I hope to see you in the east before winter closes in.
Be careful, friend.*

Rohan Death-Blade, Stag Troop

Before full dark I saw Flint coming along the ridge from the nearest stand of pines. He'd checked a trap on the way in; the limp form of some small furred creature hung from his hand, swaying to and fro as he approached. His expression was carefully guarded. It was only when he had come into the cave and set down his bag, his weaponry, and the little corpse he carried that I saw the look in his eyes.

"I'm happy to see you back safe," I said, keeping my tone steady and reassuring. The day had been momentous for me. After my visitor had gone, I had wept alone by my fire, but they had been good tears, shed for the past I had let go. Now I felt like a new-forged weapon, shining and eager. But Flint . . . What had he seen today to set such darkness on his face?

"Mm." He took out his knife, squatted down, and began skinning the creature.

"Did everything go to plan?"

"Mm."

I kept quiet while he finished his butchering job. He did it untidily, as if his mind was elsewhere. When he had reduced the catch to a few chunks of meat, he threaded them on a sharpened stick, using more violence than was quite necessary.

"I did cook a meal," I said. "We can save part of that for the morning."

Flint made a sound that might have meant anything and sat back with his bloody hands around his knees. I set the cooking pot on the fire and found a stick to stir the oatmeal mixture with. Outside, it was already night. The days were growing short indeed. I found a cloth, trickled water on it from the skin, passed it to him. "Clean your hands," I said.

It was only then that he seemed to notice the blood. He gave his hands a cursory wipe, then reached to turn over his skewered meat. "There's a change of plan," he said, not looking at me.

I was suddenly cold. So close to Shadowfell, with my tests passed, and now this. Had the Enforcers found out where I was? Had his comrades started to suspect him? "What change?"

"I can't take you on straightaway. You'll need to stay here awhile. Another three days and it should be safe to move."

"Three days?" After today, the prospect of a delay was hard to bear. "Why? No, don't answer that."

"I'll need you to lie low. I've picked up a few more supplies for you. If you're careful, there will be sufficient to last you until it's safe to go on. Stay in the cave. You'll have to go out to the stream for water and for your ablutions, but try to keep that to once a day if you can, and while you're out there, be constantly alert. Keep the knife with you. No other forays, you understand? The risk is too high."

I sat there staring at him. "You mean you're not staying."

Flint was avoiding my gaze. "I'll be here tonight, then

I must be gone. There's a matter to attend to, something I don't want you involved in. Do as I bid you and you'll be perfectly safe. I will come back for you. Three days, perhaps four."

After a lengthy silence, he said, "You've managed on your own before."

I bit back a retort. Whatever it was, he wouldn't be leaving me if he didn't need to. "I can remember you telling me I was making a pretty poor job of it," I said, struggling for a light tone.

He looked at me now and his eyes were steady, though the shadow still lurked there. "I was perhaps a little unfair in my comment. You were weak, sick. You frightened me."

"That meat is burning," I said, dropping my gaze. "What was it, a marten?"

"Hardly worth the effort. A mouthful or two each. Just as well you cooked something." A fleeting smile touched his lips. "I'll fetch more wood for you in the morning. Any sign of activity today? Friends, helpers?"

"You mean . . . No, there has been no sign of them." After a moment I added, "You need not worry that I'll be tempted to go on alone. You've succeeded in scaring me out of any such inclination."

The smile was gone. "I'm sorry I can't tell you more. Believe me, you're safer not knowing. I'll give you some explanations when we reach Shadowfell."

"I thought you weren't staying on there."

"I can stay a few days."

"I see."

"No more of this," Flint said. "Let us eat this meal, and sit by our fire together, and sleep peacefully, for this one night at least."

"You'll need to leave early, I suppose." I hated that look on his face, his mouth tight, his eyes full of unrest.

"Not so early that I cannot fetch wood and make sure you have what you need." Already I was hearing farewell in his voice.

"I'll miss you." The words were out before I had time to consider how they sounded, what he might take them to mean. I stared down at my hands.

"Look on tonight as a gift." Flint's voice was a murmur. "Time. Quiet. Companionship. I had not understood the value of such things."

I served the meal without a word, sharing the gruel-like mixture between pot and pannikin, pushing the pot over to Flint. He took the pieces of meat from the skewer and divided them between us.

"Let us forget the world beyond this cave until tomorrow," Flint said.

"Alban was different once," I said, dipping my spoon in the bowl. "Before Keldec, people told tales around the fire after supper. Sang songs. Nobody listened to make sure the words were safe."

Glancing across in the silence that followed this, I met Flint's eyes and saw there a curious expression; it was almost hungry. I remembered the little boy of my dream.

Had that child grown up with harp and whistle and the telling of tales?

"The year I was born was the year Keldec came to the throne," I told him. "I never lived in that other Alban. But I did grow up hearing stories. My grandmother knew many, and my father loved to sing. Back then."

"Your mother?"

"She died when I was three years old, giving birth to a stillborn son. Father was heartbroken, but he was a stronger man then. He still had Farral and me, and Grandmother to keep him on a straight path."

"Neryn."

I looked across at him again.

"Was your father canny too?"

I shook my head.

"Your grandmother?"

"She had a gift. The Sight, people used to call it. Sometimes she saw things that were to come. She couldn't summon her ability when she felt the need. It came of itself, as a vision in a pool or a bowl of water. Or in the flames of a hearth fire. What she saw scared her sometimes."

Flint looked into the fire as if it might hold mysteries stranger than any tale. "Did she tell you about her visions?" he asked.

"Not often. She said it was dangerous to know the future. Too much knowledge might set a person on wrong paths. If you knew something bad was coming, you might take steps to try to prevent it. The Sight doesn't work that way. You can't know if what you're shown is the certain future or simply a possible future. She didn't have time to teach me everything she wanted to. Some of it, she was keeping until I was older. But . . . well, you know what happened." I hesitated. "When I told you, it was the first time I'd told the whole of that story to anyone. About what they did to her. I was never able to say it before."

"You say she was teaching you. Does that mean you share the same gift?"

"I don't have the Sight, no. Grandmother was an herbalist, a healer. She was teaching me those skills. Which plants to gather and when; what is effective against certain conditions; how to make infusions, decoctions, salves; how to extract oils. How to set a broken limb or lance a boil. Simple enough skills; they should be no cause for suspicion. But they are. So she taught a very little at a time. I wish I had learned more."

"At Shadowfell," Flint said quietly, "there are folk who can teach you, if that is the path you wish to follow."

I did not think I would be spending time on herbs and healing. After today, it was all too clear what my path must be. But it was too soon to share the revelations I had been given. When we reached Shadowfell, I would tell him.

Beyond the cave mouth, the darkness deepened. It was a night of no stars; the moon lay hidden behind a veil of heavy cloud. We sat by our fire, exchanging a word or two from time to time, nothing of much import. We did not tell tales or sing songs, though I allowed myself to imagine a future in which I would pass on to him the stories my grandmother had told me when I was growing up, and the tunes my father had whistled, and maybe the grand old song I had sung to the ghosts of Hiddenwater and shared with a brollachan. Once or twice the two of us would glance up at the same time and our eyes would meet, and I wondered if the feeling that passed through me was the same for Flint. Not desire, not exactly, though his plain features had become pleasing to me. I liked his strong, capable hands and his well-made form. But the trust we shared was too newfound, too fragile for anything beyond the touch of hands, the occasional brushing of one body against another. All the same, our eyes spoke of something good, something deep, something that could grow and flower if the world we lived in would allow it. Something too precious to put into words. Something I would not dare let out into the light of day, not yet.

I wanted to tell him to stay safe, to take care, to make sure he came back to me. I wanted to ask what had made him so grim and quiet when he emerged from the trees earlier. I wanted to be the one who could gentle that hunted look off his face, who could reassure him that the world was not all hurt and violence and madness. But that was to assume too much. He was not staying at Shadowfell. He was going back to Keldec. The questions that hung over that choice could not be asked, not now, and perhaps not ever. They forbade any expression of tenderness. They forbade my speaking to him as if I had a right to care about his welfare. I hoped my eyes might convey, at the very least, that I was going to be lonely without him.

Sometime in the night I woke with a start to hear the voices of wolves on the wind. The sound was eerie, forlorn, a song of cold and loneliness and survival. It was a hungry season for all who picked a living in this harsh place. I moved to add wood to the fire, which had burned down to embers.

I looked across the fire. Where Flint had been lying wrapped in his cloak, there was nobody. I felt a jolt of panic. Gone already? He had said *in the morning*. He had said he would gather wood, he had told me—

"Neryn? I'm here." His voice came like a breath of darkness. He was up by the cave mouth, gazing into the night, where the pale moon now peered out between clouds, setting a chill light on the rocks around our haven.

I threw my cloak over my shoulders and scrambled out to stand beside him. Gods, it was cold! My fingers were numb; I could barely feel my feet.

Flint was as still as a man of stone. The moonlight touched his features, revealing him as a person of flesh and blood, for on his strong face the cold glow illuminated the glittering path of a tear.

Nothing to say; how could I find the right words? I laid my hand against his back and kept it there, willing some of my warmth to flow into him. We stood thus a long time. Eventually he moved, muttering something about my getting cold, and the two of us returned to the cave.

"It's freezing," I said. "Why don't we put one cloak underneath, and the two of us lie on it, and the rest of these covers can go over both of us?" And when he said nothing, just looked at me, I said, "All I'm suggesting is that we keep each other warm. If you feel responsible for my welfare, this is your way to make sure I don't freeze to death before I get to Shadowfell." I realized that I had said it; I had spoken the word aloud to him at last.

He might have said, *What about tomorrow night?* But he did not, merely helped me spread out his cloak on the cave floor. The two of us lay down on it awkwardly, side by side, and pulled the rest of the bedding over us. Without touching him, I felt Flint's unease. Without touching him, I felt the warmth from his body spreading into mine, banishing the chill and filling me with well-being, comfort, rightness. Outside, the night was quiet now. Within our haven, the fire made dancing patterns on the walls.

I fell asleep with my heart at peace. I opened my eyes at first light. I was lying on my side under the coverings and Flint was curled behind me, his body touching mine at chest and thighs, his arm flung over me. If I had been half-asleep a moment ago, I was wide awake now. I should get up, move away. To be so close to him was utterly wrong. But he seemed so peaceful; I did not want to wake him. I did not really want to move at all. *I will remember this,* I thought. *I'll remember it when I'm cold, weary, and alone.* I lay still awhile, not thinking beyond the sensations in my body. Then Flint woke, and without a word about the semi-embrace in which we found ourselves, we moved apart and rose to face the new day.

Flint packed his bag. I heated up the leftover food while he fetched more wood and stacked it for me. He gave me a bigger knife, a serious-looking weapon I hoped I would not need to use. And then we were sitting by our fire once again, and there was a quality in the silence that was more troubling than all my fears for his safety.

"Neryn?"

"Mm?"

"I have something to tell you. Something I want you to hear before I go. Will you promise to listen until I've said all I need to say?"

I did not like the tone of his voice, or the words.

"Are you sure you want to tell me now?" If he had to go away, let him get on with it before I had time to think too much. Let him complete today's mission, whatever it was, and come safely back so we could go on together. Let him perform the task without being killed or hurt or taken. The time for explanations was when we reached Shadowfell.

"Want to, no. Need to, yes. Promise me you won't interrupt until I'm finished. Promise you will listen to the end."

Now he was scaring me. What could this be? "All right," I said.

He sat opposite me, his eyes somber, his fingers twisting restlessly together. "You know, I imagine, that the king has a number of canny folk in his household." He had lowered his voice to the merest murmur. "Folk whose abilities he uses for his own ends. What is outlawed in the general community is accepted within his inner circle, and that includes the Enforcers. A talent for, say, being able to pass through walls, or to hear as acutely as a cat does, might prove extremely useful to such a person. As might, indeed, the skill of seeing into the future."

Since he had told me not to interrupt, I only nodded. My expression no doubt revealed my opinion of Keldec and his exploitation of magic. This was no surprise to me; it had been common knowledge in Corbie's Wood, and was understood all across the west. Not that folk spoke of it the way Flint did. It was a hushed comment here, a whisper there, with always a glance over the shoulder in case the wrong person might be listening.

"I . . ." He hesitated, his brows drawing together in a frown. "We spoke of the western isles before. I was not born there, but sent. As a small child, to be . . . trained. When I was eighteen years old, I went to court. My skills were of value to the king. I have been there ever since. I belong to Keldec's inner circle, Neryn. He has few friends. I am . . . He considers me the closest of those friends."

In my mind was a picture of Flint on that island, a little boy learning what an Enforcer needed to learn: how to break down a door with a single well-placed kick, how to extract a confession by torture, how to wreak terror in the king's name. How to perform those acts and survive.

How to remain obedient even when his orders made him sick. The thought of it was disturbing, and yet most shocking of all was the revelation that he was not only the king's obedient henchman but also his friend. That, I could not picture.

"I have to say to you that—" He cleared his throat and started again. "You have more reason than most to hate the king's authority. To despise those who enforce it for him. You've suffered grievous losses. You've seen the very worst of what his rule has brought to Alban. But—" He broke off once more, staring down at his hands. "A pox on it," he muttered. "There is no right way to say this."

"What? I know you are an Enforcer. I know you are connected with the rebel movement, and I can imagine how hard that makes your life. You've taken a terrible risk to help me. I understand that it isn't safe for you to explain any more, not yet anyway. What is so important that I must hear it now?"

"I . . . Neryn, I . . . What you understand about enthrallment, what you saw with your grandmother, that is not the true nature of mind-mending. It is a twisted variant, an evil distortion of what was once a noble art. People have forgotten what it was in times past; they have seen it only as this perverted mockery. Mind-mending is not the destructive practice you have witnessed. Used as it should be, to heal, it can be a powerful tool for good."

A cold snake of dread was curling around me, squeezing

at my vitals. "So I've been told," I said. "Though I never quite believed it. Flint, whatever you have to tell me, just say it."

Flint reached up to the collar of his tunic. His hand was shaking. There was a cord around his neck; I had seen it before but had not given much thought to what might be strung on it. Men often wore a lucky stone, a family talisman, a token from an employer or patron.

He drew the thing out, and it was no lucky stone, no stag amulet, no rune or sign of protection. It was a tiny transparent vial, held in place by an elaborate clasp of silver shaped like the clawed foot of a bird of prey. My shocked eyes took in every detail: the delicate five-sided shape of the container, like a long crystal; the intricate chasing on the silver talons; an area of scratching to one side, as if it had at some time been roughly handled. Around the top, just below the clasp, was wound a lock of honey-colored hair. Within the vial something stirred, something a little like smoke and a little like water.

"This is my canny skill, Neryn," Flint said, and his voice might have been that of death itself. "I am a mind-mender. You mustn't—"

My gorge rose. Spots danced before my eyes. The cave went night-dark, and blood-red, and began to turn in circles around me. I jumped to my feet and staggered outside, where I was violently sick, retching up my breakfast down the front of my gown and onto the rocks. I clutched my arms around myself as my stomach churned with spasm after spasm. My ears rang. My eyes and nose streamed. I could barely stay on my feet.

"Let me help you." He was here, looming up beside me, his fingers on my skin—

"Don't touch me!" I wrenched my arm from his grasp and bolted, stumbling over the uneven ground, slipping on the pebbles, tripping on tussock, running, running toward the shelter of the pines, anywhere away, away from him.

"Neryn, stop! Wait! You promised to hear me out! Neryn, listen to me!"

"Get away! Leave me alone!" Oh gods, I had thought him my friend, my guardian, my savior, and all the time he was one of *them*. . . .

Revulsion sped my feet, but I knew Flint could outrun me. The wood lay some hundred paces ahead. His boots crunched on the stones not far behind me. I heard his hard breathing. My chest was tight and sore; each breath hurt more than the last. In my head, throbbing pain warred with images of Grandmother staggering toward me, her eyes those of a stranger; of Garret and the little son who would grow up while his father remained a child. I dug deep within myself and summoned what I needed. The call burst from me, silent, powerful. *Hide me. Help me.*

Tendrils of mist snaked out from the dark place under the trees. The vapor moved too fast to be a natural thing, enveloping me, cloaking me in its clouds, twisting and tangling about me and drawing me up the hill toward the wood. There were shapes in it: a queen in a long gown, a fighting man whose sword flashed silver through the wreathing fog, a big-eyed child in tattered garments, a great white hound. They merged and changed even as my head turned from one to another, for none held its form for longer than a heartbeat. They led me, pushed me, swept me forward, until the darkness of the pines fell over me, and my juddering heart began to slow, and I knew I was hidden. The vapor formed a thin, pale curtain around the little grove where I stood. I could see through it to the outside, but my instincts told me nobody could see in. It seemed to me that some of these trees that hedged me around were . . . not quite trees. I held myself still, my feet on a dense carpet of needles, my hands against the trunk of a pine. I tried to quiet my breathing.

"Neryn!" He was out there, calling. "Where are you? Come out and talk to me!"

I listened. I breathed. I spoke not a word.

"Neryn, you know I have to go soon. I can't leave you here like this, I must be sure you're safe. Please come out and listen to me. Neryn!"

His voice was uneven, cracking; he strode through the woods, one way, the other way, his face linen-pale, his fists clenched.

If it's so important to go, then go, I told him silently. *I pray to all the gods that I never see you again.*

He stayed a long time, hunting for me, begging me to reveal myself. He stayed so long that he would surely be late getting to wherever he was going. He would not find me. The Watch of the North had its own uncanny powers, and I was thankful from the bottom of my heart that they had answered my call.

I watched Flint make a final turn around the little wood, jogging now. He called my name one last time. His voice was hoarse with shouting. I saw him return to the cave and emerge soon after with his bag on his back and his sword at his belt. He took a final look up toward the wood, and then he was gone.

Even so, I stood a long time among the trees, motionless, scarcely breathing. I waited until the sun had risen higher behind its veil of clouds, and small birds were busy foraging in the trees, and my back ached from the effort of keeping still. I waited until I was sure—as sure as I could be—that Flint was really gone. Then I murmured, "My respects to you. I will leave here now," and with a shivering movement the almost-trees parted and the mist lifted to let me through.

Down at the cave I wiped off my vomit-spattered gown. I scoured the cook pot, the bowls, the spoons. I picked up the blankets and folded them precisely. Just last night I had lain there beside him. I had felt comfort in his warmth; this morning I had not wanted to get up and face the day, for it had felt good to be close to him, sheltered by him. It set my stomach churning to think of it, to picture that thing around his neck, that accursed vessel only Enthrallers wore. How could I not have seen it before?

I built up the fire and sat down by it. I drank some water from the flask. Beyond the cave mouth the sky was duller now, and the air had the strange warmth that means snow is coming.

My hair. He had cut that lock from my head that night at the farm in the Rush valley, when I'd been fighting to get a comb through the tangles. But he could have worked his foul magic on me long before that, on the very first night we were together, encamped on the hill near Darkwater. How easy for him to take advantage of my exhaustion and change my thoughts so I would trust him. So I would see him not as an agent of the king but as someone who could be my friend. If not on that first night, then surely he had worked his magic on one of the many nights we had spent in the little hut above Corbie's Wood, when I had been too feverish to be aware of much at all. What a complete fool I had been, how gullible, how stupid! No wonder my dreams had been so confused; no wonder they had been full of dark and threatening things I had no names for. No wonder I had dreamed so often of Flint himself, as a child, as a man; no wonder his story had woven its way into my sleep, as if he and I were two parts of the same whole. I had been all too ready to forgive him and to see in him a good man, despite everything he was and everything he did. He had twisted my mind with his so-called mind-mending. The Enthrallers' work was to turn strong-minded folk, folk with canny gifts, into loyal subjects of Keldec. To make them think the king worthy, a great leader, someone whose will they were honored to work. But it would be easy enough for a mind-scraper to make a person follow *him* instead. That was what Flint had done. Made me care about him. Rendered me blind to his faults. Wound my hair around his wretched vial like a trophy.

"How dare you order me to hear you out!" I muttered. "How dare you try to tell me that your gift is something noble and good! How can it be, when every village has its own ruined victim wandering about dazed and hollow and frightened? How dare you say you wouldn't lie to me? Everything you've said, every single thing you've done, is a lie!"

I sat hunched over the fire, shivering. Images filled my mind: Flint striding away down the mountain; Flint looking out into the night with tears spilling down his cheeks; Flint, always so neat with his hands, butchering a marten and spilling blood everywhere. Flint sleeping, warm against me. Flint's beautiful eyes, shining in the firelight, full of falsehoods. Flint shouting my name, his voice broken and exhausted. In my mind, words from the trickster's rhyme repeated themselves over and over. *To your lost, your slain, your broken, grant forgiveness.* But the rhyme was nothing to do with Flint. He was not lost, slain, or broken. And some things could never be forgiven.

I sat there until the fire had burned down to nothing. I spread out the ashes and sprinkled earth on top. I packed my bag. I took the last of the oatmeal, the precious supply of dried fruit, the remains of the hard cheese that we had brought from the hut. Let Flint find his own food. I rolled up one blanket and strapped it atop the bag. I put on my cloak. Time to go.

"Do what you want," I whispered, taking a last look around the cave. The place was as lonely as a tomb, its corners full of shadows. "Meddle with my dreams, put your own poxy thoughts in my head. I'll fight you. I won't be anyone's puppet. A man who lies to me will never be my friend. I don't need you. I don't want you. I'll get to Shadowfell on my own."

Chapter Fifteen

THE GOOD FOLK OF THE NORTH WERE SUBTLE beings. I sensed them as whispers on the icy wind, as creakings among the stones, as half-glimpsed, fleeting shadows, here then gone. I had wondered if I might see them more clearly when I camped for the night. But when my long day's walk was done and I crept into a makeshift refuge under the roots of a great fallen tree, the best bolt-hole I could find in the gathering dusk, no small creatures pattered in to greet me.

I did not dare make fire in case Flint was close enough to see it and find me. It would snow by morning; I felt it in the air. Tomorrow, there would be no hiding my tracks. They would lie in the white, an announcement of my presence and a signpost to my destination. But if I waited, if I stayed in hiding, I might still be here next spring, a frozen corpse tangled in the tree roots. Or bare bones, picked over by the wolves; their voices had reached me on the wind as I walked. I wondered how Flint would feel if he stumbled on my remains. Would he be sad, or merely annoyed that he had failed in his mission, whatever it truly was?

Gods, it was cold! Why had I left that second blanket for Flint? I must have been mad. I imagined sharing my refuge with the wolves; I thought how warm that would feel, how welcome their hairy bodies would be against my shivering one. Provided they did not eat me. If the only pickings here were mice and martens, it was no wonder the creatures howled so. They must be ravenous.

No cooking without a fire. I ate a handful of raw oats, nibbled a shriveled circle of dried apple, drank some water. It came to me that the cold was so intense I might be dead before morning. To die thus, through my own miscalculation, would be a sorry end indeed to my journey. *"Rise in strength,"* I whispered. *"Live for Alban's liberty."* Those stirring words had filled me with hope. Now they only served to show me my own weakness.

There were the Good Folk, of course. I could send out another call and hope they were nearby. I could ask for a hot, smokeless fire or a magical garment or a big dog to warm me. But that felt wrong. A gift like mine was not only precious, it was dangerous. I had called upon them to hide me from Flint, and they had been quick to help me. But I must not squander my gift on making my life more comfortable. If I was to be in their debt, let it be because there was no other choice.

But perhaps there need not be a debt at all. The transaction could be an exchange. The Giving Hand. There certainly wasn't much to give tonight, but I did have the remnants of the food and I could share that. If I was on the right track, if I evaded Flint and the Enforcers, I might be at Shadowfell by dusk tomorrow. I need only keep sufficient for one more meal.

In the darkness I found a piece of bark and shook out a small heap of oats onto it. I crumbled cheese at one side and laid three shriveled plums at the other. There was almost a disaster as I tripped while carrying this meager feast over to a flat rock a few paces from my bolt-hole under the roots.

"Here," I whispered into the night. "This is for you. Not much, but the best I can do right now." I did not say I was freezing. I did not ask for help. I retreated under the roots, wrapped my shawl over my head, pulled cloak and blanket around me, and tried not to think of the cold.

I waited. Images of roaring flames, of glowing lamps, of fur cloaks and woolen coverlets, processed through my mind. Pots of steaming soup. Tubs of warm water in chambers heated by bright hearth fires. Most treacherous of all was the memory of how it had felt to lie under the blankets with Flint's body close to mine and his arm over me. *Get out of my mind,* I told him. *I despise you. I would freeze to death before I let you touch me again.*

It seemed to me, as time passed and my body came close to the point where it no longer had the will even to shiver, that this really was the end, and a pretty poor one it was proving to be. My mission was a complete failure. Sorrel's death had been for nothing. The help the Good

Folk had given me, Sage's courage, the selfless aid of Mara, the patience of Hollow, had all been wasted. I should have risked a fire. Too late now. I might strike a spark, but there'd be no finding dry wood in the dark.

My chest hurt in an all-too-familiar way. Each breath seemed to draw cold deep into me, as if it would turn my very bones to ice. How did creatures survive here? How did they carry on?

Nobody would come. The place was empty. I would die all alone. Even the shades of my family, which sometimes seemed to linger close around me, were absent tonight. Perhaps, after Odd's Hole, they would visit me no more. "Grandmother," I murmured through chattering teeth. "Father. Mother. Farral." A charm to keep away the dark. A lamp to illuminate the night. But I had no sense of them at all. There was only the wilderness. Shadows pressed close around me. "Flint," I whispered, not knowing why I spoke his name.

Tap. Tap, tap. Something was pecking at the oats. Something that showed pale in the night, something white, with feathers, about the size of a small dog. Tap, tappity-tap. I dared not move lest I startle it away. I watched, clutching the blanket around me, as it investigated the cheese, sampled a little, then ate the dried plums, one, two, three. What was it, an owl? The shape was rounded, compact, the plumage neat and glossy, the legs sturdy. When it turned its head to gaze at me, its eyes gleamed of themselves, round and strange. A not-quite-owl. Perhaps that was a feather cape, and underneath it . . . I could not see clearly, but the legs seemed to end not in a set of owlish talons but in a pair of small, well-crafted boots.

"G-g-greetings," I stammered.

The creature inclined its head. What there was of moonlight showed its face to be somewhat human in shape and form, save for those great eyes.

"You'll be dead before morning," it observed. Its voice was as much an owl's as a young man's.

"I hope not," I managed. "If you c-can help me, I'd welcome that. I am . . . almost at my d-destination. One more d-day . . ."

"You seek the Folds?"

"No, I—" Wait a moment. The Folds . . . I'd heard that name before. A name the Good Folk used when speaking of Shadowfell. "I am headed for a p-place close to there, yes. B-but without a fire . . ."

"You'll soon freeze, aye. I can help. You're no' afraid of a few wee doggies?"

"I j-just need to g-get warm. . . ."

The owlish creature let out an eldritch hollow cry that sent shivers up my spine. There was a silence; the very air around us seemed to be waiting. Then came the reply: the howling of many wolfish voices. I rose to my feet, stumbling in my haste. The creature shook its head.

They were here, a circle of them in the darkness, their eyes pinpricks of light as they edged closer. My heart was in my mouth. They were beautiful, no doubt of that;

beautiful and deadly. I could smell them now, their hunger, their pride, their wildness. They padded forward, and I could see the white gleam of their teeth. Well, I thought crazily, I would at least provide a good meal for this hungry pack. I would die doing something useful.

"Go small!" The voice of the owl-like being rang out in a command, and the wolves obeyed. As they crept into my shelter, they shrank. My knees gave way under me, and I sat down abruptly. The wolves settled all around me, a squirming, jostling, licking flow of them, squeezing in close, climbing on my lap, curling by my legs and body. Each was no bigger than a two-month pup. As they pressed against me, my frozen body began to thaw. Gods, what a gift it was to be warm! It seemed I would live until morning after all.

"Aye, that'll do." The owl was keeping a firm eye on the pack. "No fighting, mind. No nipping and jostling about. Keep the lassie safe till sunup, you understand?" The big eyes met mine. "Stay in there. No going out before first light or I can't answer for what might befall you. There's blood on the air. Blood and iron."

Before I could frame words, the creature spread its wings and took flight, a white phantom vanishing into a darkness through which a few delicate flakes of snow had begun to fall. Cushioned by the soft blanket of a dozen slumbering wolf bodies, I surrendered to sleep.

They left at dawn, rippling out into the brightening world, leaving behind only their wild scent. As they passed the outermost roots of the fallen giant under which we had sheltered, the little wolves returned to their full size, not needing any command. From one breath to the next they were themselves again, their powerful, long-limbed bodies flowing away across the new-fallen snow. They moved as one. Almost before I had time to get up, to stretch, to draw breath in this new day, they were gone.

I owed them my life. In return, all I had offered was that poor apology for a meal. Truly an uneven exchange. But I knew enough old stories to understand that what I had given was sufficient. The value of the gift itself did not matter; its true worth lay in its importance to the giver. If a handful of oats represented half of a traveler's provisions, or more than half, it was a worthy gift indeed.

Perhaps, I thought as I packed my bag once more and shook out my cloak (I would smell of wolf for some time to come), my life would be worth something to the Good Folk in the long run. According to the Master of Shadows, I had demonstrated all seven virtues. I had stepped onto the road that led to becoming a skilled Caller. Once I had learned to harness my gift wisely, I could play my part in the fight for Alban's freedom. I could help change the future. But first I must reach Shadowfell. *Today,* I told myself. *Today you're walking to Giant's Fist. There will be time to worry about what's next when you get there.*

I picked my way down a narrow track to the valley floor, keeping an eye out for trouble. The terrain here was stony and difficult. There were no river flats, no fields, only broken ground tumbled with boulders whose ancient rock bore occasional patches of moss or lichen. A stream ran along a bed of gray shingle. It wound between small stands of pine, and it was in the cover of those trees that I stopped when I grew weary, stretching my limbs and catching my breath before I moved on. I did not allow myself to rest for long. If the wind got up later, the cold would be perishing. My fingers were numb, my feet aching. I tried not to think about another night spent in the open, in makeshift shelter. A little voice whispered inside me, *This would be so much easier if Flint were here.*

Many streamlets rushed down these hillsides, leaping from rock to rock in cascades of white. The waterway on the valley floor grew broader as I followed its course. I wondered if there was a lake at the foot of those mountains that lay ahead. What if this stream joined another and became a swift, wide river like the Rush? In a place like this there would surely be no bridges. What if I could not get across? I had one day's provisions left, and a scant day at that.

No trace of the white owl today. No trace of anyone, though my steps were printed plain behind me in the snow. Had Flint passed this way already? And what about that troop of Enforcers? If they were behind me, I would lead them straight to Shadowfell. If they were ahead, I might be walking into a trap.

I walked on nonetheless, wondering where Flint's true loyalty lay. Who was he really working for, Keldec or the rebels? An Enthraller's skills were a powerful weapon in anyone's hand. Fear of mind-scraping kept folk quiet, obedient, docile. People like Dunchan of Silverwater and his wife, who had died for their convictions, were rare. Would a rebel leader think to harness mind-scraping to his own ends? Would he consider using it not to make folk loyal to Keldec but to turn them against him? That could win the war. It could be Keldec's downfall. But it would be wrong. Harness an evil power to serve a noble cause and surely that cause would be sullied forever.

What was Flint really up to? He had been so convincing, with his talk of freedom and a new Alban in which folk could be at peace. I could swear he meant every word. But if he had worked his mind-scraping charm on me, of course I would believe everything he said. So maybe he had been working for the king all the time. Maybe bringing me so far along the valley was part of some elaborate plan. . . . But what plan? And if he had won my allegiance with his foul magic, how was it I could see through him now? "Curse you," I muttered. "Curse you and your clever lies."

I paused atop a rise, my attention caught by a slight sound behind me. I turned to look. Close at hand, the neat prints of my feet in their unusual shoes stood out clearly on the snow. But farther away a disturbance in the air, like a miniature whirlwind, was tracing my path. As it passed, the snow danced up, spinning beneath it. I stared, gaping. It looked like a great invisible bird going by, its wings beating above the ground, stirring the snow to hide my pathway. Where it had traveled, there was no trace of footprints.

I bowed my head in acknowledgment, wondering that I was not more surprised, and moved on. Few trees ahead; few hiding places. If pursuers came up behind me, all I could do was run.

From down here I could no longer see the stone column of Giant's Fist, for the contour of this narrow valley blocked it from view. I could glimpse the foothills ahead and the snowy peaks beyond them, but the landmark I needed was still out of sight. I must press on until the terrain opened up again. How long? Gods, let me reach the place in daylight. Let me be in those hills before I had to find shelter for the night again. Let me be somewhere I could safely make a fire.

Fresh snow began to fall, drifting down around me in big flakes, settling gently on my cloak. The air grew colder. I no longer stopped to rest, but made myself keep walking. My head felt muzzy, as if I might be close to fainting. I couldn't feel my hands. Somewhere in my mind someone was saying, *You said you could look after yourself. You've made a pretty poor job of it.*

"Go away," I muttered as the wind picked up and the snow began to move sideways, clinging to my eyelashes and coating the fold of shawl I was holding over my mouth and nose. "I will get there. I can get there." Left foot, right foot. One, two.

As the wind grew stronger still, howling around the bare stones of the hillside, whistling down from the mountaintops, the valley opened up and there it was before me:

Giant's Fist, two miles or so to the northwest. Between me and the great column lay a landscape strewn with boulders, pitted with crevices, spiked with jutting spears of stone, a nightmare of traps for the weary traveler.

"Not so bad," I murmured to myself, hitching up my bag. At least there would be places to hide if the Enforcers came. But the going would be slow. How long until night-fall? Could I cross this broken place before it grew too dark to do so in any safety?

A sound came on the wind. Was that a man's voice, calling? My heart jolted. Cold sweat broke out all over my body. The shout had come from somewhere behind me. They were on my track. They were catching up.

I glanced over my shoulder, but there was no movement to be seen on the stony way down the valley, save for a pair of hawks above, turning in slow circles.

I headed out across the uneven terrain. Everything in me wanted to run, run, to stay ahead of them, of *him,* the man who had stolen a part of me and expected me to be-lieve that was a good thing. But running would be stupid. If I fell and broke my ankle, I'd surely be taken.

My hands were clammy. My heart sounded a wild drumbeat. I made myself breathe slowly. I made myself judge each step with care, consider each choice. Should I scramble up and across that great boulder there, or slip through that narrow way, which might lead to a dead end? Should I attempt a snaking progress through the fissures and cracks, or go higher so I could fix my direction, even though I risked being picked off by an arrow?

A narrow track revealed itself, winding between the rocks. I clambered down and headed along it. At first it seemed to be taking me roughly northward, but after a while it branched and branched again. With cloud blanketing the sun, it was hard to choose my way. A right fork. A left fork. The middle path of three. My skin began to prickle with unease. I paused; I thought someone paused with me. I moved on, and sensed a furtive, near-silent presence somewhere not very far away. Someone was tracking me.

What was it Silver had said at Howling Rock? *Only the most skilled of human trackers could find us here.* And not long afterward, Flint had walked silently into our secure haven and the Good Folk had fled from his presence and his iron weapons. I held my breath; somewhere among the rocks someone else did the same. I waited, counting the beats of my heart. Nothing moved. No whisper sounded in the silence. The snow fell steadily.

My back was aching. My arms hurt. I longed to set down my pack, if only for a moment, until I caught my breath again. I held myself still, ears alert for any sound. Nothing. If I did not move soon, I might not be able to walk.

With painstaking care I took a step, setting my foot down as softly as I could. Another step. A breath. No answering step this time. Perhaps my pursuer had given up. I took a third step.

A hand came over my mouth, strong, leather-gloved, stifling any sound. A well-muscled arm pinned me back against a chest. A big knife flashed close to my face. My captor hissed in my ear.

"Not a squeak or I'll slit your throat. Now walk."

CHAPTER SIXTEEN

MY BODY WAS A JANGLE OF SHOCKED PARTS that did not seem to belong together. Walk? I could hardly breathe. The hands shifted their grip; my captor was trusting me not to speak, it seemed, for my mouth was freed and I was being half ushered, half dragged through the narrow ways between the rocks, left, right, up, down, a swifter, rougher passage than I could possibly have found for myself, until a sudden turn, a zigzag descent, and a final slide down a pebbly slope brought us onto a broad expanse of level ground, encircled by rock walls perhaps twice a tall man's height. As I was marched out into the open area, my heart pounding, I saw that there were people there, twelve, maybe fifteen of them, grim-faced folk plainly dressed in clothing of thick felted wool or sheepskin. Most of them were young, and all of them were armed. There were bows and arrows, clubs, knives, swords, staves, and other implements whose names I did not know but whose purpose was not hard to guess. I fought back my panic, looking for telltale signs: a stag brooch, an Enforcer's cloak, a weapon similar to Flint's. It would be easy enough for king's men to go in disguise. I could see nothing obvious.

All eyes were on us as we approached. The faces wore a uniform expression of surprise. I had had my own surprise when my captor first spoke, and it was reinforced when, suddenly released from the grip of those powerful arms, I turned to take a look.

The person was tall, broad-shouldered, and clad in a padded wool tunic and trousers, over which were a leather breast piece and arm braces. Strong boots; heavy gauntlets; a short sword at the belt and an ax in a sort of sling. A leather cap; a swathing cloth over nose and mouth, above which a pair of long-lashed dark eyes regarded me as if I were not a trophy, nor yet an enemy, but merely a fool and a nuisance. The warrior garments just failed to conceal what my captor's voice had already revealed to me: this formidable individual was a young woman.

She pushed me ahead of her across the open ground, up to a place where a small group of men seemed to be waiting for us. My captor had her hand on my shoulder, and her grip was not gentle. She halted three paces away from the men, keeping a hold on me.

"Found her not far away, headed in our direction," she said.

"Are they in sight?" someone asked.

She gave a curt nod. "Five miles and closing. The girl's a complication we could do without. You, take off your bag, and be quick about it." She gave me a shove, then released me. And when I stood there, wondering if the story I'd had ready for so long might possibly be of any help here, she snapped, "Now!"

I removed the bag, which was promptly taken away by one of the men. I tried to breathe slowly. I tried to think of a plan.

"Who are you, and what in the name of the gods are you doing here?" The speaker was a man like a bright blade, a man whose authority shone in his high-boned, handsome features. His hair was russet; his eyes were the hue of a highland sky in summer. He spoke as if he was in a hurry.

"Calla," I managed. "I'm heading for Stonewater. Seeking kinfolk."

A short silence.

"Stonewater, is it? And where might that be?" The man who spoke was taller, darker, a lean person with an edgy look. At the wrists of his long shirt I could see the marks of tattooing, an elaborate pattern of interlinked chains. Around his neck was another decoration, like a line of dark birds in flight. His long hair was twisted into a number of thin plaits. His eyes were like the girl's, black and shrewd.

"North." I waved a hand vaguely. "Up there."

"You'll need to do better than that," the young woman said. "We know there's no such place. And children like you don't wander about in the snow looking for family, not unless they're out of their minds." Her hand tightened on my shoulder, making me wince with pain. "Tell

329

the truth! Who brought you here? What is your purpose? Don't waste our time, girl. We don't take kindly to spies here."

"All right, Tali," the red-haired man said. "Get everyone in place and leave this to me."

She turned on her heel and stalked off without a backward glance.

"Regan?" The man who had taken my bag was back, and in his right hand was my knife, the one Flint had given me the night before that terrible morning. In his left lay the sheath I had made, with its feather and pebble charms and its intricate knots. "Take a look at this."

Regan. My heart skipped a beat.

The red-haired man took the knife, weighing it in his hands. His eyes met mine, and I saw something in them that steadied me. I sensed that here was a person who would be prepared to listen. "Where did you get this knife?" he asked. "Be quick in your answers—we don't have long."

"Someone gave it to me."

"What someone was that, Calla?"

"I can't tell you."

The man nodded. "And the sheath?"

I took a risk. "I made it."

"Mm-hm."

"What about those?" The dark man's question was quick as a dagger thrust. He was looking at my fey-mended shoes. "Made those too, did you?"

I stood frozen. I wanted to believe I was among friends. But I could not bring myself to tell the truth. Speaking out about a canny gift was like putting your head into the hangman's noose. For years now I had watched every word, treading the knife edge between trust and betrayal.

"If I could," said the red-haired man, "I'd offer you food and shelter and give you time before I pressed you for answers. But there is no time." He glanced at the other man, and a silent message seemed to pass between them. He turned his attention back to me. "What if I told you I've seen that cloak before?"

They knew. They knew about Flint, no doubt of it. I hesitated.

"Tell the truth," he said. "It's in your best interest."

"The shoes are mine. A friend mended them. The cloak was a gift."

"From the same fellow who gave you the knife." The dark man folded his arms.

"I'm on my own now," I said, shivering. If these folk were in league with the Enforcers, if I had fallen into a trap, it was already too late to save myself. If these were indeed Regan's Rebels, and that was looking more likely by the moment, I should tell them the truth. But this could be some kind of trick.

"What if I told you," the red-haired man said, "that your name is not Calla? That you are on your way north for a particular purpose that has nothing to do with visiting an old grandmother or a distant cousin?"

"If I had another purpose, would I explain it to folk who grabbed hold of me as if I were a miscreant? Would I tell my story to a stranger?"

"You might," he said, "if you and that stranger had a mutual friend."

Flint. "I have no friends," I said.

"Regan," said one of the men. "Time's short."

Regan sighed. "Let's start again. I see you're wearing an unusual pair of shoes, Calla. I notice you also have a cloak I suspect once belonged to a trusted friend of ours. You are carrying a knife of a kind that most young women don't keep about their person, a fighting man's knife with a pattern on the hilt that I happen to know very well, since I was there when the thing was made. This weapon you do not carry in its original sheath but in another whose making suggests a certain . . . ancient knowledge." His gaze was level, somber, but somehow reassuring. "We were expecting you," he said quietly. "Or someone very like you. Only not now, and not here. If your companion has sent you to us today, on your own, something's gone wrong, and we need to know what it is."

I cleared my throat.

"My name is Regan," he said quietly. "This is Fingal." He indicated the tattooed man. "And you, I think, are Flint's girl."

Oh gods! Relief washed through me, powerful enough to fill my eyes with tears. I was here. I had reached the place. I was among friends at last. "Neryn," I croaked. "My name is Neryn. And, no, I am not *Flint's girl,* for he and I have parted ways. But I am the girl you mean."

"This must wait," the dark man said, glancing around the open area. Most of the folk I had seen before were gone now, vanished as if the rocks had swallowed them. But surely they had been ordinary human folk, without the Good Folk's capacity to merge. The place was almost empty. The young woman, Tali, could be seen over by the rock wall, passing items up to a person who was crouched on a ledge.

"Tell me quickly," Regan said. "Where's Flint now? How long since last you saw him, and where?"

Such was the urgency in his voice that I answered without hesitation. "We camped not far up the valley, on the hillside, the night before last. He left the next morning. He didn't tell me where he was going, but . . . there was a band of Enforcers close by. They have been moving along the valley floor for some time, heading this way."

"Mm. I won't ask what brought you in this direction on your own; that doesn't matter now. Fingal, take her to the overhang, get down out of sight, and keep her safe till this is over. Neryn, if you want to come through this alive, do exactly as Fingal tells you. If he says keep silent, then that's exactly what you do, no matter what happens. No matter what you see. Understood?"

Be as quiet as a mouse, Grandmother had said. *No matter what you see.* I nodded, my mind filling with dark possibilities. Fingal led me off without another word.

"I hope you're not scared of blood," he said.

The overhang was no more than a slight inward curve at the base of the rock wall, with a couple of spiky bushes in front. Fingal thrust me into this meager concealment. My cloak snagged, and when I pulled it free, the fabric ripped. My companion squeezed in beside me.

"Keep down," he muttered. "Don't move and don't make a sound."

I opened my mouth to ask a question, then shut it again. There was a look on Fingal's face that made obedience the only choice. Something was coming, something I was fairly sure I did not want to witness. Between the thorny branches of the plants, I had a reasonable view of the open area. It was quite empty now; Regan had vanished along with the last of the others. No sign of warrior-woman Tali, or of the fellow who had gone through my bag. No sign of anyone. I shivered. This was not much of a hiding place.

We waited. There was not a sound to be heard save my companion's steady breathing and the occasional cry of a bird. The snow had ceased falling. As we looked out, the clouds parted to let through a pale winter sunlight. The stark surfaces of the rocks were illuminated, showing myriad shades within the gray: mouse pelt, birch bark, an old woman's long hair, the sea under a sullen winter sky, a man's beautiful, lying eyes. . . . And there within the solid rock, the forms of uncanny folk, beings molded from the living stone, strong and stark as the northern crags themselves. I could see quite clearly the massive limbs, the crushing hands, the squat bodies and strange blockish

334

heads. The chinks that were mouths; the holes that were eyes . . . I sensed too that in the cracks and crevices of the rock walls, many smaller folk were hiding, perhaps observing the incomprehensible behavior of humankind.

Fingal shifted, easing his legs. He flexed the fingers of one hand, then the other. Always, he had the knife ready to strike. His attention was wholly on the open space before us, on what was coming. It felt as if the whole world were holding its breath.

Fingal laid a hand on my arm, then touched his finger to his lips, a warning that I must maintain silence. I nodded. He turned his gaze toward the spot where Tali and I had made our final sliding entry to this place. I had heard nothing at all. But now, coming down the zigzag approach, a line of black-clad men with masks over their faces advanced steadily in near silence. The Enforcers were here.

I saw Flint straightaway. He was dressed the same as all of them. Most of his face was hidden by the plain cloth mask, and his hands were in studded gauntlets. All the same, I knew him. He was coming down the awkward pebbly slope now, moving with an unerring balance. The next man was only two strides behind him. Why were the rebels holding back? Surely the time to strike was while the enemy moved in single file through the narrow path between the rocks. And Flint . . . The rebels thought of him as a friend; they'd made that clear. Now he marched into the open area with his weapon drawn, as if leading his band of Enforcers to the attack. What was this? My heart in my mouth, I waited for a sudden arrow, a well-aimed spear, to fell him. If Tali and the others were concealed in the rocks up above us, surely at least one of them had a clear line of sight.

There was no arrow, no spear. Flint reached the foot of the descent and motioned for the others to keep coming. They poured in after him, ten men, twenty, five-and-twenty. Fingal drew in a sharp breath. His fingers tightened on the hilt of his knife.

Once all the Enforcers were on level ground, I thought they would fan out around the open area, ready for an attack. But no; they began to take off their packs, loosen their cloaks, remove their masks, get out waterskins. One or two sat down with their backs against the rocks; some stretched weary limbs; a few took the opportunity to empty their bladders. Among them Flint stood at ease, shading his eyes against the watery sun, looking casually up to the top of the encircling rock wall. He had sheathed his sword. *Do something,* I willed him, my heart racing, my body all cold sweat. *Dive for cover, retreat, draw your weapon!*

I took a long breath. Flint was my enemy. He was the mind-scraper, the liar, the man who had pretended to be my friend and had worked his evil magic on me. There he was, standing unaware in the face of certain death, and I should be glad. But I couldn't bear it. I couldn't let him die, I couldn't . . . A shout of warning welled up in me. Before I could let it free, a subtle sound came from somewhere up above us: the hollow hooting of an owl.

The rebel band poured out from the rocks, spilled down from the ledges, surged across the open ground. The sunlight flashed on naked blades; the air filled with screams of challenge. In the forefront was Tali, brandishing an ax and yelling at the top of her lungs.

The first strike felled one, two, three, but the Enforcers were quick to seize weapons, to form a defensive ring, to parry the strokes of sword and ax, to meet iron with iron. I pressed a clenched fist against my mouth, forcing myself silent, as I saw a rebel fall to be trampled by many booted feet, the brown of his tunic turned violent crimson. The space out there was a mass of struggling figures. Screams and shouts filled my ears. A rebel was fighting one-handed, his other arm dangling limp, broken by the flat of an enemy sword. He staggered. An Enforcer lifted his weapon high, ready to deliver a cleaving stroke to the head. And suddenly there was Tali. The ax swung in her hand; the blade struck the Enforcer at the waist, cutting deep. Blood sprayed, a red fountain. Tali jerked her head at the man with the broken arm, her meaning plain. *Back off. You're hurt. Get under cover.*

I did not see if he obeyed her, for the two were lost in the tumult of hacking, dodging, leaping, falling bodies. Beside me Fingal was tense with nerves, clenching and unclenching his hand on his weapon.

"Not that way, go for his knees. . . . Look behind you. . . . Gods, Bryn's down . . . ," he muttered as he craned to get a better view. There was no longer any need to keep quiet. Whatever noise we made would be lost in the shriek

337

of metal on metal, the thud of ax or club on flesh and bone, the sounds of pain.

It should have been a rout. The Enforcers had been unprepared, taking their ease, resting after a long march. The rebels had been waiting in ambush, the entire exercise obviously planned. There had been far more of them hidden here than I'd realized. But after those first losses, the Enforcers had regrouped quickly; they were the king's elite warriors. Even my untutored eye could see their skills with sword and knife, the hard control in their movements, the way they worked with each other, seizing every advantage they could. My mouth was dry. My heart hammered. Another rebel fell, and an Enforcer dispatched him with a swift downward movement of the sword. Had I reached the threshold of Shadowfell only to see Regan's Rebels fight and lose their last battle?

Flint. Where was Flint? In the maelstrom I had lost him. I scanned the field and found him by the rock wall. His sword was in his hand, its blade gleaming silver, not yet stained by blood. Surrounded by frenzied movement, assailed by screams and shouts of pain, he stood detached, poised, waiting. For what, I did not know.

"Gods have mercy," muttered Fingal. "Doran's done for, and Cass. Hold fast, boys. Hold fast." He was wound tight as a harp string.

"Go," I said. "If you want, go out and fight. I'll be all right."

"I'm under orders." It was clear Fingal wished it were

otherwise. "If Regan says guard you, I guard you. Is it true? Are you this Caller we heard about?"

A scream ripped across the battlefield. It was a sound to haunt a person's dreams. When I looked out, I saw amid the mayhem a man lying prone, a man in a dark cloak. Where his head had been, there was a mass of crushed flesh and smashed bone, white, red, gray, hideous. His arms were outstretched. His hands lay open, like those of a sleeping babe. I drew a shuddering breath. Not Flint. Not Flint's hands. *That is an Enforcer,* I thought. And in the same moment I thought, *That is somebody's son, somebody's husband, somebody's father. He was somebody's friend.*

Flint had moved. He was in the middle of the melee, swinging his sword with the rest of them. I sucked in a breath. My skin was clammy, my ears were ringing. The best of the best, that was what the Enforcers were supposed to be. Best at combat. Best at torture. Best at terror. If they won today, the rebels would be destroyed and I would be sent to the king. And Flint . . . if he was killed, his foul craft would perish with him. He was a mind-scraper. He was everything I loathed and feared, and I should be glad to see him die. But it wasn't like that. It wasn't like that at all.

Fingal made a little sound. His eyes were narrowed, his attention all on the fight. Was I imagining that the tide had turned out there, and not in the rebels' favor? A broad-shouldered Enforcer ran a man through with a sword. Another had his hands around an opponent's throat, squeezing, squeezing. Now here was Flint, approaching from behind. His knife sliced across the Enforcer's neck. The man went down like a felled tree, a river of red flowing over his dark cloak. The rebel fighter bent double, coughing and choking. Flint was already gone. I searched and spotted him striding toward a place where Tali and two other rebels stood with their backs to the rock wall, surrounded by Enforcers. A man had a spear pointed at Tali's chest; he was shouting something, perhaps ordering the others to surrender or he would run her through. Oh, she would be a prize for the king, a fine, strong weapon for his will.

Fingal's body was a coil of tension. He had his teeth sunk into his lip. Flint reached the group, and suddenly it was no longer a standoff but a fight. There could be no doubt which side he was on. One Enforcer down, and blood pooling. Another down, victim to Tali's ax. A third struggling, pinned by two rebels. Only for a moment; three more Enforcers charged in and the tide turned again. Tali was on her knees. Flint and his opponent were rolling on the ground, each with knife in hand, each an eyeblink away from death.

And there was Regan, charging forward, slicing with his knife, distracting Tali's opponent for long enough to let her scramble to her feet and snatch up her fallen weapon. Beside them, Flint twisted away from his own adversary, then dispatched him with one sharp blow. *"Yesss,"* hissed Fingal.

Someone whistled, a high, clear signal. My companion

cursed under his breath. A new line of Enforcers was coming down the track, weapons at the ready. Well-aimed arrows stopped two, but the rest stepped over their fallen comrades and kept coming, dark-cloaked, menacing, unstoppable. Only six of them, but at this extreme, six might be all it would take to win the battle.

"We're gone," said Fingal with bleak certainty. "Unless there's some magic you can work to get us out of this."

Magic. Oh gods, my canny gift. Could I use it here?

"If there's something you can do," he added, "it'll need to be quick."

My whole body was shaking. "I don't know . . . maybe I could . . . ," I mumbled, peering out of the hiding place at the confusion of flashing blades, the struggling men, the dark cloaks and bloodstained tunics, the limp forms of the fallen, the fierce eyes of rebel and Enforcer alike. *Think of something, Neryn. Now.* The fresh group of Enforcers was down the path and onto the level ground. The six organized themselves in tight formation, two men with spears at the front, others behind with sword, knife, ax, metal balls on a chain. I could see how it would be: they would march forward as a group, cutting down anyone in their path.

Now! Quick! I tried to find the place within me that was strong and powerful. I closed my eyes and called as I had up on the fell, when I had asked the Good Folk to hide me from Flint. *Help! Help us!*

A curse from Fingal. I opened my eyes to see Tali down again, an Enforcer standing over her with club raised to strike. *Help! I need your help!* Nothing from the rocks; nothing from the shadows between the rocks. No uncanny warrior, no old man full of tricks, no Good Folk big or small. Yet I knew they were there; I had seen them. What was I doing wrong?

"We're finished," said Fingal.

A shriek from Tali. A twist, a turn, and she was on her feet, leaping out of range a moment before the Enforcer's club came down. Flint's sword was a bright streak of light as he swung it two-handed, severing her opponent's head. A roar of outrage from one of the new Enforcers. They had seen what happened. Now there would be only one target before their eyes: the comrade who had done the unthinkable and turned against his own.

"Stand strong," breathed Fingal. "Give them your best."

The formation was moving steadily forward, its progress barely slowed by a couple of rebels who attempted single-handed strikes on its flanks. I must act before the six were within range of Flint and Tali. Something was stopping the Good Folk from helping me, something was getting in the way. . . . Oh gods, why hadn't I thought of the obvious answer? Cold iron. This place was full of it. But not all uncanny folk were weakened by its presence—that had been proved in the defile. And what were those great blockish beings I had seen in the rock walls if not stanie men?

"Let me out," I said to Fingal. "Quick."

To his credit, he asked no questions, but scrambled out

of our bolt-hole and stood guard—one man with a knife in the midst of a raging battle—while I climbed out after him. I fixed my gaze on a point in the stone wall, above and slightly ahead of the slowly advancing formation of men, and sought desperately for the right words.

Fingal sprang in front of me, cursing, his weapon ready to strike. We'd been seen. An Enforcer with a knife in each hand was heading straight for us. My heart hammered. A rhyme. It had to be a rhyme.

Fingal stabbed forward with his knife and danced about, making himself a target. The Enforcer had drawn first blood: Fingal's tunic bore a dark stain on the sleeve. It had not slowed him. Still he ducked, swung, parried, his breath coming in gasps.

"Son of a dog!" yelled the Enforcer, forcing Fingal back with a series of slashing movements, using both his knives. I backed too, almost falling as my skirt caught on the low bushes screening the overhang. "Die in your blood, filthy traitor!"

In my mind, a little Flint was alone on the shore, sweeping his stone warriors away with a brutal stroke of the arm. The verse: I had it. Quick, before the Enforcers moved past the spot. I reached for the being that stood in the stones above them, an ancient, slow creature that had probably seen a dozen such battles, a thousand such deaths as these.

"Stanie Mon, Stanie Mon, stand up ta'," I chanted in a shaking voice. "Stanie Mon, Stanie Mon, doon ye fa'."

With a cracking, a splitting, a violent, thunderous crashing, the stanie mon fell. The men standing in its path had no chance. One moment they were there, frozen to immobility by the immense sound above them, the next they were gone, crushed beneath the great chunks of stone. A cloud of dust sprayed out across the open area, coating rebel and Enforcer alike. It rolled over us, rushing into my nose and eyes, making me cough and choke. There was a sudden sharp movement right by me, and a gasp, and a man fell to the ground lifeless. Fingal had seized his opportunity.

"Great gods," he spluttered now, putting a hand to his eyes. "What was *that*?"

Momentarily the battlefield was quiet, save for a breathy, sobbing sound from somewhere out in the swirling cloud. It was the sound of a man in terrible pain. The dust settled to reveal a great rough gash in the rock wall opposite us, and the pieces of the stanie mon lying as they had fallen, massive head, giant body, huge outstretched limbs. Around him, an army of gray ghosts still fought a dozen desperate small battles. There was Tali, covered in dust, and Flint by her, peeling the mask from his face. Thank the gods, they had not been crushed.

"Black Crow's curse!" exclaimed Fingal. "You did it, didn't you? With your little rhyme, you brought that whole thing down. You've won it for us. By all the gods, I don't believe it."

"Fingal!" someone shouted from over by the rocks, and as Fingal strode away in response—perhaps he thought I could defend myself by magic—I saw that not all the rebels had escaped the fall. Tali and Flint were still standing, but by the heavy slab that made up the stanie mon's right arm, a young fighter lay trapped. His leg was pinned beneath the great block of stone. Even if all the men here tried to lift at once, I knew they could not shift that slab so much as an inch.

Fingal had gone to crouch by the fallen man, touching his brow, his neck, giving calm instructions to one or two others. As for the fight, the rebels had rallied and were swiftly accounting for the last of their opponents. The battle seemed all but over. *You've won it for us,* Fingal had said. Rebels victorious. King's men routed. But this was no victory. Beneath those rocks lay six dead men, and I had killed them. That they'd been Enforcers made no difference at all. A moment ago they'd been standing there fit and well, and now they were crushed and broken. This was the worst deed of my life.

Bile welled in my throat; my heart beat a furious rhythm of denial. If this was what it meant to be a Caller, I didn't want it. How could I ever risk this happening again? Forget Shadowfell. I would move on alone, I would find somewhere to live all by myself, as I had once told Flint I intended to do. I was not fit for the company of man or beast.

The sounds of battle were dying down. Since I was no longer under guard, I moved, making myself walk over to the fallen rocks and witness the result of my blunder. I watched quietly as someone brought Fingal a bundle, which when unwrapped proved to be full of healer's supplies—knives and other implements, rolled cloths, stoppered jars, and little linen bags of herbs. An intense discussion was taking place not far off, to do with rocks and levers and ropes.

Regan strode over to us. He had a long, jagged cut across his brow, and his handsome face was shiny with sweat. Blood was trickling down into his eyes. The front of his tunic was stained red. "I told you to stay under cover," he said, looking from Fingal to me. "You could both have been crushed." He squatted down by the trapped man. "Garven," he murmured. "You fought bravely, lad. Lie quiet now. We'll get you out." He rose to his feet, and a look passed between him and Fingal. "Give him something for the pain," Regan said, "and then we'll talk about what comes next."

Fingal was already measuring something from a little vial into a cup, adding what might be mead, stirring it with a bone spoon. "She did it," he said, glancing up at Regan. "Neryn. She said a verse and the rocks fell down. She made it happen."

Regan's attention was suddenly all on me, the blue eyes narrowed. "Is this true?"

"It's true." I wondered how I was going to tell him that I never intended to use my uncanny gift again. For the expression on his face told me he saw its possibilities and thought them good. It told me he saw me for what I could be: a weapon, and a powerful one at that. I found that I could not say what I knew I should, for the look in his eyes was all hope, and hope was in short supply in Alban.

"Tell me what you did," Regan said. "What kind of gift is this, that you have the very rocks at your command? We heard from Flint that he might have found a Caller, but none of us were quite sure what that meant, only that it was a gift of great potential. I see that much is true. The battle was all but lost. You intervened and it was won. We owe you a great debt. If you stay with us, if you aid our cause, victory may be closer than we ever imagined. What you did . . . how did you make it happen?"

It was hard to find words. Was this a win or a loss? A remarkable exercise of magical power or a disastrous attempt to do something I barely understood? Perhaps it was both. I only knew it made no difference whether I killed an ally or enemy; he was still just as dead.

"Fingal spoke of a rhyme," Regan said. "What kind of rhyme? A spell, an incantation? Is this a charm like those sung by mind-menders?"

Gods, I wished to be somewhere far away, all alone, and for my deed to be undone. Yet if that were so, Regan and his comrades would be dead. I cleared my throat. All over the open area the rebels were finishing the day's dark business. Knives moved with swift purpose across throats; swords stabbed efficiently downward. There would be no prisoners taken in such a conflict. Rebels were stripping the dead Enforcers of anything useful: warm garments, weaponry, boots. Their own dead they carried to one side of the area. Here the fallen were laid down gently and covered each with a cloak. Four at least; grievous losses for such a small band.

There was Flint, kneeling by the form of a dead Enforcer. He was very still, his face ashen pale. What was he doing? Someone moved across, blocking my view, and I saw him no more.

"Tell me, Neryn," Regan said, his eyes never leaving my face. "This gift of yours is remarkable. It's critically important to us. A rhyme. Surely not just that."

Garven had had his dose and was quiet now. Four or five rebels were grouped around him, one offering a waterskin, a second supporting his head, the others speaking softly. Fingal got up and came over to us, his face grim. "There's no way we can lift those rocks," he said to Regan, "though the men want to try with ropes. I'll have to take off Garven's leg. But he's trapped high. I don't like his chances."

"Black Crow save us," muttered Regan.

"He's trapped because I didn't know what I was doing," I made myself say. "If I had full mastery of my gift, I might have been able to control the stanie mon's fall more precisely. I didn't realize how perilous a Caller's ability was until today, and I'm more sorry than I can say."

"We're fighting a war," Regan said. "We have wins and losses. Some of us are injured, some of us die. We can't think of this in any other way or we'd be unable to go forward. But for you I would have lost my entire battle group today, and likely I'd be lying in my own blood alongside them. What did you call it, a stanie mon? Isn't that a creature from a children's game?"

"Regan?" Fingal was waiting for some kind of command, some acknowledgment from his leader.

"If it's the only way to get him out, then take the leg. We'd best let the fellows try the ropes first, though anyone can see those stones are too heavy to move."

With a curt nod, Fingal headed back toward the trapped man. It would be a grim choice. I knew enough from helping Grandmother in her healing work to realize how unlikely it was that a person would survive such an injury, let alone with a leg that could bear any weight. Garven had been a fighter. He would fight no more.

Tali had come up behind Regan; she was as tall as he. She had taken off the cloth that covered her lower face, revealing a decisive jaw, a neat, straight nose, and a full, curving mouth. She was younger than I'd thought, perhaps only a year or two my senior. She had a tattoo around her neck that was the same as Fingal's, a pattern like flying birds, maybe crows. "They're saying you did this," she said, and the gaze she turned on me matched the bitterness of her tone. "A charm. Magic. It's a pity your magic makes no distinction between theirs and ours. We were told a Caller would be a priceless asset. If this is a demonstration of your gift, it makes you more trouble than you're worth."

"Enough, Tali," Regan said. "Neryn, is this really as simple as it seems? You speak a rhyme and the being obeys your command?"

"It's not just that." I struggled to find the right words.

For as long as I could remember, I'd been keeping my canny gift secret. I'd scarcely let myself breathe a word about the Good Folk, or the power of cold iron, or the special knacks and tricks that some human folk possessed. Even with Flint, I had been guarded. Speaking of such things openly felt as perilous as leaping from a cliff top into empty air. "I mean, with a stanie mon it is mainly just the verse, and the magic doesn't work unless the rhyme is in the correct form. But only a Caller can summon uncanny folk in this way, or so I believe. And there is a . . . there's another part to it, but I can't describe it to you. I have no words for it."

It was a sensation I had felt only on those occasions when I'd been conscious of calling directly to the Good Folk. I had reached down, reached in, touched something deep and old. . . . "It's a feeling," I said. "Ancient and powerful. Stronger in some places than others. It's being connected with earth and water, wind and flame. Understanding what exists within those things. It links me with the uncanny folk of Alban, no matter what form they take. I see them when other people can't. If I call, they will come." I hesitated. "It's said that a Caller can be far more than this, but only with special training."

"A stanie mon." Tali's voice dripped scorn. "Could you not have bid this stanie mon spread itself only over our enemy? Could you not have given a little thought to what you were doing?"

"You think I'm happy that I hurt one of your comrades?" I snapped, unable to hold back my anger. "I did what I did because Fingal asked me if I could help. It did look as if you might be losing the battle. And although you may not think much of me, I believed Regan's Rebels were worth saving. I've wanted to join you since my brother was killed fighting the Enforcers three years ago. I had to act quickly just now. I did the only thing I could think of that might turn the tide for you. But I'm new to using my gift. I haven't learned how to harness it. What happened . . . As I said before, I deeply regret it." And when neither Tali nor Regan said anything, I added, "A stanie mon only responds to the simplest verses, the kind children make up. You can't ask such a being to do anything complicated. I bade him fall, and he fell."

Tali's expression changed. The bitterness and hurt were replaced by the look of someone thinking hard. "But—" she began. "Doesn't that mean you can—"

I realized what had occurred to her. "Maybe," I said, my heart beginning to race. I looked over toward the great prone form of the stanie mon and the little group crouched by the trapped man. "I didn't use the rhyme *fa' doon deid*—I could hardly tell the stanie mon to kill himself. So perhaps I can get him to stand up again." At Regan's soft whistle I added, "I don't promise this will work. As I said, I'm new to doing it. But I will try." I never wanted to use my so-called gift again. I did not want the power of life and death in my hands. But I must try this. If I did not, that man would die or, at the very least, lose his leg. And what about the stanie mon? He might lie there for hundreds of years, unable to move until another Caller came to chant a new rhyme in his stone ear.

"Gods save us," murmured Regan. I saw him thinking, *What if it goes wrong, what if this ends with more deaths, more injuries?* But he did not say it. He glanced over toward the trapped man again. "All right," he said. "You'd best try this charm."

Folk were busy all around the open area, dealing with the aftermath of the battle. Flint was by another dead Enforcer now, kneeling again, his face ashen white. As I watched, he reached with gentle fingers to close the eyes of his fallen comrade. He was murmuring something. Words of farewell, I thought, and words of regret. There were ghosts in his eyes. Understanding came to me. How crushing a burden Flint must bear as he lived his double life, friend turning to foe as he crossed the line from one loyalty to the other. I did not know how a man could rightly bear such a load. No wonder his head was bent. No wonder his shoulders were bowed. No wonder his face wore an expression that jolted my heart. My own misgivings were nothing to his.

"It's hard for him," said Regan quietly, following my gaze. "Neryn, will you try this now? We must get our wounded away quickly if we're to reach Shadowfell before dusk."

I eyed the great pieces of the fallen stanie mon. It seemed impossible that any force could ever shift them.

"You'd best clear everyone well away," I told Regan, "in case something goes amiss."

Regan looked at Tali, and Tali, after giving me a sideways glance, went off to issue a few crisp orders. The area cleared immediately, the rebel forces moving well away from the rockfall. Flint rose slowly to his feet. He looked straight at me, and I looked back, my feelings in turmoil. I dropped my gaze; I must think of nothing but the stanie mon, the call, the opportunity to put right a small amount of the damage I had done.

"We're ready," Regan said.

There was nobody close now except him and the trapped man. And one more: for beside the prone form of Garven, Fingal still crouched, one hand holding the warrior's wrist, the other laid on his brow.

I asked a question with my eyes. Regan answered it with a slight shake of the head.

"You should move back," I said, and the rebel leader did so without a word.

I tried to clear my mind of everything: Flint's white face, my guilty conscience, Tali's scorn, the carnage of the battlefield. I tried to find the part of me that could reach out and touch the heart of a stanie mon. I had wronged this peaceable creature. His life moved with the long, slow order of stone; his great shoulders bore the summer sun, the winter snow, the storm and sleet and rain of this lonely place; he lived with the thunder and the torrent and the high, sad cries of owl and eagle. I had made him kill. I must not leave him lying here, sprawled and broken. I must see him safely back to his rightful place.

"Help him, Neryn." Fingal spoke softly from where

he crouched beside the injured man, right by the massive stones. His eyes met mine without a trace of fear.

I gave him a nod, drew a long breath, summoned the strength deep inside me. I should be explaining to the stanie mon, expressing respect, gratitude, apology. But I couldn't. What I had to say must be contained in the brief lines of a rhyme, or he would not understand it. "Stanie Mon, Stanie Mon, fine and braw," I chanted. "Stanie Mon, Stanie Mon, stand up ta'!"

Nothing stirred. I kept my gaze on the fallen stones, but I sensed the silent audience of rebels behind me, perched up on the rocks and watching with some fascination. I made myself breathe steadily.

A subtle creaking. A shudder in the ground beneath my feet. The stones began to move of themselves, rumbling, rolling.

"Hold still, friend," said Fingal, and moved to kneel over Garven, making of his own body a fragile shield. Tears sprang to my eyes. I scrubbed them away. I would not attempt another rhyme. I must trust that the stanie mon could get himself up without doing any more damage.

"Move back, Neryn!" That was Regan, calling from some distance away. But I did not obey. I stepped forward and crouched down close to Garven, taking his hand in mine.

"You'll be all right," I muttered, praying it was true. "We'll get you out."

"*Neryn!*"

That voice was not Regan's. I heard running footsteps, and then Regan saying, "No. Wait."

For the stones were assembling themselves in some order, creaking up from the ground, forming themselves into a great figure with stocky limbs, a slab of a body, a chunky square head with holes for eyes, a slit for a mouth, a look that was neither smiling nor frowning, simply . . . there. As the pressure lifted from his leg, Garven let out a howl of pain.

"All right, lad." Fingal's voice was remarkably steady. "Lie quiet."

The stanie mon raised himself to his considerable height, looming above us. He lifted one massive arm and touched his lumpish hand against the spot where his heart might be, if such a being had a heart. The eyeholes seemed turned in my direction.

I got to my feet and copied his gesture, laying my hand on my heart, then bowing my head. I hoped he understood, for I hadn't another rhyme in me.

He took two lumbering steps. The ground shook under his enormous feet. He seemed to lean into the rock wall, in the place where it was gouged and broken, and ease himself against it, and with a knitting and a mending, he became once more part of it. A few shards of stone tumbled down; a small cloud of dust eddied up and dispersed. The stanie mon was gone.

Chapter Seventeen

After that, everyone was busy. Fingal splinted Garven's leg. My offer to help was politely declined; there were plenty of folk to place the lengths of wood and wind the bandages while Fingal held the bones in position. Whether the limb would mend straight, whether this young warrior would ever use it again, I did not know. It seemed to me the bones might be so shattered that no healer could mend them, but Fingal evidently thought it worth trying.

As for those others who lay broken on the ground, I made myself look at their pitiful remains. I made myself bear witness to what my gift had wrought. *You will remember this,* I told myself. *You will see it night by night, in your dreams.* And I looked across to where Flint was standing a short distance away, watching me. I wondered if this image had the power to displace the false thoughts he had put into my mind. I did not know which would be worse. I wondered what horrors walked through Flint's dreams.

Suddenly I was so weary I could hardly stay on my feet. I sat down on a stone, watching as folk gathered the enemy corpses into a heap. The rebel dead were securely tied into cloaks or blankets, ready to be carried home. Folk were slinging packs on their backs, gathering weapons, getting ready to move on. A makeshift stretcher had been assembled for Garven, who now lay white and silent with his leg neatly strapped.

A steady stream of folk came over to thank me for what I had done, and, I thought, to get a closer look at me. Tali was not the only woman among the fighters; at least three more introduced themselves. Everyone seemed to think I had won the battle for them. There would be a welcome at Shadowfell, no doubt of it. The end of my long journey was in sight. I should have felt happy, but all that was in me was a deep weariness, as if my bones were those of an old, old woman.

Regan was busy giving orders. Tali was supervising the passage of the dead, the wounded, and the supplies up over the rocks. I judged that she was Regan's second-in-command. I wondered where she had learned to fight as if she did not know the meaning of fear. It was people like her the rebels needed, people who were all courage. People who did not doubt; people who did not make mistakes.

Someone was standing beside me. He had come up with barely a sound.

"Move away," I said, not looking up. "I can't talk to you." In my heart a small battle raged, for all I could see was his

357

blanched face, his haunted eyes, the gentleness with which he had bade his comrades farewell and safe journey. But he was an Enthraller, and that sickened me.

Flint drew in a sharp breath and let it out slowly. "I didn't intend you to see this," he said quietly. "That's why I told you to wait—to get this over first, so I could bring you to Shadowfell in safety. Why did you—"

"I can't do this," I said. "I can't talk to you as if everything were the same as before. How can I ever—" I stopped myself from saying the rest. *How can I ever trust you now that I know what you are?* It was not fair to judge him thus. Yes, he was a worker of magic, a man who meddled with other folk's minds. He had used his canny gift for a destructive purpose. But so had I. I had done the same thing he had, and for the same reason: because I wanted Alban to be free.

I looked up at him. He had not lied to me; he had only held back what I need not know. Alban was a land of secrets, and both Flint and I were long accustomed to holding our secrets close. In the end he had confided the knowledge he knew might send me running. He had laid it bare before me, and for reward, I had turned my back on him.

"Flint!" Regan called. "Neryn!"

The rebel leader was standing with Tali over by the rocks, near where Fingal had been busy tending to the wounded: splinting a man's arm, giving another a draft, wrapping a wound on a woman's leg.

I walked over, and Flint walked beside me. I did not look at him. It made no difference; I felt his presence in every part of my body. It was a curious sensation, like being pulled two ways. I wondered about the charm of enthrallment, and whether my confused feelings owed something to that.

"Is all well?" Regan asked.

Flint responded with a noncommittal grunt, and I saw the limpid blue eyes of the rebel leader fix on him with disconcerting directness. Regan, I thought, could see right inside people. He was reading Flint now, and did not like what he saw.

"Pity you couldn't have let us know part of your troop was following on later," he said. "Close thing. But for Neryn, we'd have been finished."

"There was no way to get the information to you. When I sent you the message to be ready for them, I knew only that Boar Troop had been directed to come on along the valley. And to disregard any orders I might give them to the contrary. That part I guessed. Someone at court suspects me. I got a veiled warning."

Regan was looking grim. "You'll be hard put to explain the disappearance of a whole troop when you return there." He gave me a glance, then said, "We'll talk more of this later. Thank the gods Neryn came through this unscathed. Our secret weapon. We weren't expecting her to turn up on the brink of the ambush, and on her own."

There was an awkward silence.

"If there's a difference of opinion between you," Regan said slowly, "a disagreement of some kind, I want it resolved before we reach Shadowfell. You'll walk together." And when I made to protest: "That's an order."

"There's something I must say first." I had to get this out before the door was thrown open for me and these people's hopes rose too high. "I know you need me, and I understand that my gift could help you. I want to be part of the rebellion; I've wanted to join you since I first heard of Shadowfell. But I can't use the Good Folk to kill and maim. Doing that would make me no better than Keldec. There must be some other way."

"So you'll fight a war as long as nobody gets hurt?" Tali held her voice quiet, but the anger vibrated in it. "What are you, a child of three? Besides, we have no alternative now but to take you with us. And keep you. You know our names and our location; you're witness to what we just did here, to what Flint did. Do you imagine we're going to send you off home with your little bag over your shoulder and that knowledge in your head?"

I made myself take a deep breath before I answered. "You seem to think I'm a half-wit," I said. "If you let me join you at Shadowfell, I will prove you wrong. I've been honest about how I feel. I understand how my gift could help you. I believe the Good Folk have a part to play in the fight for freedom; indeed, I don't think we can win it without them. But . . . I wonder if there is a subtler way to involve them. Give me time and perhaps I can discover what that is." This was not the moment to tell them how long it might take me to travel three ways, find three powerful Otherworld beings who most likely did not want to be found, and persuade them to teach me the wise use of my gift.

Flint started to speak, then thought better of it.

"You'll come with us, Neryn," Regan said, as if that had never been in doubt. "If it helps, think of it this way: at Shadowfell you're out of the king's reach and he can't make you into a weapon against us. That in itself is an achievement for us, never mind canny gifts or battles won. Perhaps you don't realize how significant you are. What you did today—I'm still hardly able to take it in. It was an astonishing feat. We'll speak more of it when we're safely home, with our dead laid to rest and our injured tended to. Now we must move on. Don't forget what I said. There's no room for personal differences at Shadowfell. Sort it out, the two of you."

I was going to have to tell them. "This is no small thing to be resolved in the space of a walk," I said. "Flint is an Enthraller. The vial around his neck has a lock of my hair twisted around it, hair he cut from my head with his own hands." My stomach felt hollow and sick; my words felt oddly like a betrayal. "I know he is one of you, but I'm not sure I can ever—"

Regan raised a hand, silencing me. "Gods save us, man," he said mildly, looking at Flint, "couldn't you have explained this to her?"

"It's best if I don't come on with you." Flint's voice was deathly quiet. "Now I know Neryn's safe, there's no reason for me to stay. I must be over Three Hags pass before the snows are too deep. I'll head straight back."

"This is ridiculous!" Tali's dark brows were drawn into a ferocious scowl, not directed at me this time, but at Flint. "The two of you travel all the way from Summerfort together, and now you can hardly manage a civil word to each other. You deliver us a whole troop of Enforcers, then you want to slink off back to court without spending so much as a single night in our company. As for you"—the glare was suddenly turned on me—"you demonstrate a weapon that could win the war for us, then tell us you're not sure you want to use it. This is madness!"

"I'd hoped we might have your company for a few nights at least, Flint," Regan said calmly. "I want your opinion on the plans we're preparing for next spring. And I can help you with your explanation for Keldec."

This wasn't a leader's order but the request of a friend. After a heavy silence, Flint said, "Long enough to give you an opinion, that's all." His face was winter white.

"When did you last eat, Neryn?" Tali asked, out of the blue.

"Some time ago."

"Eat now, then," she said. "It's a hard climb, and you'll have to keep up. Be quick about it; we're ready to leave. You have supplies?"

I rummaged in the bag that had been returned to me, crouching to take out the cloth that held my precious sprinkling of oats, my scraps of wizened fruit, my last morsel of cheese. Regan moved away to speak to Fingal. Flint and Tali stood side by side, watching me.

I walked to the rock wall with the cloth in my hands. I knelt down to spread it flat, then divided its meager contents into two equal portions. "I offer you a share of this small meal," I murmured. "I'm sorry for the violence that stained this place of peace today. I'm trying to do what is right." I stayed there a moment with my eyes shut while the bustle of activity continued around me. Then I opened my eyes and ate my half of the rations, because Tali was right: without food I would be unable to keep up.

I rose to my feet. My head spun. Tali was beside me in a moment, her arm coming out to steady me. "Not much of a meal," she commented. "No wonder you're skin and bone. I'm going to walk in front of you, and I want you to tell me when you need a hand. Ready to go on?"

"I'm ready."

Each of the dead was carried over a brawny comrade's shoulders. Garven was borne on his stretcher; the other wounded fighters walked, supported by their friends. The three of us were at the back of the line, Tali first, then me, with Flint coming last. Tali offered to carry my bag for me. I said no; she already had her pack and weapons. I was glad of the apparent thaw in her mood, for this was going to be hard enough without her hostility.

A small number of rebels had stayed behind. Nobody had explained why, but as I took a last look behind me, I saw them dragging the sad remains of the crushed men over toward the piled-up bodies of those slain in battle. I wondered who would pass this way. It was a remote place, chill and inhospitable. What was it Flint had told Regan? That the Enforcers had come along this valley against his advice. That someone had told them to disregard his orders. No wonder he had looked so stricken when he came up to the cave that last night. He had realized there was no stopping them; he had been obliged to send word to Regan, setting the ambush in place. And after he left me, after I showed him my disgust, he had gone on with them, knowing he was leading them to their deaths. I had seen on his face, after the battle, that those men had been his friends. They were the companions he had trained with and fought alongside, the comrades with whom he had established a warrior's trust. I had learned today, as I watched them fight and die, that an Enforcer was not a monster, only a man who had taken a wrong path.

Despite the difficult terrain and the need to convey the dead and wounded, the rebels maintained a brisk pace. I did my best to keep up, fixing my gaze on Tali's back as she marched ahead of me and trying to breathe deeply. Behind me, Flint held his silence. There would be no obeying Regan's command to settle our differences unless I made the first move.

We negotiated the area of broken ground to find ourselves on the banks of a river. It was spanned by a fragile-looking construction of twisted and knotted ropes, suspended from poles dug into the ground at either end. Beneath this bridge the water churned and tumbled, icy blue-gray under a darkening sky. The sun had shrunk behind the clouds again, and the air was still and cold. We waited while the dead and wounded were borne across, while the rebels passed over in turn. Tali crossed before me, walking backward as steadily as if there were no river, no drop, no shaking movement with every step. When I wobbled, she took my hand to steady me. Flint waited on the near side until we were safely over, then made his own sure-footed way after us. He had, I guessed, not wanted to shake the bridge with his greater weight while we were on it.

We rested briefly on the far bank. Fingal dosed Garven again. Folk drank from their waterskins; the injured rebels sat down to rest. From somewhere behind us, within the area of broken rocks, a dark plume of smoke was rising. Its smell came to us on the wind, filling our nostrils with death. The look on Flint's face made my heart clench tight. *You have done this before,* I thought. *Over and over. But that makes no difference. You will never be at peace with it.* I had to talk to him. I had to face what lay between us. What words could bridge such a chasm?

"You're wrong about him."

I started. I had been so deep in thought that I had not seen Tali come to stand beside me.

"My grandmother was destroyed by an Enthraller," I said. "Flint is an Enthraller. No matter what kind of hero he is, no matter how courageous or loyal to the cause he may be, if he's one of *them,* he can never be a friend to me."

Tali glanced at me. "I don't know what happened between the two of you, and I don't want to know," she said quietly. "But you'll need to sort this out quickly. I take it this is not just some kind of lovers' falling-out?"

The expression on my face must have given her the answer, for she went on. "Did you ask him to explain what he does and why?"

"No, I didn't ask him. I didn't need to." But that was not the full truth. Flint had tried to tell me and I had refused to listen. "I despise what he does," I said, as if that might excuse me.

"Then you despise us and you don't belong at Shadowfell," Tali said, a terrible quietness in her voice. "Flint shoulders a crippling burden. He takes risks that would drive an ordinary person crazy with terror. Think twice before you speak harshly of such a man. We've got the key to Alban's future at Shadowfell, the last light of freedom in a realm turned to the dark. I saw what you did today. Your gift is a weapon all right, a weapon to make or break our venture. And Flint is a weapon. He's our link to Keldec, our eyes and ears at court. Regan needs both of you. But you won't be welcome at Shadowfell if you can't keep an open mind. And you won't be a friend to the cause if you weaken the best man we have."

She might just as well have hit me with that ax of hers. I felt stunned, winded. "Weaken him," I echoed. "What do you mean?"

"Just ask him," Tali said, shouldering her pack again. All around us, folk were getting ready to move on up the path into the hills. "Ask him about that thing he wears around his neck. I don't care if the lock of hair belongs to you or his favorite dog. Flint wouldn't meddle with a friend's mind. Not even on the king's orders."

As we climbed, my gaze kept turning back toward the smoke from that fire, thick and heavy in the stillness of late afternoon. It was the color of stone, of bone, of storm clouds. It hung like a sad shroud over this empty land. The thought of it weighed me down. Was the only way forward a path of violence and death? To fight for the cause of freedom, must I learn to perform deeds that sickened me to the core?

Up and up we climbed as the day grew darker. The narrow track wound between high bastions of stone, their chinks and crevices bare of any life. I thought of Grandmother and the wisdom she had tried to pass on to me. I thought of Farral dying, his breath the rustle of a breeze through dry reeds, his last whispered words a blaze of courage. *Keep fighting, Neryn! Keep . . . fi . . .* I thought of my father and his wager, and the chancy-boat burning. I thought of Flint's white face and haunted eyes. There was no need to turn my head and look at him; I held his image deep within me.

Grant forgiveness, said a little voice inside me. *Grant forgiveness, set them free.* In Odd's Hole, facing the Master of Shadows, I had believed my tests all completed. But maybe there was one test left.

Gods, it was cold! My chest was aching, an unwelcome reminder of that lost time in the valley when I had been too sick to make sense of the world around me. I had to keep going. I could not let these brave folk down. I had to reach Shadowfell. . . .

The world turned around me; I put out a hand to steady myself against the rock wall.

"Neryn." Flint spoke from just behind me. "Please let me help you."

He sounded hesitant and sad, as if he was quite sure I would refuse but could not stop himself from asking anyway. In that moment, something changed inside me, as if a window long shuttered were opened to let in the light.

"All right," I said. "Just for this steep part."

He moved forward and offered the support of his arm. We climbed on together. Above us, rock walls, dark skeletal trees, a dimming sky. Below us, far, far below, a sudden glimpse of the stony terrain that housed the place of death. The smoke still rising. The air whispering a tale of coming snow. Around Flint's neck the dream vial hung, moving from side to side with his steady steps. Inside it, the vaporous contents performed a slow little dance. The warmth of Flint's body flowed into mine. I felt his strength, his endurance, his courage. The revulsion that had sent me running from him only a day ago was gone. I felt safe.

"Tell me," I said. "Tell me what you didn't tell that morning, when I wouldn't listen."

I felt him take a long, uneven breath. "Are you sure?" he asked.

"Just tell me. What is in the dream vial?"

"I told you once that I was sent away to the isles to be trained when I was quite a small boy," Flint said. "Not trained in warfare, Neryn, but in the skill I was born with, an ability to touch folk's minds as they sleep, to soothe the suffering, to calm the disturbed, to make some sense of grief or loss. Mind-mending is an ancient craft, worked through dreams. It comes to us as your own gift does, from an ancestor who is not of humankind. There is—was—nobody else in my family with such a gift, and when it first showed itself in me at an early age, it frightened my kinfolk. Like your own ability, if not governed well, it can become destructive. You have seen that firsthand.

"At that time Keldec had not yet come to the throne, and such matters could still be discussed without fear. My parents discovered that there was a master mind-mender in the western isles, and they sent me to live with him when I was five, to learn the right way to use this gift. I stayed there thirteen years. I was my mentor's only student, and he was thought to be the last of his kind. Keldec became king not long after I began my training, and while I learned my craft, he set his stamp on Alban.

"Once trained, I had a choice. I could hide my gift and hope for times of change, or use it openly. There was only one place where I could do the latter, and that was Keldec's court. I made myself known to him, and in time he called me there to join him."

"So you became an Enthraller." Let this tale have a conclusion I could bear to hear. "And an Enforcer. When did you learn to fight?"

"I met Regan. Here at Shadowfell he does not talk about his past; nobody does. But I met him in the isles, when we were young. His family was in a position to offer me an education alongside their son. That included a warrior's training. My mentor encouraged it. Regan and I made good rivals; we learned from each other. Not long before I went to court, there was a . . . catastrophe. That story is Regan's to tell, not mine. It made him the man he is today; it gave him a thousand reasons to do what he's doing here at Shadowfell. And it gave me a reason to offer my services to Keldec. On the surface, a loyal warrior and occasional practitioner of magic. Beneath the surface, something quite different. The king trusts me. He accepts that I prefer to do certain things my own way."

"Flint," I made myself say, "doesn't the king expect you to use your gift for his purposes? Why else would he want you at court?"

There was a silence. "I have done that, yes," he said heavily, and my heart sank. "He has a number of Enthrallers, none of whom have been trained as I have. Perhaps two in three times, they succeed in winning a person's loyalty for the king while keeping the victim in his right mind. The third . . . I have no need to tell you what can happen if that particular process is applied without due care, Neryn. I will give you the truth, whole and unadorned. I have never done what was done to your grandmother; my teacher made sure I had mastery of the gift before he let me go out into the world. Once or twice I have used my ability to turn men to the king's way of thinking. Regan and I spoke of this, long ago. To do what I do, to provide Regan with a window into the heart of Keldec's court, I must have the king's complete trust. That means there are certain commands I must obey. If I did not, Keldec would soon begin to doubt my loyalty. I do not perform such deeds lightly. I wear the weight of them every moment of every day. But it seems to me the cause of Alban's freedom is more important than anything. If I began to question his orders, the king would have no choice but to destroy me. He knows how strong I am, and what my gift allows. He could never let me go. I would make too powerful an enemy."

"Besides," I said, torn between horror and sympathy, "if you did not perform the enthrallment, the job would be given to another, with one chance in three that the victim would become . . . what my grandmother became. Gods, Flint. This is hideous. Regan expects more from you than any man should be asked to offer."

"I want to see Alban free. I want that place where you and I can sit by our fire and talk about anything that pleases us, and sleep under the stars with our hearts at peace. If I must tread a dark path to reach that place, I will do it. Not for Regan. Not for myself. Only because the alternative is unthinkable."

"But," I said, trying to understand, "if your gift allows you to change people's inner convictions, their long-held beliefs, why can't you perform an enthrallment on Keldec himself? Couldn't you turn him into a good man, a king who would rule Alban with fairness and justice? And if not that, don't you have the skill and opportunity to—"

"To assassinate him?" Flint's mouth twisted into a grim smile. "I have the skill and opportunity to do so; enthralling him would be somewhat more difficult. But if you remove a tyrant in anything other than an open and visible way, another tyrant soon stands up to replace him. Keldec has influential retainers. I'm not speaking only of the Enforcers, but of councillors and family. Regan and I have discussed this. We want to remove him fairly, publicly, with the support of Alban's chieftains. That will take time. Today's was a small victory. Winning Alban back is the work of many years and many people. We're only at the beginning."

We climbed some way farther; it seemed to me the slope was leveling out.

"We're nearly there," Flint said. "Are you all right?"

"Flint."

"Mm?"

"You didn't perform an enthrallment on me?"

"No, Neryn, though perhaps, now that I have told you my story, you will not believe me when I say that. It's a common belief among the folk of Alban that Enthrallers wear stolen dreams around their necks. That belief is fostered by those who work for Keldec: fear of such charms keeps people compliant. But in truth, most Enthrallers wear a glass replica of the traditional dream vial, and it holds nothing at all. Some add one vial each time they use their craft, as if keeping score." He lifted his fingers to touch the little object that swung on its cord. "Mine is no replica. It is a crystal taken from a particular cave in the isles, a place of deep spiritual power. What you see in this is the movement of water, of mist, of clouds. In the old times, each mind-mender was given a shard from that cave when he completed his training. Thus we carried out into the world a token of light and goodness. My mentor passed this to me when I left him." Flint hesitated. "I do not think I will see him again," he said. "But while I wear this, I feel his wisdom, and that gives me the strength to go on. Sometimes he comes to me in dreams, and I wake with new heart." He glanced down at me. "You're crying," he said.

I could not speak. There was too much in me. I raised a hand and dashed the tears away. "Why is there a lock of my hair wound around the vial?" I asked when I had my voice back.

Flint's features were suffused with a blush. It was a remarkable sight. "That night at the farm, I would have tossed the lock into the fire, but something made me slip it into my pouch." He spoke as if it was hard to get the words out. "I forgot it was there. Much later, while you were recovering from your illness, I rediscovered it. Perhaps . . . perhaps I anticipated how you would feel when I told you the truth. That when you learned exactly what I was, you would turn your back on me forever." His fingers went up to touch the little talisman. "I wrapped your hair around my mentor's gift. Thus, I thought, even when you were gone, I could hold some part of you close. But it was not mine to keep. If you wish, I will return it to you now." He hesitated. "I did not take this for purposes of magic, Neryn. But . . . because of what I am, once the token was with me, it played a part in opening my mind to you, and yours to me. We dreamed of each other; often each of us understood, without words, what the other was feeling. I did not expect that."

We climbed on in deep silence. After some time the ground leveled and the land opened out. We had emerged on a high fell, with the snow-crowned peak of a mountain to our north. To the south, far below us, I could see the river, the bridge like a little thread, and the broad, treacherous expanse of stony ground. There was the rising smoke, a duller hue now, as if, after its first fierce hunger was sated, the fire had begun to lose its appetite for human flesh. There was the valley down which I had traveled; I could see, in the very distance, the peaks of the Three Hags. Beyond them, beyond my eyes' reach, lay the far valley, the road to Summerfort, the chain of forests and lakes that led all the way to Darkwater, where my father had died in flames. So long a journey, and not only in miles.

"All right?" Flint asked again.

"Mm."

The rest of the party was gathered not far away, waiting until everyone had caught up before moving on. Regan came over, narrowing his eyes as he looked me up and down.

"We're almost there, Neryn. The next part's not such a steep climb, but it's tricky. Can you manage?"

"Yes." The terrain ahead was gently sloping, featureless, not at all tricky.

"Be careful" was all Regan said. "It's easy to get lost in the Folds."

The Folds. The Good Folk had mentioned that name. And speaking of the Good Folk . . . What was that over there? A creature of some kind, hunkered down pretending to be a patch of lichen? And up there? That was no ordinary stone: there were beady eyes peering out of that crack. And a feathery tail was twitching down at the base of that gnarled old tree. . . .

"You'll need to wear this, Neryn." Tali fished a long strip of dark cloth from her belt. "Stand still. I'll tie it for you."

She came behind me and put the thing over my eyes, pulling it tight. My heart lurched in fright.

"No, Tali." Regan's voice. "Neryn's one of us."

A short, tense silence. "It's the rule," Tali said. "Strangers must come in with their eyes covered." I heard in her voice that the rule had never been broken before.

"Flint has spoken for her," Regan said. "Would you challenge that? Untie the blindfold."

Her fingers caught in my hair, inflicting pain that was perhaps not accidental. The cloth came off. I did not see her face as she rolled it and stowed it away.

Everyone was assembled on the open hillside. Men still bore the bodies of their dead comrades over their shoulders; the wounded leaned on their friends. On his stretcher, Garven lay with eyes closed, his face all shadows. Time was passing. The distant hills were darkening, and the sky was the hue of a seal's pelt.

"Move on!" Regan called. "Neryn, keep your eyes straight ahead and concentrate. In the Folds, the land is not quite as it is in other places."

It surely was not. In the Folds, nothing was as it seemed. What looked to be an open fell proved to be a maze of twisting, turning ups and downs, where bare-limbed trees and thorny bushes sprang up without warning and unbroken ground acquired treacherous hollows and cracks as we set our feet on it. Sudden waterfalls plunged down the hillside and vanished into crevices; a broad lochan appeared where a moment before there had been nothing but dry stones and withered grasses.

Regan led the way with a confidence that, under the circumstances, seemed nothing short of reckless. The others followed, as sure-footed as mountain goats. The men carrying the stretcher, the fellow with the broken arm, the woman with the heavily bandaged leg, all moved ahead with steady purpose. I wondered if they saw what I saw: that on every surface, under every odd-shaped stone, and within every shadow—shadows, under a sunless sky—there were Good

Folk. Their bright eyes followed us as we passed. This was a place of potent magic. Even without them, I would have felt it, for it hummed in my bones and pulsed in my blood. Alban's power, Alban's strength, Alban's ancient wisdom.

Flint did not say any more, nor did I. I needed time to consider what he had told me, to come to terms with it, to find the courage to accept that enthrallment need not be the vile practice I had witnessed—that a man could be an Enthraller and still, somehow, remain good at heart. That a man like Flint—*Flint*—could speak tender words and blush like a boy filled me with a treacherous warmth. I must set that aside. Even if I could come to terms with what he had told me, there was another aspect of this that I must confront.

For I would soon face the same choice Flint had faced when he had made his decision to go to Keldec's court. A man should not betray comrades who trusted him, no matter who those comrades were. He should not lead his fellow warriors into an ambush and help the enemy kill them. But what if that enemy was fighting for the cause of freedom and an end to tyranny?

I did not think I could justify calling the Good Folk to perform acts of violence. But what if those very acts helped restore Alban to what it had been, a realm of peace and justice? Perhaps such questions had no answer. Perhaps the answer was that right could prevail, but only at an unbearable cost.

We moved on. I should have kept my eyes on the deceptive track, but I turned to look back. Nothing of the tortuous path we had taken was visible, and nor were the folk whose soft footsteps I had heard behind us as we walked, the small folk whose murmuring voices I could hear even now. All I could see was the empty fell, feature-less and barren. The Folds. I understood why it was so named, for the earth itself changed here to trap, to trick, to isolate. And to hide; how could any man who did not know the right way hope to find those who dwelt in such a place? No wonder the rebels had chosen this as their base, even though it lay so far from human settlements. My mind teemed with questions.

I turned back and almost walked into a rock wall that had not been there a moment ago. Flint put a hand out to steady me.

"Careful. Stay right next to me. The entrance is through this way."

A passageway between the rocks. Deep shadow. The pinpricks of eyes in the chinks, the creak of leathery wings overhead. Regan and the others had moved on ahead with-out looking up.

Before us was a doorway into the mountain. A man-made doorway—it bore the marks of tools—though no door was there, only an opening into a shadowy inte-rior. As our party approached, a very large man holding a spear stepped out. Behind him stood two more.

"Regan, Tali, welcome," said the spear carrier, and brought his weapon back from its attack position. "What news?"

"Sad news. Six dead, ten wounded. Garven's leg is crushed. Flint is with us, and a young woman." Regan looked back down the line at me. "Flint's girl, the one we heard of."

I opened my mouth to deny the name, then shut it again.

"The enemy?" inquired the guard.

"Accounted for." Tali slipped this in casually.

"All of them?" The fellow sounded deeply impressed.

"All of them," Regan said. "We left some of the fellows down there cleaning up; they'll be here before nightfall. We'd best get Garven inside. Tali, show Neryn the women's quarters."

As folk dispersed in various directions, a somber Tali led me along a passageway illuminated by hanging oil lamps, past several openings, and into a chamber housing six pallets, two storage chests, and various items of female clothing hanging on pegs. A lamp stood on one of the chests. The place was warm; a fire burned on a small hearth at the far end of the chamber. Along one wall were three shuttered windows. The sound of men's voices came to us from somewhere within the network of shadowy passageways.

"This is where we sleep." Tali sat down on one of the pallets and began unfastening her boots. "That bed's free." She pointed.

I set my meager possessions on the foot of the pallet she had indicated, the one farthest from the fire. What was this place, a catacomb in the mountain? These must be caves, surely, for the entry had led straight into the hill. From outside there had been no sign of any house or enclosure, nothing but the rocks. Yet these walls were of carefully laid stones, and the windows . . . Where did that chimney come out? There had been no sign of smoke as we approached.

I sat down on my bed. "Is this Shadowfell?" I asked, feeling foolish.

Tali tugged off one boot and bent to remove the other. "Mm-hm."

Someone twitched the door hanging aside, and the chamber was suddenly full of women. Women setting down knives and axes and swords by the door; women striding across to remove their warrior gear, to lay helms, breast pieces, arm and leg braces on their pallets, and then proceeding to strip off their clothes with no trace of embarrassment. They threw their discarded garments in a heap on the floor, between the pallets.

They told me their names again: Andra, Sula, Dervla. An older woman came in carrying two huge buckets of water, followed by another woman with a small bathtub. Milla. Eva. I knew I would not remember who was who. I was suddenly so tired I couldn't keep my eyes open.

"Best get your things off," one of the women said, glancing my way. "You look as if you could do with a wash."

"I have no clean clothes."

"Milla will find you something."

Sula was unwrapping the makeshift bandage Fingal had wound around her leg earlier. "Black Crow's auntie, this bites like a creel of lobsters. A hot soak will be just the thing. How's your injury, Tali?"

"Fine. It's nothing." Tali had stripped swiftly to her leggings and undershirt, then flung her shirt onto the pile. She had tattooed bracelets all the way up her arms, intricate spirals and twists and snakes. Her hair was shorter than a boy's, a mere finger's length, and night-dark. "Wish I'd been quicker. I could have saved Bryn." Her tone was gruff.

"You fought like a demon," Andra said. "You couldn't have done more."

"It was his time," added Sula.

Tali's face was turned away from us; she was studying the wall with apparent fascination. "How could it be his time? He was barely nineteen," she muttered. "Accursed Enforcers! They're a stain on the fields of Alban. Every man lost is a man too many. Every man slain is a man Regan needs and hasn't got. I should have saved him." Her fists were clenched tight.

Sula raised her brows but held her tongue. Dervla was crouched by the heap of clothing, scooping the garments into a linen bag. She glanced over at me.

"If you want your things washed, throw them over," she said.

I took off my shoes. I set them neatly side by side. I unfastened my cloak, unwrapped my shawl. I felt odd, as if I were somewhere far away, watching this happen to a stranger with my face. Somewhere inside me a dam was waiting to burst.

Milla had filled the bath. I saw no sign of steam rising and wondered if these hardy folk bathed in cold water.

Tali rolled down her leggings to reveal a great livid bruise on hip and thigh.

"You'd best let Fingal have a look at that when you've bathed," Milla remarked, turning a critical eye on her. "You could do with something to bring down the swelling."

"It's nothing," Tali said dismissively. "That brother of mine is going to be busy enough without tending to my scratches."

So Fingal was Tali's brother; that explained the matching tattoos. I cleared my throat. "I could dress it for you," I said. "My grandmother was a healer, and she taught me basic skills. If Fingal can give me some materials, I can make a poultice that will relieve the pain and stop your leg from stiffening up. If you like."

Tali was about to deliver a withering refusal—I could see it in her eyes—but something halted her. "Later, maybe. Right now you look too worn out to lift your little finger."

She stripped off her remaining garment to reveal a lithe body, muscular and rangy. For all its athletic strength, her form was womanly in its curves and hollows. I was staring. I turned my gaze onto the bath, by which Sula now stood, passing her hands over the water in an elaborate pattern. It was almost as if her fingers were dancing. Their intricate movement held all our gazes: Tali, standing like a warrior statue; Andra and Dervla by their pallets; Milla and Eva with buckets in hand.

Sula closed her eyes. She drew in a breath, then let it out slowly. There was a sudden stillness in the underground chamber, as if something unseen had drawn breath with her. The fire flickered and flared; abruptly, the room went winter-cold. Before I could reach for my cloak, I saw steam rising from the bathwater. Sula opened her eyes, blinked a few times, then reached down to dip a hand in. "Just right," she said.

The others were looking at me now, as if they expected me to say something—to ask how this had been done, or to express the shock and disgust a loyal subject of Keldec would feel required to show after witnessing such an open demonstration of canny work.

"That's a useful talent," I said quietly. "I had thought perhaps I was to be put to the test with a cold bath. In fact, any kind of bath is a luxury for me, as you can probably see. Since I didn't earn my place by fighting, I'll go last."

"Good for you," said Milla with a grin. "Get on with it, girls. Supper will be ready before you are at this rate." She glanced at me, sizing me up. "Eva and I will fetch you some clothing—that's if we can find anything that won't swamp you. Slip of a thing, aren't you? What have you been living on, twigs and leaves?"

"Thank you," I murmured as the two of them went out, taking their buckets with them.

The preternatural chill that had gripped the chamber when Sula worked her charm soon dissipated, allowing the fire's heat to warm us again. Since I was to be last, there would be time for me to finish undressing later. I lay down, my head on the pillow. Somewhere, a long way away, I could hear the other women talking, accompanied by the splash of water and the clank of the bathtub as one got out and the next took her place. My mind drifted, floating away to another realm, a place without blood and fear and hard choices. I slept.

DISPATCH: TO STAG TROOP LEADER OWEN
SWIFT-SWORD (TO BE PASSED FROM HAND TO
HAND)
Summerfort or the Rush valley district, time of the first
snow

The king is aware that your current mission is of
some delicacy and requires extended periods of absence
from formal duties. You will understand, in your turn,
that this approach is open to misinterpretation both
among the local populace and among our retainers at
Summerfort.
The king is concerned by some inconsistencies
between the information that has reached us through
our observers and the content of certain recent dispatches
in your hand. He believes this can only be resolved by
your personal attendance at court.
King Keldec anticipates your return to Summerfort
before snow closes Three Hags Pass. You will then ride
on to Winterfort in company with Boar Troop. On your
arrival at court, you will provide a full account of your
activities since the Cull began in the west. Your king is a
patient man. Do not stretch that patience too thin.
On behalf of Keldec, King of Alban

Owen, come home, curse you! I need you here.

Chapter Eighteen

THE NORTH WIND HARRIED HIM FORWARD, WHISTLING in his ears. *Too late. Too late.* There was no forgiveness, of course; a man who did the things he did could not expect that. But if only she had said something, if only she had let him know with a word, a gesture, a look, that she understood, then he could have left without this heavy stone in his chest, this burden that grew harder to bear with every passing season. If only he could have stayed a little longer, given her another day, two days. If only he could have seen the color come back to her wan cheeks, and the haunted look leave her as she realized that finally, at Shadowfell, she could be safe. They would not meet again until spring, and only then if Keldec gave him leave to return to the north. By then . . . by then, who knew how many more ill deeds he would have done, how many more orders he would have forced himself to obey, all for a cause that sometimes seemed as remote as the stars in the night sky? He shivered, casting his glance from side to side, eyeing the shadows under the rocks, the dark places where trees huddled close, the many bolt-holes where an enemy might be concealed, ready to pick him off with an arrow. *Neryn,* he thought. Her name was a charm to hold back the dark. *Neryn, I'm sorry.*

I woke with a start, sitting bolt upright in the dark. Flint. Gone. Gone without a word. But, no, I was here in my bed at Shadowfell, with sleeping women all around me, and it had only been a dream. A vivid dream, conjured by my own confusion and the tale he had told me as we climbed the hill. Sorry? There was nothing to be sorry for.

The fire was down to ashes and the chamber was bitterly cold. Someone had piled blankets on me; under their warmth I had slept soundly, until the dream shocked me awake. I had missed both bath and supper. Yet my hair was damp and smelled of herbs, and I felt wonderfully clean, as if I had been scrubbed from head to toe. I was wearing a capacious nightrobe whose sleeves came down over my hands and whose folds were tangled around my legs under the blankets. The others must have bathed and dressed me when I was asleep.

Somewhere beyond the doorway of this chamber, I could hear voices. Was it morning? The shutters were closed fast, but lamplight from out in the hallway illuminated the room dimly, showing me the forms of the other women: Sula, curled up neat as a cat under her covers; Andra, sprawled on her back; Dervla, visible only as a tuft of fair hair and a mound of blankets. Tali's pallet was empty. So perhaps it was almost day. I should seek out

Fingal and get the makings of the poultice I had promised. And I must talk to Flint.

Items of clothing lay over a stool beside my bed: woolen leggings, a shift, a plain blue gown, a warm shawl. There was even a comb, though one of the women must have done a thorough job on my filthy, tangled hair last night, for it was not only clean but fastened into a neat braid down my back. I must indeed have been weary.

Evidently they had not managed to feed me any supper. My belly felt hollow and my mouth dry. I scrambled into the clothes, which were only a little too big, slipped my feet into my shoes, and ventured out into the hallway.

I followed the voices. A look in the first doorway showed me two men in states of undress and several others sleeping. I averted my eyes and hurried on past. I turned a corner, thinking the place was a little like a rabbit warren, and came to a sudden halt. A set of stone steps spiraled sharply downward, apparently into a bottomless well. A chill draft eddied up from the depths, and I stepped back hurriedly, remembering Odd's Hole.

"Careful," someone said right behind me, making me start in fright. It was Fingal, fully dressed and carrying a covered bucket. "It doesn't pay to walk about backward here—there are too many twists and turns. Looking for breakfast? It's this way."

"How is Garven?" I made myself ask.

"Still alive." With a glance at me, he added, "No point

in feeling guilty about what happened. It's war. People get hurt. What you did saved lives. Remember that."

He led me to a chamber with a broad hearth on which a fire burned. As in the bedchamber, the windows were shuttered. The place housed a long table, benches, shelves holding various platters, bowls, and utensils. It all looked surprisingly ordinary. There was Milla with her sleeves rolled up, stirring something in a big iron pot that, it seemed, had just come off the flames, for the contents were steaming. A savory smell filled the place. Eva was setting out bowls and spoons. Two men sat at the table, talking in low voices. Neither of them was Flint.

"Ah, you're up," Milla said, giving me a smile. "And looking a great deal better, I must say. Now sit down and let me feed you. Nobody expected you to fall asleep quite so suddenly or quite so soundly. No, you don't," she added as I opened my mouth to protest that there were other things I must do first. "Sit, eat. Don't say a word until it's all gone."

Hungry as I was, I could not finish the helping she gave me. The food was wonderful, a thick broth with real meat in it, but so rich I knew I would be sick if I ate it all. As I sat there, the table filled up with men, all of them looking somewhat grave, though Milla got a few smiles as she ladled out the food. I remembered that some would have kept vigil over the dead last night, and that today they would be laying their comrades to rest.

Fingal did not sit down with us, but handed Milla his

bucket and went off carrying a pile of clean, folded cloths. He looked too busy to be asked about the poultice, or about anything. All of a sudden I felt very much alone.

"One more mouthful, Neryn," Milla said, watching me. "Good. That's enough; I see you won't get through all of it. Little and often, that's what you want. Build up your strength slowly. If you need the privy, it's down there." She pointed through yet another doorway. "Good idea to knock before you go in. Men greatly outnumber women here."

I cleared my throat, feeling awkward. "Do you know where I might find Flint?"

She shook her head. "Can't tell you. He and Regan were in early for breakfast. If you find one, maybe you'll find the other."

"Is there anywhere I shouldn't go? I don't know how this place is laid out or what rules there may be. . . ."

Milla smiled. "You won't go anywhere you're not allowed, because there'll be someone to stop you. If you want my advice, the best place for you is back in bed. Take things one step at a time." After a moment, she added, "But I see you won't do that. Go down that passageway there, turn right, then right again before you reach the men's sleeping quarters. Our dead have been laid out in the practice area. You might find your man there."

"Thank you." I felt a flush rise to my cheeks; ridiculous. Everyone seemed to be leaping to the same conclusion about Flint and me.

Last night's dream clung close around me as I made my way through the hallways. It had been like another person's dream; clear proof, I might once have believed, that I was an Enthraller's victim. I had walked in Flint's shoes. I had thought his tender thoughts. I had felt his hurt and his loneliness as if they were my own.

Now, in the clear wakefulness of morning, I felt the profound truth of that dream, and knew that it had proved quite the opposite. He had not lied to me. He had never wished me ill. Always, he had been my protector and guardian, my friend and companion. He understood me. He even understood why I found it so hard to believe in him. I had fallen victim to the malady that beset all of Alban, turning neighbor against neighbor and friend against friend. After the massacre at Corbie's Wood, I had been unable to trust anyone. In the years that followed, the years of flight and hardship, I had lost my clear-sightedness, the inner sense that allowed a person to know right from wrong. Flint's honest eyes, his gentle, capable hands, his kindness, and his courage were not parts of an evil plan to make me believe in him; they were real. If I had trusted my instincts, I would have known this long ago. What had brought him walking through my dreams was no fell charm, but something quite different.

And now I must find him and tell him. I must give him the words he needed so badly to keep him warm through the long winter to come. It was a small enough gift after all he had done.

The passageway opened to an expanse of hard-packed earth surrounded by a high stone wall. Half the area was roofed, half open to the sky. It was bitterly cold. The six dead men lay in the covered part, each on a blanket. The sun was not yet up, but lanterns illuminated their still forms. Their faces were washed clean; their hair had been combed; cloaks wrapped their bodies, concealing the terrible damage of that hard fight. Beyond the roofed area, the lantern light caught, here and there, a softly falling snowflake.

Two silent guardians kept vigil over their comrades. Regan's arms were folded, his eyes distant, his handsome features grim. Tali leaned on a spear. Her gaze was on Regan. While he guarded the dead, I thought, her job was to guard him. There was a look on her face that made me wonder if I had been wrong about her. Perhaps there was more to this warrior girl than hard edge and hostility.

I halted, reluctant to intrude on them. The dead men had fought their last battle alongside Regan and Tali. They had likely been good friends, for the community at Shadowfell was small. That dining area would accommodate forty people at most. Not a great army. At least not in numbers.

I cleared my throat. "I'm sorry to interrupt you," I said. "I was looking for Flint. Milla said he might be here."

Regan's shrewd blue eyes and Tali's fierce black ones turned toward me in unison. There was a moment's silence. Then Tali said, "Flint's gone."

I felt my heart skip a beat. Gone? He couldn't be gone. But my mind showed me the dream, and Flint heading back along the valley toward the Three Hags without saying a word to me. "It's not even light yet," I found myself protesting. "He wouldn't leave without telling me."

"He said not to wake you." Tali's tone was flat and final.

"But why? Why so soon? He came all the way up here to talk to Regan. What difference would it have made to wait just a little longer?"

"Some information was found on one of the dead." Regan spoke evenly, as if practiced in calming the agitated. "Flint believed it best that he head straight back to court. He's been gone some time now."

No. Wrong. This couldn't happen. He couldn't go. I hadn't said what I must say; I hadn't spoken the words he needed to hear. "I can catch up with him, I'll run all the way," I babbled, trying to remember how to get out through the branching passages. "I must speak to him, I won't hold him up, I'll just—"

"He'll be far down the mountain by now." There was no sympathy in Tali's voice; this was a plain statement of fact. "Well out of sight. He moves fast when he's on his own. You won't catch him."

"I will. I must." I turned tail and fled before either of them could speak again. I ran this way, that way, blundering down wrong turnings, almost bowling an unsuspecting man over. I found the chamber where I had slept last night, slept all too long and soundly. I ran past the doorway and down the passage toward the outside.

There were guards at the entry, of course. They stepped out and blocked my headlong flight before I could reach the open air.

"Let me through, please!" With every passing moment, with every breath I took, Flint was moving farther away.

Heading out into the cold, cruel world that was Keldec's Alban; walking straight back to his perilous, lonely life as a spy at the heart of the king's court. Facing choices fit to break the spirit of the strongest man. Without a single kind word, I had let him go. "I must catch up with Flint, I must talk to him!"

The guards looked me up and down. "On a day like this, with no cloak?" one of them asked, not unkindly.

"Flint's been gone a good while," said the other. "You've no hope of catching him now." Neither of them moved. Both were big, solid men.

"Please," I begged, beyond caring what anyone thought of me. "Please let me try. It's important, or I wouldn't ask."

They looked at each other. "No going in or out without Regan's say-so," one of them said. "And certainly not on your own, dressed for indoors. That would be foolish."

"Here." A voice spoke behind me, and I felt a thick cloak drop around my shoulders. The voice was Tali's, crisp and authoritative. "It's all right, Donnan, I'll go with her." She stepped past me, giving me a sidelong look. "Fasten that cloak and put the hood up; it's cold out there."

She still had her spear; it had been joined by an ax on her back and a knife in her belt. She looked sufficiently menacing to scare off a horde of enemies.

"Thank you," I murmured as we made our way out.

"He'll be too far ahead, I told you." Tali set a fast pace; I scurried to keep up. "There'd be no point in lying about a thing like that. But there's a certain point on the hillside where you might catch a glimpse of him. If anyone can spot him, I can." A pause, then she added, "I have sharp eyes. Sharp enough to cause me trouble in certain quarters, if it's noticed."

So she too had a canny gift. If I stayed here, I would probably find that Shadowfell housed a number of unusually talented men and women. Sula with her ability to draw heat into water; Tali, not only a fearsome warrior but possessed of unusual eyesight. And Flint, a mind-mender. "I must talk to him, Tali," I said as we crossed the Folds. This morning, under the falling snow, the place seemed no more than the featureless fell on which we'd emerged the day before. No traps, no tricks, no sudden sharp descents. An easy passage. Had my urgency communicated itself to the very earth beneath our feet? No human woman had so much power, surely.

"It's not going to happen, Neryn," Tali said bluntly, not looking back at me. "It's too late. And maybe that's just as well."

"What do you mean, it's just as well? He needs to hear this, it's important—"

She stopped walking and turned abruptly, and I almost crashed into her. "There's something you should understand," she said. There was a new look in her dark eyes now, not quite compassion, but the very slightest softening of their combative glint.

"We must keep walking! Don't just stand there!"

"You listen first, then we walk on." She folded her arms. "This is a war. A long, hard war. When you're fighting a war, there's no place for softness. There's no time for personal feelings. When you do the work we do, you can't afford to develop attachments. That kind of thing must wait until the war is won. A wife, a husband, a sweetheart, a child, each of those is a chink in a warrior's armor. Each is a weapon in the enemy's hands, a key to extracting vital information. A man like Flint will sacrifice his life before he gives up secrets. He might not be so ready to sacrifice yours."

Great gods. How long before this war was won, half a lifetime? "Tali, please walk on," I said. "I understand. I'm not about to make some kind of declaration to Flint, I just need to . . ." *I need to put my arms around him and tell him that it will be all right. I want to kiss him on the cheek, and hold him for a little, and share some of my warmth. I want to say thank you. I need to see that terrible sadness leave his eyes.*

She walked on and I followed. "Anyway," I said, "I am nothing like a sweetheart to Flint. We are friends, that's all. Comrades of the journey. Now that I am safely delivered here, he can forget me."

Tali turned her head to give me a penetrating look. "You didn't hear him last night, telling Regan the story of your journey all the way from Darkwater," she said. "You didn't see the look in his eyes. And you can't see the expression on your own face right now. Come on, then, let's make this quick."

It had seemed to me we were walking quite fast already, but she picked up the pace. By almost running, I managed to keep up. Snow was falling lightly, a scatter of dancing flakes across the open ground. Here and there, a small drift had formed at the base of a stone or around the gnarled roots of a lonely tree. The air seemed alive with magic; I felt it in every part of my body. Somewhere very close at hand there was a gathering of Good Folk. Their presence seemed to hang over the whole of Shadowfell, and whether it was protective or menacing or simply indifferent, I could not tell. But they were here. Here in force.

"Tali," I said, a little breathlessly. "Are there—uncanny folk, Otherworld folk, at Shadowfell?"

She did not answer straightaway. When her reply came, it was unusually tentative. "There must be. The place is . . . Well, you can see what it is. And from time to time we get . . . help. Supplies of one kind or another. Useful changes to the way things are organized. But they don't come out. We never see them." She turned her head. "It sounds as if you might be able to see them. Even talk to them."

When I said nothing, she added, "Your gift could be critical to our winning this war, Neryn. I hope, for the sake of Alban and all of us, that you can bring yourself to use it again. It's powerful. It's what we need." Not a criticism this time, not a whipping for doing the wrong thing, but a statement, woman to woman. I had not expected this from her.

"It's only what you need if I know what I'm doing," I said. "And I'm not sure I can find someone to teach me."

"Teach yourself," Tali said. "That's what I did. I surely didn't learn to fight the way a boy does, from his father's master-at-arms. See that outcrop over there, the one that looks like a crouching cat? That's the spot. If we climb up, we might be able to catch sight of him."

She went up ahead of me, agile as a squirrel. I followed, a little prayer repeating itself over and over in my head: *Let him be there. Let him still be in sight.*

Tali reached the top. I heard her suck in her breath. "Great Boar's bollocks!" she exclaimed. "Where are his weapons? And what in all Alban is *that*?"

My heart performed a somersault. He must be still within reach, perhaps close enough for me to call out to him and be heard. I scrambled up beside Tali, who was perched atop the rock formation staring down the hill, her expression pure amazement.

At the foot of the rocks, Flint's pack and rolled-up cloak lay on the snowy ground. The hilt of his sword could be seen protruding from the concealment of the cloak. A mere twenty paces from his belongings was Flint himself, sitting on a large stone, deep in conversation with a small personage in a hooded green cape. Sage. Sage, here in the Watch of the North. Sage, who had battled my enemies like a true warrior and lost her dear friend in the fight. Sage, whom I had thought I might never see again.

There was no need to call out. The moment I moved, the two of them turned their heads and looked straight at me. Flint rose very slowly to his feet. He looked as pale as he had in the aftermath of the battle.

"Neryn!" Tali spoke in an undertone. "Is that one of the—"

"She's a friend," I said. "I'm going down to talk to Flint."

"Not on your own, you're not." She followed a step behind me.

"If you're coming, you'll need to leave your weapons behind," I said.

"My job is to protect you. Maybe I can do it barehanded, but I prefer not to put that to the test."

"They fear cold iron. The Good Folk. It hurts them. No wonder you haven't seen them at Shadowfell; the place is bristling with weaponry. Why do you think Flint set his sword and knives aside before he went to talk to her?"

We were climbing down the way we'd gone up, and for now were out of sight of Flint and Sage. My heart was drumming. I felt as nervous as if I were going to battle.

"I need to be able to see you," Tali said. "I'll keep my distance, but I'm not giving up my weapons for a . . . a whatever it is. I can't do my job properly without them."

So she had not been moved by sudden sympathy to accompany me down the mountain. She was here to guard me, under Regan's orders. Because, after all, I myself was a weapon, a particularly valuable one. "Don't frighten her," I said. "She's come a long way to see me and taken a risk every bit as great as mine or Flint's."

We came around the base of the rocks and back into view. Tali gave Flint a nod, then stationed herself beside his belongings. I'd rather have done this without her shrewd eyes fixed on my every move. But never mind that, because Flint was here, he was waiting for me, and what I saw on his face made everything worthwhile. I walked down the snowy path toward him, hoping I could find the right words, hoping he would understand, hoping . . .

But first there was Sage. I crouched down beside her. She looked tired; her eyes were less bright than I remembered them. Nonetheless, her sharp little features wore a look I could only describe as dauntless. The two parts of her broken staff were neatly strapped atop her pack. Where her cloak had been torn in the fight at Brollachan Bridge, it now bore lines of tiny, neat stitches. The scorch marks still showed, but they were overlaid with delicate embroidery: a pattern of sorrel leaves.

"Sage, I can't believe you're here," I said quietly, finding that my eyes were brimming with tears. "You're over the border, in the Watch of the North. Why have you taken such a risk?"

"What kind of a welcome is that, lassie?" She held out her arms and I embraced her, feeling how fragile her little body was beneath the layers of her clothing, as frail as a forest bird's. "Let me look at you." She subjected me to a long examination, at the end of which she smiled and nodded as if satisfied. "So you're here at last. You found your way to Shadowfell." She glanced at Flint, who stood silent beside us; she looked up the hill toward the straight-backed, vigilant figure of Tali. "Why am I here? I heard a rumor. It's being whispered that the Master of Shadows is back, and making mischief wherever he goes. If that might be true, you need to know it. Besides, it came to me that perhaps I was wrong about this fellow and I'd best give him a chance to explain himself. And as for the border, I've come to the conclusion that it's time for a rule or two to be broken. We'll get nowhere if we can't even trust our own in this benighted place. I'm here to help you, lassie. You'll be needing some guidance with the Master abroad. And since your fellow here's leaving, it seems I've come just in time. If the folk of the Folds are not inclined to extend a welcome, I've a friend or two I can call in to speak for me."

"The Master of Shadows," I echoed, wondering if I should tell her now, straightaway, or leave it until the two of us were alone.

"Aye, a Big One in person. Folk have seen him here and there. Or so they say. He's a tricky creature at the best of times. A shifter and changer, a player of games." Sage's eyes were shrewd as she examined my face. "You don't look surprised, Neryn."

"I have a tale to tell," I said. "Most of it can wait for later, but . . . I met someone unusual, and I was told, more or less, that I'd shown all the virtues. There was a rhyme; six of them in the first part, only one in the second. Exactly how I demonstrated the first six I'm not sure. The seventh was plain enough." After a moment I added, "You don't look surprised either."

Sage grinned. "I heard the tale of yesterday's battle and how you turned the tide. I wish Silver could have seen that; it would have silenced her doubting tongue. By the time we met you by Hiddenwater, you were well on your way to passing the tests. She and her band were slow to believe it, thinking as they did that there was only one way to meet each requirement. Fools. What was it you showed the night your grandmother was taken but Strength of Stillness? As if that weren't enough, you did it again with the urisk. As for Flame of Courage, without that you'd never have endured those three years of hunger and flight, though Silver would probably say you didn't prove yourself brave enough to be a Caller until you got over Brollachan Bridge. Canny Eyes? We all know you've had those since you were a wee bairnie."

"Open Heart?" I queried, fascinated.

"You need to ask me that? It goes along with the Giving Hand, Neryn. You've been taught to share what you have. Not just your meager supplies, but your love and compassion. You made time for that poor fellow in the cottage, the one who's not right in the head—oh yes, we know about that, we're everywhere—and you stopped to listen to the sad ghosts of Hiddenwater when nobody else in a hundred years had spared them a word, let alone sung them the song they wanted. Who knows what that fine act may lead to one day? As for Steadfast Purpose, that was what I saw at Brollachan Bridge, for I guessed how badly you wanted to run back and help us; I knew what it must have cost you to go on. But you never lost sight of your mission, lassie. You put Alban first, as it appears this fellow of yours does, and all of them up there." Sage nodded in Tali's direction.

I was humbled by her words. It seemed to me that she and her small companions exemplified the fine qualities of the rhyme far better than I ever could. "The second verse ends with *Live for Alban's liberty*," I said. "That's what we must do."

"We'll talk more later," Sage said. "You don't have long, your fellow here tells me. Say your farewells, or whatever you've come to say. I'll wait over yonder, as far from that guard of yours as I can safely take myself. She's got the smell of death about her."

So small, so brave, so wise. "It's good to see you," I said with a lump in my throat. "Where is Red Cap? Did he come with you?"

"Never did manage to shake the wee fellow off. Aye, he's close by, and his bairnie with him. It's good to see you too, lassie." She made to move away, then halted, fixing me with her shrewd gaze. "One thing. You said you demonstrated the seventh virtue. Could be there's one step further to go with that one."

She moved a short distance away and settled herself under a wind-blighted tree. Up the hill, Tali had not moved.

We stood gazing at each other, Flint and I. Now that I had found him, now that we were together again, all my words fled. *Grant forgiveness,* a voice whispered in my mind. *Set them free.*

"A message came," he said shakily. "There was no time. You needed your sleep." He lifted his fingers to touch my cheek, sending a shiver through me. "I'm sorry I must leave so soon," he said. "More sorry than I can say."

"But you were never going to stay." The words that

came out were the wrong ones; all I could think about was that this was the last touch, the last look, the last memory. It was a long time until spring.

"That was before we came up the mountain. Before you said you would listen to my story. When you heard it and did not shrink from me, I thought . . . I wanted to stay longer, Neryn. It isn't to be. It seems someone has raised doubts about my loyalty, back at Summerfort. When I heard Boar Troop was coming along the valley, I tried to halt them, to tell them that any rumors they'd heard of rebel activity in these parts were untrue. I told them I'd checked already, thoroughly, and that the stories had no foundation. I'm not only a troop leader, I'm the king's confidant; in the past they would have accepted my word. At the very least, their leader should have delayed the advance. But he did not. That told me I was being watched. It told me they were under orders from someone higher up, someone who suspected me. I tried a second time, when they had traveled farther, and again my counsel was ignored. So I was forced to send a message to Regan, setting up the ambush. And to leave you on your own. Safe in the cave until it was all over. At least, that was the plan."

"You went with them yourself," I breathed. "You chose to—"

"To lead them to their slaughter?" His tone was bitter. "The situation was dire. They were dangerously close to Shadowfell. Since they would not go back, it was necessary to make sure they went on, and that they ended up exactly where Regan wanted them. And then to ensure nobody returned to Summerfort to tell the tale."

"I had thought, earlier, that they were following me. That was what the Good Folk believed."

"They knew of your existence, certainly. They played their part in pursuing you earlier. They believed I was still looking for you. But Boar Troop was not dispatched up the valley to find you, Neryn. They were sent to hunt out rebels, and to check on me. The document Regan's men found yesterday confirmed that."

"Then . . . when you go back . . . how can you possibly explain . . . ?"

"I'll find the right words. I have done so before and I can do so again."

"But this . . . the loss of all those men . . . You'll be in terrible danger."

"I can look after myself. Don't let it trouble you."

My tears welled anew. I blinked them back. This was not a time to break down and weep; it was a time to be strong. I did not want to be a chink in Flint's armor. I did not want to be the person who weakened him and made him vulnerable. And yet, the language of his touch was not the language of comrade to comrade, friend to friend. It went far deeper than that.

"When I saw the battle, when I saw what you had to do . . ." I was finding it hard to catch my breath. "I wondered how you could make yourself act like that, over and over, season by season, year by year. I wondered how you could bear it. And then . . . when I called the stanie mon, when I made him kill, I began to understand. What I did sickened me. It filled me with guilt and shame. But if I hadn't done it, you and I and Regan's fighters might all be dead now, and there would be nobody to stand up against Keldec's might. The life you lead . . . it horrifies me. It's like the worst nightmare I could imagine. You must feel as if you're constantly struggling to tell right from wrong. You must dream of your deeds and your decisions every night, and rise every morning wondering where you can find the strength to go on. And, somehow, you find it."

He bowed his head. "I am not worthy to be your friend," he said. "Nor the friend of any right-thinking man or woman. What I do . . . it sets me apart. It sets a stain on me that there's no removing."

"Look at me, Flint," I said. He raised his eyes; I tried to see beyond the pain to the true heart within. "You are a good man," I told him. "I saw that in you from the start, but trust was a hard lesson for me to learn. You are brave beyond imagining. Alban is fortunate indeed to have such a man fighting for her freedom. Don't doubt yourself. You're treading a hard path. . . . I wanted to tell you . . . I wanted to say . . ." Now even the right words were not enough. Instead, I put my arms around him and laid my head against his shoulder.

Without a word he gathered me close. I felt his heart beating, quick and strong. A warrior's heart.

"Our time will come," I murmured. "When all this is over. When peace comes again. When Alban is restored to herself. Tali is right: saying any more only makes things harder for both of us. But . . ." I drew back so I could see his face. His lovely eyes. His strong, sweet mouth. His plain, scarred features. He had shaved his head since I last saw him; he was the hooded man of Darkwater again, the stranger who had won me in a game of chance and fled with me into the forest. "I will dream of you every night," I said. "I will count every day until spring. Be safe, Flint."

"Every night, you will walk through my dreams," he said. "That will be nothing new; you have done so since I first met you." He stepped back, releasing me. I felt as if my heart would crack in two. "Neryn," he said. "What you said . . . the words you just gave me . . . that was a gift beyond price. A flame to light me through the harsh winter and bring me home again." He glanced up toward Tali, then across at the small figure of Sage, who was sitting quietly under her tree, gazing at nothing in particular. "I'm glad you will be among friends," he said. "I must go, Neryn."

I nodded. With misery welling up in me, I tried to smile. There were words I wanted to speak, but Tali's warning was in my mind, stark in its premonition of danger. *You won't be a friend to the cause if you weaken the best man we have.* So I said nothing. Instead, I put the tips of my fingers to my mouth, then reached to lay them against his lips.

Braver than I, Flint bent to touch his lips to mine. His kiss was quick and light, yet full of promise. "Be safe, my heart," he whispered.

Then he moved away. He spoke to Sage, thanking her for her willingness to speak to him and for coming to find me. He went up to collect his weapons; he exchanged a word or two with Tali. I stood very still as he came back down. I did my best not to let any tears fall.

For a moment he stood before me again, holding his weapons wrapped in the cloak; I saw that he would not take them out while Sage was close by. I gazed at him, storing his image away for the long, cold season to come. I managed the smile. "Until spring," I said.

He smiled. It was a smile such as I had never seen before, full of joy and sadness and love and farewell. He gave a little nod, then turned and strode off down the mountain on his long journey back to court.

"That's him away." Sage was beside me, though I had not seen her move. "And your last virtue proven. You've some work ahead. That's if you're ready to test this gift of yours." The bright eyes subjected me to a searching look.

I thought of blood and death. I thought of courage and honor, pain and sacrifice. I had seen all of them on my journey. I had seen comradeship, vision, selflessness, patriotism. I had experienced friendship, goodness, love. Despite everything, they still existed in the dark realm that was Keldec's Alban. "I'm ready," I said. "Ready to be strong. Ready to take risks. Ready to learn."

"Aye, well, we'll do that together, my kind and your kind," Sage said, gathering her meager belongings. "That's if you and I can convince them. I'll slip off now and seek out Red Cap. I sent him to find a corner to shelter in, away from your warrior friends. When you're ready, call me and I'll come." Before I could say a word more, she had vanished into a fold of the land, leaving nothing behind but a set of small footprints going nowhere.

Gods, it was freezing. I pulled my borrowed cloak around me as I made my way up to the waiting Tali.

"Home," she said. "Regan won't thank me for taking out a living, breathing girl and bringing back an icicle. Was that really one of the—"

"The Good Folk," I said as we made our way back around the rocks and up toward Shadowfell. "Yes, an old friend of mine. Her kind are all around us here. But they don't come out unless it suits them. I've always been able to see and hear them."

Her dark eyes were full of wonder. For the first time, I thought, she recognized in me a strength equal to her own, despite our great differences. "Would they show themselves to me?" she asked. "Could I learn to talk to them?"

"Yes, if they wanted it, and if you were prepared to lay your weapons aside for long enough. Sage didn't hide herself from you just now. And Flint saw her earlier, even though I was not here. Saw her and spoke to her." I hesitated.

"What?"

"That's what we need to work on. Understanding. Co-operation. It won't be easy. The Good Folk prefer not to mingle, even among themselves. In times of trouble, their answer is to hide away until the storm passes. But . . . if we're to win, we'll need to change that. I don't know if it's possible, Tali. But I believe we must try."

"So you'll do it? You'll help us?"

"I don't think I have any choice." How could I expect of Flint what I would not dare myself?

We walked on steadily. The silence between us was different now: the tension was gone from it. The mountain was quiet. Under the falling snow its rocks and crags and fissures lay in folds of gray and violet, mysterious and remote. *Her ancient bones brought me to birth. . . .*

"We can do it," I said. "We must believe that, or we can't go on. We can win this, all of us together. All of Alban's children."